EVA WOODS

you are here

SPHERE

SPHERE

First published in Great Britain in 2022 by Sphere

1 3 5 7 9 10 8 6 4 2

A CIP catalogue record for this book
is available from the British Library.

ISBN 978-0-7515-8531-5

Typeset in Baskerville by M Rules
Printed and bound in Great Britain by
Clays Ltd, Elcograf S.p.A.

Papers used by Sphere are from well-managed forests
and other responsible sources.

Sphere
An imprint of
Little, Brown Book Group
Carmelite House
50 Victoria Embankment
London EC4Y 0DZ

An Hachette UK Company
www.hachette.co.uk

www.littlebrown.co.uk

Eva Woods grew up in a small Irish village and now lives in London, where she dodges urban foxes and tuts at tourists on escalators. She runs the UK's first writing course for commercial novels and regularly teaches creative writing.

Eva also writes thrillers under her real name of Claire McGowan.

you
are
here

JUNE 2019

OK, Ellie told herself. This was a good choice. It was perfectly sensible to be thirty-eight and hiding under your childhood single bed, even if there was a cardboard box poking into your back and enough dust down there to build a life-size model of yourself. That was an idea. Perhaps the model could take on everything she had to do today, and she could carry on hiding under the bed. Would he even notice the difference?

There was another knock at the door, louder than the one that had sent her scurrying under the bed in the first place, heart hammering.

'Ellie! Hurry up! The makeup lady's here and she's very cross you've not had your colours done yet!'

Ellie held her breath. *I'm not here. I'm not here.* But then, where else could she be? The only window was too small to climb out of when you were a size fourteen, and the entire house was mined with relatives and friends. There was no escape from it, from this day, from her entire life. Her wedding. It was supposed to be a happy day, wasn't it? She wasn't supposed to be hiding under beds or contemplating escaping out the window. So why had her mother's knock thrown her into a panic, sent her diving for the floor? She'd been lying awake for hours before it, turning things over in her mind. Clearly, something had gone very wrong.

Her mum knocked louder. '*Eleanor!* I don't have time to babysit you, I've got to steam my hat!'

Briefly, Ellie wondered how one steamed a hat – in a saucepan, like a pudding? – but that was not important right now. What was important was how she was going to get out of this situation. Because she wouldn't be under the bed in her fleecy sheep-printed pyjamas, choking on dust, if she wanted this, would she? She'd be flinging open the curtains like Snow White, coaxing birds down to perch on her fingers, filled with joy and hope. She would have already showered and had her hair and makeup done and put on the fancy wedding lingerie her chief bridesmaid had persuaded her to buy, which made her cringe to even think about. She would be ready, instead of hopelessly lost, lying awake since four going back over every choice that had led her here, wondering if it was the right one. Endlessly weighing up the pros and cons of getting married today.

She coughed out dust. 'I'll be down in a minute!'

She just had to buy some time, figure out what to do, make sure it was what she wanted. Her mother's slippered footsteps retreated, creaking down the stairs, and Ellie let out a breath. In her head she was already drawing up plans. Step one, get out of her pyjamas and find clothes that weren't made of satin or lace. Step two, escape from this room without being seen. That wouldn't be easy. Given that she'd spent all her teenage years sleeping in this same small space, she knew it wasn't possible to make it out without being rumbled by the creaky board on the upper landing, or the fact that her mother, sister-in-law, friend, various assorted cousins, and Auntie Joyce were all milling about the lower floor. Step three, find transport. She had no idea where her own car was – brides, it seemed, were not allowed to do things like drive themselves or put their own makeup on or make decisions. Step four, get the hell out of here. The train station? The airport? A quick ferry from Hull?

The urge to run was almost as overpowering as the dust, but no, that wasn't what she wanted, not really. She couldn't do that to him. And anyway, she *wanted* to get married – she'd said yes, hadn't she? She just needed a little time to think, maybe talk to a few people and get advice, reassure herself. Soothe her nerves. Everyone talked about wedding jitters, didn't they? Perhaps this was it. Ellie wriggled out from under the bed, noting that the standards of her mother's cleaning had really gone downhill since she was young. Everything went that way eventually, if it was left.

Her undignified writhing had dislodged the box that was under there with her, and now Ellie recognised it. It had once held Tunnock's tea cakes, and suddenly she wished she had one of those, sweet and sticky as a cloud. She'd been dieting for months, forgoing chocolate and buttered toast and cheese and glasses of wine, and for what? To squeeze into a dress that didn't fit? To look good in photos?

Inside the box was a dusty collection of items. Several notebooks, dog-eared and faded. Ellie realised with a shock that these were the diaries she'd kept on and off through her childhood, the beginnings of novels she'd begun and abandoned in her teens. She'd forgotten all about them.

Other treasures too. A toy stethoscope. A snow globe of the Eiffel Tower, from when she'd become obsessed with moving to Paris after too many viewings of *Amélie* at university. A Barbie doll dressed as a bride, a gift from her Aunt Joyce which had never really interested Ellie all that much – ironic, given that today was her actual wedding and she was spiralling into panic. A model of a New York taxi, the yellow paint chipping. And a small globe, which still spun wonkily on its axis. The places she had planned to go. The countries she was going to live in.

Ellie sat back on her heels (buffed and pedicured down to the dermis) and felt tears prick her eyes. This was why it hurt to go home. Here in a box were all her old dreams, the way she'd thought her life would turn out. Travel, discovery, being a doctor, being a writer. Love, friendship, marriage. She picked up the paperback books and saw they were from the Choose Your Own Adventure series, ones she'd spent an entire summer reading, holed up in the bay window of the living room downstairs, shutting out the world. Crocodile attacks, quicksand, pirates, aliens, villains and heroes. She'd been obsessed with the idea that choices shaped your life. But in these books, if you took a wrong turn and ended up eaten by sharks, you could just skip back a few pages and try something else. Decisions were not fatal. Not like in the real world.

She ran her hands over the embossed covers, dated and worn. So many places in her life where she'd made choices and decisions, picked one path instead of another, all of them leading her to today. And here she was, thirty-eight and about to get married. What choices exactly had led to this moment? Was it just one, or a series of them? If she could go back, and find that vital decision, whenever it was, and do something different, would she be here now, crouching on her not-very-clean bedroom floor, crying over a box of childhood tat? Impossible to know.

Another knock at the door. 'Ellie! We're going to be late for the church! Katie's already had her base done and the lady's plucked out half her eyebrows and she's crying; Lucy's had a tantrum over her flower wreath; plus Popkin's eaten fourteen sugared almonds and been sick in the roses. You have to get ready!' The handle rattled. Not trusting the flimsy 1990s lock, Ellie had shoved a chair up against it.

Ellie closed her eyes. *I don't care*, she wanted to scream. *I don't care about roses and makeup and tantrums and how many sugared almonds the dog ate. I just need to think! I need time!* 'Mum, I can't . . . '

'Just get in the shower, for goodness' sake! I'll try to stall the makeup lady.' Footsteps headed off again.

Ellie took a deep breath. She couldn't hide in here all day. Time was ticking on, and people would be arriving and there'd be florists and harpists and readers and bridesmaids and drivers and *what have I done?* Panic overtook her, and her breath caught in her throat. Did she want this? Walking down the aisle with all eyes on her, trying not to trip in heels and the unaccustomed long skirt? She had to get up. Make some kind of plan. She sat up quickly, and a sudden agonising pain filled her head as she cracked it on the wooden bed frame. 'Ow! Holy Mother of Christ, that hurt!'

More knocking. 'Ellie? Are you all right? What was that noise?'

Ellie breathed hard, blinking several times. The bang on the head had cleared her mind. The wedding was still hours away – she had time to think. Maybe if she could work out the steps she'd taken to get to this precise moment, it would show her whether she was making the right choice or not, and then she would know what to do next.

CHOICE 1 – OCTOBER 1998

Mr Cole tapped the pen on his chipped plywood desk. 'So, Allie . . . '

'It's Ellie, sir.'

'Oh yes. Ellie. Um . . . ' He broke off, staring into space for a moment. Ellie waited, observing the dust motes that shimmered in the small office, sweating into her bottle-green 100 per cent polyester uniform and hoping he wouldn't notice the black nail polish on her chewed nails. But then, her careers teacher hadn't noticed much for a while. The word around school was that Mrs Cole had run off with an ice-cream van man, which explained why no one in the upper sixth had had anything that could remotely be called guidance about their future careers. He began again. 'So, you've got your six university choices?'

'I think so. But maybe I should put York instead of Hull? I mean, is it worth aiming higher?'

'It's up to you, Ellie.'

'But which one am I more likely to get into? And is it true if you put somewhere as your second choice they won't take you, even if you get the grades? Because you didn't pick them first, like? Are you better to put somewhere with lower asking grades, just in case you fail? What if your first and second choices want the same marks?'

Mr Cole blinked. 'Um ... what is it you're applying for again?'

Ellie sighed. 'Medicine. Sir.' She was tipped to get 4 As in her A levels, but when she thought about her exams, it felt like standing toe-in on a high cliff, waves crashing below. She would do OK, wouldn't she? The thought of failing made her shudder with fear. What would she do? Another year at home, retaking the exams, in her tiny room with her brother and parents fighting downstairs, the disappointment of her mum, her dad's blank stare. Mark leaving her behind, moving on with his life, meeting exciting new people at uni ... she couldn't bear it.

Mr Cole was taking notes in shaky handwriting. 'And your back-up course?'

'Well, that's what I want to ask. If I put something totally different as well, like English or history, will they think I'm not serious about medicine? Should I put something else sciencey, like biomedical sciences? Or since I'm doing my English A level, I could apply for it somewhere, and that might make me look well rounded?' It was these choices that kept her awake at night, trying to game the UCAS system. 'I mean, what I really want is to be a writer . . . ' She tailed off, embarrassed to even say that sentence out loud. 'I know it's hard. Maybe a doctor who also writes? Or maybe I should have done a language, that could be useful, work for the EU or something.' Ellie had loved her French GCSE, and harboured secret dreams of living in Paris one day, eating croissants and looking chic in a beret, but it hadn't fitted with the courses she needed for medicine. God, it was hard. Why did they expect you to choose your whole life path at the age of not-even-eighteen?

He was struggling to keep up. 'Do you want to do bio-medical sciences?'

'No, like I said ...' Ellie stopped. She'd leaned forward, irked that he wasn't understanding her, and in doing so spotted a glint in the top drawer of Mr Cole's desk. A glass bottle. Vodka. Oh dear. 'Um, it's fine, sir. I'll work it out myself.'

'You're still applying to Oxford?' She could smell it on him now, a stale fire like her uncle at Christmas when he'd had too much sherry. Poor Mr Cole. But also poor her, because how could she hope to get into a decent university if she had to rely on him to sort out her UCAS application?

'Yes, and you remember there's another form to submit for Oxford, plus a reference and samples of work? You're going to send it in for me?'

'Of course. I have it right here.' He rested his hand on a brown envelope, already stamped and addressed in his spidery handwriting. 'Don't worry, Allie. I'll sort it all out.'

'*Ellie.*'

'Oh right. Sorry.'

As soon as she got out of Mr Cole's stuffy cubicle of a room, she knew she had to find Mark. She dug out her homework diary and consulted the copy of his timetable she'd drawn onto the inside cover with her four-colour pen, so she always knew where he was. Physics and maths were Mark's subjects. He was doing six A levels, the most in the school, his calendar crammed with applied maths and statistics and other weird things. He was applying to Edinburgh, too, the only university they had in common on their UCAS forms. She'd tried to persuade him to go for Oxford, but he was dead against the idea, thought she was mad to want to be with 'a load of poncy Harry Potter poshos'. It didn't matter how many times Ellie pointed out that Harry Potter wasn't a posho. And anyway, Edinburgh was quite fancy too, wasn't it? She could picture it already, the two of them in long scarves, striding down the cobbled streets with armfuls of books, a chill in the air and autumn leaves at their feet. Best friends, like they'd always been since they were five. Apart from that weird year at thirteen when Mark's voice suddenly broke and she needed a training bra, and they stopped speaking for a while, but they didn't talk about that.

Mark was just getting out of his maths class when she strode along the corridor with its smell of boiled cabbage and blocked drains, together with a collection of spotty weirdos of which he was the least weird. Though that wasn't saying much. He looked like Harry Potter, she thought, with his glasses and sticking-up black hair. One of the other boys, whose name was Barry and who always smelled of meat paste, made a choking laugh sound. 'Hey Grant, it's your *girlfriend.*'

Ellie gave him the finger, which made him stumble away in disgust. Apparently it was fine for him to be gross, but girls had to be delicate flowers.

'What's up?' said Mark, falling into step beside her as they made their way to chemistry, which they both studied.

Ellie found it bewildering, but it was necessary in

order to get into medicine. Her other A levels – biology and English – were some classic bet-hedging. She hoped that wouldn't go against her when the universities were making their decisions. A doctor who liked to read had to be good, yes? Readers were never bad people; Ellie was convinced of it.

'Just had my "careers guidance" with Old King Cole and guess what? He was pissed.'

'No way!' Mark turned in shock to look at her, and she saw the smears on his glasses, the dried Clearasil round the spot on his nose. She had a similar one, but at least she could slather it over with Pan Stik.

'Way. Booze in the desk drawer and everything.'

Mark scowled. 'Crap. No way am I letting him near my UCAS form. Is it 'cause his wife's gone off with Mr Whippy?'

'Reckon so. I mean he was a careers teacher, he was never the best we had. But he's really hit rock bottom now.'

'I'm never getting married.' Mark pushed his glasses up his nose with one bitten-nailed finger.

'Me neither. Nothing but trouble. Now, can I copy your notes on moles?'

'Not again, El!'

'I'm sorry, I'm just not naturally good at it and you are! If you ever want some notes on *The Scarlet Letter*, I'm your girl.'

'You are such a piss taker.'

They were walking down the main school staircase now, all around them a swarm of hormonal teenagers, shouting and calling to each other, some of the boys flicking wets bits of paper over the banisters, the odd harassed teacher ineffectually telling them to stop.

'Thanks, Mark. You're the best, Mark. I love you, Mark!' She'd said it jokingly, but suddenly Mark stopped up short, right on the landing of the stairs. A girl behind them – Denise Crowley, who'd been wearing a double-D bra since she was fourteen – tutted and shoved him.

'Jesus, Grant, watch where you're going.'

'You'd think he could see with glasses that thick,' said her friend, Amelia Raglan, and a ripple of laughter rolled through the crowd of surging kids.

Ellie rolled her eyes. 'Don't listen to Jugsy Malone. What's up?'

Mark mumbled, 'Um – Bazza was telling me about this party at the weekend. His mate from maths camp.'

'Bloody hell. Bazza has mates?'

'It sounds kind of cool. This guy, his parents are loaded, right? There's even a hot tub! And they're away visiting his sister at uni in Southampton, so he's got the place to himself.'

Ellie started walking down the stairs again. She was going to be late for chemistry and didn't know where he was going with this. 'So?'

'So, do you want go?' Mark was behind her and she couldn't see his face.

'What, Bazza told you to invite any girl you know, since they've never spoken to one?'

'No! Well, yeah. But that's not it. It might be fun. If we went together.'

Ellie was frowning now. What was he on about? Go *together*? They went everywhere together, spent most week-ends in Mark's living room watching films or episodes of

Buffy, his sweet mum bringing them trays of orange squash and Bourbons arranged on a plate.

'OK,' she said cautiously. 'As long as I'm not the only girl there.'

'Honestly, El, you can be good at maths and not a total dweeb.'

'Aye, can you though?'

'You're such a tool.' They were at the chemistry lab now, and crashed in to secure their usual bench, with side-by-side high stools. Mark fished goggles from his bag. He was such a nerd that he had his own hypo-allergenic ones. 'Will you come, though?'

'Course I will, you wazzock. Nothing else to do, is there?' Ellie heaved herself up on the stool and prepared for an hour and a half of barely comprehending boredom. As Miss Maginn droned on and on about atomic weights, Ellie found herself looking over at Mark. He was making notes in a laconic way, in his neat, rounded writing – probably he already knew all this. He was the kind who read ahead in the textbook. It wasn't a big deal, was it, to go to a party together? Why had he made a point of asking like that? Something about it snagged at her, but she didn't know what.

She felt a poke on her arm. Without taking his eyes off the teacher, Mark had slid a note over to her, written in the green ink of his own four-colour pen, on a torn-off piece of file paper. Carefully nodding along to Miss Maginn, who wore the same mustard-coloured suit three days a week, Ellie unfolded it on her lap. It was a little drawing, a stick figure with frizzy hair, and an animal that looked like a mole, beside a tiny hill. Mark had written NOT THESE KIND OF MOLES ELLIE!!!!

She folded it up, suppressing a smile and digging him gently in the ribs. Of course she'd go to the stupid party. She'd never even seen a hot tub in real life.

'Ellie! ELLIE! Turn that racket down, your dad's trying to rest!'

Ellie sighed and reached over to turn down the volume on her CD/radio player, a much-prized present from the Christmas before. However, since she didn't get much pocket money and CDs cost fourteen quid each, she was still taping most of her music off the radio, catching the tail-end of the DJ talking or snatches of ad jingles. Mark, who had a part-time job in HMV, was always making her mix CDs on his family computer, painstakingly writing down the band and track name on a bit of lined paper from his file block and slotting it into the plastic case. Ellie didn't always like the songs, but hadn't the heart to tell him the Spice Girls were still her favourite band. She'd been singing along to 'Stop' at full volume when her mum banged on the door. They always had to be quiet around the house. Dad was always tired. He'd been tired ever since he lost his job as a factory supervisor, four years earlier.

Another spike of worry. How was she going to pay for uni? Her mum worked at the benefits office in town, which didn't pay much, and Dad was clearly never going to have a job again, even assuming he could even get out of bed, which he didn't many days. She'd have to get a part-time job, and she'd heard they didn't let you do that at Oxford, the terms were so short and the workload so intensive. She'd at least need to find a job over the summer, save up a bit. The car factory in town was supposed to pay well, though it was boiling hot inside and back-breaking work.

Ellie sighed. She wasn't going to think about all that tonight. She was going out, something she rarely did, if you didn't count Mark's living room. She looked at herself in the mirror. Her frizzy brown hair had been tamed into submission with copious amounts of serum and Elnett. Brown eyes ringed in liquid liner, which had taken three goes and was still a little wonky. Heather Shimmer on her lips, White Musk perfume sprayed behind her ears and knees, as she'd read about in *Just Seventeen*. She was wearing a tight metallic top she'd bought in Miss Selfridge, and a short black skirt with black tights. She wondered briefly what Mark would say – normally she wore jeans and army jackets, exactly like him. But she was seventeen. It was nice to dress up for a change. A surge of something went through her – excitement, fear, a kind of pain that was almost pleasant. God, she hoped this party wasn't totally lame.

'Ellie! Mark's here!'

She couldn't remember the last time her mother had spoken to her without exasperation. *Could you not brush your hair? Could you not have put the dinner in the oven? Could you not just be totally different?* Thank God Mark had passed his driving test and she didn't need to ask for lifts any more. Hopefully she'd do her test soon, though there was no money for lessons. She grabbed her army jacket – she hadn't totally changed – and ran down the stairs, anticipating and hearing her mother yell at her not to make so much noise.

15

Alan was hovering in the kitchen as she passed through. 'What?' she snapped.

'Eh . . . you're going out with Mark?'

'Not *out* with Mark. Just to a party like.' She looked at her brother with exasperation. Spots erupting along his jaw and cheeks, a sweaty smell that wasn't held back by his cheap body spray. God, she was so glad she was almost eighteen and out of this place. 'Are you . . . what are you gonna do?' Suddenly she felt sorry for him.

He shrugged. Fifteen was a crap age, too young to drive or get served in pubs. 'Dunno. Watch telly, maybe. Mum's on the radge though.'

'When is she not? There's a good film on Channel Four.'

'Yeah. Thanks.' He paused. 'Have fun.'

'Um – thank you.' A horn sounded outside – Mark getting impatient. She ran out, picking up the house key she'd finally been allowed the year before when her mum started working full-time. As she raced to Mark's Mum's Jetta, she could hear he was playing Oasis. This was going to be fun.

Mark didn't say much during the car journey. When she climbed in, he blinked. 'You look dressed up.'

Was that good or bad? 'It's a party, right?'

'Yeah. Yeah, I suppose.' He fumbled with the ignition. He was in the same clothes he wore all the time – a *Back to the Future* T-shirt, and black jeans that were too big for him. But he had gelled back his springy brown hair and put on aftershave, which she recognised as Lynx Africa, body spray of choice of most of the boys in her year. Not Mark before,

16

though. The smell of it fought with Ellie's White Musk in the small car.

Ellie sang along to the radio, but petered out when he didn't join in, feeling self-conscious. 'All this UCAS stuff is so stressful like,' she said. 'You know, I'm not even eighteen yet and I have to decide the rest of my life? How am I meant to do that? Pick one thing and shut down all the rest? Wrecks my head.'

'You aren't really shutting them down, though. Not in other universes.' Mark indicated carefully and made a left turn.

'Oh here we go. What you on about, Einstein?' Although Ellie made fun of him when he talked about physics, she actually enjoyed it. The way his brain worked, full of concepts she could hardly bend hers around.

'The many-worlds theory of quantum mechanics.'

'Eh?'

'It's this idea. That every single thing that's possible has happened in a different universe and timeline. So when you're obsessing about choices like, there's no point, because everything's going to happen anyway. Somewhere, anyway.'

'Not to me, though.'

'A different you.'

'So how many universes are there?'

'Infinite.'

'But . . . '

'Infinite is infinite, El. Anything that can happen *will* happen.'

Ellie tried to digest that. Was it comforting, or just terrifying? 'Well maybe that's true, but I still have to choose a university in this universe, and I'm proper freaking out I made the wrong decision.'

He glanced at her. 'You should do what your instinct tells you. Your gut.'

She hesitated. That was writing, English, journalism. 'But I might not get a good job ...'

'Come on, El. You're seventeen, you've got time to make some mistakes and try different things. You want to write, yeah? And you're good at it.'

'I don't know about that.' Mark was the only person who'd ever seen bits of her work, painstakingly typed out on a computer at school, saved on a floppy disk.

'You're good at it. Trust me.'

'It's not really a job, though, you know? I need to earn.' She needed up and away from this town, was what she meant. From her home. Her mother.

'You'll always be grand, no matter what you do.'

'How do you know?'

'Because. You're smart. You're strong.'

Ellie felt herself blushing. It wasn't like Mark to pay her a compliment. Usually they just slagged each other off mercilessly, or spoke only in quotes from *Buffy* or *Friends*. 'But ...'

'El, don't worry so much. It's the here and now. You're here now – enjoy it.'

She nodded, unconvinced. Soon, they were pulling in at the party house, a large bungalow with a two-car garage. The windows were vibrating to the sounds of that song 'Brimful of Asha'. Ellie got out, staggering slightly on the grass verge in her heels. Mark gave her a look. 'Can you walk in those?'

'Course I can.'

They made her a little taller than him, she realised. They rang the bell and Ellie saw that there was already an empty bottle of Smirnoff Ice in the flowerbed. Someone's parents were going to be mad when they came back. The door was opened by a guy she recognised vaguely from the year below, who wandered off without saying anything. Ellie relaxed a little – clearly, this was an OK party. She had feared finding a bunch of Mark's maths nerd friends sitting about playing Pictionary. But there were a lot of people here, some she didn't even know, who must have been from the other school in town, the posher one. She hung her jacket over the stairs and saw Mark take in her tight top and short skirt, and blink again.

'What?' She felt self-conscious – maybe she looked stupid like this.

'Nothing. Come on, let's find Bazza.'

They pushed their way into the kitchen, where the music was louder and the table was covered in different types of booze. Ellie was impressed – she never dared try to buy it, even though she was almost eighteen and most of the shops in town couldn't have cared less. She picked up a WKD and looked around for a bottle opener, determined to have fun even if Mark was in a weird mood.

Sometimes, there were nights when everything came together. The right combination of people, everyone in a good mood, the best music playing, the stars all aligning, chats with randoms in the queue for kebabs, taxis available and cheap, weather not cold or raining or windy, no wait

19

at the bar, no bad energy. This party was like that. It was true there was a hot tub, and people were stripping off and getting in wearing just their undies. Ellie had no intention of exposing her M&S cotton pants and bra to the world, but the splashing and shrieking and bare flesh on view, the glimpses of dark nipple through wet material, did add a fun, edgy feel to the party. People were just the right level of drunkenness – loose and friendly but not lairy. She knew from experience they had an hour, two hours tops, before it turned, so she'd better join in. She downed two WKDs in quick succession and picked up a third, wandering through the rooms of the house. Mark, deep in conversation with Bazza about their maths homework, watched her go, as if he'd like to say something, but didn't.

In the conservatory, she spotted a knot of people she didn't know, several girls and two boys, most likely from the other school. One of the boys was strumming a guitar, an Oasis song. The other boy struck her right away, as if the rest of the room had faded into soft focus. Floppy brown hair, fraying leather bracelets round sinewy wrists, a denim shirt with rolled-up sleeves. *Oh, hello.* He caught her eye, too, and smiled, it being the perfect night that it was, the planets in conjunction and her horoscope in the right house and everything firing as it should. Ellie didn't stop to talk – this being the night it was, she knew he would find her. She wandered out to the garden, where the over-excited hot-tubbers had spilled water all over the patio. She sat down on a wooden bench, feeling the cool night air on her bare arms, slightly drunk and happy. This was one moment in her life: she was seventeen years old and trying to decide what to do with the rest of it. This time next year she might be hundreds of miles away, with different friends, a different world. Mark might not be there. There was sadness in that thought, but also a tiny flare of something like fear, or even excitement. She could change if he weren't right beside her, someone who'd known her since she was five. Who knew who she'd meet or what she would do? And they'd always be friends no matter what – wouldn't they?

'Aren't you cold?' A voice above her. The boy from the conservatory. He'd come to find her. Ellie's heart raced with this new possibility, where she could be a girl – a woman – that men came after, instead of developing hopeless crushes on people who never looked at her and instead hooked up with thin blonde girls from the year below right in front of her eyes.

She smiled up at him. 'You could keep me warm.' Who was she? She never said things like that – she could almost hear Mark snort with derision in her head.

The boy sat down beside her, the sleeve of his denim shirt grazing her arm. His skin was dizzying – warm, smelling of CK One, his pulse beating beneath his chin. *Oh.*

'You must go to Parkside, yeah?' He had a posh accent, barely Geordie at all.

'Yeah. I'm Ellie.'

'Adam. Just finished at Northolt.'

What a great name, and he was a year older, practically at uni. A warm feeling was growing in her solar plexus. 'So, were you Liam or Noel?' She jerked her head back at the Oasis-players.

He laughed. An amazing sound. 'God, so pretentious, taking a guitar to a party. I tried to stop him.'

Then, and Ellie wasn't entirely sure how this happened, everything got fuzzy and intense and she was very aware of her own heartbeat, and his fingers were brushing her neck, and he was kissing her. He tasted of Juicy Fruit gum. His tongue was in her mouth. *Oh.* Wow, what a night.

He detached, and it took her a second to catch her breath and realise a girl was standing over them, hands on her hips. One of the ones from the conservatory. She was extremely pretty, with very straight, very shiny black hair, and dressed like Ellie normally would be – combat jacket, ripped jeans. She stared at Ellie.

'So. Who are you, and why do you have your tongue in my boyfriend's mouth?'

Then, as if that wasn't bad enough, Mark appeared behind the girl in the conservatory door, staring at Ellie with his eyes colder than she'd ever seen.

'I'm really so so sorry. I'm mortified.'

A tense half-hour later, filled with crying (Ellie) and shouting (the girl, whose name was Michelle, and Adam, who was now her ex-boyfriend) and stony silence (Mark, and what was it even to do with him?) Ellie was being driving home by Michelle. She wasn't sure how this situation had arisen, but she knew Mark had at some stage disappeared, leaving her at a stranger's party where she was suddenly the subject of a trial by teenage girl. She was absolutely furious with him for that.

'I didn't know – I mean, he never said he had a girlfriend.'

Michelle sighed, eyes on the narrow country road ahead, lit only by the odd cat's eye and the distant orange glow of the city. 'It's fine. He never does say. I'm glad, really. You've done me a favour. At least he'll be gone to uni soon and I won't waste my time waiting for him while he snogs other girls in the student union.'

Michelle Allenby was Ellie's age, at Northolt High School, but she was dazzling in her confidence, her self-assurance. She had a Chinese mother, Geordie father, a spirit that was all her own. Ellie was utterly mortified – she had kissed someone else's boyfriend! She wasn't that kind of girl. At least Michelle didn't seem to blame her, but Mark clearly did, and that gave her an anxious burn in her stomach, part anger and part guilt. She couldn't bear the idea of him thinking badly of her, even though she was cross with him for leaving her.

They were almost at Ellie's house now, and tears filled her eyes again, thinking how she'd tripped out with such high hopes for the night, in her silly short skirt, and how terribly everything had ended up. The story would be all round both schools by Monday morning. Ellie Warren, boyfriend stealer. Slapper.

'Listen.' Michelle put the handbrake on with a vigorous pull. 'You seem cool, Ellie. You must be – he only goes for the cool ones. I heard you write a bit.'

'How did you—'

'Oh, when I saw Adam sitting with you, I asked who you were. That guy you came with said you were this amazing writer, working on a book even?'

Ah, Mark. Talking her up before throwing a strop at her. 'Well – I like books. Dunno if I'm any good, though.'

'I'm an actress.' Michelle said it with no self-consciousness. 'We have a theatre group, at our school. If you ever wanted to be involved – write a bit, help us stage things, act if you want – that would be really cool. I believe in artists working together.'

And before Ellie knew it, the girl had written her phone number on Ellie's forearm, with a marker pen she'd fished from the glovebox, and Ellie was out and standing on her front drive. The light had gone on inside the house – she'd be in trouble for the sound of engines and voices. Mark usually dropped her up the road a bit. An artist? An actress? Who was this girl? And suddenly Ellie realised that there could be an even more exciting outcome to a night out than meeting a boy. Meeting a friend, for example.

A few weeks later, the UCAS letters came. Ellie was invited to an interview in Edinburgh to study medicine, and to one at Oxford to study English. It was time to make a choice.

Edinburgh

Ellie had been at university for exactly two and a half days, and she was already face to face with a dead body. An elderly man, his skin shrunken and shrivelled, his teeth loose, his internal organs yellow and fatty. She knew this because their tutor, a ruthless Glaswegian called Dr Alistair Menzies-Fraser, had already sliced their cadaver from chin to groin with a gigantic buzzing saw. The boy next to Ellie, a broad-shouldered rugby-playing type, turned pale and began to sway on his heels.

'Here. Puke into this.' A nearby girl, her hair tied back in thick braids, seized a kidney-shaped metal dish and held it out to the rugby boy, who heaved up purple-coloured bile into it. The girl examined it with interest. 'Red Bull,' she said, with scientific curiosity. She had a strong Scottish accent.

'Are the contents of Mr Stevens's stomach more interesting to you than this poor wee man's liver, Miss Carney?' barked Dr Menzies-Fraser.

Ellie quailed at even being in the line of fire of his wrath, but the girl didn't seem bothered. 'I'm conducting a double-blind study into the corrosive effects of energy drinks on the digestive system,' she said coolly. 'Sir.'

The professor stared her down, fluid dripping from his saw and onto the tiled floor. Ellie felt her own stomach heave.

'Very good, Miss Carney. Now, who can tell me what this piece of viscera is?'

All the medical students surged forward to get a better look at the poor man's innards. Ellie glanced at the girl with naked admiration.

'You're so brave.'

The girl shrugged. 'I spent my gap year in a refugee camp in Sudan. No bother dealing with these old bastards. You just have to not show fear, like with a dog.' She held out a hand, the one not holding the dish of Red-Bull vomit. 'Laura.'

Ellie shook, feeling the girl's confident grip, her rough palm and short sensible nails. Round her wrist were various twists of leather and festival armbands, the mark of the gap year student. 'Ellie.'

25

She wished she'd brought more to university than her provincial education, her final year spent driving about with Mark singing along to obscure indie bands, putting on terrible plays with the drama group Michelle had cajoled her into joining, and holed up in her room desperately trying to get the grades she needed for this course. After the strange night of the party, Mark had been normal with her again, and said sorry for leaving her there. Ellie hadn't been able to stay mad at him for more than a few days, so they'd made up. Michelle had become a good friend too, the three of them often driving to gigs in Newcastle or Sheffield, or fighting over what film to watch at the local multiplex – Ellie always pleading for *She's All That* or *10 Things I Hate About You*, Mark insisting on something nerdy set in space, Michelle preferring the Oscar winners, sure she would star in one soon.

Ellie moved forward, part of an eager gaggle hanging on the anatomy professor's every word as he pointed out with his saw the liver, the pancreas, the bile duct. It was just like the model in Ellie's sixth-form science class, but rendered in real life, in yellows and purples and pinks. It was fascinating. And terrifying. This was someone's actual body. At least they were dead – she could hardly imagine what she'd do if faced with a real-life alive person, depending on her to save them.

'Here's the spleen,' said the professor. 'You'll notice if I cut here' – more buzzing and a disturbing squelching sound – 'what's released is green in colour.' Two more students turned around, bolted for the stainless-steel sinks along the walls and threw up into them. Ellie closed her eyes briefly, but held firm as her stomach lurched.

Laura Carney looked at them with disdain. 'Lightweights. These lot'll no make doctors. Your stomach OK, Ellie?'

'It's grand,' said Ellie resolutely. She was thinking to herself, with a sense of wonder: *Can I do this? Really?* She'd always assumed she'd be a doctor, but now, confronted with actual blood and guts, she felt only a rising panic.

As they exited the anatomy lab a while later, hands scrubbed to a sore pink, Laura and Ellie naturally fell into stride. The other girl was tall, and wore flat DM boots and a sensible anorak. She wasn't girly or shiny like the others in Ellie's halls of residence, which echoed day and night with the hiss of hairdryers and body sprays.

'What you doing now?'

'I was going to meet my friend Mark. He's in the Physics Department.'

'Is he sound? Like, not a total physics nerd?'

Ellie considered it. 'He's kind of both, I guess.'

'All right so.' As if it was the most natural thing in the world, Laura looped her arm through Ellie's. 'I'll tag along.'

Ellie marvelled at her confidence. Imagine just inviting yourself along to things! Imagine just knowing your company would be welcome.

By the time they'd reached the student union, along streets which all contained some beautiful or interesting building, students in hoodies and scarves all over the place, a babble of excitement in the air, Ellie already knew Laura's life story. Her parents had come here from Ghana to go to medical school and never left. She'd spent her gap year working with Médecins Sans Frontières, she played bass guitar, she didn't eat meat. Ellie was hopelessly intimidated, and desperately wanted to be her friend.

They rounded the corner into the cobbled square where the students' union was. Ellie saw Mark on the steps, talking to a handsome boy in a beanie and long black coat. It was only September, but it was Scotland, and an autumn chill filled the air already.

'There he is.'

'The hottie in the hat?'

'Eh, no. The Harry Potter-looking lad.'

Laura squinted. 'Oh, aye. He's cute too.'

As Ellie and Laura crossed the square towards Mark – who she saw with something between affection and exasperation was in his usual *ThunderCats* T-shirt and frayed jeans – and the boy he was standing with, whose name she didn't know, Ellie had the strangest feeling that every step she took in the fading sunlight, in the September of the year she was eighteen, in her first term as a medical student at Edinburgh, was walking her towards the rest of her life.

Later, many hours later, Ellie was queuing at the bar in a loud and scuzzy pub somewhere off the Royal Mile, waving aloft one of the weird Scottish tenners that didn't look like real money. It was warm in the pub and she'd stripped down to her vest top, her hoody tied around her waist. She wasn't entirely sure how they'd ended up here, such was the force of Laura Carney's personality. She had swept Ellie, Mark and the handsome guy off Mark's course, whose name Ellie had not managed to learn, into a wild pub crawl from the student union to several dive bars in the city. Somewhere along the way they had lost the handsome boy, who'd been last seen queuing for a deep-fried Mars bar.

Ellie finally caught the eye of the barman, a short, bearded man in a Slipknot T-shirt, and screamed out her order for three vodka Red Bulls – Laura's suggestion, as it both got you drunk and let you stay up. Ellie's heart was already beating so fast she could hear it buzzing in her ears as one of her favourite songs came on, the Green Day one about being paranoid or bored. She glanced over while the barman opened three tins of Red Bull. She blinked – what she'd seen didn't make any sense. She looked again, saw the same thing.

Laura Carney was kissing someone, arms around their neck, stooping down a little because she was taller than the boy. And the boy was … Mark. Laura and Mark were kissing.

Well, that was fine, wasn't it? Even if Ellie felt a bit like a gooseberry. She liked Laura, and Mark was her best friend. It would be cool if they got together. That was why they'd come to university, after all, to meet new people, make friends, fall in love. She just hadn't quite expected it to happen so soon. As the barman slammed down three glasses and she handed over the money, Ellie ignored the small pocket of cold that had formed just under her ribs, and tossed back her drink.

Oxford

'Ohhhh, hiiiii, I totes didn't see you there, darling.'

Ellie blinked. Did people actually talk like that? She

looked at the girl who'd just arrived on her corridor, lugging several huge cases. Did eighteen-year-olds here have Louis Vuitton luggage and swishy, highlighted blonde hair? Apparently so.

'That's all right,' she mumbled, backing into her room, narrowly missing an ankle-swipe from a suitcase that probably cost more than she'd earned in her entire summer job on the tills in Boots. She'd been in Oxford for one hour, since her parents had dropped her off and had to be forcibly dissuaded from arranging her room for her, and she'd already had one small cry and put up her collection of postcards with Blu Tack on the cream-painted walls.

When she'd thought of Oxford, she'd pictured a wood-panelled room, maybe with leather armchairs and a four-poster bed. Instead, she was in a modern 1960s block with industrial blue carpet in the hallway, one manky fridge already stuffed full of someone else's yoghurts, and a small room with the kind of cheap chipped furniture you might find in a very downmarket Travelodge at a motorway service station. Her clothes, the pictures of her family and friends (Mark and Michelle in pride of place), and the new cheap toaster and kettle her mum had bought her in Argos, seemed too few for the space, and the bedclothes were a depressing maroon colour. Had she made a mistake, choosing to come here? Even when she'd travelled down for the interview – staying in a much nicer, much bigger room on the other side of the college – she hadn't been sure. She wouldn't get in, surely? Not Ellie from the small northern town who'd never even eaten sushi. But she had got in, miraculously, and it had seemed daft to turn down Oxford.

Mark had been annoyed. He hadn't said anything, but he'd retreated from her, and they hadn't been as close during that final year of school. They still hung out, but usually with Michelle, hardly ever just the two of them, and Ellie couldn't remember the last time she'd been round to sit in his front room and eat Bourbons or drink orange squash. It was sad, but she could hardly turn down Oxford for him, could she? It was a once-in-a-lifetime opportunity. But now she was here, her doubts had returned. It was dingy, and everyone seemed really posh so far. And Mark was in Edinburgh, meeting new people, probably having the time of his life.

Ellie had been hovering in her room, feeling deflated and too scared to go to the college bar, when this blonde girl arrived in a cloud of expensive perfume. She had sunglasses perched on her head and was carrying what Ellie was fairly sure was a real Marc Jacobs bag.

'Hellair, I'm Verity.'

'Ellie.'

'Your surname must be a "W", darling, if we're next door? I'm Wyven-Holborn.'

'Er . . . Warren.'

Verity didn't turn her nose up. 'Well, Ellie, I think it's time to break out the gin. What do you say?'

Ellie had never drunk gin in her life. It was something adults liked, bitter and strange. But she'd realised already that being at Oxford was going to involve a radical overhaul of her entire personality, wardrobe and voice.

'Aye, cool,' she said, trying to sound as confident as her new next-door neighbour. She suddenly felt how strong her accent was, though it had been considered fairly posh at her school.

An hour later, Ellie was fuzzy-drunk on three gin and orange juices, swigged out of a variety of mugs they'd found in the communal kitchen, and felt she'd known Verity all her life. The other girl seemed to have no filter at all, and had updated Ellie on her parents' recent divorce – all the posh luggage was apparently a guilt gift – her affair with a ski instructor the previous spring, and the nose job she'd had when she was sixteen. Verity was studying history of art, which Ellie hadn't even known was a subject.

At some point, the bottle of gin entirely drained, Verity smacked it down on her desk and declared it was bar time. 'Tonight is very important, Ellie darling. The people you meet, they could end up being your lifelong friends. And trust me, we want our pick of the top totty before it gets creamed off.'

'You mean . . . boys?' Ellie had avoided affairs of the heart since the disastrous time she'd accidentally kissed Michelle's boyfriend at the party. Michelle found it hilarious and told the story as often as possible, but Ellie was deeply ashamed. Partly because it was someone's boyfriend, but mostly because of the way Mark had looked at her. The disappointment in his eyes. Now she was at uni, she supposed finding a boyfriend was the next step. Or even just kissing someone. She was embarrassed she'd got this far without ever having sex. Surely no one else in the whole college was still a virgin.

Verity had turned her head upside down to brush out her long blonde hair. She flipped it up, revealing fresh rosy cheeks. Expensive skin and teeth. She pulled a hoody over her vest top and jeans, but managed to look glamorous all the same. Ellie was in a Little Miss Naughty T-shirt, bought in New Look, and jeans and trainers. She knew she didn't look the same as Verity, despite wearing almost identical clothes. But why? It was impossible to tell what the difference was, only that it existed.

Verity linked Ellie's arm. 'Absolutely boys. Seen anyone you like yet?'

'Eh, no, not really had the chance like.'

'Then let's head down there! I am absolutely determined to get over Thierry, so I need to get under someone else. Come on, darling.'

Ellie had never met anyone like this, so posh, so open, so polished, but all the same so kind and friendly. Grabbing her room key, she followed her new friend out into the quad, which, she was learning, was Oxford-speak for the square of lawn in the middle of the college, which you weren't allowed to walk on except in summer term.

Already little knots of girls and boys stood about the entrance to the bar, a glass-fronted room on the other side of the quad from Ellie's block. Two minutes' stumbling distance, if even that. Everyone was casting looks at each other, sizing up the talent and the opposition. Who would become a friend, a lover, an enemy? So many of the girls were like Verity, tall and beautiful and shiny. Ellie caught sight of a cute boy, about her height with brown hair and dimples, an Irish accent saying something about football. She might have liked to talk to him, but Verity pulled her on.

'Come on, darling, I really need a wine or two now.'

Three gins was already more than Ellie had ever drunk.

She cast a quick look back at the boy, who smiled at her. Ah well. It was only the first day. She had years to get to know everyone here. And as she tagged obediently after Verity, into the cool wooden exterior of the bar, she felt suffused with a wonderful sense of possibility, that anything might happen to her, and she was in exactly the right place for when it did.

JUNE 2019

Ellie was pressed against the wall of the staircase, listening hard to the voices in the kitchen. She hadn't dared risk a shower, but instead pulled on the tracksuit Verity had bought her to get her makeup done in. It was pink velour, not her style at all, and had BRIDE printed over the bum. In the kitchen were Verity – a top financial consultant whose father owned most of Jersey – and Ellie's cousin Hannah, who worked in Sainsbury's on the deli counter. Nonetheless, they were chatting animatedly about *Love Island*. Ellie could smell slightly singed hair, and knew Katie would be trying to repair hers in the kitchen. She was obsessed with her hair, long and blonde and curly. A child's voice was saying, 'Mummy, I don't WANT to wear these shoes. Mummy. *Mummy!*'

The front door was ahead, the door to the kitchen ajar. She could make it. Holding her breath, realising too late she was still in her slippers, Ellie ran forward and opened the front door, threw herself out of it. Through the kitchen window she glimpsed Verity's head, her shiny blonde hair, expensively highlighted, twisted into braids. She'd done that for Ellie's wedding. It was all in motion, too late to stop it now – wasn't it? She pulled her phone from the impossibly tight pocket of the tracksuit and texted Verity.

Emergency. Make excuse and meet me in garden.

She heard the trill as her text was delivered, and Verity stop talking for a moment, then mutter something about needing a bit of air. A moment later she'd opened the front door. Ellie pulled her friend against the wall, out of sight of the windows.

'Darling! What are you doing?'

'God, I don't know. Freaking out. I'm doing the right thing, aren't I? Getting married?'

Verity's face, aggressively made up, softened. She was still wearing jeans and a Breton jumper, her hair coiled and plaited. She looked like she'd stepped from the pages of *Elle Bride*. 'Wedding-day jitters?'

'Yes. No. I don't know, I guess it's something about being in my old room. I just can't stop thinking about the past.'

She'd been thinking about the first crunch moment of her life. The choice she'd made in her last year of school, after poor Mr Cole had messed up her UCAS forms and Oxford had invited her to interview for English, not medicine. Choosing that would mean a different career, not being a doctor, a different life. It had been an agonising few weeks, trying to decide. In the end she hadn't been able to turn down Oxford, and that had become her life, the friends she'd made – Verity, Camilla who would be at the church later battling her twin toddlers – the experiences she'd had, the jobs she had ended up with. It was a lot to choose at eighteen.

Often, she thought about her other life, the one she might

have had if she'd stuck to the plan and gone to Edinburgh with Mark. Laura had been on the medicine course there, and perhaps they would have been friends. Then, who knew, everything might be totally different. But she couldn't think that way – she'd go mad. She had chosen to go to Oxford and that was it. This was her life, there was no turning back. She had to think about the present, not the past. What was she going to do?

Verity patted her arm. 'This is totally normal, babe.'

'Is it? Did you have jitters?'

'Oh, darling, you don't know the half of it. I had to be restrained from climbing out the window of the church. Remember, I was absolutely green walking down the aisle?'

Ellie only remembered her looking beautiful. 'Why weren't you sure? You had doubts about Sebastian?' Verity's husband was a bond trader, handsome and absolutely loaded, but Ellie had never quite seen the point of him all the same.

Verity shrugged. 'Just doubts. It's such a big step, and I was determined not to end up divorced like Mummy and Daddy.'

'But it was OK?'

'Of course it was OK! We're very happy.'

Ellie could hear vague noises from inside the house, footsteps on the stairs, doors opening and closing. Her wedding was already in motion. And she loved him, didn't she? The man she was supposed to marry? It wasn't a flash in the pan thing – they'd known each other for years. He was good to her, unlike some of the men she'd gone out with in the past. She was more than ready to get married – she wasn't far off forty. Schoolfriends had been married for years and had even teenage kids. Why had Ellie dragged her heels for so long? She didn't want to think about the answer to that.

Make a decision. Do something. She looked at her reflection in the front door in dismay – she had dust in her unwashed hair, and a swelling bump on her forehead. She hadn't even showered yet. Upstairs, her wedding dress hung on the back of the door, shrouded in cream cotton. She couldn't put that on. Not yet. If she did it would all be real, there'd be no turning back. She just needed to think about it for a minute. Go back over her life, try to work out if she was exactly where she was meant to be. She squeezed Verity's hand quickly.

'Stall for me with Mum? I just need some space.'

Verity looked alarmed. 'Well all right, darling, but your hair! Makeup! It takes ages.'

'I'll be back. I promise.' And Ellie fled.

CHOICE 2 – DECEMBER 1999

Ellie squinted up at the house as her mother's car drew to a stop outside. It looked smaller. That wasn't possible – it was exactly the same house she'd grown up and spent her entire life in – but it did look smaller all the same. Maybe that was the effect of spending the last ten weeks at Oxford, surrounded by old stone and towers and gargoyles and bridges, all of it casually heaped together as if the world had enough beauty to throw it away.

'Come on, then,' said her mother, irritably. 'I'm not carrying your bags for you – you might have servants at Oxford, but you're home now.'

'I don't have servants,' Ellie snapped back, bitterly regretting that she'd ever told them about the scouts who made her bed and emptied her bin. Their main purpose, everyone was sure, was to spy on you and make sure you weren't having illegal room parties (officially defined as six or more people in a room with music) or, God forbid, putting things on your wall with Sellotape. As soon as term ended, the college wanted the students out so they could clear the rooms and rent them to conference guests at vastly inflated fees. Ellie wasn't sure who'd want to sleep in her lumpy single bed under the high draughty window with its view of the spires, though she had all the same been very sad to strip out her belongings and head off for the train with her suitcase and rucksack. She'd had the very strong sense of leaving behind all that was fun and exciting, heading back to the dreariness of her provincial home. Other people were picked up by their parents in spacious people carriers, whereas Ellie had to make her own way on the train. And her mother was clearly in a foul mood, snapping at her all the way from the station. It was hardly Ellie's fault she'd not been able to find anywhere to park.

Now, she lugged her baggage into the house, noticing how chipped the paint was on the door, the muddy marks of her brother's shoes in the porch. It was hard not to compare it with Verity's mother's house in Buckinghamshire, where she'd spent a weekend mid-term. Floors kept shining by a daily cleaner, bunches of flowers everywhere, Verity's mother elegant and interested, hugging Ellie hello. Her own mother hadn't hugged her at the station, too panicked about getting a parking ticket, and she didn't offer one now they were inside either. Instead, she tutted at the dishes in the sink. 'Someone couldn't have washed these? Frank?'

Ellie's dad appeared, holding his favourite mug of tea, in a soft old golf jumper. He was out of bed. That was a good sign.

'There she is.' He enfolded Ellie in his arms, and she breathed in his familiar smell of Imperial Leather and wood smoke. 'Hello, pet.'

'Hi, Dad.'

'Back to slum it with your poor peasant family, aye?' But he said it more kindly than her mother would have.

Her mother sniffed. 'Dinner's at six, Ellie. I'm sure you're used to more Continental ways now, but Alan gets hungry, he's a growing lad.'

'Where is he?'

Her brother had not come to say hello. She hoped he was all right. She'd only spoken to him once or twice all term, when her mother had put him on during the stilted phone calls Ellie made from her room, using phone cards that rapidly ran out. She'd given her family the number, but they rarely called. She wasn't sure why. *Oh, we thought you'd be busy,* her mother always said, and Ellie would feel a stab of guilt because, yes, she was often busy, in the college bar or out at the Turf Tavern or having dinner at Pizza Express, spending too much on cocktails at the Grand Café, a place Verity loved. Having fun. Flirting, being young. Studying, too, late nights behind the glowing windows of the Radcliffe Camera. Why shouldn't she do all that? But the guilt nagged at her all the same.

Her mother hadn't answered. Sighing to herself, hefting her rucksack, Ellie said: 'I'll go up, then. Dad, can you help me?'

'I'll bring your case up in a minute, pet.'

'Oh, Ellie.' Her mother looked up from the post she was sorting through, biting her lip in annoyance or stress. 'We did make a few little changes to your room. You'll hardly notice.'

Hardly notice? That was pushing it a bit, Ellie thought, ditching her rucksack on the bed, which now had a neutral blue duvet cover, and surveying all the new things in her room. The exercise bike, the sewing machine, the racks of thread and wool. Her posters and pictures had all been taken down, and her desk swept clear of her trinkets and toiletries. Even her books were gone somewhere.

'Under the bed.'

She looked up. Her brother was in the doorway. He looked pale and spotty, in a Manic Street Preachers hoody.

'What is this?'

'She had this mad clear-out. I wouldn't let her chuck your stuff though, it's under the bed in boxes.'

'Oh. Ta, bro. You all right?'

Alan shrugged. 'Got the computer now, so, you know, that makes a big difference.'

'Don't you go out and meet people, see friends?'

Another shrug. 'I have friends on there. Honestly, El, you'll see. In a few years the internet will be totally normal, not sad.'

She couldn't picture it. There were computers at college, and some people had their own in their rooms, used for chatting on MSN Messenger and illegally streaming films, but most of Ellie's communication was still done in person, or by leaving notes in the college pigeonholes. 'Hmm, if you say so.'

An electronic beep sounded through the door, drawing Alan's head as if on a wire.

'Better go.' He paused a second. 'I'm glad you're back. Mum, she's – well, she works every day now. She's so stressed, like, all the time.'

'Dad seems better?'

'Yeah. You know, I think he actually is. So.'

And Alan was gone. Ellie sat down on her bed, looking

42

round at what used to be her room, feeling how quickly she'd been erased, as if she no longer really had a home. She didn't entirely belong in Oxford, with her northern accent and lack of knowledge about port, but clearly she didn't belong here any more, either. Half-heartedly, she unpacked a few things from her rucksack, the hefty Victorian novels she was supposed to read over the break, her college hoody, which she knew she couldn't wear about town without attracting ridicule, the snow globe of the Eiffel tower she'd bought on the whirlwind week-end when Camilla and Verity had dragged her to Paris on the Eurostar, which Ellie could not really afford but couldn't bring herself to regret. She shook it and stared at the twinkling image inside, trying to recall how it had felt to see it in real life, lit up and shining against the sky, the dark silk of the river, the smell of croissants from every bakery, the taste of rough red wine on her tongue. Camilla was studying French and planning to spend her third year in Paris, lucky thing. She was probably having a wonderful Christmas break, with her aristocratic family in their large Norfolk house, all roasted goose and twinkling lights and roaring open fires. Verity was in the bloody Caribbean! And Ellie was here.

She pushed herself up. Wallowing wasn't going to help her. Instead, she was going to enjoy her Christmas break, starting by getting rat-arsed with Mark. Just like old times.

The landline was on a little table in the hallway, where it had always sat, so that Ellie's mother could stick out her head from the kitchen, eagle-eyed for pre-6-p.m. calls. Ellie dialled Mark's number, which she would surely always know by heart.

'Hello?' His mum.

'Hi, Mrs Grant! It's Ellie.'

Was there a slight hesitation? 'Oh, Ellie, pet, how nice to hear from you. Back from Oxford? How is it?'

She'd be answering this question a lot over the next few weeks. 'Oh, you know. Posh, hard work. The buildings are lovely. Is Mark there?'

'Hmm, well, actually, pet, he's just in the bath. I'll tell him you called?'

Since when did Mark take baths? Maybe this was some new Edinburgh thing he'd picked up. She wouldn't know – it wasn't as if they'd talked all term. Ellie had been so busy, overwhelmed with all the work and socialising crammed into the short term – three black-tie events a week, some-times – but she had sent him some emails from the university computer room, tried to call him a few times from her new mobile, but the number she had was for a communal phone on his staircase, and half the time no one answered or else they did it in silly prank voices, or no one had heard of a Mark Grant.

'OK. Well, eh, I was hoping maybe we could do some-thing tonight. Or tomorrow. Will you tell him?'

'Of course I will, pet. Bye now.'

Ellie looked down at the phone, the dial tone sounding. Had Mark ever not been in when she called him? He never went anywhere, did he? Pushing down her sense of uncer-tainty, a feeling that something just wasn't right in the fabric of the world, she rang Michelle's number instead.

It was weeks before she saw Mark in the end. December had worn out, Christmas had been and gone, a strange and exhausting one. Ellie's mum had been in a constant routine of making and cleaning up meals, refusing all help, never even sitting down with them to watch a film. Alan was in his room, the electronic beeps of his computer drifting out into the hallway. Ellie hadn't seen him go outside all week, and worried about him. If he got his A levels he was going to study computer science at university, so her parents seemed to think his online time was all educational. Ellie still couldn't believe her parents had actually bought a computer. And what about her own education? She'd handwritten all her coursework and didn't have a laptop at university. She had the feeling they were just shocked Alan was taking his A levels at all. Ferociously bright, he'd always found school a bit too easy.

A few times he had reluctantly let her into his room, which smelled of cheesy Wotsits, to check her Hotmail. Verity had sent her a long screed from Barbados, where her divorced parents and their new partners were all staying in the same hotel. *Major drama, darling.. Luckily the bartender is cute and I have an unlimited tab for daiquiris.* Ellie had hardly had time to reply, Alan hovering over her, his neck red with acne against the collar of his polo shirt. At least her father seemed better this Christmas, getting out of bed and even helping her mum make the gravy, watching *Gone With The Wind* with her on Christmas Day. Ellie and he had gone on a few walks in the chilly air, and he'd done his best to ask her about Oxford, but she had the feeling it was impossible to explain without sounding twattish, all her talk of scouts and High Table and Formal Hall, gowns and sub fusc and Collections. It barely made sense to her, that world, and she knew it was elitist and silly, but all the same she loved it. It was hard to explain how it drew you in, the beauty of the spires on cold, still winter mornings, the frost on the grass at Christ Church Meadow, the history all around you, the sense of young brains firing and fizzing and hearts breaking and all of them cooped up together in three small quads. It was her place, but she couldn't share it with people from her old life.

Even when she met Michelle for a drink in the Blacksmith's Arms, their old haunt, where the barman had always served them Smirnoff Ices without checking their IDs too closely, her friend was full of questions, but with a hint of judgement.

'So, do you all get dressed up in ballgowns and drink champagne on the lawn?'

Ellie actually had done that several times – the ballgowns, at least, even if the 'champagne' was Cava from Tesco. Michelle was at drama school in London, desperately edgy, dressed in a black polo neck and slim jeans, her eyes heavily lined. She had her own lingo too, about the Tube and clubs she went to in East London and warehouse parties and the Stanislavski method. They were on different paths, and that was OK. But Mark. Why hadn't he called? She'd rung to invite him to the pub and he supposedly wasn't there again – out on a walk, his mum had said.

Squashed round their old table at the pub, feeling his absence, she asked Michelle about it: 'I tried Mark earlier. Did you invite him?'

Michelle just shrugged. 'He'll get in touch when he's ready.'

What did that mean?

'Have you seen him?'

Michelle took a drag on one of the thin French cigarettes she'd started smoking – Ellie knew her hair and clothes would stink when she got home. 'Oh yeah, he came down once for a conference thing. We went out on the lash. Good times. I always knew he'd be one of those boys who come into their own at uni.'

He'd been in London and not told her? She could have gone down. It was barely two hours on the Oxford Tube, which was actually a coach that went between the cities. But they hadn't invited her. Why?

The night wore on. There was a slight reserve between her and Michelle, a bit of competitiveness over whose college experience was cooler, but Ellie soon realised she could not compete and began to self-deprecate, always safer.

'Honestly I feel like such a provincial. So many people secretly have yachts or second homes in France, and here I am – I went to Calais once on a day-trip with school.'

Michelle lit her seventh cigarette. Was this why she'd stayed so slim, when Ellie had piled on what they called the Freshers' Fifteen, subsisting on chips and cheese and late-night toasties? The historic buildings didn't have kitchens, and hall food was both expensive and disgusting, so often they just scavenged for nutrition as best they could.

'I know,' Michelle admitted. 'I used to think I was kind of a big shot, I won't lie, but turns out I was a big shot for Longton, not London. I swear there's like four people in my class whose parents have Oscars. Just hanging around the house, like. Doorstops.'

'That's privilege, isn't it?'

'It sure is. But hey, El, you made it there – that's half the battle, right? You got there without the same leg-ups. And you're as good as they are.'

'I don't know if that's true,' Ellie said, thinking of the tutorials where she sometimes fell silent, with no idea what people were talking about.

'It's Oxford. They don't take people on charity!'

'Well, same with you – RADA don't let in any old scummers, do they?'

Michelle shrugged. 'Probably had to fill their working-class quota.'

'Fucked that up then, didn't they. Did no one tell them your dad's the richest man in Truckleton village?'

Michelle laughed. 'That's right, my dad the major land-owner. Three acres complete with hot and cold running cows.' She paused. 'You don't regret it then? Oxford over Edinburgh? English over medicine?'

Ellie had spent many hours thinking about this, quizzing the medics in her college about their workload. Would she have enjoyed that – getting up for 9 a.m. all-day lectures? She couldn't deny she loved English, immersing herself in ideas and arguing about the intentions of long-dead authors, drinking coffee in the faculty café and lying in bed reading.

'Nah,' she said. 'I can always do post-grad medicine. Lots of people do that. And Oxford – I know it's twatty, but it really is special.'

'Course it is. You'd have been mad to turn it down.'

Michelle had never said that before, and Ellie felt a big wave of relief. She'd done the right thing – even if it had meant stepping away from Mark. Maybe that was why he

48

hadn't called. He might still be annoyed at her for the choice she'd made – but she'd made it, and she couldn't regret it.

After that, things were more relaxed, as the Smirnoff Ices (for Ellie) and neat tequila (for Michelle, who seemed to doing everything she could to avoid calories) flowed and so did the conversation. At about ten to eleven Ellie was fighting her way to the bar to get last orders in, waving a tenner in the air. 'Sorry, sorry – need to get past – thank you!' She flashed a smile at some hulking townies and they let her through. There was one person ahead of her, gathering up a handful of pints. 'Sorry, can I just . . . ' She slipped in beside them. It was Mark. Mark was at the bar.

Ellie just stared at him, then realised she had to say something. He looked the same – same glasses with the wonky leg, same faded old *Doctor Who* T-shirt. Same old Mark. 'Hi.'

'Oh. Hi.' He had his usual order as well, a pint and two packets of crisps, one salt and vinegar, one cheese and onion. To be ripped open and shared with the table, like they always did. But who was he with?

'I'm with Shell, did she not . . . ?'

'Oh yeah, she said. Didn't think you'd be here though.'

'What, the pub we always come to?' Ellie knew she sounded cross. 'Who're you out with then?'

'Oh, Bazza and the lads.'

The physics geeks, no doubt arguing loudly about whether the new *Star Wars* film was good or terrible.

'OK. Well. Come and say hi at least?'

He followed her to the table. Michelle did a double-take.

'Bloody hell, it's Grantman!' They hugged, her arms wrapping round his thin back. 'You're like a beanpole.'

'You can talk.' Mark looked her over critically. 'Going for the actress size six, are we?'

Michelle rolled her eyes. 'I don't have a choice. Believe me, there's nothing I'd rather do than grab those crisps and shove them in my gob, all piled on top of each other, as God intended.' She looked at Ellie. 'Did you forget the drinks?'

'Oh. Crap, I did.'

Ellie fought her way back to the bar, and by the time she'd argued Joe the landlord into serving her – 'I've rung the bell, Ellie, you know the law' – and come back, Mark was gone and Michelle was texting on her Nokia. 'Did he leave?'

'Oh yeah. They're going to Pancho's apparently. Said we could join them but can you imagine? Dancing to Steps with half the Physics Set? No thanks.'

Ellie looked over at the door. She might have quite liked to dance with Mark, messing about and laughing as he stuck his hands over his ears whenever they put on pop, lobbying the DJ for some obscure indie music which would definitely not get played. And why hadn't he come with them tonight? Why had he gone out with the nerds instead of her and Michelle?

She brooded over it all night and the next day, staying up too late listening to the sounds of Alan's computer in the next room, wondering why he never got into trouble for making noise when people were sleeping, looking at the pile of hefty novels she was supposed to read for the following term. As a child around Christmas she would have lain awake wracked with excitement, ready for her Doctor Barbie or Fisher Price Big Yellow Teapot. Things were simple then. Now she was assailed by worries on all sides. Why her mother was so snappy and unhappy. Why her father seemed increasingly forgetful, making cups of tea and leaving them on the side to go cold, or asking halfway through a film what it was they were watching. Why Mark didn't want to see her. Whether she'd ever fit in at Oxford, if she'd pass her beginning-of-term exams, inexplicably called Collections, whether she'd get a boyfriend or lose her virginity, which now she was nineteen was becoming an embarrassment. Eventually, her eyes drooped shut on the red and green of the fairy lights she'd looped around her curtain pole, which her mother had complained would scorch the lining, and she fell asleep.

Then the next morning, a surprise – her mum knocked on her door while she was still skulking under the covers.

'Honestly, Ellie, it's after ten. You might be allowed to lie in your bed all day at Oxford, but—'

'I have a nine a.m. tutorial,' Ellie snapped, sick of this. 'I don't lie in bed all day. What is it?'

Her mother blinked, as if surprised to be answered back. 'Phone for you. It's Mark.'

Mark! Ellie sat up hurriedly, smoothing her hair and wishing she wasn't in pyjamas, though he'd hardly be able to see her. She ran downstairs to the phone (her mother had never seen the point of buying a cordless).

'Hello?' Her heart was racing. Ridiculous.

'El.' The familiar voice. 'Sorry about last night. I just already said I'd see the lads.'

Lads, indeed.

'I wanted to hang out and the holidays are nearly over! Tonight, maybe? The pub?'

'I'm heading to London today – staying with a mate for a

few days over New Year. A group of us are going.' He sounded different; she didn't know exactly how. Older, maybe.

'Oh.'

He paused. 'Maybe you could come down too? Watch the fireworks? What do you think?'

Ellie and Mark had always spent New Year together, staying in to watch horror films, agreeing that it was the worst night of the year to go out. And this year was more hyped-up than ever – the millennium. She wasn't sure about going to London. She'd only been there a handful of times – and who were these new friends? It seemed wrong that Mark had friends she didn't know.

'I'll have to ask Mum.' She couldn't afford the train fare by herself.

'OK, well, let me know. I'm thinking a pub somewhere.'

'Sure. OK.'

A slight pause, filled with all the things they needed to say to each other. Three months' worth of catching up. 'Um . . . OK, we can talk then I hope. You've got a phone now, yeah? Give me the number and I'll text you where to meet.'

She did, and he hung up with a swift goodbye. Ellie sat on the stairs, greasy-haired and sleep-stained, wondering what on earth it meant.

Her mother was not keen. 'What about this Y2K bug? They say planes might fall out of the sky and trains crash and that. You really want to be out in the world with that happening?'

'Mum, that's just a conspiracy theory.' But Ellie was a tiny bit afraid too – she'd make sure not to be on any form of transport at midnight.

'Well, what if something happens in the city? You know what you're like, not street smart.'

That stung. 'I've been at university by myself for nearly three months!'

A sniff. 'Oxford. It's hardly the real world, is it?'

Unexpectedly, her dad stepped in. 'Let her go, Judy. She's a grown woman now. Why shouldn't she celebrate? A new millennium; she'll want to see that in somewhere with a bit of life. It's history being made.'

Her mother scowled. 'And I suppose you'll want money.'

'No,' Ellie said, too proud.

Her dad winked at her, and once her mother had stormed out to the shops he slipped her fifty quid.

'Just have a good time, pet. It's all over before you know it.' She didn't know if he meant New Year's Eve, or her youth in general, or something else, but it was money and a free pass, so she was going.

'Oh, come on!' The orange numbers on the Tube sign had just frozen and reset themselves to read '10'. Ten minutes! She didn't have ten minutes. She wasn't sure she was going to make it by midnight. Especially not when everywhere was rammed with drunken, singing idiots. Ellie, sober and irritated, wished she'd followed Michelle's advice and slipped some booze into her handbag for the train journey. Her friend was at a drama school party somewhere in Camden and had begged Ellie to join her – *there'll be fit lads and vodka jellies, honest* – but Ellie had stuck it out. She'd promised to meet up with Mark. He'd told her to go to the Oxo Tower, and she wasn't sure what that meant. Was it a pub? He'd said something about it having a great view of the fireworks. No doubt it was some London thing she didn't understand.

She would definitely be late, though. Stupid, stupid, stupid. She cursed herself for not leaving in time, missing the earlier train, having to get the late one, which had crawled to London stuck at endless red signals. It wasn't like her to be late. She wasn't a girly girl, unlike Michelle, who wouldn't set foot outside without three coats of Heather Shimmer lipstick. But she'd been nervous for some reason, taken too long straightening her hair, and there was a definite singed smell when she breathed in. Now it was already 11.08 p.m. and she was going to be late for Mark. It was mad they hadn't met up over Christmas, when he'd been just a mile away, and now he was off staying with strangers. Her mother had raised that as an objection, too – where was Ellie going to sleep tonight? At Mark's friend's, Ellie had said, though in truth it hadn't been mentioned. Was that what he'd meant, or would they stay up all night, get the first train home to Newcastle, knackered and screwing up their eyes against the dawn, as they had once or twice that final summer? Would there be a big group as she was imagining, who'd stay out partying till dawn? Would she have to stand up for hours, being jostled in some expensive and crowded London bar? God, she was out of her comfort zone. Ellie already felt worried about the idea of getting no sleep or having to kip on someone's floor. Or did he mean something else – had he arranged somewhere for them to stay? She had no idea.

Ellie put aside her worries and concentrated on actually getting there. She could go up and try to find a bus or taxi, but it all depended on the traffic. Wait ten minutes for the

Tube, or run all the way up the escalators to the street and risk the bus? Tube, bus? Tube, bus? Come on, just decide! She was wasting even more time dithering. Her phone didn't work underground, so she couldn't check if Mark was there already and waiting for her, or if he and his friends had moved on to another pub. *Just decide, Ellie.* It didn't matter either way. It was just one night, as her mother always said. She'd be turning her nose up at the New Year's revellers around Ellie now, surging onto the platform with nowhere to go, whooping and singing snatches of 'Auld Lang Syne' and dressed up as superheroes or Elvis or the Spice Girls.

Tube or bus. Ellie made a decision.

The bus

It was rammed on there, too, boozy-breathed partygoers filling the space, talking and singing loudly. Someone had been sick near the back seat.

The bus had been a bad choice, she realised. Stuck in a tide of people spilling out onto the streets, it had barely moved an inch in the last half-hour, and she was crammed in the elbow of some sweaty man dressed as Dr Evil from *Austin Powers*, a rubber cap over his head. She blinked as a drop of sweat fell from his chin onto her face. Happy bloody New Year.

The bus lurched forward, stopped again, and all its lights went out and the engine stopped. A chorus of groans went up.

'For fuck's sake, it's almost midnight!' someone shouted.

Ellie glanced at the watch Dr Evil was wearing. Eleven forty-nine. Bloody hell, she really might miss it.

Inspiration struck. They weren't that far from the place now – just a few streets and a bridge, and if she ran . . .

'Can I get off?' she yelled. 'Please, can I get off?'

She knew London bus drivers had all kinds of ridiculous rules about not letting you off unless you were at the designated stop. He met her eyes in the mirror – a weary man, working just another shift while everyone else got drunk and snogged – and took pity on her. The doors whooshed open, and Ellie, along with a few others, wriggled out and into the crowd. Cannoning by people, she ran through Leicester Square, past Burger King and the cinemas and the bright tatty lights. Not real London, Michelle always said contemptuously. For the tourists and out-of-towners. But it seemed everyone was there right now, and getting in Ellie's way. Eleven fifty-one. She jumped over a half-eaten burger that was spilled like roadkill on the pavement. Eleven fifty-two. She dodged a gaggle of bare-legged girls taking photos of themselves in front of one of those creepy human statues. Eleven fifty-three. She weaved skilfully through a gang of drunk boys in football shirts, one with a traffic cone on his head. She was going to make it. She . . . fell right over the open guitar case of a busker who was belting out 'Angels' and sprawled on her face, scattering coins everywhere.

'Oh God! I'm so sorry – are you OK?'

She blinked up at him. Bits of her hurt. Her knees, her palms where she'd put them down to stop herself. They stung and burned and she knew she'd have scabs tomorrow. And all the germs of Leicester Square embedded in them.

The busker had stopped at the top note of 'through it *allllll*' and was helping her up, but the guitar was getting in the way, and bashing her on the head, and for a few moments they just struggled, apologising to each other and falling over themselves. Ellie realised a small crowd had gathered and someone was even recording it on a camcorder. They'd probably send it in to *You've Been Framed*.

'Here, here.' She scooped up his change and dropped it back into the guitar case. 'I'm sorry.' She had to go.

'Hey, stop a minute, you're in a bit of a state.'

'It's just I'm late for—'

'You're bleeding.' He pointed down and she saw that she was indeed leaking blood and grime from both knees. Oh God. She didn't have time for this.

'It's OK. I just need to clean it and ... are you OK?' Because the busker had now gone white and looked like he might throw up.

Faintly, he said, 'It's just I ... I really can't stand the sight of blood.'

'Really? Um, well, do you have a tissue or something?'

'No.' He was the colour of a kiwi fruit now.

Oh God, this was all she needed. But she felt responsible, for being late and clumsy, for interrupting his set, making him sick. And he was right, she really had to clean her knees before they got infected. They'd begun to throb and sting now. Mark would understand, wouldn't he? She'd had an accident. She'd text him once she got inside, try to catch up with him and his mates later.

'Look, come with me. We'll go in somewhere, I'll clean myself up, you can recover a bit. Sound OK?'

He gave her a wobbly smile. 'What are you, a doctor or something?'

She could have been, or at least on her way to being, if she'd made a different choice once. Elle stared at the ground, littered with chips and rubbish. 'No. No I'm not.'

Arm in arm, they staggered towards the Leicester Square Burger King, which on New Year's Eve resembled one of Dante's circles of hell (or so she imagined – she only pretended to her tutor that she'd read Dante). People were fighting over chicken nuggets and puking and singing. Ellie removed her torn tights in the loos (indescribably dirty) and went at her wounds with a tissue soaked in hand soap. She might have a scar, but at least she hopefully wouldn't die of septicaemia. She glanced at the time on her phone – she could never make it now, it was almost midnight. Quickly, she typed a text to Mark.

So sorry total nightmare fell over will explain.

She waited for it to send, but it didn't. Network overloaded, maybe. When she came out of the loo, the busker was hovering, holding two milkshakes. 'Um . . . I wanted to say sorry. Are you all right?'

She was very conscious of her bare legs, her tights now discarded in the bin. Three quid down the drain. 'I'll live.'

He held out the milkshakes. 'Peace offering – chocolate or strawberry?'

She chose chocolate, of course. 'Do you know what time it . . . ?'

Just then, the crowd began to chant: 'Ten . . . night . . . eight . . . '

The year 2000 was almost upon them and she wasn't

going to make it to Mark. She rooted in her bag for her phone to see if he'd replied, looked up to find the busker watching her. Then it was midnight and everyone was whooping and cheering and hugging, and it seemed perfectly natural to turn to each other and hug. He smelled of sweat and the leather of his guitar strap, and aftershave, and for a moment among all that chaos he put a finger under her chin and just looked at her, and Ellie seriously thought her insides might melt like her milkshake. She hadn't noticed how good-looking he was – fair indie-boy hair that flopped like Brett's from Suede, tall and lean, hazel eyes and a mouth she suddenly couldn't stop staring at.

Then he leaned towards her and gently placed a kiss on her lips. No tongue. Just a warm, soft mouth, promising delights to come. Ellie would think about this moment for a long time after, the way her whole body seemed to dissolve, her stomach turning over itself. 'Happy New Year,' he said, and she couldn't say anything back for a long time.

The Tube

At last, the train was here. She was glad she'd waited and not run off for the bus. Ellie managed to squeeze on, carried forward by a human tide. It was hard to breathe inside, hot and reeking of booze and perfume, but she had only a few stops to go. Then she was fighting her way out at Waterloo and up onto the street. Only twenty to twelve; she was going to make it. Congratulating herself on being too boring and sensible to wear heels, she kicked up her DM boots and ran

59

towards the river, and soon the glowing letters of the Oxo Tower – a pleasing palindrome – came into sight. It was a big building, it seemed. She wondered why Mark had wanted to meet there. Maybe his new friends were fancy.

She found the lift to where he'd said to meet, pressed buttons. *Come on, come on.* The journey seemed to take for ever, soaring over London, silent fireworks already lighting up the sky in the distance. 'I'm here! I'm here!' She stumbled from the lift and into the restaurant, breathless and sweaty, aware of lights and the clink of glasses and murmur of conversation. God, this was a really nice place. Mark was there at a table with a white cloth, looking anxious, his knuckles clenched around a bottle of fancy Italian beer. He was alone. Confused, she hugged him, breathing in his familiar smell of pencil rubbers and Lynx Africa. There was something else, too, which she didn't recognise. A new type of laundry detergent, maybe, not the one his mother had used for years, a smell Ellie associated with being at his most weekends between the ages of eight and eighteen. Presumably Mark had finally started washing his own clothes.

For a moment, they looked at each other, searching for changes, details that showed they weren't themselves any more. His blue eyes behind his old glasses. New black shirt – an actual shirt with a collar, which before this she'd only ever seen him wear to do work experience at a local chemicals lab. 'Are we – this is a restaurant?'

'Well, yes, that's where you usually eat food.'

She and Mark had literally never been to a restaurant together, unless you counted McDonald's. 'And – it's just us?'

'Who else did you expect?'

So not the big gathering she'd been imagining. Just them. 'I thought – eh, never mind.' Ellie nudged the green-glass bottle, the same shade as their old school uniform. 'Drinking poncy beer now? Snakebite and black too good for you?'

'Mate, they don't have any. I asked them to put your dinner on a silver plate though, since you're up at Oxford.'

They smiled at each other, and Ellie was surprised how glad she was to hear that *mate*. They'd barely talked since that day in September when he came to wave her off as she set off in her Dad's overloaded car, giving her a friendly biff on the arm. Ellie had been surprised to find tears pricking her eyes as they pulled out of the drive, her parents already bickering over what route to take to Oxford.

'So. How is it then? Full of poshos?'

'Full of poshos,' Ellie confirmed sadly. 'There's a few cool people, though. I'm in the Indie Music Soc.'

'You have a soc for it? La-di-da. We just go on pub crawls and jump around to awful sweaty bands until we vom in the street.'

'Oh come on, it can't be that bad.' Ellie felt a little stab of guilt that she hadn't visited. Oxford was so full on, everything crammed into eight-week terms, and it had whizzed by before she'd had time to draw breath. 'So, why are we here then?' She turned to take in the dazzling views, London strung out like the fairy lights she'd threaded along her wall in college, until she'd been made to take them down as a fire hazard.

'Oh, you know.'

She noticed Mark had picked the label off his beer with

his thumbnail, and opened her mouth to make the usual joke about sexual frustration, but something stopped her. She wished the waitress would come. When she did, Ellie ordered a gin and tonic, and saw Mark raise his eyebrows.

'Fancy. Off the beer?'

'Oh, you know. It makes you fat, doesn't it.' She jiggled her stomach under her dress, a skater-style vaguely goth design in black velvet and lace.

'For God's sake. You're not fat, El,' he said crossly. 'Drink gin if you want. Whatever.'

'OK, I will.' The mood had soured for some reason, and she didn't know why. When the gin came, she downed it, and they both asked for seconds.

'Almost midnight,' Mark pointed out.

'I know. Why are we here, Marko?' She came out with it without thinking, a straight true question, looking him right in his blue eyes. 'I mean, if the millennium bug hits we might get stranded up here. They say planes might fall out of the sky and lifts and electricity stop, all that. Mum was on about it.'

He pushed his glasses up. The frame was cracked where Darren Johnson had kicked a football into them in Year Ten. How well she knew him – or had done, anyway.

'No reason we can't come to a nice place, watch the fireworks.'

'Yeah, but we never do stuff like this. It's us.'

'Is it us?'

'What do you mean?' Ellie's heart beat faster under her velvet.

'I mean, you've changed, El.'

'I haven't.' She was cross now. 'I just started drinking gin – what's wrong with that? People can drink different things.'

'You hardly called. Like, ever.'

'*You* hardly called.'

'I emailed. It's the twenty-first century, almost. Or it will be in ... three minutes.' He checked his watch and that was the same too – Casio with a tiny splash of luminescent green paint on it. It made Ellie's heart ache, in some way she didn't understand. For the past, the kids they used to be, and now here they were playing grown-ups in a posh bar.

'I'm sorry,' she said. 'It's been crazy. I never realised it would be so full-on. There's essays, and lectures, and black-tie events and parties and socials and bops ... '

'Speak English,' he chided.

' ... and I'm just this chubby northern girl there, and yes I know I'm not chubby-chubby, but I am by the standards of all these gorgeous lasses whose parents live in Dubai or Jersey or whatever, and here I am, I don't even know you're supposed to serve red wine at room temperature.'

'Did you put it in the fridge? Oh, El.'

She glared at him. 'Who died and made you sommelier of the year? That means a wine expert, by the way. Dunno if you have those at Edinburgh.'

'We've got Snakey B sommeliers up there. My student union does them in three different colours.'

'See, if you'd told me that I'd have been up like a shot.'

He laughed, and so did she, and whatever that awkward moment had been, it was gone, and they were El and Mark again.

She tried again. 'I am sorry. It was just – it's so mad there. I hardly had time to breathe.'

He shrugged. 'It's OK. I guess we both needed to settle in, make friends.'

It was there between them, the decision she'd made to go to Oxford, and not Edinburgh together as they'd planned.

She said, 'And did you? Make friends?'

'Some.' The thumb was back, scratching. Ellie suddenly realised they weren't talking about friends. They were talking about girlfriends. And boyfriends. Mark stared at the table. She willed him to look up, but she knew that when he did, something between them was going to change, and nothing would be the same again.

'Mark?'

Around them the chant went up. 'Ten ... nine ... eight ... '

He raised his eyes. Bright blue, so familiar, squinting a little in the low light.

'Seven ... six ... '

'What, El?'

'Why are we really here?'

'Five ... four ... three ... '

'El ... '

'Two ... '

Ellie leaned forward.

'One ... '

At the stroke of midnight, as a new year and century and millennium dawned, as the lights did not go off or planes fall from the sky, Ellie raised her mouth to Mark's, and it tasted like beer and toothpaste and coming home.

JUNE 2019

As Ellie crept around the pebble-dashed side of the house, waiting for a clear moment to run, she found she was thinking about how strange life was. Choices, big and small, and how they affected everything. If she hadn't gone to Oxford, Verity would not be her bridesmaid, here to give her advice. Then there'd been that Millennium Eve where she'd not managed to meet Mark, and everything had changed and now here she was, trying to break out of her mother's house on her wedding day like Tim Robbins in the *Shawshank Redemption*, except wearing a pink velour tracksuit.

It would be fine, she told herself. She just wanted a moment to herself, in her special childhood place, where she'd gone when her mother was on the warpath or boys didn't notice her or she fell out with friends. Just a minute to clear her head, think over her options and be sure she was making the right decision today. That was OK, wasn't it? Like Verity said, all brides got the jitters, it didn't have to mean something bad. She would find some breathing space, think it over, make a list of pros and cons. Maybe meditate or something? It would all be fine.

But just as Ellie had reached the back of the house, and

spotted an uninterrupted route over the back fence and down the field to the river, she heard a voice drifting round from the front. The slam of a car door. A Scottish accent, assertive, ringing. Oh God. Laura was here. And Ellie knew who would be with her. The absolute last person she needed to see right now.

CHOICE 3 – MAY 2002

Ellie sat in the crowd, nervously clutching a gin and tonic. It was now officially 'her' drink, after falling in with a booze-swilling crowd at Oxford. Admittedly, some of them were poshos – Camilla and Verity in particular – but she loved them, and they were her gang. Her girls.

God, she wished they were here tonight. The audience in the Camden bar was embarrassingly small, and she kept willing someone else to come through the door. The bar stamp was smudged on the back of her hand. Once, those hands had always been dirty with something – highlighter ink or pen notes to herself or temporary tattoos that drove her mother mad. Now she painted her nails and sometimes even went to a salon. Verity had been appalled that she'd never had a manicure. 'Dear God, darling, do they still send you down the mines in Newcastle?' Ellie hadn't even asked Verity to come tonight – she wouldn't have been able to bear her friend's well-meaning confusion at the venue. *Oh whatever wine they have, darling – a Pinot, maybe?* The bar didn't even sell wine. She'd had few other friends to invite, and that worried her too. She was twenty-one – should she not have a full and exciting life? Mark was too far away and in any case things were still weird with them. She had invited Michelle of course, but she was touring a student production of *The Importance of Being Earnest* in Scotland, sending long grumpy texts about midges and haggis. *Honestly I've put on five pounds, this is actual hell, will bring you back some tartan tablet.*

A nervous-looking man had come onto the stage, cradling his guitar like his first-born. It was covered in stickers and had a rainbow strap.

'Er . . . hi,' he said, his voice cracking into the microphone. He was tall and lean, stooping, wearing a long-sleeved Radiohead top, a scruff of beard on his chin. 'My name's Steve Wilmott.'

Ellie clapped enthusiastically, and saw his eyes search for her in the crowd. She'd never get tired of that feeling. She gave him a thumbs-up.

'This is a song I wrote for someone special in my life . . .' Ellie beamed around her. *That's me! I'm the special someone!* 'It's called "Needing You".'

And he began to pick out the notes, and then his voice rang out, smoky and worn, the voice of a sixty-year-old boozehound, not a boy of twenty-three whose parents had sent him to music lessons but hoped he'd become an accountant. Steve. Ellie's boyfriend. The Leicester Square busker, whose guitar case she had fallen over two and a bit years ago. She still had a small scar on her left knee, silver and pale. Sometimes Steve kissed it when they were in bed, which made Ellie feel weak all over, so it was lucky she was usually lying down at the time.

She and Steve did a lot of lying down. It had been a revelation to her, that kissing and touching and all that . . . stuff, was enjoyable when you actually fancied someone, and they weren't licking at your face like a friendly dog. After her accident on New Year's Eve, when planes did not fall from the sky but life changed all the same, Ellie and Steve had become an item. Her first boyfriend, first love, first sex. She'd transitioned from an awkward northern girl, out of place and intimidated at Oxford, to someone vaguely cool, who went down to London most weekends, danced at gigs, even took drugs once or twice, though she'd been too terrified of dying and ending up on the news to actually enjoy herself. Steve was her refuge from feeling so out of place at university, a glimpse of a different life where it wasn't only grades and exams that counted.

The time had gone by in a blink. Three years of university, drinking and studying and watching *Neighbours* at lunchtime. Sitting in traffic most Fridays just itching to get to Shepherd's Bush, where he'd be waiting for her coach, and they'd grab each other and kiss hungrily while the other passengers pushed past them muttering about getting a room and so on, and Ellie and Steve didn't care one bit. Weekends were spent in his rumpled bed in the house he shared with four other boys. Stepping into the shower was an act of supreme love and sacrifice on Ellie's part; once she'd found a fag butt in there. Steve had barely changed his sheets in the whole time he'd lived there, despite her gentle urging. But it didn't matter. Her virginity hadn't lasted a month with him, and now she felt different, grown-up. Life had finally started.

'That was great!' They were waiting for the bus home to his flat in Ladbroke Grove, a steaming bag of chips in her hand, the stamp from the bar smudged off with nervous sweat.

Steve's mood had dipped. 'Come on, El. There were like ten people there.'

'But you have to start somewhere. Today it's smaller rooms, but tomorrow it could be . . . '

'What? A stadium tour?' His voice was low and morose, and she suddenly had no appetite for the chips. Steve never thought about dinner. He was so thin she could run her hands over his ribs like a piano keyboard.

'What do you want to do now? We could watch a film or something, download it?' This was how they spent much of their time, squinting together at his small laptop where he BitTorrented films in poor definition.

'Internet's been cut off. Charlie didn't pay the bill.'

'We could stay out? Find a late-night bar or . . . '

'I'm skint.'

Ellie's heart sank. She knew what that meant – another night in his scuzzy living room, watching Steve and his housemates get stoned and argue about Tarantino films, while she drank warm Foster's and tried not to be bored. 'I'm sorry about the gig.'

He gave a wan smile and squeezed her hand. 'At least I have you.' He cupped her face on the dark street, rested his forehead against hers. Ellie's heart turned upside down, as it so often did when he looked at her like this. As if she was everything – his muse, his support, his world. It was like plugging into an electricity grid. 'You'll never leave me, will you, El?'

'Of course I won't,' she whispered. And he took her home, and under the duvet with its unwashed cover, he turned her mind and body inside out, till she lay beside him, breathing hard, running her hands over the lines of his shoulders. It wasn't his fault he felt things so keenly. He was artistic, volatile, creative. All the things she wished she was – she hadn't even looked at her novel in two years.

Suddenly he sat up on one elbow, dislodging the manky duvet. She could see his face in the glow of the streetlight outside, the planes of his cheekbones, the glint of the stud in his ear. How sexy she'd thought that, how daring. How much it had pissed off her mother, who'd only met him once for an awkward lunch at Zizzi's in Oxford. Mark would never do a thing like that, he'd just quote infection statistics and studies about the impact of body piercings on employment prospects. Though why she would think about Mark now, she didn't know. Neither of them had made the journey between Oxford and Edinburgh (a long and expensive one, she told herself often) in the previous academic year. They were busy. Exams. New friends. She'd heard from Michelle he had a girlfriend, Laura someone, who he'd met at a student union gig.

Mark still hadn't forgiven her for not making the bar on that New Year's Eve years ago, though she'd texted him to explain. Eventually, around half twelve, he'd replied to say he wasn't there any more and not to bother coming. Slightly miffed, Ellie hadn't answered, even though she had nowhere to stay that night. Instead, she and Steve had spent all night walking round to stay warm, until the first trains started north, and Ellie had boarded one, bleary-eyed and freezing but tingling all over. She'd explained again to Mark about falling over, making it sound a tiny bit worse that it was, and they were still speaking, but she hadn't seen much of him

71

since getting together with Steve. On their one meeting, the guys had got into a bantering argument that wasn't really banter about the merits of Nirvana versus Pearl Jam, and she hadn't organised another one.

'It's going to be good, isn't it?' said Steve now.

'What?' she mumbled, pushing thoughts of Mark aside, ignoring the brief stab in her heart, the cold-stomach fear that they just weren't friends any more.

'This summer. When we're together all the time.' Ellie had an internship lined up at a women's magazine, organised through a friend of Verity's mother, so it seemed to make sense to live with Steve when she moved down. The idea should have been lovely, but somehow a little shiver went through her.

She sat up. His elbow was resting on her arm and it was a bit painful. 'Are you sure it's a good idea?'

'What are you going to do otherwise? Go back north and pull pints in the local pub?' One thing she'd never loved about Steve was his constant jokes about her hometown. It had a multiplex now! What more did he want? 'And we can actually spend time together, more than a few weekends here and there.'

She thought about it, living in London, working in a fancy magazine office. Shops, restaurants, theatres, all on her doorstep. Coming home to Steve for cuddles, someone to eat dinner with and watch TV and tell about her day. But on the other hand, coming home to Steve slumped in the living room with a joint, moaning that another record company had sent back his demo. Being the only one who'd ever wash a dish, or put the laundry on, or remember to buy milk.

'I mean . . . we'd be living together.'

A short hurt silence, then: 'Do you not want to be with me?'

She was being stupid – where else was she going to stay? It wasn't like she could afford her own place on the unpaid internship. She didn't know how normal people broke into journalism, without vast family wealth behind them. 'Of course I want to be with you. All summer long – amazing. And maybe we can save up to go travelling?'

He pulled her close. 'I don't need to travel. I've got everything I need right here.'

It should have been romantic, but for some reason all she could think about was that night more than two years ago, when she'd run through Leicester Square and literally fallen for him. Would things have been different if she'd waited for the Tube instead of the bus? If she was a different, more patient person? If she'd made it to Mark in time for midnight? But she wasn't; she hadn't. She had met Steve and now here she was, in love. On a path.

Steve had fallen asleep now, giving out wheezy stoned snores. She supposed she would never know what the alternative future could have been.

The next morning, Ellie had to be up early to get back to Oxford for her tutorial. It was frowned upon to leave college overnight in term time, especially with her finals coming up in just a few weeks, but she'd felt she had to support Steve. Not that he seemed to feel supported. He didn't get up to take her to the bus stop, as she crept about his shared flat, brushing her teeth in the disgusting bathroom, squeezing the last millimetre out of the toothpaste. She couldn't face the shower so had a wash and rub-down with the only towel Steve owned, a pale grey colour that had perhaps once been white. He sat up in bed, his breath smelling of cigarettes and kebab.

'Bye, then.'

Ellie's heart sank a little. Had she annoyed him? Not praised him enough?

'Bye. Look, it was a really good gig, honest. It's just – people don't always have vision, right? The public.'

That seemed to cheer him up a bit. 'Yeah. Maybe. Just need to find the right audience.' She bent over to kiss his clammy forehead. 'See you soon,' he mumbled, and she went out into the cold dawn alone.

Ellie fell asleep as the bus inched through the Hyde Park traffic, though she should have been revising, and woke up stale-mouthed at Thornhill Park and Ride, gathering her things, trying to get into the mind set for her tutorial. She got off at George Street and walked briskly back to college, let herself into the quad with her wicket key, waved at various people standing about in rowing clothes. Verity was in the corridor, sitting on the ground by the fridge with her legs propped up on the wall, talking to Camilla, who was drying her hair in her room with the door open.

'Honestly, it was absolutely epic, he chundered in a flower bed and ... Oh! Darling, you're back! You missed the *best* night.'

That was always the way, Ellie thought. When she was here, she missed Steve, the way his body curled around hers at night, his warm breath on her neck. But she was missing so much else as well, and it would only get worse if she moved in with him after uni.

*

'ARRRRGH!' A few weeks later, Verity stopped in the middle of the high street, threw her mortar board to the sky and yelled, catching it neatly and shoving it onto her shiny hair.

Ellie was swigging from a champagne bottle. 'What are you doing?'

'We're finished! I don't have to look at another revision note again – I can immediately forget everything I know about the Renaissance, thank God.'

Ellie laughed. Her mood was buoyant too, like the helium balloon looped around her wrist, a gift from Camilla, who'd come to meet them out of their final paper as was traditional, with flowers and booze and a shower of confetti. Exams were over, and she could stop existing on Red Bull and stress and get rid of the uncomfortable black tights and gown she'd had to wear to sit the exams, another archaic Oxford tradition. But all the same, something nagged at her, pulled her back down to earth. If exams were over then university was over, and the rest of her life beckoned. And it didn't seem quite as exciting as it should have.

Ellie shook confetti from her hair, the harsh glitter of it sparkling between cobblestones as they made their way back to college from Exam Schools. A holiday mood in the air, streamers and party-poppers and balloons, wine bottles already abandoned empty on corners, though it was barely noon. Verity tucked an arm through hers. She managed to make her sub fusc look glamorous, with an expensive linen shirt and black fishnets, her caramel-coloured hair shiny over her shoulder, bits of confetti glinting in it.

'You're not rushing off, I hope, darling?'

Most weekends Ellie was straight onto the coach to London. But this time she'd told Steve her final exam was tomorrow. Why had she lied? He'd have wanted to come and meet her, that was why, and she couldn't bear the idea of him hunching along the edge of the crowd, chippy at all the posh people, even though he'd gone to private school himself, and she'd have to introduce him to her college mates and go back to her room with him instead of drinking cava on the quad with everyone else. She'd travel down in the morning, surprise him, explain she'd got her schedule mixed up or something like that. She just wanted one night without him, before moving in with him for ever. Accepting the rest of her life, ready and waiting for her. That was OK, wasn't it?

'Not at all,' she said to Verity. 'Are we bopping tonight?'

'Of course! We're finalists – everyone's going to buy us drinks.' She plonked a pair of deely-boppers on Ellie's head. 'This is it, darling. Our last night. I intend to make the most of it.'

Tomorrow Verity's mother and stepfather were picking her up and sweeping her off to Barbados, and then in a few weeks she was starting a (paid) internship at her father's firm. And Ellie? She had the internship, but no way of earning any actual money yet. She tucked the panic away to worry about later.

'Can't wait.'

There were two kinds of boy at Oxford. Type one was loud, did a lot of sports like rugby and rowing, went around in packs with bow ties draped about their necks, and talked in a kind of slack-jawed drawl. They'd all been to private school together and just knew the world was ready and waiting for them to step into.

Type two was nerdy and nervy, wore black jeans with white trainers, twitched when girls spoke to them, and often carried a calculator in their pocket (and they weren't just pleased to see you). Although they knew everything there was to know about physics or maths or chemistry, saying hello or making conversation was apparently an undiscovered secret of the universe.

Ellie was not much impressed by either kind, and for the past three years had simply avoided them, glad to be able to escape the college bubble and run off to Steve. But now, somewhere around midnight, at the very end of her time at university, her finals done, her revision notes thrown joyfully into a bin on the High Street, she found herself strangely regretful she'd never dipped her toes in the waters of Oxford men. Because, very occasionally, one came along who was neither nerdy nor entitled, who was confident without being a twat, who knew how to speak to women as if they were people and not just horses to be whistled for and fondled when drink was taken.

Connor Mullins was one of them. The boy who'd caught her eye almost three years ago, crossing the quad that first day, but she hadn't stopped to talk to him, and somehow they'd never really interacted after that, despite being in the same year in a college of four hundred people. It was like that – you settled early into cliques during Freshers' Week, and didn't always move out of them. She was sorry about that because Connor was lovely. He had a soft Irish accent that made everything, even 'Have they run out of Archers?', sound fun, meaningful, exciting. Spiritual, almost. And, standing as she was in what the college called a 'bop cellar', i.e. a murder-dungeon with sweat dripping from the head-crackingly low ceiling, currently filled with heaving bodies in various states of academic dress, if she could even be thinking the word spiritual, he must have something about him. Either that or she was very, very drunk.

'Hm?' she said.

'The Archers cocktail thing. Have they run out?'

'Oh, yeah. Think they're down to the vodka and Kahlúa now.' It was the end of year 'drink the bar dry' disco, or bop, and Ellie, having just finished her exams, was still dressed in her sub fusc garb of white shirt, black skirt and tights, black ribbon tie, and drooping black gown. She had definitely lost her mortar board somewhere, fifty quid down the drain, but she didn't care because university was over. What lay ahead she had no idea, and thinking about it made her take another large gulp of her cocktail, which was why she was already so drunk she was swaying on her New Look heels.

'Ah well. It's a load of shite anyway, isn't it.'

How did he make 'a load of shite' sound so sexy? Ellie squinted up at him, aware she was slurring her words slightly.

'We never talked, did we, Connor? Three years and maybe a few words.'

'Ach now, that's not true. One time you asked me where the lodge was. In Freshers' Week.'

'You remember that?'

'Sure I do,' he said, easily. 'You always remember your first college crush.'

Ellie was suddenly aware of every detail. The sweat

trickling under her bra. The slushy ice in her plastic cup of cocktail. The music thudding through the walls and juddering her bones – Toploader's 'Dancing in the Moonlight'. Somewhere in the middle of the crowd, Verity was throwing herself about with wild enthusiasm. She must have been hammered – she normally avoided college bops and only listened to hardcore trance. Was Connor Mullins, with his lovely accent and quick smile and Interpol T-shirt . . . was he saying he'd had a crush on her, Ellie Warren? Wasn't he going out with a girl in the second year, someone who got up early to go rowing and had huge boobs? 'You and Marianne . . .'

'Ah, sure that's been over months, Ellie. Are you so out of touch with the college grapevine? What about you and your muso fella?'

She shrugged to indicate it was complicated. How to sum up the last few years of her and Steve? Only two and a half years, but it felt like ten. Sometimes, she found it hard to believe she was only twenty-one, as if she'd lived a whole life already, and every step she'd take was mapped out for her far in advance. She'd never fitted in at college, always uncomfortably on the outside, conscious of her lower-class roots. She played it up sometimes, peppering her sentences with *canny* and *haway the lads*, things she never would have said at home.

'And where did you go?' one tall boy had drawled to her at a party, the collar popped on his rugby shirt.

Ellie had blinked, clutching her Smirnoff Ice. 'What do you mean – what school?'

'Yah, what school.'

What did he mean? Surely he wouldn't have heard of her secondary school? 'Um . . . Parkside High.'

The blank look, then his eyes skipping over her to someone more important, more connected. Ellie hated that. Hated the sound of her voice, meek and regional beside their ringing tones, hated the fact half their sixth form had come to Oxford so they knew people in every college, as opposed to no one at all, like her. Hated her cheap and fraying clothes from New Look or Miss Selfridge. Verity thought nothing of dropping a hundred quid on a top from Karen Millen, which she'd often burn with stray cigarettes on the first wearing. Most of all she hated how she'd spent three years at a legendary university, one of the best in the world, and still didn't feel good enough, not remotely. Perhaps that was why she'd stayed with Steve, who worshipped her, at least in between bouts of depression. All her summer holidays, when others travelled to Egypt together or interned at businesses or went to festivals, had been spent in Steve's flat in London. The first year she'd worked in a call centre near Heathrow and again seen nothing of the city. She'd spent most of the second year ferrying him to and fro between therapy appointments, then staying awkwardly in the spare bedroom of his parents' house in Surrey (they weren't allowed to sleep in the same room, despite almost living together in London). She felt his parents looked down on her in the same way her fellow students did. Not posh enough, not good enough. Maybe she would never be.

She certainly had never cheated on Steve, not even close. It was a long time since anyone had looked at her like Connor Mullins was now, admittedly squinting a bit like she was. He took the plastic cup from her hand, his fingers cupping the bones of her wrist.

'I live just upstairs, you know.' He pointed. 'I've some decent alcohol hidden away. You want to have a drink with me, Ellie Warren?'

She knew what he was asking. And he was so lovely, with his smile and his accent and the smell of his after-shave, even over the reeking sweat of the bop. She looked past his shoulder – Verity was locking tongues with Alex, her on-off hook-up, who she'd sworn off weeks before for the tenth time. It was a blurry night. No one would notice what she got up to, and anyway, she was leaving the next morning, supposedly to move to London for Steve and her internship. She'd have to look for something paid too – she hadn't applied for the graduate journalism schemes on the big nationals, assuming they would be for people who weren't her, more confident or connected or just better. Many of her fellow students had jobs lined up already at management consultancies or banks, where they'd start on thirty-five grand a year, a sum Ellie could barely take in. Others were going on to law training contracts or con-version courses, after the more fanciful arts degrees they had allowed themselves, or gap years in India or teaching English in Japan.

If she didn't move in with Steve, what would she do? Go back to her parents? That was the most depressing thing she could think of. An Oxford graduate, answering phones in the toilet showroom she'd worked at before she went to uni, or in the Blacksmith's Arms, IDing kids who'd been years below her at school, listening to sleazy old men bore on and look down her top. No. She couldn't go back, move into her old room with the exercise bike and Swiss ball and her mother carping at her to make something of her life. Even her brother was gone now, in his first year of a computer science degree at Manchester. He'd had his pick of places, her mother liked to boast. She'd clearly forgotten the years she'd spent trying to persuade Alan to go out and have fun, enjoy the weather, whisking open his curtains and threatening to put a lock on the computer. Her nerdy little brother had moved out and Ellie, the Oxford star, was sure as hell not moving in.

The thought of her future – living permanently in Steve's flat, which he now shared with four random people, his old mates, even Bonzer who was usually so stoned he didn't know what month it was, having found jobs and moved on with their lives – ran through Ellie like an electric charge, and her hand jerked, spilling some cocktail onto her shirt, pink blooming red over the white. 'Shit!' This was her best shirt, and she'd need it if she had to take up waitressing, as looked increasingly likely.

'Vanish,' Connor Mullins said. 'I have some. We'll get that out in a jiffy.'

Oh God, he was adorable. He stepped back, still holding on to her wrist.

'Are you in, Ellie? We might never see each other after tonight. This is our chance to catch up on three years of knowing each other but never actually talking.'

Ellie paused, the moment of choice in front of her. The lovely boy. The music. The final night of university, of three years mostly spent writing essays and on the phone to Steve and reading novels on the Oxford Tube. Not having enough fun. Michelle was already auditioning for professional roles, living in a flatshare with three other actresses, all thin and glamorous and scary to Ellie. And as for Mark – well. He was graduating with several offers from tech firms – that area was booming and Mark was top of his class, not that he would ever have told her so himself. Michelle was her conduit to him now, which seemed sad since she only knew him through Ellie in the first place. His girlfriend Laura was apparently a medical student, and didn't Ellie have a little stab of jealousy every time she thought of that, the life that could have been hers. She wouldn't have to worry about what to do with herself in that parallel world, she'd just be a doctor and it would all be simple. If she hadn't done English, if she hadn't taken the offer from Oxford, if she'd followed Mark to Scotland. If everything was different, but she was so sick of thinking that way, worrying over past decisions. Oxford had brought with it many joys, and like Mark had once said, everything had happened in different universes. So it didn't really matter what Ellie did. She was only twenty-one and a good-looking, good-smelling boy who wasn't her boyfriend was holding her hand.

She made a decision.

Yes to Connor

Slowly, the world came into focus. A maroon college-issue bedspread. Not hers. She had her own bed linen, colourful patterns to brighten up the drab room. This was definitely her college, but a room she didn't recognise, an L-shaped layout, a vague smell of boy and unwashed laundry. An empty bottle of whisky on the floor, the fumes making her sit bolt upright. Oh God, she was going to be sick. Oh God. Oh God. She counted to ten, praying she wouldn't, and it seemed to work. The room stopped spinning and her stomach settled. Ellie looked around, her very bones filled with existential horror. Where was she? What had she done?

'Morning,' said a sleepy Irish voice beside her, and from under the tangle of bedclothes Ellie made out some unfamiliar limbs wrapped around hers in the single bed. Not Steve's. Fair, fine hairs, smaller hands, a different smell. Then she saw the Muse posters on the wall, the stack of vinyl in the corner, and she remembered.

She was in Connor Mullins's room.

Calm down, calm down, maybe you just passed out. She assessed the situation. She was naked on top but – she pulled the duvet round her breasts – she had pants on underneath. So maybe it was OK, maybe they hadn't done anything. 'Connor, did we . . . ?'

'Ah, we misbehaved all right.'

'Did we have sex?' She blurted it out.

'Depends what you mean by sex.' He rubbed his eyes. She tried not to notice how cute he was in the morning, his brown hair sticking up, the curves of his shoulders and ribcage. Shorter than Steve, sturdier. Solid. Memories were coming back of the night before. His tongue in her mouth, desire surging through her in a way she hadn't felt for years, her hands tugging his hair, his arms pinning her to the bed, straddling him, her bra flying off . . . Sure enough, there it was, looped around the light fittings. 'You passed out before we did the deed.'

'But we did . . . other stuff.'

'We did,' he confirmed. 'Hey, are you OK?'

She was rocking herself, clutching the duvet over her nakedness. Her mouth felt sour and rough. 'Oh Connor. I did a really bad thing.'

His face hardened. 'Your muso?'

She nodded.

'Not over after all?'

'Not . . . exactly.'

Not at all, in fact. She knew that whenever she found her phone there'd be dozens of missed calls from Steve, frantic about where she'd been all night. He'd have called her room phone too, he'd know she hadn't gone back there. How would she explain? Oh God. She felt sick.

'I see.' The atmosphere had chilled. He was getting up, pulling on his jeans – even in her distraction she noticed how nice his bum was. 'I didn't know, Ellie. You kind of misled me on that one.'

'It's my fault. I . . . ' How to explain that, drunk as she was, she'd felt she deserved something nice for once? To kiss this lovely boy, who seemed to like her. Just once, in three years of looking after Steve? She hadn't thought about his feelings, or Steve's, just her own selfish joy, to kiss his mouth and run her hands over his back, muscled from rowing. 'I . . . things are hard. It's complicated.'

Connor shut his chest of drawers with a snap, pulling a T-shirt over his head. 'The way I see it, these things are actually pretty simple, Ellie. You're either with someone or you've got your tongue down some daft fella's throat.'

'I'm sorry.' She felt wretched.

'I liked you, you know. Always thought there might be something between us, if we ever managed to collide at the right time.' He picked up his towel and soap. 'I'm going for a shower. You have your room key?'

'I . . . I think so.' Even if she didn't, she wasn't going to stay here another second.

'I won't tell anyone, Ellie. I'm not like that. But maybe you should talk to your fella, yeah, if this is the kind of thing you're going to get up to? It's hardly fair, is it, on me or on him.'

How to explain that it wasn't the kind of thing she got up to, that she'd been scrupulously faithful all this time? That she'd cared for Steve and taken all his sad, spiralling calls for years? That she always made sure to be back in her room by one at the latest, to have her mobile charged up, to check it every hour, just in case he needed her? That she'd gone to every gig, listened to him rant for hours about the music industry, helped him with his song lyrics at the expense of her own studies? She couldn't. She just nodded, feeling the shame rise up and drown her.

'I know. I will.'

Creeping out of Connor's block, Ellie was horrified to round the corner of the staircase and run straight into Verity, still in her sub fusc, bare-legged and carrying her heels. Of course – Alex Monroe, her hook-up, lived in this same block.

'Oh!' Verity just stared, slowly putting it together.

'I . . .'

'I saw you talking to Connor last night.'

'I – I think I just passed out, he was taking care of me . . .'

That didn't make sense. Her own room was closer to the bop cellar than Connor's. She saw her friend register her lie, nod slowly.

'It's none of my business, El, but – he's a really nice guy, Connor. Don't mess him about.'

Verity was not Steve's biggest fan, but she took a dim view of cheating since her long-term boyfriend Pablo had been revealed to be running a chalet girl on the side during his ski season. It was this betrayal which had prompted Verity's uncharacteristic cameo at a college event last night.

'I know. I know. I didn't – I won't.' Leaning into her lie.

Verity just nodded. 'Well. I better shower and get ready, Mummy will be here soon.'

They walked the short distance back to their block in silence. Ellie shut the door on her own room, its familiar posters and photos illegally Blu Tacked up, her kettle and mugs and clothes, and realised she still had to pack it all up and vacate it so they could clean it for conference guests. She approached her phone like an unexploded bomb, and there they were – forty missed calls and dozens of texts. *Where are you. What are you doing. How could you do this to me. Please call, baby, I'm so worried. How could you, you slut.*

Ellie paused. How to even reply to these? Her hand hovered over the keys. She couldn't think what to say that would not be a terrible lie. She'd just go and see him and hash it out. She'd have to tell him the truth – he'd be able to see it in her face.

Outside in the corridor, she heard a door slam, and the

posh tones of Verity's mother. 'Come on, darling, we're parked on double-yellows.'

'Yes, yes, just a minute, Mummy!'

Verity was leaving. She wasn't even going to say goodbye to her best friend of three years. Ellie's heart sank even further. She really had messed up.

A few hours later, still feeling raw and ashamed, she trailed her suitcase and two laundry bags – all she had to show for three years of university – to Steve's flat. She still had her key from the previous summer, and this one stretched ahead, and after that the rest of her life. Steve had not replied to her texts that morning, so he was angry at her. She'd tell him the ringer had got stuck on silent the night before, or she'd been in the bop cellar and had no reception. Maybe he'd believe her? Unlikely. No, she had to tell him the truth. But then what? If the conversation unravelled to its logical conclusion, it would all be over between them. Maybe that wasn't the worst thing in the world. But Ellie still felt sick at the conflict ahead.

As she reached his door, trundling her bags, the straps eating into her shoulders, Ellie stopped up short. There was an ambulance parked outside.

Not him, she told herself. A neighbour, some old lady slipping in the shower or having a stroke, nothing to worry about. But she knew it wasn't.

A crowd of people were standing around in the front garden, including two boys she vaguely recognised as Steve's new flatmates, and one she didn't know at all. It was him who spoke to her, wearing a grey suit and tie. 'Are you Ellie?'

She could hardly speak. 'Wh ...' Her breath wouldn't come, as if she was winded.

'Don't look. Come on.' He was turning her away, grasping her shoulders, taking her bags from her, this total stranger. Something was being loaded into the back of the ambulance. 'Ellie, please, you shouldn't see this.'

She was struggling to get a grip on what was happening. 'I'm sorry, who are you?'

'I'm Paul – I live here.'

'What?' Surely there weren't any rooms spare. 'And – what are you saying? Where's Steve?'

'Ellie, I'm sorry. He must have done it this morning, early on. I was trying to get ready for work and ... anyway, we got him in time, Ellie, it's going to be OK.'

She opened her mouth, and shut it again, dimly aware that this good-looking stranger had taken her things and now she felt so light, like she might float off. She ignored him, ducking her head over his shoulder so he was almost embracing her, in time to see the gurney the paramedics were loading in, the body on it tucked in with a blue waffle blanket, and at the top of it Steve's face, drained of blood.

The next hour unravelled in a blur. The boy – young man – who'd held her, whose name was Paul, called a taxi and came with her in it and paid the bill, seemingly invested in this situation, though Ellie had no idea who he was.

'Don't you have work?' she'd said, her face almost too numb to form the words.

'I called them, it's OK. Said there was an emergency.'

'What do you do?' She was trying to make small talk, pretend everything was OK.

'Banking. It's not important.'

When they reached the hospital, Paul spoke to the receptionist and came back shaking his head – they weren't allowed to see Steve yet. So Ellie sat in the waiting room for another hour, crushing a plastic cup between her hands. She'd barely slept in days and still had glitter from the previous night under her nails. How could life change so much in an instant?

She'd gathered a few reluctant details from Paul in the cab. Steve had taken an overdose of paracetamol in the shared bathroom, but been found in time, by Paul in fact, who'd had to get up for work.

'It was, um, pretty messy. Glad you didn't see it. But the ambulance came in time, I'm sure of it.'

'And – you said you'd moved into his room?'

Steve had lost his room and he hadn't even told her. Maybe he'd been trying to tell her last night. Or maybe he'd been asking for her help, which had not come.

Paul squirmed. 'He couldn't make the rent, so, yeah. We all agreed he could sleep on the sofa till he found a place. But he – I don't think he was doing so well. Not sleeping, not applying for jobs, smoking too much. You know. Didn't think he was this bad though.'

Had she known? She'd barely spoken to him properly in weeks, in a blur of finals panic, and last night, when he'd perhaps been reaching out to her in desperate need, she had ignored him. Climbed into another man's bed. This was her fault. The guilt was so huge it made her gasp, and she might have cried out, except just then a blue-scrubbed nurse or doctor (how did you tell?) was standing in front of them with a clipboard.

'You're here with Steven Wilmott?'

'Yes. Yes. Is he OK?' Physically, she meant. Clearly he was not OK in other ways, not at all.

'Come with me. One at a time.'

Leaving Paul in the waiting room, she followed the nurse or doctor down a grim, windowless corridor to a small room. In the bed lay someone who looked like Steve, but pale, so pale he was almost green-tinged. Various tubes went into him. Ellie moved forward, then her legs gave way and she sank to her knees by his bed.

'Oh. Oh baby, I'm so, so sorry. I'm sorry.'

She could feel the truth lodged in her throat, but how could she tell him now? It would push him over the edge to know of her betrayal. She'd just have to carry it, like a stone inside her.

'Hey.' Steve's voice was croaky and weak. 'El, it's me should be sorry.'

'No, I'm sorry! I should have answered my phone. I just – I was just . . . '

'Hey, you didn't do anything wrong. I know you were out with your friends, having fun. I know it was your last night with them. I just – I get myself into these panics, like I'm convinced you're off with someone else. Someone better, less crap. Smarter, cooler.'

That was exactly what she'd done, but she could never tell him now. Her tears soaked into the hospital blanket.

'This is my fault,' she sobbed.

'Hey, hey. Come here.'

She climbed up on the bed and lay her head on his shoulder in its usual place. He smelled of cigarettes and something else, medicinal. He was in a hospital gown, soft and faded. Unbelievable how close his heart had come to stopping, his breath to ceasing in his thin chest. She couldn't bear it. She would do anything to make him better, keep him here, atone for what she'd done.

'It's not your fault. It's me, I have a problem. I should have admitted it, gone home, asked for help. I can't manage London, El. It's too expensive and I'm not good enough, I'm not strong enough for music or even a job.' And what did that mean for her? She'd have to give London up now as well. Not that she had a job there, either.

'What will we do? We've got no money, and your parents won't want me staying with them. I guess I'll have to move back home, find work there.' The thought was so depressing she started to cry again.

'Oh El, please don't. I have an idea how we can get Mum and Dad to help us – give us the deposit for a house, maybe. So we can be together always.' He was so tender. He cupped her face and pulled it to face him, his eyes intense. Suddenly she knew what he was going to say and panic flared in her chest. *Oh God, don't say it, don't* . . . 'Ellie Warren, will you marry me?'

Marry him. She was only twenty-one, it was mad! Be with him for ever. Be his wife, support him through everything. The idea filled Ellie with a wild and gushing fear, deep as a river. But how could she say no, when her last rejection had almost cost him his life?

No to Connor

Ellie turned her key in the lock of Steve's flat, and opened it to the familiar smell of weed.

'Hey, it's me.' She was exhausted from humping three years' worth of her belongings on the bus from Oxford.

She'd woken up that morning in her own bed after just a few hours' sleep, nursing a hangover from sugar and bad alcohol, and felt flat as a pancake. Yes, she'd done the right thing in detaching her wrist from Connor Mullins's hand, and going upstairs to her own room, locking the door, even if she'd lain awake for at least an hour twitching with frustration, picturing the curve of his smile and the dimple that appeared in his cheek. Had she made a terrible mistake? Was she going to regret not kissing him, or even possibly more? Well, she'd never know now.

Then the phone had rung. It was 1 a.m., but of course it was ringing. She'd thought about ignoring it for a minute – saying the ringer was on silent – but knew it would upset him, and she had this dark nameless fear that if he got upset he might do something to himself. She didn't know what. Just . . . something.

So she'd picked it up, and there was Steve, half-crying, half-shouting. Where had she been. Who was she with. Didn't she love him. And Ellie, tired, drunk, exhausted from finals and buzzing with the desire to go back downstairs and kiss Connor Mullins full on his laughing mouth, had shouted back. The row had been epic. She was sure everyone in the block had heard. The words came back to her now. She'd called him pathetic, a drain, a vampire sucking her dry. He'd called her a whore, a slut, a heartless bitch responsible for all his woes. *It's over*, she'd screamed. *I can't do this any more.*

When she woke up she'd known with a sinking heart she had nowhere else to go but to his flat, despite all this. It wasn't their first row. No doubt they would thrash it out and he would cry and she would too and they'd hug and kiss and watch bootleg episodes of *Buffy* on his old laptop. Her life, for the foreseeable future. She'd packed up her things, taken down her last postcards and photos from the wall, her heart hollow at leaving behind her Oxford life for good. Humping her bags out in the early dawn, she'd passed Verity staggering back from Alex Monroe's block, still in her exam clothes, and they'd said an emotional farewell.

'I can't believe you won't always be in the next room, darling,' Verity had mumbled into Ellie's hair. She smelled of booze and expensive perfume and was missing an earring.

'I know. But we'll be in the same city at least, right?'

Verity was starting an internship (paid, of course) at her father's company, once she got back from the three-week Caribbean holiday her mum and stepdad were taking her on later that day.

'We have to meet up all the time. Promise me, you wench!'

'I promise.'

And as Ellie had walked away from college to the bus station, she'd looked back to see Verity waving and waving from her mullioned window, blowing kisses until Ellie was out of sight.

'Steve?' Now, she walked through the empty rooms of the flat. The other flatmates must have been out at work, those boys she had never actually met but sometimes slept on the other side of the wall from. Steve was never out, though. Where was he? Her heart sank at the row ahead – she'd never actually told him it was over before. But he'd know she hadn't meant it, and she hadn't done anything wrong, that was key. She'd made the good choice, the right choice. She'd said no to the lovely boy who wanted her, and picked this. Steve. A future with him, because she loved him, didn't she? Even if it was hard sometimes.

In the living room, nothing but a silent TV and a new chair in place of the one Steve usually sat in, a cheap armchair with clean upholstery. No sign of the usual ground-in ash and cold, undrunk cups of coffee that Steve always left around him.

'Hello?'

Noticing that the place was a lot cleaner than usual – like, a lot – and that there were groceries in the kitchen, clean towels and loo roll in the bathroom, Ellie pushed open the door to the bedroom she and Steve had shared last summer and likely would again.

The room was different. She spun around, confused and wrong-footed. The bed, which had a clean navy bedspread on it pulled tight, had been moved against the window. There was different furniture, in a functional pine, and the shelves were lined with different books and framed photos. She peered at one – a boy in cargo shorts and a vest top, hugging various people. A family shot. The same boy cuddling a dog. This wasn't Steve's room.

What the hell was going on?

'Hi.'

Ellie turned around, her heart in her mouth. Was she

going to be murdered? God, she hoped they'd use a flat-tering shot in the press, not the one she'd carried around on her university ID for three years, which looked like a police mugshot.

'I'm guessing you're Ellie?' It was the boy from the photos, but older, with his hair neatly cut, wearing grey suit trousers and shirt with a red tie. He had a handsome, alert face, smoothly shaved. And Ellie was ... standing in his room. 'We knew you had a key still but not how to get in touch with you.'

'I'm sorry but ... where's Steve?'

The strange boy – man, really – sighed. 'Look, it shouldn't be me telling you this but ... he's gone.'

'Gone?'

'His parents came this morning and took him to rehab. He kind of had a freak-out last night, something about you breaking up or ...? I don't know. It all got a bit much, I guess, the skunk and the booze and not working, and he ... well, at least he's ready to get help now.'

'But ... what's happened to his room?' She tried to rack her brains for the last time she'd actually spoken to Steve, except for texts and the screaming last night. Weeks, maybe, with her head deep in finals madness. Was it possible all this had happened and he hadn't told her?

'He couldn't afford the rent any more. I moved in to cover it, so he's been sleeping on the sofa. Er, I'm Paul by the way. I work with Tim?' He held out his hand and she shook it, her mind reeling. Who was Tim? One of the unknown flatmates?

Ellie's hungover head was spinning. 'Why didn't some-one tell me?'

'We couldn't get in touch with you, like I said. We thought you'd probably turn up at some point.'

'Why didn't *he*?'

'Um . . . I think he thought you'd broken up?'

Well, of course, because she'd said it was over. But she hadn't imagined he would take her at her word.

'Oh.'

'I'm sorry,' the boy said, sympathetically. 'Will you be OK?'

She was very aware of her huge pile of belongings, the case and laundry bags abandoned in the hallway.

'So what do I . . . '

Suddenly, Ellie was panicking. She had no paid job and her one toe-hold in London, this flat, was suddenly gone. And her boyfriend was no longer her boyfriend. No more Steve. A door had suddenly been opened and cold air was blowing in. She was standing there in the suspiciously clean hallway of a flat she had no right to be in, with nowhere else to go, and nothing at all to show for the past three years of her life.

The boy was still looking at her. 'Is there someone you can call or . . . sorry, I have to go to work.'

Michelle was still in Scotland, Verity would have left for the airport already, Camilla was in France at her parents' villa. Who else was there? Ellie could only think of one person, and she just had to hope that, despite the distance between them, he would still answer the phone to her.

JUNE 2019

Ellie had grass up her nose. The urge to sneeze was over-powering, but she couldn't because Mark and Laura were standing outside her bloody house, just metres away from her. She was on her hands and knees crawling through the field behind her parents' house, where the grass was at its midsummer height. Why weren't they moving into the house? She couldn't help but overhear – Laura had a clear, ringing voice, all the better for shouting over the hubbub of A & E.

'I still don't see why we have to be here.'

'She's my oldest friend, Laura.'

'Is that how you'd put it?'

She heard Mark sigh. 'She's your friend too. Isn't she?'

'I know, but . . . Jesus Christ, will it not be a wee bit awkward? You know. With everything.'

'Well, what do you want me to do, Laura? Turn the car around and leave?'

Ellie had never heard Mark speak to his wife like that before, so grouchy, and her response was equally cold.

'I want you to have listened to me and RSVPed no in the first place. I mean, do you ever think how it feels for me, to have to stand here and smile and pretend it's all fine, with a bloody big smile on my face?'

'You didn't have to come.'

'Oh aye, send you here by yourself, that'd work. You don't think people would have questions? I don't want to have to explain it to everyone, not today.'

'It's her wedding, Laura! As in, she's getting married! Why can you not see that?'

Ellie heard a few steps on the gravel, the noise of a woman's heels. Laura rarely wore heels and her gait sounded unsteady.

'Why can *you* no' see that means nothing?' But her voice had softened. 'Look, take my arm.'

'I can manage, OK?' The sound of scraping. Mark must be on his cane today, and Ellie's heart hurt – she knew what it would cost him to be leaning on it today of all days, how he would hate it and try to do without it until he got white and shaky with tiredness.

'Come on. Please.' A short pause, then their footsteps moved on in unison. They were together, after all. Those were the facts of it. *They're together. They're married.* Same things Ellie had been telling herself for years.

But as she crawled to her feet, brushing grass off herself and out of her hair – her mother was going to go spare – and reached the small stream at the bottom of the field, she found she couldn't shake Laura's words from her head. What exactly did she not want to explain to everyone? What was going on?

CHOICE 4 – JULY 2005

The beauty editor, Carina, wrinkled up her long and beautiful nose as she scanned Ellie's copy. Ellie stood by her desk sweating into a polyester top from Jane Norman, beyond her budget.

'Hmm. You've used the word "sparkly" three times here, Ellen.'

Ellie did not correct her; she was too afraid. 'Um, OK. What else can I . . . ?'

'Shimmery. Glittery. Spangly. Iridescent. I thought you studied English?'

'Yes,' said Ellie humbly. 'Sorry.'

Carina tossed the page back with a flick of her manicured fingers. 'Have another go.'

Ellie took the piece of paper and went. Before her first internship on a women's magazine, she'd thought she was quite a good writer. She'd had four features published in the *Oxford Student* paper, and a play put on by the drama group, which at least ten people had seen. But three years later, her work – she was now on her fourth unpaid internship – was a daily exercise in humility. She knew nothing about fashion, beauty or celebrities, it seemed; she couldn't write an exciting feature or even a pull-quote; she was too shy to ring people up and ask about their sex lives, and as for doing vox pops – going out in the street to sample opinions from passers-by – she would rather die.

I could be a doctor by now, she thought, sitting down at her desk again. No one even knew her name here. They just called her 'the workie', didn't include her in their pub trips, and laughed at her behind her back, she was pretty sure. *I could be saving lives right now, instead of writing about sparkly, sorry, shimmery eye shadow.* It wasn't that she didn't like this world – she was dazzled by the designer clothes piled up in corners, the lipsticks and eye pencils rolling on desks, and the shiny pages that came from the printer, smooth and beautiful. The casual way the staff writers talked about interviewing Gwyneth Paltrow at Soho House – this was a world she wanted into, but she felt she was peering in through the window like a grubby Victorian urchin. She wasn't good at magazine journalism, it seemed. She could knock out an essay on George Eliot that got a first, but that skill was of absolutely no use here.

It was three years since Ellie had broken up with Steve, after turning down the offer of a night with Connor Mullins. At least she told herself that was what had happened, conveniently ignoring the part where she'd turned up at Steve's door to find him gone. Back then, adrift in the city with nowhere else to turn and nowhere to stay, she'd tried to summon the courage to press on Mark's number in her phone. *Screw your courage to the sticking place.* She'd thought of the terrible student production of *Macbeth* she'd stage-managed the previous term, where the second year playing the lead, a real luvvie called, of all things, Aeneas, had overdone the Stanislavski method and came onto stage having cut one of his fingers open in order to drip with real blood. He'd been carted off to the John Radcliffe Hospital, screaming about what philistines they all were, and his understudy, a nervous chemist from Wadham College, had a strong south London accent which turned the play into 'Macbeff'. Mark would have enjoyed that, would have understood why student theatre was so intrinsically hilarious but why Ellie loved it all the same. The ring tone had sounded very loud in Ellie's ear, and for a moment she'd listened to the panicky thud of her own heart and almost hung up.

'El?' His voice through the phone was so familiar, exactly as it always had been, too loud and hurried, with its Geordie accent still strong, that for a moment her throat was full of tears.

'Hey. Um, yeah, it's me.'

'I can hear that.'

An awkward pause, taking in the last three years during which their friendship had yellowed and wilted like a plant that's gradually being starved of water and light.

'I . . . Marko, I need help.'

And she'd poured it all out to him, and he'd come to get her, carrying her bags and letting her sleep on his floor until Michelle returned from Scotland and Ellie moved onto her sofa. They now shared a flat in Camden, and Mark and Ellie were firm friends again. Ellie still marvelled at it sometimes, noticing the way he cleaned his glasses on his old band T-shirts, the marker stains on his fingers from writing on whiteboards at work, how even his grown-up suits and ties looked like school uniform, somehow. How could she have gone so long without him? But now it was all OK. A friendship like theirs never really died. She was a Londoner now, with strong opinions about the Tube, a job of sorts, a group of friends who spent weekends in pubs or jumping up and down to indie music at Koko then curing their hangovers with greasy bacon sandwiches at cheap cafés.

Ellie spent the rest of the day torturing her copy into a different shape, then emailed it back to Carina, who didn't respond, just swanned out to get a vampire facial, which sounded horrific to Ellie. It was five o'clock – she supposed she'd better go home. It wasn't like they paid her to be there – she'd saved up to do this placement working in a branch of Debenhams for three months, her feet aching in cheap heels and being driven slowly insane by the CD that looped the same twelve smooth jazz hits. She looked about the room, the large windows offering a glimpse of nearby Marble Arch. Her one work friend, Yolanda, who covered the fashion desk and got paid a princely £11,000 a year, didn't do Fridays, needing to pull extra waitressing shifts to fund her season ticket in from her parents' house in Essex. Ellie didn't have that option, even supposing she could bear to live with her mother again.

'Bye then,' she said, to the remaining staff in the office.

No one looked up.

'Jesus, El, you really need to get up.' Michelle had little time for life crises. She marched into Ellie's room the next morning and thrust the curtains open, letting in a sickly yellow light. Ellie winced and hid under the covers.

'It's Saturday!'

'It's nearly twelve, you lazy lump.'

'I'm having a crisis here. I don't know what to do with my life. I'm no good at journalism. And I haven't had a boyfriend in three years.'

There had been hook-ups, yes, and even some dates, people she met in pubs or through friends, but nothing serious. She couldn't even look up Connor Mullins and ask for another chance, because he'd gone to teach English in Japan, all of which Ellie knew because of a new website called Facebook, which she'd become slightly obsessed with.

'That's because you're taking time, prioritising yourself after years with Steve, emotional vampire that he was.'

'I know, I know. But ...'

'Trust me, you don't need that kind of boyfriend, a Home Counties wannabe-creative living off the bank of Mum and Dad. You're grand as you are.'

A southerner was what Michelle meant. Ellie felt she'd been reclaimed somehow since breaking up with him, her accent moulding back into the familiar old curves of her natural voice. She hadn't even realised she'd changed it, changed herself. It was only talking to Michelle now, teasing and gossiping in their old manner, that she realised a strangeness had grown up between them since Ellie had been at Oxford. She'd sometimes felt a silence when she told a story about bops or Matriculation or eighth week, but wondered if it was her paranoia talking. Now she knew it wasn't, and she'd grabbed hold of her old life not a moment too soon, before it was gone for ever.

'What about work, though? It's OK for you, you always knew what you wanted. I just ... can't decide.'

Often, she returned to her choice at seventeen not to study medicine. She could still do that now. Or she could stick to journalism, get her head down and accept it would take time to earn any money. Or finish the novel that was still languishing, now transferred to a USB stick in the drawer of her bedside table. Or follow Connor Mullins's lead and teach English, in Japan or China or anywhere. Do a TEFL course or Erasmus. Live in Paris, maybe, one of her long-term dreams. She could just imagine her mother rolling her eyes at that. *You have to think of the future, Ellie! You can't put it off for ever. What if you want children?*

What if indeed? She did want that, always had done – a husband, a house, two or maybe three kids. She was twenty-four, though. Surely there was time?

'I'm turning the shower on,' said Michelle, who was dolled up to the nines for the audition she had later that day. 'You better be in it, Warren.'

Ellie sighed. There was no point in expecting coddling from old friends. They'd known you too long to be gentle.

'Then what?'

'Then you sort out the rest of your life. Decide what you want, if you're sticking with journalism or doing some-thing else.'

'There are no jobs in journalism. You have to work for free for like a year.'

'Oh no, imagine being in an industry where you have to slog and work for free,' said Michelle, with heavy irony. She'd been struggling to get into acting for years now, and had even been told several times that 'ethnic' looks were not in demand. Michelle was beautiful and a brilliant actress, too.

It was insane. 'What is it you really want to do, El? What happened to medicine?'

Ellie sat up, reluctantly. 'You know what happened. I got into Oxford and couldn't turn it down.'

'But you can still go now, can't you? Post-graduate?'

'I'm too old.'

'Bloody hell, El, you're twenty-four! That's not too old for anything. Except maybe crimping your hair and lying around feeling sorry for yourself all day. Come on. I'll make you a deal. If you've applied for at least two things by the end of today, I'll take you out to Pizza Express – how about that?'

'Stop trying to bribe me.' It was working, however. Ellie really loved those dough balls.

'Just decide, you daft bint. Choose something.'

As if it was that easy, Ellie thought, dragging herself up from her dank nest. As if making a simple choice wasn't the most terrifying thing in the world, sending your life spinning in the opposite direction like a crazy game of pinball.

Later that day, she was feeling quite proud of herself. She'd had a shower, washed her scuzzy hair, put on an old sundress and slipped her feet into worn-down flip-flops. She'd found the local library and got a slot on a computer, since she still didn't have her own laptop. Calling up the search engine, she felt overwhelmed with choice. What did she want to do with her life? Journalism or medicine, those had been her choices in her teens. Medicine would involve a graduate course, four years more study and no earning. She'd have to ask her parents to fund her, take out more student loans. Her heart sank at the idea of broaching it with her mother.

Ellie typed in *how to break into journalism*, bringing up dozens of results for courses. She knew these would cost thousands of pounds, and weren't really necessary when you could go straight in and do work experience. But maybe it would speed up the process if she had a qualification. News journalism was not for her, she knew. Features, opinion, magazines, that was her area. A journalism MA would also involve some working for free, but perhaps less than the four years the medicine course would take. And she could work in a pub in the evenings to make rent.

That was also dispiriting, however – the idea of working all day and all night and earning seven pounds an hour, if she was lucky. How did people manage it? Just transfer from university to London, find jobs, rent flats? Her former college mates were all doing well in law or banking or management consultancy. Ellie had shunned those jobs during the so-called milk-round presentations, and now she was just drifting, caught between possible futures, sometimes too broke to buy lunch, hiding her homemade sandwiches in the work fridge among the nail polishes and energy drinks. She was twenty-four and the pressure to choose between different lives was immense. Any false step now might define the rest of her future, and so she remained, stuck.

Of course, leaving London was always an option. She could take a post-uni gap year, like she'd read about in *Cosmo* the previous week – go overseas, volunteer, travel. She began to google TEFL courses, which brought up thousands of options as well. That was also expensive. Why did everything she wanted to do cost money? Couldn't she just get a job, as her mother would say? But she didn't want to get stuck in some marketing or admin role for years. She was no closer to any answers. But she had to apply to at least two things, because she really wanted the dough balls Michelle had promised.

Twenty minutes later, she had filled in most of a graduate application for medicine. There were two places to do it, basically – London or Newcastle, the latter of which was a bit close to home. But she was just filling in a form, not making a decision, and it turned out there were bursaries available. Luckily she'd already done chemistry A level before her plans had bounced off track and she'd gone to study English. Did she regret that? No, of course not. She wouldn't have met Verity or Camilla, or lived somewhere so beautiful for years. Probably she wouldn't have met Steve, either, as she'd only stumbled over him because she was meeting Mark that time.

Mark. He was the right person to advise her, she suddenly realised. He'd known her the longest, and always encouraged her to follow her dreams, even when people told her they were impossible.

Ellie sat in the hot library, sweaty fingers on the keys. Her time was almost up – she'd have to finish this application another time. Make a decision, Michelle had said. Well, here she was doing just that, and deciding to see Mark. She gathered up her cheap print bag and made for the exit, her place quickly taken by an older man in a stained cardigan. Outside in the blinding sun, she unlocked her phone.

Hey, Marko, are you free? Need to pick your brains.

He'd be busy. At the seaside, maybe, or playing tennis or in a pedalo or drinking Pimm's in a park. All the things you imagine other people doing on a perfect sunny day, when you yourself are adrift, with no plans. An ideal summer, always happening elsewhere and to other people. He'd probably not even answer. After all, he had a girlfriend, was likely feeding her strawberries as they reclined on a patterned rug and—

Sorry am at football.

Ellie stared at it, then texted back.

Eh what? Is this Mark? Blink once if you've been kidnapped.

Ha ha. Corporate thing. The worst but can't get out of it.

Ellie couldn't help but feel disappointed.

Then he texted again: *Drinks in the week instead?*

Sure. He wasn't out with Laura, anyway. Laura was probably busy saving lives. The thought of Mark's girlfriend always made Ellie feel vaguely itchy and ashamed. Yes, Laura was amazing, tall and beautiful and kind, a doctor in A & E, a volunteer in soup kitchens, played the bass guitar. It was impossible not to like her. And yet Ellie was jealous of her successful career, her confidence and sureness. It was a nasty side to herself that she didn't like.

Then Ellie caught sight of the time. She was going to be late for pizza if she didn't get a move on.

An hour later, she slid into a seat in Pizza Express near Charing Cross, fourteen minutes late for Michelle, who was already halfway down a plate of dough balls. 'Cheat day,' she said, through a mouthful of garlic butter.

'Sorry I'm late!'

'Any insights?'

Ellie sighed, perusing the menu, asking herself the usual questions. Choose something healthy or what she really wanted, a vat of carbonara and garlic bread? 'Oh you know, a million options as always. France, Japan,

South America ... go back home and do medicine ... stick at journalism and try to be better ... write my novel. Blah blah blah. You're so lucky you always knew what you wanted.'

'I'm not so sure it wants me,' sighed Michelle, pushing the last dough ball over to Ellie. 'Here, I feel sick.'

'You better not be developing bulimia.'

'Honestly, it's hard not to. My tutor told me I was too fat yesterday.'

Ellie spluttered. 'That's outrageous. You're gorgeous.' Michelle was a size eight at the most.

'You're right. Let's order more dough balls.'

'And pasta.'

'And a pizza to share.' Food on the way, Michelle peered across the table at her friend. 'So? How are you going to decide what to do?'

'Mate, I have no idea.'

As a steaming pizza made its way to them, glistening with cheese and oregano, deep pools of fat and crispy crust, Michelle said: 'Look, just apply for everything. Work hard at this internship. Write your novel too. Then see what sticks. Can't hurt, right?'

'I suppose,' said Ellie, losing interest in anything but the pizza.

*

This season's hottest colour is orange. The colour of fizzing Berocca, of tropical sunsets, or orange Fruit Pastilles, which as everyone knows are the best ones. Go bold and brave in these fab shifts and jumpsuits, or settle for a pop of colour via jewellery or shoes.

Several days later, Ellie looked at what she'd written. She

was quite proud of it. It wasn't easy to get a thousand words out of orange being the new pink (based on one esoteric Italian designer having used it in his runway collection). She printed the copy and passed it to Carina, who pursed her glossed lips and held it in the odd splay-fingered way everyone at the magazine handled things, to protect their manicures. Since leaving university three years earlier, Ellie had also got manicures every week. Even if she couldn't afford the bus and had to walk home, she wouldn't forgo her beauty regime. Everyone at the magazine took it for granted that you couldn't be expected to live without foundation and facials and several new items of clothing every week. Ellie did her best not to think about the mountain of personal debt she teetered on. Everyone she knew had credit cards and overdrafts (except for Mark, the boring bastard, who lived within his means and even saved part of his income towards a house deposit every month). It would be fine once she started earning. Which surely she had to, someday soon?

Carina raised a groomed eyebrow. 'Is this true what you've put, about orange being used in Buddhism?'

'Well, yeah. Think of those monks in robes.'

'Hmmm. Yes.' Carina set the paper down, delicately. 'See if you can get in a bit more of that. Spirituality plays well with our readership.'

Ellie waited. 'But other than that . . . it's OK?'

Carina tapped at her computer. 'It's . . . quite good, Ellie.'

Ellie almost fell over. Finally! It had only taken three years to get praise from someone for her writing. It was almost comical. She, who'd dreamed of winning the Booker Prize and writing stirring, important novels, had been reduced to tears several times over copy about mascara or Britney's divorce or how to do gel nails. And what was more, she cared. People were going to read these words, perhaps millions of people. Girls like her, growing up in depressing villages where the height of glamour was a meat raffle down the church hall, would be turning these glossy pages full of questions. How to be grown up. When to have sex. How to be beautiful. And it was Ellie's responsibility to answer. Or it would be when she finally got to write something proper. Maybe things were turning around.

'Oh, Ellie?'

She turned to see Kai, the editorial assistant (a job Ellie coveted, which meant she wrote most of the magazine, while the editor, a glam American no one ever saw, just breezed in and out of Soho House and put her name to it). 'Janine was thinking we should do something about the Olympics bid. You know, it's being announced tonight.'

'Oh yes.'

Despite having zero interest in sport, Ellie was feeling oddly patriotic at the idea that London might get to host the Games.

'Hottest British athletes, how to take up sport – but nothing aggressive, something nice like fencing or judo – you get the idea. Not one of those sports that gives you thunder thighs.'

Ellie ignored all the problems with that statement, as she so often had to working at the magazine. 'You want me to write it? A feature?'

'Sure.'

'Great! I mean, I'll get on it.'

Finally, a feature. Excitedly, Ellie pulled her keyboard towards her, noticing too late that she'd already chipped her nail polish. No matter. She bet Martha Gellhorn had never worried about her manicure.

The next few hours flew by as Ellie happily researched her piece. Eventually, she looked up and saw the beauty editor's desk was empty. In fact, most of the desks were vacant, computers turned off.

'Have people gone already?' she said to Kai, who was putting on her jacket, a Max Mara filched from the beauty closet – one perk of working here, but one that Ellie was not yet senior enough to be allowed.

'Yeah, summer hours, you know. Head home, Ellie. Nothing will get done today.'

It was four o'clock. A long summer afternoon and evening stretched ahead, in the most exciting city on earth, sun warming the pavements and drawing people out to pubs and restaurants. And what did Ellie have to do? Nothing. Absolutely nothing. Maybe she should work on the novel she'd been incubating for years, tortuously adding and deleting words. But the idea of wrangling with that unwieldy beast on such a beautiful afternoon felt like searching for synonyms of *sparkly* – ultimately futile. She'd slaved at the magazine all week, doing phone interviews and research and waylaying people in the street for vox pops, arranging couriers and making coffee. All she'd seen of London for weeks was the Tube and and a quick trek round the shops on her lunchbreak while shoving down a homemade cheese sandwich. She wanted some fun.

She looked out of the window. Brilliant July sunshine shone down on a grimy London street, traffic crawling around Hyde Park. She nipped to the loo, sprayed Sure under her arms, fluffed up her hair, popped a mint into her mouth, dabbled Rimmel powder over her shiny forehead. As she stepped out onto the summer street, the smell of petrol and barbecued meat rising up from the hot pavement, she realised she had nowhere to go. Michelle was out of town at an audition, Verity would be working till seven at least; likewise Camilla. Mark would probably be working too. But she decided to risk calling him all the same. She stood on the hot street listening to the dial tone.

'Warren.'

How good it was to hear his voice, not taken for granted even after three years of being friends again.

'Grant. How's it hanging?'

'Not bad. Well, I'm currently waiting for a mate who isn't coming because he's got tickets for bloody Wimbledon. Honestly, why do so many men insist on loving sport?'

'No idea. You wouldn't want to be there?'

'Are you kidding me? Drinking overpriced booze and eating strawberries with a load of people's rich parents from St Albans? No ta.'

Ellie wasn't even sure where St Albans was. 'So you're all alone.'

'Yeah, had the afternoon off. Nursing a pint in a beer garden, on my tod.'

'Is it nice?'

She sensed him shrug. 'It's OK. Standard Wetherspoons, but it's cheap.'

'I thought they were paying you megabucks to discover the next quark or whatever.'

'I wish. Anyway, you know me, penny saved and all that.'

'Tight as a duck's arse, you mean. Where is it, this beer garden?'

'Near Victoria. Place called the Princess Alice, or some other bloody monarchist rubbish.'

'Would you like some company, to help deride them?'

Just a simple thing to offer, from one friend to another. So why did she feel nervous, her stomach lurching under her Top Shop tea-dress?

She heard him pause. 'You're off work?'

'Got out early. I heard about this pub near London Bridge, that plays good indie music –the Three Goats.' Another long pause. What was his problem? They'd gone drinking hundreds of times.

'Or you could come here? I already have a table.'

'If you like, lazy bastard.'

'No it's not that, it's just ... we can go to your place if you want.'

'I don't mind.'

'Well, make a bloody decision, lass! It doesn't make a difference really.'

The Princess Alice

Ellie thought about it for a second. 'Meh, I'll come there. First one's on you though.'

'As long as you're not going to drink a gin cocktail or some other fancy crap. This is Wetherspoons. They're practically northern.'

Ellie felt a smile break out over her face. She was twenty-four, the sun was shining, she was going to drink beer in a garden with her best friend ever. 'A pint'll do me. See you then, petal.'

Ellie took the Tube to Victoria, buoyant despite its strong smell of underarms and the air so clammy you could almost bite it, and ran the last few streets to the pub, dodging tour groups. Her heart felt like it was bursting suddenly, with possibility, with youth. She wasn't past it. She had plenty of time to make her mind up about her career. There were endless opportunities.

She found the pub, her breath coming faster than it should, even with the run, and pushed her way in through the throng of people on the pavement, smoking and drinking beer, faces turned up to the sun, shoulders turning pink. London just felt different when it was hot. As if everyone woke up and stood up straight and looked around themselves properly, music seeping out of open windows, the smell of barbecues and sun cream on hot skin. Tomorrow it might rain, so they had to make the most of it.

There was the door to the beer garden, and her eyes adjusting back from the dark of the pub. Mark was sitting under a tree, reading a Terry Pratchett book. He was wearing a suit and white shirt, the jacket slung over his chair, shirt sleeves pushed up. He looked like a grown-up. She stopped for a moment, just watching him, an odd impulse in her legs to turn and run.

He seemed to sense her there, and looked up from his

book. Across the crowded beer garden, full of braying City workers and women in high, painful shoes, they looked at each other. Same old wonky glasses, same old Mark.

'There you are, Warren. Late as always.'

'Just working on my Pulitzer-prize winning piece about how to take up fencing without ruining your hair.' She hesitated at the pub table – she felt awkward for some reason.

So did he, it seemed, as they did the hug dance, and he punched her gently on the shoulder instead. 'You all right then? How's the job?'

'Yeah. I mean, it's kind of shallow, I guess . . . but it's fun. Glamorous. You know, a bit of a lift.'

'We could do with some of that at my place,' said Mark gloomily.

She noticed he'd already finished his pint, while hers was still untouched, and hurriedly changed the subject away from his job at the big tech giant. He hated it, but it paid a ridiculous amount for someone of their age. He was always talking about leaving and setting up on his own.

'Another?' She took out her fake Louis Vuitton purse (three pounds from the market) and he waved it away. He earned literally ten times what she did.

He went to get more drinks, coming back with two of each hooked into his hands. 'We have to celebrate that we might get the Olympics, after all.'

'Cheers.'

'Cheers.'

They clinked and Mark took a deep gulp. She hoped he wasn't drinking too much.

'Where's Laura?' she asked.

'At the hospital. As always.'

'Ah. Just you and me then?'

'Eh . . . I guess so. No Michelle?'

'She texted to say she had a last-minute audition in Brighton, she's staying over with a mate.'

'Have to hand it to her, she doesn't give up.'

'Like I gave up on medicine.' Ellie sighed, taking a gulp of the cold, foamy beer.

Mark made a little violin movement. 'What about your writing? You did all those plays at uni.'

'Not really. One or two.'

When Steve had come to see her first play – a tense two-hander about an unhappy couple trapped in a rowboat – all he'd said was, 'Hmm, yeah, still it's just your first go, isn't it.'

'Are you not still writing the novel?' said Mark, wiping away a beer moustache.

'Well, yeah, I am, but it's hard. I'm so busy at work, you know.' He was looking sceptical, and she knew he was right to be, so she changed the subject. 'Hey, I saw they've got a Millionaire machine! Remember we cleaned out the one in the Coach and Feathers back home?'

'Course I do, they barred us and I tried to give them some big speech about discriminating against us for our intelligence.'

'I remember. You were lucky they didn't take you behind the bar and mince you into those dodgy burgers they served. Fancy a go?'

Mark felt in the pocket of his suit trousers for some change. 'Why not? I bet I can still take you on, Warren.'

How nice this was, Ellie thought, following him into the

118

beer-smelling dark of the pub to the machine. How good to have Mark back in her life. How had she ever coped without him? It was so great they could be friends, past whatever strange nervy awkwardness there'd been at that school party, then the years of not really talking after they hadn't met up on New Year's Eve. Everything was now back on track.

At 7 a.m., Ellie woke up with a start of horror. She hadn't ... had she?

A leg stuck out of her floral duvet cover. Hairy. Familiar.

'Oh Christ,' she said out loud.

Mark sat up, his hair almost standing on end with an existential dread that Ellie recognised in herself. 'Shit. Where am I?'

'You're ... at mine.' Oh God. Oh God, what had happened? How?

'What?' He rubbed his eyes. She could smell his body, sweat and old aftershave. It wasn't a bad smell at all, not to her. She would have liked to press her face to his chest and breathe it in, if everything hadn't been so awful.

'I don't know, we must have ... shit, how much did we drink?' All she remembered was the dark pub, downing pint after pint, laughing, reminiscing. Simply being, in a cosy golden bubble. With Mark, who understood her totally. But how had they ended up here, in her bed? Maybe nothing had happened. She looked tentatively under the covers. Both of them were stark naked. Memories came back, grappling on the bed, her head hitting the backboard with surprising, sexy violence. With Mark. After all this time. And she'd been too drunk to remember it properly.

119

A memory suddenly came back. 'That New Year's Eve years ago, the millennium – we talked about it last night.'

He was getting up – a flash of white bum – looking for his clothes, which were tangled with hers on the floor. 'Did we?'

'Yes. You said – Mark, you said it was just you waiting for me that night! Not a whole gang. It was meant to be just you and me, like – well, like a date.'

'Not a date,' he mumbled, pulling on his T-shirt. 'Shit. I'll be late for work. I don't have time to change. Oh Christ. This is bad. This is really bad.'

She hadn't been thinking it was good, but all the same it wasn't nice to hear the panic and regret in his voice. Laura. Oh God. She liked her. Everyone liked her. 'Mark! We have to at least talk about this. What did you want to happen that New Year's?'

He met her eyes for a painful moment. 'I don't know. I just – I wanted to see you. I'd missed you.'

'And you'd booked a table – for the two of us?' It was all the opposite of what she'd imagined, some noisy pub with a big gang. 'You never told me.'

'Yeah, well, you didn't make it, did you? You met Steve.'

'I hurt myself! You said not to bother coming.'

Mark was looping his belt through his trousers. 'I was annoyed. Look, it was a long time ago, El.' And since then he'd met Laura and they were together. So why had he brought it up last night, after the Olympics announcement when the pub had gone wild, people hugging and cheering, and Ellie and Mark ordered more and still more drinks?

'I'm sorry. Mark, I'm so sorry. Can we talk at least?' What did it mean? Mark had feelings for her? He'd wanted something to happen between them that night years ago? 'And the party, where we met Michelle that time, you were really pissed off at me – was that why? Because I kissed that stupid boy?'

He sighed, looking round for his wallet and phone. 'I took you to that party. And next thing I find you with some guy's tongue down your throat.'

Ellie was stung. 'I had no idea! You have literally never given me any indication you saw me as more than a friend.' Assuming he did – she wasn't sure what was happening. 'Please talk to me.'

'Later. I need to get to work now. I'm sorry.'

And he was gone.

Ellie lay in bed for another half an hour or so, feeling thoroughly dejected. She was going to be late for work too. When she dragged herself out, she saw Michelle at the kitchen table in her rollers and very dirty towelling robe. Oh God, she must have come back early. She tried to tell from her friend's face whether she knew.

'Mark crashed,' she said, brightly, taking down a packet of Shreddies. 'We drank way too much.'

'I heard.' Michelle pushed away her coffee cup and stood up.

'I . . .'

'El. Save it. I don't want to know.'

Ellie began to tremble as her friend left the room. She'd spoiled everything, messed it all up. She'd maybe ruined things for Mark and Laura, and she could see on Michelle's face how little she thought of Ellie right now.

She was just sinking down at the table when she heard a

text ding on Michelle's phone, then an intake of breath and her friend was suddenly back in the room. 'El. Turn the radio on.'

'What's happened?'

'Something on the Tube ... they're saying a power-out but Laura's just texted it's a bomb. Maybe several bombs.'

Ellie was moving to the radio, the name *Laura* spiking at her before she took in what Michelle had said. 'A bomb? Jesus Christ.'

'Yeah. And Mark hasn't made it in to work.'

The Three Goats

'Bit dead, isn't it?' Ellie wished she hadn't insisted on coming to the pub near London Bridge, which was somewhat lacking in atmosphere. There was one bored barmaid, with pink hair, and a group of middle-aged men in polo shirts talking loudly about speed boats. Her pint was flat, too. And to add insult to injury, the music they were playing was UB40, Mark's absolute nightmare.

'Yeah, not your finest choice.'

Ellie looked around her. 'There's no TVs even – we'll miss the Olympics result.'

'You really care that much?' He looked at her quizzically. 'Ellie Warren, who faked a broken ankle to get out of running the six hundred metres?'

'I suppose not. I have to write this feature on it is all.' How proud she was, to have an assignment, even if it was only a puff piece in a magazine.

'Oh yeah?'

'Which Olympian has the best hair ... how to pole vault in hotpants ... matching your nail polish to the different flags ... that sort of hard-hitting stuff.'

She was gratified to hear him laugh, a low chuckle that she'd always loved. Mark was hard to amuse.

'That's great.' He chinked his pint against hers. 'You've been waiting ages for a feature, haven't you? They paying you?'

'I think I'll get basic freelance rates.' She loved even saying that, though the rates were pitiful compared to what he earned. She was finally making some progress. Maybe sticking with journalism was the answer after all. She remembered she'd wanted to ask his advice about what to do with the rest of her life, admit how lost she was. 'Marko – what ...'

Ellie broke off, because Laura was coming towards them, still in her scrubs. She looked radiant despite her twelve-hour shift and no makeup, lit up with adrenaline. 'Oh – look.'

Mark wiped beer foam from his mouth. 'Oh, yeah – her hospital's right near here. I kind of had to ask her along.'

Ellie tried to quell the ridiculous disappointment that was dragging her stomach down. Stupid of her – she should have just gone to meet him, but she'd wanted to impress him with her knowledge of pubs. That had very much backfired. 'Oh yeah, no it's great, lovely to see her. Hi, Laura!'

'Hiya, Ellie. Hey, sweetheart.' She leaned over to kiss Mark; Ellie looked away.

'Good shift?' said Mark.

'Amazing. Just resussed a grandma who collapsed in the

lift. Boom, down she went, heart stopped, and I brought her back. Like she was literally dead.'

'Pretty normal day then.'

Laura laughed. 'Actually, it is. Never a dull moment.'

Ellie found herself putting on a rictus grin, as Laura slid in beside Mark on his side of the booth. She'd been about to ask his advice, confess how adrift she was, both in work and romance. But now that Laura was here, she felt she couldn't say anything.

Laura glanced at her phone. 'We got the Olympics, by the way.'

'Oh, that's nice,' said Ellie, no longer all that bothered.

'To the Olympics,' said Mark, lifting his glass. 'Who knows where we'll all be in 2012?'

The next morning, Ellie stared at herself in the bathroom mirror, rubbing a small space clear of the steam. She looked tired and drawn despite not staying long after Laura's arrival. Ellie always felt drab after seeing her – she was so full of energy, her skin always glowing despite the lack of sleep her job entailed. Beside her, Ellie just felt boring, and frivolous, and . . . well, not enough. Her hair was frizzy and dull, horribly dry from the air conditioning at work. Her brown eyes sat behind dark bags. It had been a slightly awkward threesome, Ellie trying not to lapse into the bantering shorthand she and Mark had always shared, and Mark trying to find some common ground between the two women. She'd made her excuses after two pints and headed home, feeling cheated of her heart to heart with Mark. Maybe she'd just stick at journalism, see if this piece worked out well for her.

Ellie showered, put on a pencil skirt and polyester blouse, made some cheese and pickle sandwiches, squeezed her feet into uncomfortable heels and set out for the Tube station. She was so busy musing over the night before that she didn't notice until she was almost there that crowds of people were walking away from the station. Outside, a man in an orange jacket was waving people from the gates. Great, all she needed was to be late. 'What's happened?'

The man glanced at her. 'Power outage or something.'

'Will it be back?'

He shrugged. 'Try a bus, love.'

Ellie glanced at the time – almost nine. She usually got in for half past. She wandered to a nearby bus stop and scanned the signs to work out which one she needed for Marble Arch. But when one came, it was already full. And the next. It was now ten past, so Ellie decided she would walk. It wasn't all that far past Euston and into Soho. She set off, cursing her stupid heels.

After forty minutes of limping through London, Ellie was growing alarmed. She kept hearing sirens in the distance, and hundreds of people were walking the streets, too, as every Tube she passed was closed. Could the whole system really be down? It was going to cause chaos, but on the other hand she could hardly get into trouble for being late if everyone was. She kept checking her phone, but the text she'd sent Kai had not even gone through, and nothing had come in. That was really weird. Had the power issue taken phones out too?

As she reached Marble Arch, the streets were weirdly empty. A police car sped by, sirens blaring, sending a chill through Ellie. What had happened? It felt like a disaster film. Still she kept walking, not sure what to do except head to the office. When she arrived, she could see things were strange there, too. There was no one behind the reception desk, and the usual security guard was missing from his post. Ellie fished out the pass that would let her into the building, deeply worried now.

'El!'

She turned. Mark. Mark was there, outside her office, in a suit with his tie askew.

She didn't understand. 'What are you . . . '

'You're OK?'

'I'm fine. What's going on? The Tube's down.' Mark worked in the City – how had he even got here? He must have walked, like her.

'Laura got called into work.' He hesitated. 'They're saying it was a massive bomb on the Tube. More than one, proba-bly. Multiple Tubes.'

'Oh my God. Really?'

Who would do such a thing? When she'd first moved here her parents had worried about IRA bombs, though that already seemed far in the past. Her mind began to churn – who might have been on the Tube that she knew? Michelle had texted to say she'd got back to the flat just after Ellie left, and Verity went to work at six so she could fit in a gym session. Camilla, maybe. Yolanda, who came into London via Liverpool Street each day. But Mark was here, Mark was safe. As Ellie stood there watching him, a woman staggered past. Her head was bloodied, and she was clutching a tissue to it, talking into a phone at the same time. Ellie turned to Mark in horror.

'What is this?'

'It's a terror attack,' he said grimly. 'I had to see you were all right. I walked the whole way – texts aren't going through. I was so worried.'

Ellie tried to take this in. He'd come all this way to check on her? Out of everyone in London?

'Why?'

'Because, El . . . ' Mark raked his hands through his hair and she saw he was ashen. 'God, it's such a mess. But I love you. I've been in love with you for years. Since school. Since that New Year. I was going to tell you then but you didn't come, then you were with that prick Steve for so long, and then it was too late because there's Laura, and she's a really good person, the best. I've been trying not to say it for so long. But I love you, OK? This morning when I heard the news, all I could think about was you.' He stared at her, blue eyes boring into hers. 'Say something, El. You feel the same, don't you?'

Ellie tried to draw in breath. London was under attack, people were dead, the world was upside down. And here was Mark telling her he loved her, all the little puzzle pieces falling into place. Why he'd been strange with her at that party years ago. The real reason for the weird New Year's Eve plan.

An alarm was going off in the building, almost drowning out her reply, so she stepped closer, an inch from his arms. She knew she'd be safe there. Had always known it. It made so much sense, as if shock and fear had thrown things into sharp clarity.

'Of course I do,' she said.

JUNE 2019

Ellie had made it to the stream now, the little brook running through the field behind her parents' house, where she'd spent so much time as a child. Sailing paper boats and twigs, daydreaming, splashing about and getting her clothes wet so her mother would scold her yet again. Like so many things from childhood, it looked smaller, no more than a trickle over sandy ground. All the same, she kicked off her slippers and dangled her pedicured feet in the water. It was cool and gentle and she felt her breath slow. So. She'd run away from her wedding and was now lurking in a field like Tom bloody Sawyer. She'd hidden from Mark and Laura, who seemed to be having some kind of bust-up. And even thinking about that, the merest hint that what had seemed so solid and unassailable was perhaps not, gave Ellie heart palpitations. Caused her entire world to slip and slide.

She was getting married! She should be happy. Someone loved her, and she loved them, and her mother was actually pleased with her for the first time Ellie could ever recall. Some women said they'd dreamed of their wedding day since they were little, but Ellie honestly never had. She'd been more interested in making up dramatic stories with her dolls than playing brides, re-enacting medical emergencies that Barbie would then cure through her surgical expertise, Ken standing by as nurse (Ellie had always been a feminist).

Why had she even invited Mark to her wedding? She still couldn't look at him without being swept with a guilt so tangible she could feel it rushing through her body. Of course it was a mistake, to stir up the sediment of the past, of what might have been, on a day when she was supposed to be making the biggest and most final choice of her life. She was supposed to be sure, and in just a few hours someone was going to ask her, in front of witnesses, exactly that. If she was sure. And she wasn't. Because Mark was here, and he and Laura didn't seem to be getting on, and Ellie had never forgiven herself for what had happened to him because of her. Was it possible that, after all, she hadn't come between him and his true love, kind and capable Laura, but that instead her guilt had ruined everything, sending her fleeing from the country, afraid to speak to him for years?

What if his true love had been *her*?

Ellie looked down at her feet in the chill, clear water of the stream. Her pedicure was a discreet French polish – she'd wanted a bright colour, orange or red, but her mother had been horrified. *You need to look elegant, Eleanor!* She wondered how much of today, her wedding day, had actually been chosen by her, and how much she'd been overruled by her mother and groom.

Oh yes. Her groom. He was probably getting ready himself at the hotel he was staying at, on the other side of town. It was really just a pub with rooms, nothing special and certainly not what he was used to, but the best Ellie's hometown had to offer. She'd travelled so far from this little mill town. Yet inside she still felt like the same unsure teenager, constantly criticised by her mother and angsty about boys. And maybe, just maybe, in love with Mark. Because she always had been, hadn't she? They'd just missed each other so many times. So many doors she hadn't opened. So many paths she hadn't walked down. And now it was her wedding day and she was due to get married in three hours. Her mother would be absolutely doing her nut, yet here Ellie was sitting in a tracksuit with her bare feet dangling in a stream. She hadn't even washed her hair or showered yet.

Three hours. It wasn't very long to decide what she was going to do with her life, but all the same, when she looked back, she knew she'd made enormous choices in less time than that. Often with no thought at all, unaware that a tiny decision had changed the course of her life.

She had to get some advice. Obviously she couldn't talk to Mark, and Verity hadn't been much help. Who else was there? Ellie pulled her feet out from the stream, wiped them on the grass and set off back to the house.

CHOICE 5 – NOVEMBER 2005

A sharp winter sunshine was glinting on the river as Ellie walked along. Often, in Paris, she saw herself as if from the outside. A character in a film. There she was, strolling past the *bouquinistes* with their green wooden stalls selling old books, postcards, prints of Babar and black and white photos of the old city. She wore flat black lace-up boots – French women didn't do heels – and a calf-length navy skirt with gold elephants printed on it, which she'd found in a second-hand shop in Montmartre, and a black polo neck. Long silver earrings brushed her shoulders, and her hair was piled up in a knot. These were the clothes of a Parisian, not a tour-ist, and Ellie knew she was accepted by the way shopkeepers nodded to her and waiters tolerated her GCSE French. On the surface, life was good. She lived in Paris, finally, in a cute studio apartment near the Sacre Coeur, reached by going through a little courtyard with bay trees in pots, and up five flights of rickety wooden stairs. Her neighbour, Madame Vallotte, was always plying her with macaroons and sweet mint tea, and downstairs the *boulangerie* started sending up the warm yeasty scent of baguettes from 5 a.m. onwards. She loved it here – the cafés, the fashion, the food, the museums and art galleries. Moving to Paris had always been her secret dream, and now she was living it.

She definitely wasn't thinking about Mark.

After that terrible day, 7 July 2005, when Ellie, Michelle and Laura had trawled London's hospitals looking for him, realising with a growing sweaty terror that he must have been caught up in the bombs – mobile networks were down, but he'd have found a phone box, he'd have gone to his office and called if he was OK – nothing would ever be the same. It was getting dark by the time they found him in UCH, unconscious in a hospital bed, white sheets tucked around him. Ellie tried her best not to think about what she'd seen that day, the trail of blood on the floor, footprints tracked through it, which no one had yet had time to mop up, the terrified relatives badgering shell-shocked hospital staff, the ceaseless noise of ringing phones and bleeping machines and running feet. The sense of barely controlled chaos, the fear that everything was breaking down and there might be more bombs, that death could strike at any minute.

Laura had been calm and decisive, even when living out the worst day of her life. She knew where the trauma centres were and how to find out the names of patients. When they found him, Ellie had frozen in the doorway. 'Is he ... OK?'

Laura was seizing his chart, pushing her way past the exhausted nurse looking after him. 'I'm a doctor. Sorry. Please let me look.'

How pointless Ellie had felt at that moment. What useful skills did she have? She could type and recommend lipsticks and knock up a good PowerPoint. What good was that when people were bleeding and dying?

'What's wrong with him?' Michelle had her hand pressed to her mouth, horrified. 'Is he ... ?'

Laura flipped the chart. Her face was grim. 'He's OK. But they've had to amputate his left leg. His artery was severed – he must have been nearly dead. He tourniqueted himself. God! He thought to do that while losing all that blood.' She blinked. 'What I just don't get is why he was at Aldgate. It's not on his way to work. Ellie, he was out with you last night, aye?'

Ellie had felt the room spin, seen Michelle's angry look, known, in her bones, that when Mark woke up he would not want to see her ever again. This was her fault. If she hadn't met up with him last night this would never have happened. Mark would have been on his way to work as usual that morning, his leg would still be attached to him, and he never would have cheated on Laura. If she hadn't gone drinking with him that night, if she hadn't got so hammered, if there hadn't been a quiz machine and she hadn't suggested tequila-shot forfeits, if they'd gone to the other pub even, maybe – if, if, if. If she hadn't been in love with Mark for most her life. Because that was what she'd had to admit the night before, drunk on tequila and his presence, buoyed by the country's optimistic mood after the Olympics announcement, sealed in a happy bubble where she didn't think about Laura or anyone else at all. She was in love with Mark, and so when he'd suddenly revealed he'd had feelings for her at school, and that the strange New Year's Eve had been intended as a date, as their heads had begun to inch closer and closer across the sticky pub table, ringed with booze, she hadn't done anything to stop it. It was impossible

133

to say who'd made the first move, if either. They had both wanted it. But the next morning, it was Mark who'd been pale with guilt, who'd rushed from her flat without even saying goodbye, and who because of her had been on the wrong train, not his usual line, and standing three metres from a man who'd strapped explosives under his clothes, who had detonated a dense pack of nails and debris, used his body as a weapon, sent shock-waves and metal and glass flying out into the unsuspecting carriage full of people, and one large piece of metal had severed Mark's femoral artery and he would have bled to death on the floor of the Tube carriage if he hadn't had the presence of mind to remember the first aid he'd learned in school, a class Ellie had also been in though mostly focused on flirting with Darren Johnson, and used his tie to stem the flow of blood from his thigh.

Michelle and Laura were looking at her for answers. 'Um – yeah. But only till the pubs shut.' Technically true.

Laura shook her head. 'I don't get it. Maybe he had a meeting I didn't know about.' They didn't live together, so she wouldn't know he hadn't gone home. Please God she didn't know and would never find out. Michelle had approached the bed, casting a final bitter look at Ellie, and it was just all too much. Before she knew it, she was staggering down the corridor, running out into the street, gulping stale London air. The next day she'd quit her job at the magazine, left the money for two months' rent in an envelope on the kitchen table for Michelle, with no note of explanation. She'd dropped off her few bits of furniture at a charity shop, packed the rest and lugged it to the Eurostar, where she'd bought a one-way ticket to Paris. That night, she had slept in a cheap noisy hotel near the Gare du Nord and wept herself dry.

She hadn't seen Mark, or Laura, or Michelle since. He had lived. But he would never be the same again, and Ellie had been so guilty, so terribly wracked by it, that she'd run away, fled the country. Mark and Laura got married three months later, Mark walking down the aisle with his new prosthetic. Ellie had been invited, which told her Mark had never mentioned the cheating to Laura, but she'd made up an excuse about having to work in Paris. She knew that her absence would raise eyebrows, but she just couldn't face it, sitting there as they made their vows, Michelle's hostile looks and her own seeping guilt. So she'd stayed away. Her life was here now. The thing she had always wanted – to live in Paris, to be sure what she was doing with her life – but it had come at a terrible price. Mark and Laura had moved out of London since he could no longer negotiate pavements and escalators, assuming he'd ever be able to face going on the Tube again. They were in Glasgow now, where Laura was from, making a new life. Ellie just had to stay away and not ruin it further. She'd chosen a different path – not a doctor like Laura, not a journalist. She'd missed her chance with Mark on that New Year's Eve almost six years before, and that was it.

One thing about shocking tragedy is that it resets your priorities. Realising she did not want to spend her life writing about makeup, Ellie, with enough money to live on in Paris for three months (it was cheaper than London), told herself she'd find a new career there. She had some shifts in an English-speaking bookshop on the banks of the Seine, a magical place with a piano nestled in among the books. All those years she'd told herself she couldn't possibly move to another country, that she'd never find a place to live or a job, that she'd be too lonely, that she couldn't quit work to write a book, and it turned out that all you had to do was go ahead and do things and they happened.

She was almost at her flat now, already thinking with quiet relish of sitting in her wide window looking down on the busy street below, propping her feet on the radiator and sipping a strong coffee from the little silver pot she boiled on the stove. Damn, that was a point, she was out of coffee.

Ellie hesitated. She should really do some shopping, but she'd already spent the morning wandering about staring at things, her main activity in Paris, and she'd promised herself she'd do some work today. Because, although she could barely admit it to herself, Ellie had started writing a book.

The idea had come to her a few weeks after she'd arrived in Paris. She'd spent her days walking the baking-hot, empty summer streets, many shops and restaurants closed down for the month. Loneliness, guilt and regret were her only companions, since she knew no one in Paris. Did she even regret it, sleeping with Mark, finally, after so many years? Even after everything that had happened, she couldn't seem to. And that was the worst thing of all, maybe.

The days were long and quiet, heating up soup from the Monoprix at the end of her street, buying baguettes and croissants, trying to fill a hole with carbs and sugar. She had to do something eventually other than cry – no point trying to look for a job in the summer in France. So one day

136

she had found herself in a beautiful stationery shop on the Rue de Rivoli, which was still open for the tourists at the Louvre. She'd caressed the thick creamy paper, the cover bound in blue-flowered fabric, the gold edges. Too nice to write anything in, really. And yet. All the same she found she was taking the notebook to the counter and paying a truly unbelievable amount for it – she'd even stammered, 'C-combien?' only for the disdainful and extremely chic assistant to confirm the sum.

She'd brought it home, found a pen in the bottom of her old work satchel and sat in her spot by the high window with the beautiful book on her knee, a small bitter coffee on the bare floorboards beside her. In a water glass she'd shoved some stocks she'd bought from a flower stall, hoping the sweet, heavy smell would drive out the aroma of cigarettes in the flat. She'd looked about her – tiny bathroom she could barely turn around in, bed and table with two chairs, little strip of kitchen with a mini-fridge, no washing machine, no lift, no air conditioning against the pressing heat of August. But it was the first place she'd ever had to herself. Pushing the leaky old pen into the perfect paper, she had started to write. Just words.

It had no sense and no structure to begin with, but somehow it was coming together. A story about a man and a woman, growing up on the other side of the world from each other, not even knowing the other was alive, but somehow made for each other all the same. Every morning Ellie showered in the claustrophobic and damp bathroom with the whirring fan that barely worked, made coffee, picked up the pen, looking out over the rooftops of Paris, the Eiffel Tower soaring in the heat haze across the river. And she would write, scrawled words and fragments of scenes and dialogue, slowly the story of these two people – Ben and Natasha – coming to life in her head. It wasn't much, just some ink and paper and a permanent crick in her neck, and she was often lonely and tired and frustrated, with the ever-present worry about not having a job – even this tiny flat was five hundred euros a month – but all the same it was the most thrilling thing Ellie had ever experienced. She was writing a book. Finally, after all these years thinking and talking about it, she was doing it. And there were other joys of living in Paris, so many that despite the tragic circumstances, despite Michelle's silence, the emails and texts Ellie had sent her which she'd totally ignored, and her mother's anger that Ellie had dropped everything after three years trying to get into journalism, she could not regret coming here. The rattle of the Metro, with its stale-popcorn smell. The rapid fire of French on the street, which she increasingly found herself able to understand. Flower markets and bars that stayed open all night and vintage boutiques and the Seine glinting in the autumn light. And the food. Dear God, the food. Steak frites and terrine and cheese and wine and cakes, and the bread and, above all, the pastries.

If she wrote five pages first thing, she'd allow herself to go down to the bakery for an almond croissant. The first day she'd moved here, she had queued up, shyly pointing and paying her euro, then, standing in the street, she'd pushed aside the greasy brown paper and taken a bite of the warm, melting, sweet flaky pastry. It was so good she'd stopped short, an older woman with a shopping trolley tutting impatiently around her. Could a pastry change your life? If so, it had happened to Ellie. Yes, she was lonely and broke and hadn't answered any of the messages from her work or family or friends (none from Mark or Michelle). Despite all that, the croissant was maybe good enough to make up for it.

Now, several months on, having filled the beautiful notebook and bought herself a cheap laptop, typed it all up, noting with growing excitement that her word count had ticked over the fifty-thousand mark – half a book, at least! – she was reluctantly admitting it was time she left Paris. Despite the endless beauty of every day here, she didn't belong in this city. She knew no one and the weight of loneliness, her voice rusty with lack of use, was starting to get to her. Her mother was right – she was halfway through her twenties, high time to figure out her career, meet someone, settle down. The idea of leaving it too long, never having kids, was terrifying to Ellie, and clearly that was not going to happen in Paris. She'd have to start looking at coaches to the UK, since she couldn't afford the Eurostar. Back to a drab British life, with no idea where she'd live or what she'd do. Getting a job might mean she didn't have time to finish her novel, and she was so close with it. Maybe she should do a big push before she went home – starting today.

Ellie stood at the corner of the street for a moment, dithering. Should she go to Monoprix and stock up on groceries? Or just buy a coffee at the bakery downstairs and spend the afternoon writing?

Bakery

'You are confused?' A husky, tobacco-raw, red wine-infused, male voice.

Ellie was startled out of her reverie; she'd been staring at the rows of cake in a sort of daze. Yes, she'd had her morning croissant earlier, but it would take more strength than she had to go into the bakery and just buy a coffee. There were so many cakes to try. Reds and greens and yellows, glazed fruit brighter than jewels, puffs of satiny sweet cream, crisp almond pastry. How everyone in Paris wasn't enormous she didn't know.

'Um, no.' Shyly, she switched into French. '*J'aime regarder les gateaux, c'est tout.*' I just like looking at the cakes – her French had improved enough to make little jokes, even.

'English?' Like many Parisians, he refused to humour her attempts to speak their language.

She looked at him properly now, depressed he could tell so easily she was British. The speaker was a tall, stooped man of around thirty, shaggy dark hair, a tweed jacket, a sensitive, amused face. Ellie felt the bottom drop out of her stomach, and suddenly, she couldn't have eaten a single bite of *religieuse*, the meringue- and chocolate-infused cake that was the most delicious and overwhelming of all.

'Yes.'

He held out one nicotine-stained hand, the fingers long and graceful. 'You are, I think, Ellie?' He pronounced her name with a high e at the end.

'How did you ...'

'I am Serge. Upstairs.'

The mysterious pianist who lived above her! Sometimes, late at night, she lay awake listening to faint tinkling notes. More than once a particularly beautiful melody had made her cry, thinking of all she'd lost, all Mark had lost. Once or twice he'd had parties, and a lonely Ellie had left the window open so the sounds of laughter and music dropped down to her, feet tripping on the stairs, loud French voices. It had made her feel even more alone, but she'd never actually seen her neighbour, apart from his post in the hallway marked *Serge Lemoine*, and thought what a sexy name it was. Ellie stood up straighter. It wasn't every day she was accosted in a bakery by a hot, piano-playing Frenchman. Subtly, she checked his hand for a ring. Nothing.

'I hope I will not annoy you with my playing?'

'I'm sure you won't,' said Ellie, who'd been known to take a broom to the ceiling when her upstairs neighbours in London insisted on having loud screaming sex at four in the morning. 'Maybe I can . . . ' Daringly, she bit her lip. 'I'd love to hear it properly sometime. I mean, I love the piano.'

What had got into her? Was flirting just easier in a different country, a different language?

'*Ah, oui?* Then you must come. Join me for some wine, around ten p.m. perhaps, tonight?'

It was as easy as that. People in Paris were like that – they asked you round, they hosted you. Not suspicious like London, closing the doors and shutting themselves in. Ellie blinked. Why the hell not? It wasn't like she knew anyone else here. And after all, she would only have to go up one flight of stairs. 'Um, sure. A *plus tard*, then.' See you later.

He smiled at her accent, and she realised he was still

holding her hand, his long index finger pressing into her palm. She pulled it away, blushing, and turned to the woman behind the counter. 'Um, a coffee please, a *café*, um . . . *petit café, s'il vous plaît*.'

The *boulangere*, a roly-poly woman with arms the size of car tyres from beating out baguettes, poured a tiny espresso into a paper cup and held out her hand for Ellie's euro.

'*Vous êtes de retour, alors*,' she said to Serge, with slight hostility. So you're back.

'*Juste pour te voir, Adeline*.' Only to see you. The more intimate *tu* a touch flirtatious, a little daring to an older woman.

The baker, who'd seen many things over her long years of hammering out bread for the inhabitants of the 18ème, rolled her eyes. But Ellie had already downed her espresso, strong and black as tar and silty with brown sugar, and her nerves were fizzing and jangling, and she was in Paris and had a date (maybe?) with a hot pianist, and she thought she'd never heard a sexier voice in all her life.

There was something quite thrilling about dressing to see a man when you could hear him moving around above your head, the occasional scrape of furniture or trill of music, a loud cough, the run of water. Ellie dug out a dress she'd bought in a vintage shop in her first week, optimistically, then never worn since she had nowhere to go here. It was red and strappy, with a full swinging skirt. She drew around her eyes in liner and brushed her hair upside down, wishing Michelle was there to give beauty advice. Or that Michelle was speaking to her. But there was no point mourning the past when she couldn't change it. She lived in Paris now, she was a writer (admittedly a totally broke, unpublished one), and she was going upstairs to see what transpired. She clutched a bottle of red from Monoprix – you could get good wine here for very little – and, strangely out of breath, climbed the short dusty flight of stairs from her apartment to Serge's. He was playing music – jazz, something with a saxophone. She raised her hand and knocked, on the verge of running away in fear, leaving Paris, going home with just her laptop and red dress. Because something told her tonight was going to be one of those strange moments she experienced from time to time, when she glimpsed a pattern in her life, a larger architecture. When she felt that every step she took was somehow vitally important.

The door opened, releasing a smell of smoke and garlic. Serge was in a loose blue shirt, sleeves rolled up. He was gorgeous. So incredibly sexy Ellie could hardly walk forward, and she only realised now she'd forgotten to put any shoes on, but somehow that worked, the elegant dress and the bare feet, her hair loose, her body giving off waves of a musky perfume she'd bought at a stall in the *marché aux puces*.

'Ellie,' he said, and her name in his mouth was even sexier. 'I am happy to see you.'

Monoprix

'You're sure you want to come back?' said Michelle, looking around Ellie's small studio apartment, now stripped bare, her scant possessions, amassed over the past five months, packed into three cases. 'It's so beautiful. And the cakes in that bakery downstairs – man, it would be worth ending my career to eat one of those every day.'

'I know,' said Ellie, ruefully pinching the extra weight that had settled around her middle from those very cakes. 'But it's not home, you know? I miss people.' She'd stuck with the decision she'd made several weeks before, standing on the street dithering between buying groceries and writing. It was time to leave Paris, and nothing had happened since to change her mind.

'People?' Michelle arched her perfect eyebrows.

She paid £100 a month to have them shaped, which she could afford now she'd landed a lead role on a hospital drama called *Crash* (even Michelle got to be a doctor, a fact Ellie thought about often). This trip over to see Ellie and help her move back to London was the first time off she'd had in months. Although Ellie had loved being in Paris, and eaten a lot of memorable cakes, she hadn't really made any friends, and certainly not had a romance, which seemed a little sad in the city of love. So she was going home to try and pick up the threads of her tattered life. It was almost Christmas, and the shops were decked out with even more sumptuous cakes and jewelled fruit and intricately moulded chocolate figurines, any animal or object you could imagine. Huge shimmering trees in public squares, ice skating, hot wine, lovers kissing on each street corner, cosy in berets and scarves. And yet, because Ellie was alone, it all left her hollow, and so she was giving in. At least the time had allowed her almost to finish her book, and when she thought about it she felt a small tick of excitement in her stomach. Going back to the UK – that made sense if she was trying to find an agent and publisher. And why not? People did it all the time. Why not her?

'Yeah, just – people.'

'You mean Mark?' Michelle was wrapping a blue glass vase in old newspaper. 'That's the people you miss?'

'No, I don't mean Mark.' Crossly, Ellie bent down to wiggle a hairpin out from an ancient floorboard. 'I highly doubt we'll be seeing each other once I come back.'

The sore place in her heart was still tender when pressed. It had taken a long time for Michelle to forgive her for what had happened that day in July and finally respond to one of her anguished texts. Even longer for Ellie for forgive herself, if she ever had. She knew it was no one's fault Mark had been on the wrong Tube line, on the wrong train, on the wrong day. Just blind fate. One of those things. And yet he wouldn't have been on it if not for her. But Scotland was far away. She wouldn't have to see him, and face up to what she'd done. He and Laura were married now. Sometimes, when Ellie wanted to torture herself, she went through the wedding photos on Facebook: Laura, her capable shoulders rising out of a plain white silk dress, Mark leaning on a stick. Her mother had asked her at least ten times now why she hadn't been at the wedding, and she knew Laura must think her a horrible person, not to turn up to her oldest friend's wedding, her wounded, miraculously alive friend. Abandoning her friend, skipping the country while he was still in hospital. Perhaps Laura still wondered why her husband had been on the wrong Tube line that day – or perhaps she knew it all, the entire shameful incident. That was something she, Ellie Warren, had done, and just had to live with.

Michelle could say a lot by saying nothing at all. It was one of the things that made her such a great actress.

'What?' said Ellie.

'Oh, nothing. It just seems a shame, you two not speaking, that's all.'

'Don't you like Laura? Is he not happy with her?' Ellie knew she shouldn't ask these questions. She only did it to hurt herself.

Michelle shrugged. 'Oh, Laura's amazing. I'm just not sure she's amazing with Mark.'

Ellie turned away, suddenly annoyed, and carried on wrapping plates in bubble wrap. 'What do you mean?'

'Well, she's so . . . so strong and fearless and sensible. And he's sort of – he's a romantic soul, under all the maths and physics. And you – well, he was always besotted with you, that was obvious the minute I met you guys.'

Ellie shrugged, angry tears stinging her nose. What was the point in saying these things? 'I didn't know.'

'How could you not, El? Why do you think he was in such a radge at that party we went to, when you accidentally kissed dumbass Adam?'

'He never told me! He never even explained the stupid New Year's thing was just me and him – I'd never have stood him up if I'd known that. He never *says* things.'

Michelle shrugged. 'I think he was planning to that night. And then, well, Steve.'

And what bitter regret Ellie had at that, the wasted opportunities. 'Well, it's too late for that now, isn't it? They're married. The best thing I can do is stay away, leave them to it. Believe me, I didn't want to lose him. But I've done enough damage.'

A pained moment went by, and she felt Michelle's hand on her shoulder. 'Come on, Grumpy. It's your last night in Paris. Let's go out and celebrate, drink lots of *vin*, lower their opinions of British people even more. What do you say?'

An hour later – Michelle required vast amounts of time to get ready, which was probably why Ellie felt like a scarecrow walking down the street beside her – they were finally clattering down the narrow stairs of the apartment building and into the courtyard it was built around. Unlike a Frenchwoman, Michelle was wearing huge heels and a skintight top with holes cut out of the shoulders, and lots of makeup. Ellie, more acclimatised, was in a jumper and flats, despite Michelle's complaints about her failure to dress up. It was also far too early to go out, at seven. The clubs wouldn't open till eleven. All the same, Michelle would not be deterred, and so off they went.

That's when it happened. After five months of living in that apartment building, getting no closer to the pianist upstairs than the sound of his notes drifting down through the ceiling as she lay in her lonely bed, sniffing his cigarette smoke in the stairwell, or hearing his feet on the steps as he went to buy his morning baguette, she now ran into him.

She knew it was him right away, in his tweed jacket, with an aura of smoke around him. He was gorgeous, standing against the courtyard wall, holding his cigarette in that graceful pinch that French people seemed to be taught at birth. He wore a loose red shirt and jeans, dark hair falling over his lean, sensitive face. '*Bonsoir*,' he said politely.

Michelle stopped up short, almost his height in her

towering heels. *'Vous avez du feu, monsieur?'* Do you have a light? *'Et aussi une cigarette?'* she added cheekily, as he fumbled for the lighter in his pocket. He laughed, and held out the packet.

Ellie frowned at her impeccable accent, remembering that Michelle had done an arthouse French film the year before, and had had to spend six weeks in an isolated farmhouse in the driving rain near Strasbourg. At the time, Ellie had been pleased she wasn't an actress herself. But now Piano Man was cupping her friend's hand, helping her light a cigarette. She knew Michelle smoked from time to time, but why right now?

'We'll be late,' she said pointedly, even though they were vastly early.

'It's Paris.' Michelle could even do the French shrug. *'On a du temps.'*

The man smiled between them. *'Bien sur, il est encore tôt, mademoiselle.* You are my neighbour, I think? The lady who play the . . . Beyoncé?'

Ellie blushed. She'd gone through a long jag rotating 'Irreplaceable' with 'Survivor' when she'd first moved in, weeping into glasses of cheap red wine. 'Hi. Ellie.'

'Serge.' He took Michelle's hand, locking her eyes with his dark ones. *'Et vous?'*

'Moi, c'est Michelle. Enchanté!'

For a moment, Ellie thought he might kiss Michelle's hand. They were staring at each other, and she almost backed away from the force of the energy between them, a tangible thing. She would have blushed and stumbled had someone looked like that at her, but Michelle held his gaze

148

for several moments, only narrowing her dark-rimmed eyes into a kind of scowl. Then, she laughed.

'Well, Serge, pal, I think you better come with us.'

That was it, Ellie thought, with a sinking heart, as they made their way down the cobbled lanes of Montmartre, everywhere glowing bars and quirky shops and green-painted shutters and the abandoned easels of the tourist painters. She was going to spend her last evening in Paris watching two people fall in love, and neither of them was her. If only they'd gone downstairs a few minutes later, or a few minutes earlier, or Serge had finished his cigarette faster, and not lingered in the courtyard, if it had been raining or he'd already had plans that night. It could so easily not have happened.

The next day she was shaken awake by Michelle, wearing a familiar man's red shirt and nothing else, her hair tousled. She looked beautiful, sexy. Exhausted. 'Shh. It's me.'

'Where've you been?' The night had dissolved into gin cocktails at Serge's, booze poured over sugar cubes and set alight, and at some point she'd just left them to it and gone back downstairs, put in earplugs so she wouldn't have to hear their laughter and possibly worse. 'Up there all this time?'

Michelle sat on the bed, hugging her long, bare legs. 'Oh El, he's really something. So sexy. Like, "I could eat him with a spoon" sexy.'

Ellie had never seen her friend like this. Michelle hadn't had a serious boyfriend since useless Adam back at school, throwing herself into her work and occasionally getting embroiled in passionate flings with other actors, which would usually end when one of them took a job out of town.

'You're not coming back with me today, are you,' said Ellie, resigned to carrying all her own bags.

'I'm sorry, love. I can have your stuff couriered for you? Or bring it when I come?'

'When will that be?'

'Honestly, I've no idea. I've no work booked over Christmas, so why not hang around?' Lucky Michelle. Staying in Paris, and with a sexy man. 'Look, you can have my flat to yourself – how about it?'

Ellie had been planning to sleep on the futon, but it was a seriously nice flat to have to herself, high over the river in London, paid for with the proceeds of *Crash*.

'All right, then.'

'Thanks. I'm sorry – I just need to see where this goes.'

'Don't be. I'm going to star-fish in that big bed of yours every night and buy a load of premium-rate channels on your TV.'

Michelle giggled, a sound Ellie had not often heard. 'He doesn't even have a TV. Oh, Ellie, it's so romantic! A garret room, a musician, Paris . . . '

It was. So much so that Ellie couldn't help but wish, in a small selfish part of herself, that she'd run into her sexy neighbour before he'd had a chance to meet chic and confident Michelle. What might have been.

Six months later, Ellie closed her eyes and leaned over the rail of the boat, feeling the spray on her face. All around her was a navy-blue sea, occasionally lightening to a pale green or turquoise where it lapped brilliant white beaches. On the cliffs above were houses so gleaming they hurt the eyes, adorned with the blue of the Greek flag.

150

'Glad you came, then?'

Michelle was wobbling across the deck on ankle-breaking wedges, holding a slushy cocktail in each hand, the unnatural pink of bubble gum. When she'd announced she was having a destination wedding, Ellie had privately rolled her eyes – so pretentious! – but she had to admit it was beautiful. Tomorrow, in a tiny white church on a hill, in front of a congregation made up half of semi-famous people from the acting and music worlds, half of shell-shocked Northumbrians, Michelle would marry Serge. It was only six months since they'd met in that courtyard in Paris, but Michelle had had an offer to work on the American reboot of *Crash* in LA, and if Serge was going to go with her, they needed to be married. Neither of them seemed to have any doubts about it. LA was also a big centre for music, so he was excited about his opportunities there.

Ellie envied them, not just their passion for each other, which bordered on awkward when you had to eat lunch across from them sticking their tongues in each other's ears, but also their confidence. That they'd picked the right person, that their love would endure, that moving to America was the right choice for them. She'd agonised about leaving Paris, and had only gone in the end because she hadn't met anyone herself. She wanted this, she had to admit – a wedding, a husband. A family, perhaps, in a few years. She was twenty-five and both Mark and Michelle were married, or would be by tomorrow. Verity was engaged to a hedge-fund manager called Sebastian and Camilla was still with her college lawyer boyfriend. Why couldn't Ellie make it work? A deep-buried worm of panic that she only

151

let herself think about on dark, sleepless nights told her she'd missed her chance of love, through something as stupid as getting a bus instead of a Tube one night.

'S'all right, I suppose.'

Ellie reached out for her cocktail, feeling the condensation on the plastic cup, licking the sweetness from her fingers. Michelle was wearing a bikini top and cut-off denim shorts, showing her honed abs and long brown legs; Ellie was in a wide-brim hat and a patterned maxi dress. Her fair northern skin tended to burn as pink as the lobsters they'd taken on board earlier, to grill on a beach.

It was the most perfect day imaginable, sea shining silver in the sun, sky the colour of cornflowers, the gentle rock of the waves and the turquoise depths below the boat. 'I don't want a hen do,' Michelle had declared. 'I just want a nice relaxing day, good food, good drinks, and you, El.' So that's what they'd done. The sun overhead, the blue of the sea, the smell of sun cream on her hot skin, baked to a kind of biscuit warmth. Michelle beside her, throwing her tanned face up to the powder-blue sky, radiating happiness like a low hum. They'd already swum off the boat, the rocks on the sea floor visible metres below through the clear cool water, and eaten grilled fish and seafood and delicious pitta bread dipped in tzatziki and balsamic vinegar. Ellie's body felt happy, as gleeful as a dolphin in the waves. But her heart, beating under her strappy dress, was still leaden. Because tomorrow, or possibly even later on today, she was going to have to see Mark for the first time in a year. And he was coming alone, since Laura – his wife! – had to work, because she was a doctor, someone

152

with a proper, responsible job. Unlike Ellie, who had nothing but time.

'Come on, pet,' said Michelle briskly, downing her cocktail. 'It's my hen do, or sort of. Chin up.'

'Sorry. I'm so happy for you!' And she was. But it burned a little, in a dark part of herself, that Michelle now had the big part on the TV show and the theatre offers, and the handsome French musician desperate to marry her in a clifftop church. Since returning to London six months before, Ellie's life had gone nowhere. She'd sent her book out, got little response, decided to rewrite it, and was still sitting on it today. In the meantime, she made ends meet pitching freelance articles to the same magazines she'd worked at, and copywriting for various websites for a pittance. This wasn't how it was supposed to be. Moving to France was supposed to be her grand new beginning, the start of a new story, a sweeping love, a brilliant career. And it had been, but for Michelle and not her.

She felt Michelle's head drop onto her burnt shoulder and tears hazed her eyes. 'You'll be OK, El. What will be, will be.'

'You really believe that?'

'Course. We just do what we can, and things turn out all right.'

Ellie wasn't so sure. 'You don't think it's all to do with choices, tiny little things like turning left instead of right on the street one day? Something so stupid and so small you don't even notice you've made the decision, but the rest of your life is totally different all the same?' Like not turning up to see Mark that night in 1999. Like breaking up with

153

Steve, or never meeting Steve. Like sleeping with Mark that night in July 2005, changing the course of his life. Choosing Oxford over Edinburgh, deciding not to study medicine after all. It was like Mark had said once – every possible choice existed, so that meant there were thousands of Ellies, millions of her, living millions of different lives. Sometimes it was overwhelming.

Michelle shrugged. 'God, El, stop rambling on and go and get us some more cocktails, you daft bint.'

Later, so fuzzy-headed on cocktails she barely remembered getting off the boat, she and Michelle tripped back to the hotel through bright-lit cobbled streets, tavernas and shops and restaurants bubbling with sunburnt people, a holiday mood in the air that made it impossible to feel sorry for herself. She would be OK. She was only twenty-five! Plenty of time to find love, publish a book, figure out her path in life. It would all be fine. As they entered the cool lobby of the hotel, Ellie saw someone standing there, back turned. A man about her height, in a white linen top and slacks, the back of his neck red and sweaty. It looked like – yes.

Mark turned around. They just stared at each other.

'Hi,' he said, eventually.

Her first thought was: *I wouldn't have known.* Standing there on two feet, there was no sign of what he'd lost, and that helped with the guilt. The last time she'd seen him he'd been running from her flat, into the path of a bomb.

'Er – hi.' Her mouth felt dry and gummy. Beside her, Michelle was rolling her eyes, then pushing forward to hug him.

'So glad you're here, Marko. It wouldn't be a wedding without you! Now hurry up and check in, we're having dinner with Serge and my parents in an hour.'

Over Michelle's smooth brown shoulder, not a trace of sunburn, Mark's blue eyes were still locked into Ellie's, and somehow, all the guilt and shame and regret she'd carried was simply evaporating, as if she only needed to see him for it all to be OK. It hadn't been her fault. He didn't blame her. Everything was all right.

JUNE 2019

Ellie snuck back around the side of the house, aware of how entirely ridiculous she was. Past the living room, where through the window she could see her mother in a high feathered hat, talking agitatedly to someone on the phone. 'Well I don't see what she could have needed to do so urgently on her wedding day! She hasn't even had her hair styled yet! Where on earth is she?'

Ellie moved on, feeling her way along the pebble-dash of the wall, which as a child she had worked loose and thrown into her father's roses. It was many years now since anyone had tended them, and her mother had replaced them with concrete slabs a while ago. She had to get back inside, and find one particular thing that she thought might help her make her decision, soothe her jangling nerves.

Inside, the kitchen was strangely deserted. Her heart lurched – people had perhaps started heading to the venue already. What was she doing? She wasn't even dressed yet! She heard voices from the living room – Verity was having her makeup done, chatting to the lady about a recent trip to Majorca. Verity would have stayed in a five-star hotel and flown first-class, but she was good at talking to anyone.

Where were Katie, Lucy, Nigel? Ellie went to the cupboard under the stairs, hoping the box she vaguely remembered was still in there.

It was dark under the stairs, spiders lurking in corners. Full of junk, a rolled-up old rug, tennis racquets, a pair of wellies Ellie hadn't worn in decades. And there was the box, just as she recalled. She pulled the cord of the light, shut the door after her to prevent discovery by her mother, and lifted the photo album from the box of her old uni books. *Tom Jones. Mrs Dalloway.* All covered in her own boxy writing, these texts she'd once found so important, worried over so much. Never thought of again once her exams were done.

The photo album began in Ellie's childhood, and the very first picture was of her and Mark at a bowling alley for her ninth birthday. She'd managed to get a strike somehow, a feat she had never again repeated. God, he'd been such a nerd, with his wonky glasses and sticking-up hair. Her own frizzed like a halo, above the daring double-denim outfit she'd chosen. How young they were. More pictures, mostly with Mark in too. A school trip to the zoo. Birthdays, Christmases. In those days, taking photos meant having a camera in the first place, and the money and ability to take the film to the chemist to get it developed. Most of them had strange rings of light on them, or people's thumbs in the foreground. Nothing like the slick and packaged shots everyone knew how to take these days.

There was a brief peak of photos in her university days. Fancy dress, black tie, many pictures of Ellie looking drunk and dishevelled. Clutching a bottle of champagne after her last exam, arm around Verity. She'd broken up with Steve the very next day. Quite a few shots of him, too, with his guitar in most pictures, the one camping trip they'd gone on where it rained so much all of Ellie's socks had been wringing wet and she'd almost had a nervous breakdown halfway up Snowdonia. Nights out in London, Ellie holding up her first magazine byline and smiling wide enough to bust her face. More of Mark, a few of Laura creeping in. Karaoke, club nights, picnics. Then Paris. A lot of moody shots of the city. After that, she must have got a smartphone and stopped printing out pictures. Ellie sighed – these were just pictures, after all. She'd hoped for some clue in the smiling faces from decades ago, a sign of what she should do. Was this right for her, to be getting married today? Was she just thrown by normal bride worries, and by overhearing Mark and Laura's mysterious conversation? Or was she making a terrible mistake? The girl in these pictures was so gauche, with her curly brown hair and bad clothes – wide-legged cords! Little Miss T-shirts! – but Ellie missed her all the same. That sense of optimism, the blank possibility of the future, with so many decisions still unmade. Unfortunately, she could tell there were no answers to be had in these snapshots of the past.

CHOICE 6 – DECEMBER 2007

Like most of the time Ellie and Serge spent together, it should have been magical. He was giving a concert in Paris, in an ancient church with stained-glass windows lit by candles. The audience was packed with journalists, reviewers, rich classical music fans, and Serge was up front in his tails, his face rippling with emotion as he played Rachmaninov. The heartbreakingly romantic music thundered from the long, sensitive fingers that had given her so much pleasure in the two years they'd been together. Ellie was sitting in the front row in this ridiculous, stunning dress, which she'd found in one of the dusty little vintage shops in the back streets of Montmartre, a sparkling silver bodice and floaty net skirt. Serge had advised her on hair and makeup enough that she knew how to make herself look chic in a French way. She was his, his girlfriend, and she was clapping till her hands were sore. Afterwards, they would go to some bistro where the food would be melt-in-your-mouth delicious, as almost every meal she had in Paris was, and they'd be feted by his agent and tour manager and the papers might take a picture of her and include her name as *partner of the acclaimed pianist*.

But even as Ellie clapped and clapped, her heart was like

ash inside. She was miserable, despite her dress and the surroundings and the music and promise of wine and gourmet food and, later on, the way he would peel the dress from her, his body still wracked with energy after his performance, that could only be burned off by devouring her. None of it mattered. Because of a tiny moment she'd witnessed before the concert, when Serge strode out to a waterfall of applause, and silence dropped, and he flipped his tails to take his seat, spread his hands over the keys, took a deep breath. Ellie always loved that moment, like the one right before a first kiss. Like the night she'd first climbed the stairs to Serge's flat, two years before, every inch of her body straining for his touch as they talked and listened to music and ate pâté and cheese and drank red wine, long into the night. Waiting for it. Anticipation, stillness. Dynamite.

But then there was Claudette, the girl who turned his pages, and as she darted forward to stand beside him, Serge had briefly stroked her hand with his little finger before launching into the piece. And by that, the simple familiarity of how he touched her, Ellie knew it had happened again. Claudette was a typical petite French girl, with bobbed *Amélie* hair, able to look sexy and innocent in dungarees or an evening gown. Beside her, Ellie felt like a big British heifer. As she sat there, clapping and smiling, her heart was breaking. It had happened again, and he'd promised after last time, sworn to her, it would stop, that he loved her, he would be faithful. And they'd been happy – exciting years of music and food and travel in his falling-to-bits Mini, sex that made her skin tingle and burn. But she watched him, where his eyes went. There were pretty girls everywhere in

160

Paris – soloists, orchestral musicians, publicists, journalists, managers. Girls on the Metro or in bars or at bakeries, as Ellie had once been. She wondered why she had stuck, become his girlfriend – perhaps because she lived downstairs, and avoiding her had been too difficult, so they'd seen each other every day for two months and then it had seemed obvious to move up to his apartment and save on the rent.

Not wanting to ruin his night, despite everything, she smiled and shook hands, posed for pictures. She went to the after-party at a restaurant, trying to understand the rapid French of Serge's muso friends, and not cry all through the onion soup and steak and crème brûlée and innumerable bottles of red and everyone giving up on the effort of talking to her as the evening went on and she couldn't quite follow the conversation. She held her tears in all the way in the taxi, listening to a manic Serge go on and on about his choice of phrasing, and all the way through the little courtyard with the potted trees and up the creaking stairs and past the apartment that had been hers for a while, now rented out to transient Airbnb guests, until they'd shut the door behind them. Knowing that, the moment they were alone, she would burst into angry sobs, and they'd fight and scream till their throats were raw. He'd hold that against her too, as he was doing another interview the next day, and Ellie was already wondering if they'd send a pretty young journalist again. Oh God. Would it never end?

Even meeting Serge in the first place had seemed like a miracle. She'd lived beneath him for months and never seen him, only to run into him that one day in the bakery, slavering over the cakes. If Ellie was less greedy, or hadn't been too lazy to go to Monoprix, maybe she wouldn't have met him, and her entire life would once again have been different. Likely she would not have stayed in Paris, but gone back to London as planned, tried to pick up the threads of her life there. She'd have finished the book she was working on, too, probably – she'd been doing so well at it, the words flowing out of her every morning as she sat in her high window over the city, a strong coffee cooling at her feet. Maybe she'd even have sold it, got published.

Once she'd met Serge, she had stopped writing, and she wasn't sure why. Maybe there wasn't room for two artistic people, when his creativity, his temperament, took up so much space, pushing hers out. Ellie had to be the one who thought about paying the electricity bill and buying washing powder, posted back his contracts and took his jackets to the dry cleaner. She'd made herself that person, without him ever asking. Because maybe – and she really didn't like to admit this – maybe the truth was she'd just been playing at writing, too afraid to send it out and get rejected, waiting all the while for another man to fall in love with. And she had certainly found him.

'Ellie. You must come out now.'

Silence. Ellie tried to find the words to tell him how wrong he was, how cruel, how unfair, but her mouth was as empty as her eyes were full. The tears caught, blurred and spilled down her cheeks. She'd been locked in the bathroom for the past hour, and although she knew it was melodramatic to be sitting on the cold 1970s lino wearing a vast concoction of an evening dress, the silver net skirt shot through with sequins, and her makeup smudged, all the same that was what she felt like doing.

'I . . . ' A fresh bout of tears bubbled up. 'How could you, Serge? You said you loved me.'

He broke into French, as he always did at times of stress, and although hers had improved a lot since she'd lived with him, she couldn't follow the long babbling stream through the heavy wooden door. Ellie lay her head against it, weary and broken. She wished she could be the kind of chic French woman who shrugged her shoulders at infidelity, acknowledged that monogamy was hard. But the idea of his hands, his pianist's hands with the long fingers, running over another woman's body, drove her absolutely out of her mind. The first time had been after just a few months of dating – Sasha, a tall blonde Russian who ran front of house in a theatre where Serge sometimes played. She'd found out when the message popped up on his phone. He hadn't even bothered to change the settings.

Serge had been surprised at her reaction, as if he hadn't even thought they were exclusive, and Ellie had driven herself mad trying to remember if they'd ever discussed it, or if she'd just assumed it because they spent most nights together in his saggy double bed. 'But it is business,' he'd said, surprised and grumpy at her tears. 'You may do the same, Ellie. It is natural.' Ellie had never been able to bring herself to take advantage of this offer, and in the end he'd apologised, covered her in kisses, promised to be hers alone. They hadn't left the bed for ten hours.

And yes, it had occurred to her that this was what she deserved for sleeping with Mark two years ago, betraying

Laura. Ah, Mark. Like a small pilot light in the back of her brain, never quite going out. She hadn't spoken to him since she'd come to France, though she scanned his Facebook obsessively for signs that Laura might be pregnant. So far, nothing. Maybe they'd wait till her career calmed down a bit; the early years of a doctor's training were too full-on for children. Laura didn't post much online; too busy saving lives, no doubt. Mark posted about holidays and various stages of his rehabilitation. He seemed to be getting about really well on his prosthetic leg, but Ellie still couldn't think of it without the deep burn of guilt. Maybe she wouldn't have stayed away for so long if she wasn't sure it was all her fault. The loss of him could still paralyse her, every time she saw a man on a Paris street wearing a black coat and coloured scarf, or with glasses and dark hair like Harry Potter.

Outside the door, she heard the sound of a jazz record scratching on. Serge had vinyl still. He played them on an old wooden record player. He was that sort of man, one born out of time. He would never do a triathlon or give up smoking, which she hated, or stop drinking wine at lunchtime. He'd never get an office job, or want to move to the suburbs and buy a sensible car. Ellie just had to take him as he was, or leave him. She almost wished he would dump her and save her the trouble of choosing. Because she'd never been able to do that, just make decisions. The weight of it, determining the course of her life, had always seemed too much.

She opened the door, after scrubbing her puffed face with a flannel, smearing mascara onto it. He looked up. He was in an old green armchair by the window reading a book, cigarette burning in his hand.

'You are feeling better?'

As if she had a cold or something. Not a broken heart. Except, it wasn't broken, was it? There were only so many times you could say that before you realised hearts were very elastic things. They could bend and bow under the weight of an amazing number of heavy, painful things.

'I . . . is there any wine?'

'*Bien sûr.*' He got up and poured her a glass, the red liquid glowing in the crystal she'd found at the flea market for a few euros.

'Just *un petit peu*. Thanks.'

This isn't my life, Ellie thought. French flea markets and expensive wine and a man who smoked and played jazz records . . . it was all sexy and exciting, but it didn't belong to her. It should have belonged to someone like Michelle. Michelle would have had the confidence to lash down Serge's wandering ways, and she enjoyed rows, and even smoked now and again. She knew how to dress, like French women all did, and no one ever made her feel inferior. Michelle was currently single, after an unhappy showmance with her co-star in *Crash*, the hospital drama she starred in, had broken down. Whereas Ellie probably should have been living in a London suburb or some affluent town, in a new-build three-bed with a small neat garden, a sensible car outside, and beside her in the bed . . .

Well. Maybe a man who didn't smoke and drink every day and who had a steady job (Serge was always either broke or loaded, coming home with armfuls of foie gras and Armagnac), who always saved part of his salary and paid into a pension. Who cut the grass on weekends, walked the dog. She sighed. There were so many moments where, if she'd just done a different thing, she could have had that safe, settled life. But now she was so far away from it, it was impossible to see her way back, like losing your path in a dark wood. Did you keep walking on the one you were on, hoping it might lead somewhere better, or plunge back into the branches and thorns and darkness? She honestly didn't know. And was that even what she'd wanted, or would she have chafed against such a safe life? Been bored, worked at some dull job that stifled her, so in the end she'd blow up her life just to feel something? Her life here was amazing in so many ways, glamorous and exciting. Serge would never bore her, and after two years she still went weak when he ran his fingers over the back of her neck. And Paris! She lived in Paris, and it was as wonderful as she'd always hoped.

She didn't hear him at first. 'Hm?'

'Claudette she is ... *enceinte.*' Ellie knew that word. It meant ... her hand began to shake, disturbing the wine in the glass, and her stomach lurched in shock. A baby. That meant ... but ...

'No. You don't mean ...'

'*Oui.* She is pregnant. I am sorry, Ellie, I do not know how this can happen.'

There was a loud smashing noise, and Ellie looked down to see her bare feet splashed in Merlot. She had broken the glass from the flea market. 'Oh ...' Mechanically, she stooped to pick it up, stepping back and ...

'Ellie! Stand still, *la verre!*'

Too late. A large shard went right into her instep, and the pain was sharp as a knife, and as Ellie swayed, her own voice howling in pain in her ears, Serge lifting her up, blood mingling with the wine, she was only glad that now, at last, she found herself able to break.

He was good in a crisis. He wrapped her foot in a towel, leaving the glass in as you were supposed to, and carried her down all five flights of stairs in his strong piano-playing arms, leaving spots of blood she would scrub up the next day. He hailed a taxi, and convinced them in rapid persuasive French, bundling euros into the driver's hands, to take them to hospital. Ellie was oddly calm for the ride, feeling the slow pulse of her blood into the towel, over the white cuffs of Serge's shirt. Neither of them said anything. What could they say? Within ten minutes she was in a cubicle, her bleeding staunched. She'd just need stitches and then she'd be fine, though her dress was ruined, with poppy-red splashes of her blood around the hem, and Serge had to give the driver a fifty-euro cleaning fee. Her foot would be all right, at least, but nothing else would. He'd got someone pregnant. And that was not the only problem.

The doctor rattled aside the curtains round her bed. Serge had been banished to the waiting room, and she was glad, because she didn't want him to hear this. Not yet. The doctor was an efficient young woman in a hijab. '*C'est Ellie? Mademoiselle Warren?*'

'*Oui.*'

'*Il n'y a aucun problème au niveau du pied. Je vous donne une pilule, et ensuite on fera des points de suture.*' Your foot is all right, I'll give you a painkiller then we'll do stitches.

Ellie hesitated, groping for the words. '*Est ce que c'est dangereux?*'

167

'*Dangereux?*' The doctor sat down, pulling a suture kit towards her.

'*Pour le bébé,*' said Ellie, hands creeping to her stomach.

Because there was a reason she'd not drunk much wine that night, a reason she'd have been willing to give Serge another chance, even after the revelation that he was having an affair. She'd known since that morning, when she slipped out to buy a test from the pharmacy while he was rehearsing, that she too was pregnant. At first she'd sat in the tiny bathroom and stared at the pink lines, asking herself *How. How did this happen.* Then, channelling Michelle – *Pet, you came off the pill cos you were gaining weight and Serge only uses condoms like twenty per cent of the time.* It was true. How stupid she'd been. But she'd never imagined he would get someone else pregnant too.

Ellie hadn't got her head around the news yet – she would have told him after the concert had things been different, had she not witnessed that small caress of Claudette, just one finger brushing her hand. Maybe he would have been happy, maybe she'd never have found out about Claudette or the other pregnancy in that parallel world. She was twenty-seven, which felt too young to have a baby, but really wasn't – many of her school friends already had several children. Ellie had always wanted a family, several kids, a home. Why not take the chance that had presented itself to her, the baby she was already growing? And what genes – handsome, talented, brilliant French genes. Cheating genes. Hurtful genes. Ellie thought she was seven weeks or so along. Time to do something about it, if she wanted to.

The doctor nodded, unsurprised by the news. She didn't

know Ellie; she had no reason to realise how momentous this moment was.

'*Non, c'est pas dangereux.*'

As she numbed the skin, Ellie felt the needle slide into her flesh, aware of its movements but not hurting. In a way Serge had left her like that, too. Numb. She'd never dreamed she'd be expecting a baby and not even sure if she had a partner, a home or any money. For years now they'd been living hand to mouth, Ellie doing translations and copywriting, her novel abandoned. How would she support a child in a foreign country, especially if Serge left her, as seemed to be his plan? He'd be paying for two families, which he definitely couldn't afford. She'd have to go home to her parents, and at the idea a shudder went through her, so much so that the doctor had to ask her to keep still.

'*Désolée,*' said Ellie, as her tears dripped onto the doctor's arm. Lying on a bed in a Paris hospital, in a blood-stained evening gown, with a needle in her foot and a baby in her womb, she contemplated the next step in the rest of her life. What was she going to do?

Don't have the baby

Ellie looked at herself in the mirror. Same mirror she'd stared in all through her teenage years, willing away her spots or inexpertly plucking her eyebrows. Now she was older, but not necessarily any wiser. Her body looked largely the same now the brief fullness her middle had taken on for a few months was long gone. She wasn't pregnant any more, and indeed her family didn't know she had been. No one knew except Michelle, who'd arranged for her to go to a clinic in London after she'd packed two bags of belongings, all she had to show for her years in Paris, and left on the coach, not even able to stretch to the Eurostar. She was coming back with less than she'd left with. Serge had made it clear immediately that he was leaving her for Claudette, and the pregnancy made no difference. He had another baby on the way, and urged her as strongly as possible not to have the one she was pregnant with. For three long weeks Ellie had agonised over the decision – was it the right thing to do? She'd always wanted a child, yes, but she was young still, she had time. And it was hardly ideal to have one whose father had already chosen another woman, another family. And she hadn't enough money to support herself, let alone a child, in a foreign country with no family and few friends nearby. Even though she hated to do what Serge wanted, she'd agreed this was the only way. A conversation with Michelle had swayed her.

'El, it's not the right time. You want to be free of this bastard, not tied to him for ever.'

'It's not the baby's fault.' Ellie's voice had choked with tears.

'I'm sorry, pet, I know. But it's not a baby yet – it's just . . . a possibility.'

Yet another future that might have been: walking the streets of Paris with a buggy, bringing up a chic French child who'd ask for kale smoothies in a pretty accent and wear adorable designer dungarees. That was stupid. She'd never be able to afford designer clothes for her kid, or possibly even smoothies. So she'd let Michelle arrange it, and after a night in her friend's spare room, bleeding into a large pad, she'd taken the train north. To her family, her fate. The homecoming she'd done her best to resist, because it meant she'd failed. Failed at medicine, failed at journalism, failed to finish the book she'd started in Paris. Failed to hold onto love, with Steve, with Serge. And Mark. The biggest failure of all.

Ellie was temporarily distracted from her self-pity spiral by a creak from the hallway outside. She dashed to the door. There was a very tiny window to catch her brother as he made his way between the bathroom and his room. 'Alan!'

He had his hand on the doorknob and regarded her warily. He was wearing his usual uniform of black jeans and a hoody, his hair greasy. She wasn't sure how often he showered.

'What?'

'What are you up to?'

He shrugged. 'Online.'

As always. It had been a sad surprise for Ellie when her brother finished university and moved straight back into his old room at her parents'. He earned money – quite a lot, apparently – doing online stock trading, which Ellie didn't understand even a little bit. Her mother barely tried to hide her disapproval at having two children back under her roof, both failures. At least Alan had a good job. Ellie was making coffees in the café at the local National Trust centre. Sometimes she took her laptop out and opened the file of her novel, stared at it, clicked out of it again without typing a word. It seemed insurmountable. As if the person who had written these words, scribbled into a fancy notebook in a Paris garret, no longer existed.

'You want to watch a film later?' she asked.

Alan's face twitched. 'Not with Mum.'

Ellie nodded – their mother was incapable of sitting down for long enough to watch something, always jumping up to tidy or batch-cook or iron. And as for their dad . . . well. She wasn't entirely sure he *could* follow a film.

'Well, we could go out?'

'Out?'

'Yeah. Pub or something. Cinema?'

Alan looked shocked, as well he might – he and Ellie had never done anything just the two of them, she didn't think. But she worried for him, growing stranger by the day, never seeing natural light, wilting like a neglected plant. And she was lonely. Mark was in Glasgow with Laura, happily married by all accounts, and Michelle was in St Lucia shooting a thriller with someone from *Dawson's Creek*. Serge was in Paris in his love nest with Claudette and their son – Olivier. When she wanted to hurt herself she went through their pictures online. Her own child would have been born about now. Imagine that, a whole different life, a car veering sharply round a hairpin bend onto another path. But there was no point in thinking like that, because there was no child. She'd done the right thing – even if her life currently sucked absolute balls, and her odd brother had a better social life than she did (albeit entirely online).

'I don't drink,' he pointed out. 'And what's the point paying ten quid for a film when it'll be out on DVD soon?'

'Yeah,' she conceded, defeated. 'All right.'

Alan shut the door behind him, with palpable relief, and Ellie contemplated another night explaining the plot of *Midsomer Murders* to her father, while her mother darted in and out criticising her for everything she did – her hair, her clothes, her posture, her overwhelming lack of success. Everything.

It was about an hour later that it happened. Ellie had gone back to her room after dinner – Alan didn't come down to eat with them, of course. Her mother had banged down plates of sausage and mash, boiled peas rolling off the edge. Although Ellie's mum was the only member of the family with a full-time job, she didn't let anyone else do any cooking, so their meals were always rushed, uninspiring.

'Did you apply for anything else today?' she said, plonking down Ellie's plate.

Ellie dragged her fork through the stodgy mash. 'There's nothing around here.'

And it was true. After the recent financial crash the only available jobs in a twenty-mile radius were at the chicken factory, and since she didn't have her own car, even getting there would be a struggle.

'To think you could have gone to medical school,' her mother sighed, sitting down to fret at her own meal. She was too thin, worried and always angry.

By contrast, Ellie's dad, in his well-washed green jumper, was methodically eating his dinner, not saying a word. He said less and less these days.

'I do try,' mumbled Ellie, forcing down a mouthful of potato. It was gluey and already cold.

'You need to try harder. I can't be supporting all three of you until I work myself into an early grave.'

'Alan's earning.'

Her mother cast a fearful glance at the ceiling. 'He never eats. I wish he would have just one proper meal.'

Ellie didn't really blame him – her mother's cooking was a sad comedown after Paris.

She turned to her father, who hadn't spoken at all since sitting down. 'Dad, I was thinking we could go for a walk tomorrow,' she said, recognising the bright cheerful voice she was putting on, as if talking to a child.

Her mother sniffed. 'Nice for you to have time to go for walks.'

'The café's shut on Tuesdays, you know that.'

Ellie had worked every weekend for the past three months. She ate a bite of sausage, wondering what Serge was dining on right now – not that he would dream of having dinner at six o'clock. Some delicious cassoulet maybe, or a cheese plate washed down with a fine wine. Claudette was probably feeding the baby, radiant and still tiny. It stabbed her in the solar plexus. She hadn't told her parents why she'd left Paris, or about her own pregnancy. It was amazing that but for one decision she could have been a mother, and instead she was back living with her parents as if she was a teenager again, being told to brush her hair and help with the dishes.

Her dad had not responded to her comment, his eyes wandering somewhere above Ellie's head. She glanced up – nothing but blank wall.

'Dad?'

'Umm?' He had a gob of mashed potato on his chin.

'A walk tomorrow?'

'Oh aye, aye.'

She wasn't sure he'd entirely understood. Did her mother not notice any of this? That her father was untethered, that Alan locked himself up with the curtains pulled and barely spoke, and that Ellie was silently imploding with misery? She had to change something. She couldn't bear it.

Her mother was already on her feet, scraping dishes, her meal hardly touched. 'I'll do those,' said Ellie.

'No, no, you don't do them right.'

'All right. I'll go and look for some more jobs then.' Assuming there was enough internet bandwidth left, with Alan gobbling it all up on whatever he did online.

Ellie dragged herself up the stairs, feeling so tired, so old. She'd be thirty soon and had absolutely nothing to show for it, no career, no boyfriend, no child. She'd ruined the best friendship she ever had, and although Michelle was still in touch, she was gone from Ellie, hanging out with film stars and appearing in the pages of *Closer*. If only she'd recognised when she was happy – Oxford, London, even Paris until the end – and made the most of it. Because this was the pits.

She knocked on the door of her brother's room, hearing the tinny sounds of explosion and gunfire from one of his games.

'Alan? I need go to online for a bit.'

The internet bandwidth didn't stand up to two people being on it. Though what jobs she would find there, she had no idea. Maybe it was time to move back to London, take her chances. Though she'd need at least a grand to get started, put down a deposit on a flat, or even rent a room. Currently her savings were almost zero.

No answer.

'Alan?'

She knocked harder. Then she heard something under the racket of the game – a strange sound. Like a strangled gasp. Like feet pounding on the carpet.

'Alan!'

Suddenly terrified, Ellie did what she knew her brother would absolutely hate, and pushed open the door to his room. It was dark, the smell of cheesy crisps – or feet – almost overwhelming. Ellie could see nothing but the blue of the computer glow. She snapped on the light and a scream caught in her throat.

Her brother had slipped off his computer chair and was half under his desk. His body was spasming, his feet lightly drumming on the floor. His eyes rolled in his head. Oh God. A seizure. Ellie ran to him, screaming out for her mother. She pushed back the chair, trying desperately to remember what she'd learned in first aid at school. Recovery position. Head to the side so he didn't bite his tongue or swallow vomit. He was limp and heavy and she could hardly stop him falling onto his back. She pulled him over to his side, realising how long it must have been since he'd showered.

'Mum. *Mum!*'

Footsteps on the stairs, the door thrown angrily open. 'Is there any need to shout—oh!'

'Call an ambulance! He's having a seizure.'

Without her even realising it, Ellie's hands were working quickly and deftly. She had him on his side, his head in the right position, his collar loosened. He was breathing. He'd be all right if they could get help. But her mother was standing frozen, the near-permanent expression of annoyance she'd worn for Ellie's entire life now slipped into horror and fear.

Have the baby

'Shh, honey. Shh, shh.'

The baby's screaming only intensified. How could someone be three days old and so angry at the world? Ellie felt answering tears in her own exhausted eyes. She hurt all over, between her legs, her back, her hand where the cannula had gone in during her labour. Bruises and rips all over the place, her body like an overripe fruit she was trying to scoop up from the floor to salvage what she could. It wasn't right, any of this. She shouldn't have to take her baby home to a fifth-floor flat with no lift, lugging all her things and the buggy up the narrow stairs, or suffer her neighbours banging on the ceiling when the baby cried. She shouldn't have to do any of this alone – she should be resting while an adoring father took care of the child. But Serge had gone. He'd chosen Claudette, whose parents turned out to be loaded, and moved in with her in a huge apartment near the Jardin de Luxembourg. He'd left Ellie this flat, grudgingly agreed to pay half the rent until she could work again. She wasn't sure what she'd do for the rest – how could she concentrate on translation work when the baby howled all day and night like this? He'd come to see her in the hospital after the birth, but Ellie hadn't been able to stop sobbing, so conversation was difficult. He'd try to see the little girl, he promised. But Ellie could only think, over and over, that she'd brought the baby fatherless into the world, let her down before she was even born.

Ellie tried again, unfolding the cramped pink limbs of her daughter. 'Shh, *ma petite.*' Maybe she understood French better than English – perhaps she had absorbed its rhythms in the womb? Or maybe she just knew she had an absent father and a struggling, broke mother, who hadn't even given her a name yet. How had it come to this? She'd had a baby, which she'd always hoped would happen sometime, but not like this, alone in a dusty flat in a foreign country, the floorboards marked with red-wine stains where various women, including herself, had thrown drinks at Serge. A faint tidemark where her foot had bled on it that terrible night when he'd left her, even after she'd told him she was pregnant. He'd chosen the other woman, the other child.

Claudette's little boy, Olivier, had been born a week earlier, and Ellie had tormented herself clicking through all the pictures on Facebook, an adoring Serge cuddling them both on the hospital bed, Claudette still chic even in a gown that tied at the back. Meanwhile Ellie had given birth in a foreign language, terrified and adrift, unable to understand the different inflections of French healthcare, what the conventions were and what to worry about. She'd been so afraid she had almost wished for her mother, but they currently weren't speaking after Ellie had refused to go home to have the baby. She hadn't been able to face it, the recrimination and criticisms – how could she be so stupid as to get pregnant, why hadn't she left Serge earlier when it was obvious what he was like, how was she going to support the baby with no money? Michelle would have been a good birth partner, efficient and firm, but she was in the Caribbean shooting a thriller and hadn't been able to come. Ellie understood – it was the chance of a lifetime and could not be turned down. But it was a horribly alone feeling, being in hospital with no one to bring you snacks or a clean pair of pants. Besides, when she'd rung to tell her the news months before, Michelle had said, 'OK, so what are you going to do?'

'Do?'

'How does it work over there? Or you can come home and I'll take you – I know a good clinic.'

She'd been supportive, if shocked, when Ellie said she was going to have the baby, with or without its father, but the damage was done. And Ellie couldn't explain her decision. Certainly she'd always been pro-choice, and had agonised over it for weeks after Serge had left her, walking the windswept streets of Paris alone, throwing up in the tiny mould-spotted bathroom. There were so many reasons not to carry on with the pregnancy, not least a clean break from Serge. But something stopped her booking an appointment. A kind of depressed paralysis, maybe. A desperate hope he might come back. Or just the feeling that, having struggled into life somehow, the baby deserved a chance.

Now, she opened the window onto the hot July night to let some air in and laid the child in the crib she'd had to assemble herself. This place wasn't remotely suitable. She'd have to move, but where to? She could barely afford here. She'd have to find work. Sort her life out. Right now it all felt overwhelming. But as she sat there, her nameless daughter gradually soothing into softer breathing, and the noises of Paris, voices and laughter and traffic, drifted up to them, and a huge silver moon rose behind the Eiffel Tower, a certain peace crept over Ellie. She was a mother now. Whatever else happened, she'd always be that.

Gently, she touched the baby's curled fist, pink and soft as petals. That was an idea for a name. 'Fleur,' she tried. Pretty, chic. She never wanted her daughter to feel awkward or ungainly or out of place, as Ellie had for most of her life. She wanted her to feel invincible.

Fleur. It seemed to fit. And somehow a miracle had taken place, and there was another person in the world.

Her phone was ringing. Ellie roused herself from her daze, as Fleur – her new name! – murmured and strained her legs.

'Hello?'

She'd answered so fast she hadn't even checked the number. Serge? But no. It was her mother's voice.

'Ellie?'

'Yeah.' She should have rung them to say she'd had the baby. Maybe Michelle had told them.

But her mother's voice was wobbly, thick with tears. 'I'm sorry to tell you on the phone, Ellie but – you need to come home.'

Her first thought was *I can't go home, I've just had a baby.* Then her brain caught up with it and her stomach dropped a mile away. This was something bad.

'Mum?' Her mother was sobbing now, and Ellie could barely hear the words. 'Is it Dad? Mum! What's happened?'

'It's Alan.' She hitched in enough breath to push out the words. 'It's your brother. Ellie, he's – he's gone.'

Ellie couldn't take it in. Beside her, Fleur began to mewl. Distracted, Ellie juggled the phone against her chin as she lifted the baby.

'Gone where?' Had he moved out suddenly? Her mother hadn't asked even about the birth. Typical.

Then she made a noise Ellie had never heard before, somewhere between a scream and a gasp. 'Ellie, you're not understanding. Alan died. He's *dead*.'

JUNE 2019

Ellie heard a noise outside the hall cupboard, and realised she had lost track of time. Her wedding was in just a few hours, and not only was she not ready, she was now tear-stained and had cobwebs in her hair. She opened the door tentatively, expecting her mother, but was relieved to see her brother going into the kitchen. He was alone, already fully dressed in a suit and pink carnation buttonhole. He was no doubt bewildered by the chaos in the house, the hair straightening and makeup and her mother in a flap. She crawled out on her hands and knees.

'Hey,' she hissed. 'Al.'

Alan looked mildly puzzled. 'Are you not meant to be getting ready? I don't know why it takes two hours to get ready, but Mum's doing her nut.'

'I know. Al, I don't know if I can do this.'

Few things ever ruffled her brother. 'OK.'

'How did you know? I mean, how could you be sure?' Alan had been married for several years now.

'Katie wanted it. And I didn't mind, so.' He shrugged. Life was simple to Alan, and Ellie was so jealous of that. She'd never been sure of anything.

'Well, I'm not sure. I'm having a crisis here, Al.'

'OK, so, call it off.'

'I can't just call it off!'

'Why not?' He looked confused.

'Because! Mum will lose her mind, and everyone's on their way already, the hair and makeup lady's started next door, and it wouldn't be fair on ...' But Ellie could not say her fiancé's name. Panic was seeping in from her bare and dirty feet. 'Oh God, Al, what am I going to do?'

Her brother was not much of a one for physical contact, so it meant a lot that he now took her hand in his.

'Look. Whatever you do, it will be OK. Worse things have happened than calling off a wedding, right? It happens all the time on TV.'

'You're right,' she said. 'But still. There must be another way than just calling it off?'

She wasn't there yet, and the thought filled her with horror. She was just freaking out. Trying to look for answers outside herself, advice from others, old pictures and memories, the peace of nature. So far none of it was working.

He thought about it. 'Maybe if you went to talk to him? Could be this is just cold feet, like they say?'

Perhaps he was right. It was very odd, sleeping apart from her groom and waking up in her childhood room assaulted by memories, then having to get painted and curled and trussed up in a dress to be presented to him like a package. None of it was her.

'I'm not supposed to see him before – bad luck.'

Alan just gave her a look. 'If you're wanting to call it off, I'd say that ship has sailed, El.'

And he was right. In that moment, Ellie was so grateful for her blunt, practical brother that she could have cried. 'Thanks, bro. I'll go and find him.'

'How are you going to get there?'

He was right about that, too. Her car was, of course, not here because, being the bride, Ellie was supposed to be picked up and delivered. But over Alan's shoulder, on their special hook by the door, Ellie spotted her mother's car keys. She'd get into trouble for taking it, and for leaving the house on her wedding day, not getting her hair curled or her eyelashes tinted in time, but Ellie was thirty-eight and it was surely time to stop caring what her mother thought. 'Tell her I'm sorry,' she said. 'I'll be back soon. Probably.'

Alan grimaced. 'Well, OK, but I'm not falling on my sword for you. It'd take a braver man than me to get between her and her mother-of-the-bride fascinator.'

She would have liked to hug Alan, but in deference for his feelings she settled for a light pat on the arm instead.

'Thank you. You've helped.'

Then she went.

CHOICE 7 –NOVEMBER 2009

'Oh come on. Just a quick picture?' Ellie waved her new smartphone at her brother. She was very pleased with the pictures it took, up to 1 Mb in size and almost good enough to print.

'It's stupid!' complained Alan. 'I'm just holding a door key.'

'But it's for your own flat!' insisted their mother. 'We're so proud of you, darling.'

'We are,' agreed Ellie.

She and her mother had become a lot closer over the past year and a half, after Alan had almost died in Ellie's arms that night. She felt her eyes creep inexorably to the scar just above his ear. They'd come so close to losing him. Thank God she'd come back from Paris when she did, and been at home to knock on her brother's door in time to catch the seizure that was engulfing him, and that she'd remembered her first aiding and kept him breathing till the ambulance arrived. The doctors later said that if she hadn't gone in when she did, he would likely have died right there on the floor of his bedroom, wracked by the huge epileptic seizure taking over his brain, which was in turn caused by the tumour that was growing on the right side of his skull, responsible for his light phobia and withdrawn, irritable mood of the past year, which they hadn't really noticed because Alan had never exactly been a social butterfly.

And if she was grateful she'd been there to help him, that had to mean she was also grateful Serge had cheated on her, and she'd decided not to have her baby, and she'd lost everything. By hitting rock bottom she'd been there to save her brother's life, and he was with them today, thriving and healthy. Perhaps it had all been worth it, for that. It was hard to say she should have kept the baby – she could not imagine a world where she was the mother of a French child, tied to Serge for ever. A whole other life.

Alan had made a swift recovery after his surgery. He was back on his feet within months, surprising even the doctors, and had now bought his first flat, in the centre of Newcastle in a shiny modern building overlooking the quayside. Ellie was so proud of him, but it also served to underline how little progress she was making in her own life.

She had at least made one big decision, after that night when she'd held her brother's life in her hands, pumped blood through his heart with only her hands, blown air into his failing lungs. She needed to go back to medicine, at least try it. Turning away from it, because of a simple admin error when she was eighteen, had been a mistake. But look at all the things that would have been different if she hadn't. She wouldn't have gone to Oxford, or met Verity or Camilla, whom she was now back in regular contact with. They'd even been to Ibiza on a girls' holiday a few months before, which Ellie could barely afford, but which had been great fun all the same. She wouldn't have met Steve, either, most likely. Perhaps she and Mark would be together now, if they'd ended up at the same university for four years. Or maybe they wouldn't – maybe it would have been too soon and too intense and it would all have imploded. Or he'd have met Laura anyway, before Ellie realised her feelings for him, or she'd have met someone. There was no way to know. Anyway, none of it mattered, because Ellie had now begun the graduate medical course she'd considered years before and chickened out of. She'd be very old when she finally qualified, as her mother kept telling her, but she figured it was better to be late getting to her dream career than never get there at all.

Soon, Alan had lost patience with them being in his space, and Ellie stopped taking photos of him very reluctantly holding up his keys and posing on his new balcony. 'All right, I do need to do some work now, so you'll have to leave.'

She and her mother walked back to the car, which was parked in an NCP that her mother had grumbled about paying for. Ellie tuned it out more now, her mother's constant negativity and fretting. It was just how she was – she meant well.

Things had changed between them the day after Alan's surgery. After spending the night dozing on plastic chairs in A & E, waking in terror every few minutes in case Alan had died and the doctors just hadn't told them yet, she and her mother had eventually been informed that the surgery was over, it had gone well, but he'd be asleep for most of the next day. Coming home, Ellie had passed out on her bed for an hour, waking with her alarm and remembering, disorientated, that she had the day off from the café.

It seemed crazy that this was her job, making tea and replenishing the bags of crisps and having tense meetings about sandwich fillings. Her boss was seventeen years old. How had she ended up there, instead of being the one who sawed open people's heads, fixed their insides, saved lives? It had been so clear to her, sitting in hospital stewing with unbearable tension at having to wait, useless, while the staff bustled to and fro actually doing things, that this was what she wanted. An important job, a purpose in life. To help people, fix people.

When she came downstairs that day, groggy and shattered, her mother was sitting at the dining table with her head in her hands, wearing the same clothes from the night before.

'Have you not been to bed?' said Ellie.

She'd stirred. 'Didn't think there was a point. It's almost nine now.'

'Where's Dad?' He hadn't come with them to the hospital, which had seemed natural, and when they'd got back to the house he had been in bed.

'Asleep still. Amazing he can sleep while his only son's under the knife, but there we go.'

Ellie wanted to say that her father wasn't right, and she wasn't sure he'd entirely taken in that Alan was close to death, but perhaps it wasn't the time. One health emergency at a time. She faced her mother, pulling out a chair. The only two functioning members of the family.

She said: 'What are going to do? He'll need months of rehab.'

If he pulls through, she thought, but didn't say. He'd come

through the surgery but it was far from certain he'd be all right. They'd said he might not be able to talk, or walk, or even feed himself. Not for months, if ever.

Her mother's face was pinched with worry. 'I'll give up work. He'll need caring for, but God knows what we'll do for money. Your sandwich-making doesn't exactly pay the bills.'

Ellie opened her mouth to say she would work more, but she brought in a pittance from the café, and no wonder, it was the job of a teenager, not a woman almost in her thirties. 'I'll look after him,' she said. 'You need your job.'

Her mother looked up. 'You've got your own life to live.'

'Well, I don't, do I? Let's be honest.'

It was true. No real job, no friends nearby, no purpose in life. No partner, no kids.

Her mother's face twisted. 'I'm sure you're trying.'

Ellie lay her head on the smooth veneer of the table, utterly worn out, crushed by tiredness and failure.

'Look, I'm sorry, Mum. I know I'm a disappointment to you. I certainly didn't intend to be back here, making coffees for a living – not that it's even a living – cluttering up your spare room.' And her mother didn't even know all of it – her role in Mark's injury and the baby and Serge leaving her for his second family. 'I'm going to do better, OK? I promise. I'm going to get my life on track.'

But she didn't yet know what that would look like. And she'd have to stay here for months, possibly years, to get Alan back on his feet. Her dad would be no help at all and her mother couldn't do it alone. Her dad might need help of his own, even. The outlook was bleak. But even despite all that, she had determined on that morning she was never going to feel this bad, this useless again. She had saved someone's life, and no one could ever take that away from her.

Back then, Ellie had looked up from her slump to see her mother was crying. Quiet tears slipping down her lined cheeks – Ellie was horrified. She'd never seen her mother cry before, not even at her grandmother's funeral.

'Mum?'

She waved a hand. 'Oh, I'm just being silly. I'm sorry, Eleanor. You know, I never wanted to be like this – snappy and mean and angry all the time. I'm just so worried. I feel like I'm the only one holding the family together. Your brother's always been withdrawn, and this last year or so even stranger – well, we know why that was now. And you – you seemed to be doing so well, getting into Oxford, off in Paris! Then you boomerang right back and you're living in your old room, sulking about the place, working for minimum wage. It's like the past ten years never happened. And you never talk to me, Ellie! I've no idea why you came back from France, but I know something's wrong. I hear you crying at night in your room. And you and Mark, always such great pals, and you haven't seen him in years. But you never tell me any of it.'

Ellie stared at the place mats on the table, old ones with a pattern of horses and carriages, impossibly worn and dated. She wanted to say that her mother had never invited her to open up, never seemed to have time to listen or notice her. Instead she said, 'I know.'

Her mother took a deep breath. 'And as for your father, he's the biggest worry of all.'

Ellie froze. They were finally talking about it, the biggest of all the elephants in all the rooms of her family home. 'Yeah.'

'He's not himself, is he? Hasn't been for years.'

'No. Has he been to the doctor?'

'He won't go. Says he's fine – but he's not. He can hardly remember how to make a cup of tea, he locks himself out of the house so often I've had to put extra sets of keys under the plant pot, he doesn't recognise people when we bump into them at the shops. He can't follow the plots of TV shows.' Her mother looked up. Without sleep or makeup, her face was ravaged with tiredness. 'I can't take care of him by myself, Ellie, not for ever. He needs help. We need to decide if he stays here with us or . . . we look for something else.'

'What do you mean?' She knew, really, but didn't want to think it.

'A home, Ellie. Supported housing, whatever they call it.'

'An old folks' home?'

'If you want to put it that way. I'm only fifty-eight, Ellie. I'm not ready to be a full-time carer for my husband, and we've Alan to get better, too. So you and I have to decide what we do – keep your dad here or put him somewhere.'

Ellie was not even thirty yet – she too was not ready to be caring for a parent, or visiting one in a nursing home, either. Not with Alan in hospital, his life hanging in the balance. Her family seemed to be falling apart around her. No. It couldn't possibly be that bad. He was her dad! He was just a little bit forgetful, maybe.

'Mum, it's not come to that! First we need to get him diagnosed. It might not be . . . ' She couldn't say the word *dementia*, or *Alzheimer's*. It made it too real. 'It might be something treatable.' She vaguely remembered from school biology that there were treatable causes of confusion, vascular dementia, perhaps, or certain food intolerances or neurological issues. It didn't mean he was permanently gone from them, bits of him missing like Swiss cheese. If only she'd studied medicine, she might be able to help here. She might have spotted what was wrong sooner. 'I'll persuade him to go to the doctor. He'll listen to me.' She wasn't sure that was true, but she knew her dad would do anything for her.

Her mother nodded. Just then they heard the soft padding of slippered feet, and her father came in, already neatly dressed in slacks and a jumper, as if heading to the golf course.

'Well well, look at this bunch of early risers!'

'We were too worried to sleep.' Ellie watched his face to see if he remembered why they might be worried.

He nodded. 'I know, I know, but we have to carry on. Will our Alan need owt? Pyjamas? People like grapes in the hospital, don't they, though can't say I ever knew why.'

See, Ellie wanted to say to her mother? *He's not that bad.* Just a little forgetful. Just a little faded – and who could blame him, when all he did was sit about this house with a stressed, harassed woman who barely spoke to him? Maybe what he needed was a bit of interest in his life, to be more active and engaged. She would try, she decided, getting up to face her father. She would enrol in medical school but in Newcastle, if they'd let her in, and she'd live at home and help with Alan's recovery and her father, too, try to make his life brighter and busier, talk to him and take him places, maybe sign him up for some classes and teach him to use the computer. That could give him a whole new lease on life. And her mother would worry less and be nicer and happier, and Alan would get better. It would all be all right. Her family could come through this.

Yes, it would mean Ellie giving up more of her own life to stay at home with ageing parents and a sick brother, but it was the least she could do. By doing this, sacrificing like this, maybe she could atone for some of the bad things she'd done, the mistakes and misjudgements and cock-ups, the people she'd hurt and the things she'd lost. Maybe she could reset her life somehow, and make amends. Find her way back to the place where she'd gone wrong.

That had been more than a year ago, and Ellie had been true to her secret promise. She bought a dirt-cheap second-hand car with the meagre savings she'd amassed at the café. She applied for and got her place at graduate medical school, and diligently went to every lecture with kids ten years younger than herself, although she wasn't the oldest. She drove home every night while her classmates did shots off each other's abs, watched old films with her dad or walked with him through the fields on summer evenings, painstakingly taught him how to use YouTube to look up film clips and songs, took him bowling or to the cinema or out for meals in local pubs. Often, her mother came too, though she was frequently exhausted after a day of caring for both her husband and son. Alan spent a month in bed in his room, hardly able to go anywhere except the few steps to the bathroom. Then one day Ellie came in and he was using his laptop, although squinting out of one eye.

'What?' he said, when she stopped at his door with tea on a tray.

'You're ... can you see it OK?'

His vision had been blurry since the surgery, and he got tired so easily.

Alan shrugged. 'I've missed so much. Need to get back to it.'

Just as easy as that. The next day he got out of bed and walked to the petrol station and back, a little wobbly, but he made it. After that he got better and better. He'd had to quit the online job he was doing, but insisted he was working on a new project, his own company doing something called cryptocurrency. Ellie had no idea what that was, and Alan still slept half the day and got tired after an hour of screen time, but he was on the mend. They hadn't lost him, her dad wasn't in a home, it was all right. At least for a while. Because nothing was all right for ever.

Then, one day, it happened. The thing she'd been afraid of. In every slow-moving situation, there's a long period where you can close your eyes to what's going on, hope that it's all right, deny the signs. Wait so long for the impact that you can convince yourself it's not coming. They'd taken Ellie's father to the doctor after Alan's accident, as Ellie had insisted, and she'd sat between her parents in a small consulting room with a strong antiseptic smell, her eyes flicking between the model of the brain on the bookcase and the framed picture of the GP's cute kids on the desk. The GP was Asian, with a calm, soothing voice. Ellie wanted to close her eyes and be told everything was fine.

'So, Mr Warren, we have your test results here,' the doctor said, sitting down opposite the family. Ellie gripped the edge of her seat. Her father's gaze was unfocused and she wasn't sure he totally understood what was going on here – he'd been a bit baffled as to why she wanted him even to get the tests, but she'd made it sound like some kind of routine screening because of Alan's issues. 'There is some shrinkage of the brain tissue – we see it often in people who've worked for years in high-noise environments.' Ellie blinked. Was this whole thing a hearing issue from his time in the factory? He wasn't confused at all? Hope leapt in her chest, sharp and painful. Hearing loss could be fixed, or at least dealt with. The doctor went on, 'However, it's still not conclusive either way for dementia.'

'What does that mean?' said Ellie's mother sharply. 'You're telling me he's fine?'

'No, no. The symptoms you mention certainly are of concern.' Although it was hard to even sum up what the symptoms were – a feeling he wasn't quite with you when you talked to him. A wandering gaze, looking at nothing obvious. Sometimes not being sure what day it was, or even what year. Forgetting plans and names. Maybe that was just getting old? Or maybe he was good at covering things up. He could still dress himself and get about the house, but he hadn't been anywhere by himself in over a year. 'Just that it's still too soon for a diagnosis. And, in any case, I'm afraid treatment options for dementia are limited.'

That was the problem. You could identify that bits of a

person were flaking off and blowing away, but what could you do to stop it? What glue was there to put someone back together? So they'd taken him home and carried on for another year, while he slowly lost more and more of himself. But it hadn't been chronic. Not yet.

Ellie had to get up early to drive into Newcastle in time for her 9 a.m. lectures. Once, she would have been horrified at this idea – the early starts were one reason she'd perhaps dithered over medicine when she was younger – but she'd become used to it. Sometimes she even enjoyed it, opening her curtains on a grey-pink dawn, creeping downstairs to make a cup of tea, thinking of everything she'd do that day. The facts she'd learn, the scribbled notes she would take in the stuffy lecture theatre, trying to cram it all into her head. There was so much to take in about the human body, she would never learn it all. She'd become friends with some people on her course, and they'd meet for coffee or lunch in the snack bar, although all they could talk or think about was work, work, work. Studying, remembering, making notes and going over them with highlighter pen. Waiting for that day when someone's life would be in her hands.

That morning, she paused on the landing, listening to her mother's snores through the door. Now that Alan was in his own flat, his room stood empty, the door ajar, the single bed stripped and his furniture cleared of dirty cups and computer equipment. She'd never have thought she'd miss his beady, silent presence, but she did.

Downstairs, she jumped to see her father in the kitchen. 'Dad, you're up!' He was wearing a suit – that was confusing. 'What are you doing?'

He turned his gaze back from the window, and she saw he had the kettle boiling and toast in the toaster.

'What do you mean? I've to go to work, don't I? Half-eight sharp we start.'

Her father hadn't worked since Ellie was at school. And the suit didn't fit him any more, and the buttons of his shirt were done up wrong. His tie was loosely draped around his neck, as if he hadn't remembered how to knot it. Ellie felt cold dread wash over her. The moment when you can no longer deny it, or hope that things will be all right. Here it was – he had somehow lost the last fifteen years.

He looked at his watch then, and said: 'You'll be late for school, pet. Is your brother up?'

'Um ... Dad, I don't go to school. I'm at university now – post-grad?'

His brows knitted. 'What?'

'And Alan doesn't live here, remember?'

Had her father forgotten her brother's entire illness? Reset to a time when he was healthy, and his near-death hadn't brushed across them all like inky feathers? She tried to remember what the pamphlets said about this confusion – whether you should correct people or let them sit in happy delusion. But she couldn't have her father going out and starting the car and driving to a factory that had closed down in 1995. It was now a paintballing range, she thought. She had to do something.

'Listen, Dad. You don't have to go to work today. You've got the day off.'

'Oh?' He frowned at her. 'That doesn't sound right.'

'Yeah, Ron rang earlier.' She'd remembered this was the

name of her dad's old boss, dead of a heart attack on the golf course two years before. 'They've shut down. There's – a problem with deliveries. Cardboard shortage.'

'Are you sure?' He looked towards the hall phone, suspicious. 'I didn't hear it ring.'

'Absolutely, yes. Come on. Why don't we eat this toast anyway?' She wouldn't be able to go to college today, that was obvious. This was some kind of crisis. What were they going to do? Carry on as they were with him at home – putting even more safeguards in place? How would they manage if he was going to get up in the middle of the night, try to drive to places that didn't even exist? Her mother was already exhausted – a fact shown by the way she was still fast asleep and hadn't noticed her husband get up from the bed beside her and dress himself in a suit that had been packed away for years. It would be down to Ellie to sort this out. Caring for him at home would perhaps mean yet again stalling her dream of being a doctor, becoming a full-time carer for her dad, never going anywhere, never getting her own place. She'd be thirty next year and was no closer to a partner or family of her own.

The other option was what her mother had raised before, which Ellie had strongly rejected – putting her father into a care home. In with all the old people, not even sixty yet. It had seemed abominable then, because he couldn't possibly be as bad as all that, not at his age. Now she looked at him from the corner of her eye, glancing vaguely between the phone and the door, fingers agitating slightly as if rubbing away at something on his shirt. Could she live with herself if she did this? That was the choice. Put him in a home, or look after him herself, thereby giving up her dreams yet again. At the moment, both seemed equally unbearable.

Put him in a home

'That's the last box.' Alan staggered under the weight of it, sitting it down and rubbing his lower back.

Although he'd recovered amazingly since his surgery, he still wasn't strong. Partly because he still spent almost all his time in front of a computer moving only his fingers, and rarely exercised or ate vegetables. But that was OK – he was happy. The company he'd set up was apparently doing very well, though Ellie still had no idea what he did and thought it all seemed suspiciously made up.

Ellie looked about her at the small room. It was clean and cosy enough, but nothing special. A single bed, a nightstand, a wardrobe and sink, everything in cheap veneer – not much bigger than her university room, and this was where they were leaving her father, who'd once managed an entire factory of people, who still owned a three-bedroom home. He was standing by the bed testing the mattress, looking a bit puzzled.

'OK, Dad?' she said.

'Oh yes, grand, grand. So – I stay here, do I?'

She bit her lip. They'd tried to explain what was happening, but he couldn't retain it. 'Yes, Dad. They'll take good care of you here.'

Alan ducked out, probably avoiding Ellie bursting into tears again, which she already had four times that morning. 'I'll just . . . help Mum with the car.'

'So ... is it a hotel?' said her father, looking doubtfully at the tiny sink.

'Kind of. It's a place for people to live, where they have lots of nice games and activities.' She was talking to him like he was a child, and hated it.

'And – I can still watch my programmes, right?'

Maybe he'd hate it here. He'd never been one for games or joining in, preferring to read the paper and watch TV in peace.

'Of course. We're going to put your TV right there, look.'

She pointed to where it sat on the floor, trailing wires. Alan was going to set it all up for him, though he couldn't actually follow many programmes now, nothing with a plot. He liked to watch property shows, shaking his head at how much things cost and reminding Ellie over and over he'd bought their house for a thousand pounds back in the 1970s.

He was nodding, trying to make the best of a situation he clearly did not understand. 'Grand, grand. And ... I'll see you soon?'

'Of course, Dad. I'll come every day, we all will.'

But would they keep it up? Part of the reason for taking this step, which Ellie still felt so terrible about she thought she might throw up, was so she could focus on her studies, finally qualify as a doctor, almost twenty years after she'd first decided it was for her. Then she'd be into a crazy few years of night shifts, training, rotations in different parts of the country. She wouldn't have time to take care of her father, and Alan had his work and in any case didn't really know how to soothe their dad. Her mother was worn out, and now she'd at last stopped work it was as if she'd ground to a halt. After years of barely sitting down, she rarely got off the sofa, doing sudokus and watching the same property shows Ellie's dad loved. Ellie planned to move out as soon as she could – she and her mother had rubbed along surprisingly well for the past while, but she couldn't be still sleeping in her childhood single bed at thirty. She hadn't had a date in two years, let alone touched a man. That part of her life, the wild woman who wore evening gowns, drank wine with famous conductors and attended classical museum concerts, seemed gone for good. It was hard to believe it had actually happened, and wasn't just a dream, a branch of her life she might have had if she'd taken other paths. A figment of her imagination.

Her mother came in then, carrying a small lamp.

'There you are, then, Frank. Settled in?'

A tightness in her face betrayed that she too was finding this hard. She'd be living alone now for the first time in her life. Did it mean your marriage was over, if you put your partner in a home, admitted they were no longer the man you'd fallen in love with? Maybe she'd meet someone else, have a second stab at love. Ellie's heart felt sore with what this day meant, the fact that there was no coming back from it. Her dad would never live independently again, and would likely die in this poky room.

'Oh yes, grand. Are you – you're not staying with me?'

'No, love, I've explained this to you. You're staying here by yourself. We'll be in to visit, of course.'

'Oh, right. Yes, yes.' But the confusion crept back on his face, and it broke Ellie's heart.

'Where's Alan?' she said to her mother, to change the subject. 'He was going to find you.'

'No idea, thought he was with you. Go and look for him, then.'

She was giving an Ellie an out, so she didn't have to witness this painful goodbye between her parents, and Ellie gladly took it, hurrying down the carpeted stairs to the lobby, choking down her own stifled sobs. There, she was surprised to see her brother talking to someone. Firstly because he was *talking* to someone, a total stranger at that. Secondly because it was a woman, and a young pretty one, with blonde hair in a ponytail and pink scrubs. Thirdly, he was actually laughing, something he rarely did.

'There you are,' she said, going over to him.

'Hi!' said the woman, with a bright perky smile. 'I'm Katie, the nursing manager here. I was just telling your brother we're going to take very good care of your dad.'

'He's – well, he's very young to be in here.'

'I know, I know. But he's not the only one, I promise. It may take a while but he'll settle in, they always do, and really it's the best place for him. We have loads going on, lots of hobbies and activities. It's honestly nice.'

'See?' said Alan. 'I told you there was no need to feel guilty.'

'I still do, though,' muttered Ellie.

Easy for her brother to take the practical approach.

'Of course,' said Katie, smiling sweetly. 'Perfectly under-standable.' She checked a little clip-on watch on her scrubs. 'Oh, whoops! Time for my rounds. Absolutely lovely to meet you, Ellie, Alan. I'm sure we'll be seeing a lot of each other now.' And she shot off like a pocket rocket, pony-tail bouncing.

Alan gazed after her, a look on his face that Ellie had never seen before. 'Isn't she lovely?' Ellie wondered what the hell was going on. Could her brother for the first time in his life be interested in a woman?

Keep him at home

'OK, Dad. You'll be all right by yourself for ten minutes if I pop to the shop?'

Ellie was making lunch, but they'd run out of bread, and she knew her dad hated to have the heel of the loaf. He ate so little these days, often forgetting about meals, and he'd lost so much weight. She always tried to give him food he would enjoy.

'Aye, aye.'

He was seated in front of the lunchtime screening of *Homes Under the Hammer*, and seemed happy enough. All the same, Ellie dithered about going out. He'd rarely been left alone since his diagnosis, with Ellie deferring her second year at Newcastle to pick up the slack from her mother, who was out at her Tuesday Pilates class, the only time she got to herself all week. It was OK to pop out, wasn't it? The doctors had never said he was so bad he couldn't be left unsupervised. She checked the stove was off and taps not running, but she could hardly lock him in, though she would have liked to. There might be a fire or something.

'Don't move, OK, Dad? I really won't be long. Please just sit there.'

Full of misgiving, she snatched a raincoat from the peg

in the hall and set off down the road to the garage at a brisk pace. A light rain was falling, and her village looked grey and depressing. Clusters of bungalows, the roar of the main road nearby, the village hall, the shuttered-up pub that had gone bust the year before. The slight babble of the river that ran along the backs of the houses, which threatened to flood more and more every spring, so her mother had bought sandbags to keep in the garage. What was she doing with her life? She would turn thirty in a few months. Thirty! She'd imagined so many futures for herself at that age. She'd be a doctor, happily married, probably with one or two kids. Or else a writer, a journalist on magazines, a published author. A grown-up, happy and sorted, who knew about things like mortgages and hairdressers and how to dress for work. Instead she didn't even have a job – she was a student still, and one who'd put off finishing her course for even longer now to care for her father. People her age were becoming consultants already, Mark's wife among them, as the ever-helpful Facebook told her, and Ellie had swerved so far from her course in life that she hadn't even finished university. Her friends from Oxford were steaming ahead with their lives, too. Verity was now a vice president in her dad's bank, and Camilla was about be made partner in a law firm. Michelle too was basically a Hollywood star – she'd moved to LA the year before and kept inviting Ellie out to visit, but of course she had no money for the fare and couldn't leave her father in any case.

She'd reached the petrol station now, which had several years before been given an upgrade with a small M&S

attached. She picked up the bread and browsed in the yellow sticker section, adding some slightly bruised grapes to her pile. God, life seemed so bleak. Medical school had been hard work, but at least she'd seen people every day, and she'd felt focused and learned new things all the time, and was driven by the idea that every lecture took her closer to being a doctor. Of course she was so grateful Alan was all right, but even his life was going better than hers. He had friends, and even went out at weekends. Ellie hadn't been out in months. Who would she go with? Her Newcastle friends were on placements around the country, rushed off their feet with no time to meet up. Michelle was far away, and as for Mark – well. Ellie and Mark were long done. They weren't even friends now. He was just a person she used to know, someone she had so many times walked with to this very petrol station back when it was an Esso, bought Mini Milks and ice pops and those orange drinks where you had to pierce the lid with a straw.

Ellie queued up, paid on her card, thinking how little money she had left since she hadn't received her student bursary this year, and trudged home, hopelessness seeping into her along with the rain, leaving her hair in rat-tails. She opened the door and stopped in her tracks. The bread fell from her hands, forgotten.

'Dad. Dad!'

No. This couldn't be happening again. Another family member sprawled on the ground, and Ellie was on her knees beside him, trying to decipher the scene. The chair in front of the open cupboard. Her dad fallen beneath it, blood spreading from his head. The red-stained corner of the worktop. It all told a story. She'd left him, he'd been hungry and confused, and he'd taken a chair to the cupboard to look for some food. Oh God.

'Dad! Dad, can you sit up?'

He was woozy, but still conscious. The wound on his forehead was tacky but clotting. He'd need stitches but maybe it wasn't disastrous. He stared at her, pushing himself up slightly on his arm, as if too weak to get up.

'Dad, are you all right?'

He was still staring at her, and Ellie was cold all over, that same feeling she remembered from the worst moments of her life, getting the call about Mark being caught in 7/7, Serge telling her about Claudette, finding Steve gone that day.

'Who are you?' said her father, as if he had never seen her before in his life.

'It's me, Dad. Ellie.' *Your daughter. You were the first person ever to hold me, and you don't know who I am.*

'Oh. I feel a bit peaky.'

Something passed over his face, a kind of shudder that Ellie would never forget as long as she lived. As if she could see him fading away, the exact moment where he ceased to be. His head lolled back.

'Dad. Dad!' She shook him. There was no strength in his body, and it was just like shaking a rag doll. 'Dad. *Dad!*'

Ellie continued to pat his face and rub his hands for another few minutes, in desperate hope, but she already knew deep down that her father, her one champion and supporter, the person who'd loved her most in her life, was dead. And all because she'd gone out to buy bread.

*

206

A week later, Ellie buried her father, on another dreary wet day, rain thudding over the coffin lid at the interment. The church had been a blur of faces, strangers in black coming up to Ellie, her mother and Alan, shaking hands and saying how sorry they were – lots of people who'd once worked with her father. It made Ellie want to cry to see how they remembered him, how respected he had been. Some of her friends from her course had come too. Verity and Cam had come up on the train from London, and Michelle, who'd flown out from the set of her new film in LA just to be here for a day. Ellie squeezed her hand in passing, unable to say anything just yet. She still had not cried for her father, and could feel the tears storing up inside her like an underground lake – drip, drip, drip.

She turned away from the grave as the rain intensified. Her mother was muffled in a black coat and umbrella, Alan awkwardly holding her arm. He looked smart in a black suit and tie. Their father would have been proud, Ellie thought, and the idea made her choke up.

'I'll take Mum to the house, OK?' he said.

'OK.'

They were having a small wake – plates of sandwiches, a tea urn, a cooked ham. Ellie had organised most of it as a way of keeping going. Then, as she headed back to her own car, heels sinking into the damp grass, thinking how sad it was to be alone at your father's funeral, she realised one person was still standing there in the rain. She could hardly see who it was, blinking water from her eyes. A man in a heavy coat, leaning on a cane and holding an umbrella in the other. She walked a few steps closer. Rain began to drum on her own umbrella.

Mark. It was Mark. He had come for her. He didn't say anything, but his gaze was kind and steady. And the years seemed to melt away as Ellie threw her umbrella to one side, and he did the same, to leave an arm free to pull her in. Rain pelted down on her, but she didn't care. As her hands locked behind his back, and she laid her head on his shoulder – same height as hers in her heels – she knew this was the one place she could find comfort today.

JUNE 2019

Ellie wasn't used to her mum's car. The seat was so far forward she was practically crammed against the steering wheel, and she was still in her slippers, so pressing the pedals was difficult. She hopped the car out of the drive, making enough noise that her mother was sure to hear and look out to see the bride making off with her Vauxhall Corsa, which she'd need to go and pick Ellie's dad up from the nursing home. Too late to care now. Someone else could get her dad, maybe. He couldn't miss her wedding, though he likely wouldn't know what was going on. And of course she wasn't at all sure there'd even be a wedding – it all depended on the outcome of this conversation.

Wishing she'd brought her phone, she tried to remember the route to the pub. She'd been there many times before its revamp into a 'boutique inn', with rooms and rainfall showers, for eighteenth birthdays and engagement parties and graduations. One time Michelle had thrown up Archers and lemonade in its car park while Ellie held her hair back.

Michelle. If only she were around. Michelle would understand how Ellie had ended up here, on her wedding day, still not sure what she was doing. Still thinking of another man. She would understand about Mark-and-Ellie, the long and troubled history of them, how impossible it was to walk away entirely from him, even after so much water under the bridge.

There! Ellie missed the turn for the pub, swerved a full turn around the roundabout, earning herself a sharp toot on the horn from a van driver. It wasn't fair: people shouldn't beep at her on her wedding day. She wasn't supposed to be driving herself at all, or indeed doing anything for herself, including peeing alone. She was supposed to be having her hair teased and pinned, false eyelashes stuck on, and getting squeezed into the boned bodice of her dress. Instead she was on the ring road, in her tracksuit and slippers. What was she even going to say to him? He'd be so gutted. She turned off into the pub car park, stopping the Corsa not far from the site of Michelle's long-ago vomit, and sat there for a moment paralysed with indecision. What was he doing right now? Maybe having a drink with his groomsmen, or trying to tie his tie. Watching TV, perhaps – men seemed to have hardly anything to do to get ready, even on their wedding days. Running over his vows and speech. He'd be stunned to know his bride was just metres away, having a silent meltdown in the car park outside.

She had to talk to him. Maybe if she could just see him, his familiar face, press hers into his wide chest, she would be sure again. All these doubts would melt away, the feeling of worry she'd woken with that morning, which seemed so long ago. The vague unease of knowing something wasn't right, as if she was in the wrong timeline or had stepped into the wrong branch of her life. Was there a word for that?

Probably there was in German. And she couldn't even blame the conversation she'd overheard between Mark and Laura for sending her off the rails. She'd been having doubts even before they arrived. Really, she must have known for ages something was amiss. But what was it?

Ellie turned off the engine and got out, moving as if through water, putting off the difficult moment. She traipsed into reception. The man behind the desk was about her age, though badly aged, bald and portly, in a polo shirt with the name of the pub embroidered on it. His badge read *Adam Cooper*, and there was something vaguely familiar about that, someone she'd seen on Facebook perhaps? Maybe they'd been at school together? For a second she couldn't place him, and then – *oh my God*. It was *that* Adam. It was Michelle's ex, the one Ellie had kissed that night over twenty years ago. He and Ellie had various mutual friends on Facebook, and he popped up from time to time. She almost forgot her mission in her shock. This man had an ex who was a Hollywood star, who'd once gone on a date with Chris Evans. Amazing.

He looked up. 'Can I help?' He didn't recognise her. Was that better or worse?

'Um, yes. Is it OK if I go – can I go to – room ten?'

He looked puzzled. 'If you want, pet.'

Pet! God. He really had no idea who she was, the rupture he'd made in her life. There'd been a strange mood between her and Mark that night and kissing Adam had made it even worse. Maybe something might have happened if he hadn't stepped in. Of course then she might not have met Michelle, and life would be different again.

She was spiralling. She had to do this. The corridor was

dingy, the carpet a nasty pattern of swirls, fraying in places and with bits of something sticky in one place. Tired art prints of the local area. Fire extinguishers. Ellie approached the door of room ten. Inside, she could hear the noise of sport – of course he was watching sport. He was probably totally chilled, with no idea of the turmoil she'd been in all morning. She raised her hand and knocked. A few seconds delay. Maybe he was in the shower and – but then he opened it. He wasn't in his suit yet, just jeans and a T-shirt. He stared at her, puzzled, as well he might be. She shouldn't be there – it didn't make any sense.

'Hi,' said Ellie, her voice breaking. 'Can we talk?'

CHOICE 8 – AUGUST 2012

'Yes … yes, yes, yes, yes yes, YES!' Ellie's mum leapt up from the sofa, fists clenched in joy. Ellie stared at her. 'Go on, Mo! He won!'

On screen, the sweat-lathered man slowed from his sprint, arms aloft, face split with wonder as if he could hardly believe what had just happened, what he'd done.

'Mum, you hate sport. What's happened to you?' said Ellie, amused.

Her mother was so different these days. She wore jeans, she got her hair highlighted. She did Pilates and went on book club trips to the theatre and had opinions about politics.

'Oh, it's all so exciting, isn't it? Us having the Olympics. And winning! We never win anything. It's so nice to just feel, well, proud I suppose. Of the country.'

She was far from the only one – Olympic fever had gripped the nation, and most of the houses in the village were draped with Union Jack flags. Ellie was enjoying watching the Games, and as pleased as anyone that the UK was winning so many medals, but she couldn't shake off their association with the terrible events of 2005, the bombs coming the morning after the celebrations. Waking up with the slow realisation that Mark was in her bed. His swift awkward flight, the last time she'd seen him whole. Finding him in hospital after those terrible hours of searching blood-stained wards, out of his head on pain and drugs. Then her abortion, Alan's illness, her father's dementia.

These had been very dark years for her family, but the mood seemed to have turned. Her dad was settled in his care home, and although he often didn't know who they were when they visited, he seemed happy. Alan was not only cancer-free, he'd also started dating and moved in with Katie, the nursing manager of the home. Ellie still had to remind herself this was true, that her brother, who needed so little from other people, was in love and living in his wharf-front flat with his pretty, bubbly girlfriend, who seemed besotted with him.

It was amazing to think he'd only met Katie because they'd made that horrible choice to put their dad in a nurs-ing home. How sad she'd felt that day, and yet it had led to something lovely. If they'd kept her dad at home, as she had dithered over, what might have happened then? Would he still be with them, or might something have happened to carry him off already? Impossible to know. She had to stop tormenting herself with alternative paths.

At least she was out of her parents' house, finally. She had her own flat in Newcastle, where she was on rotation in the hospital there, halfway through a Geriatrics placement that made her sad sometimes, but also helped her understand her father better. It was undeniably hard – Ellie sank into bed most nights too tired even to wash her face, and cried most days when patients died or their relatives shouted at her or just from sheer tiredness. She often worked for a whole day and night without a break – it was supposed to be illegal now, but there weren't enough staff, and someone had to do it. If you were all that could prevent an elderly woman with a collapsed lung from screaming in pain all night, it was hard to clock off and go home. Home was a sparsely furnished place, since she was rarely there, so she'd come over to her mother's house to watch Mo Farah race. It would have seemed unthinkable only years ago, but Ellie could now spend the day with her mother and not want to strangle her, even enjoy it a little. They had their shows that they watched together – *Grey's Anatomy* was a big one, and her mother would touchingly defer to Ellie's medical knowledge throughout, even though that glamorous hospital was a world away from the shabby NHS ones she worked in. Soon she would be a fully qualified doctor, out in the world, responsible for people's lives and deaths.

Her stomach lurched at the very thought. Ellie stood up as the footage switched to the commentators in the studio. 'I'll make more tea.'

Her mum was still glued to it. 'Put the milk in first this time! I can always tell when you don't.'

Ellie rolled her eyes, stooping for her mother's mug, which was one she'd bought in Paris, the Eiffel Tower making the handle. How had she ever been that chic woman, effortlessly throwing out French idioms and eating escargot? A lifetime ago. As the kettle boiled, she thumbed through her new smartphone, which still seemed impossibly exciting and high-tech. It took photos that were better than those from any camera she'd owned, and could store her music and play videos and everything. It also meant you could be logged into Facebook all the time – no need to go upstairs and take out your laptop and boot it up. Sometimes Ellie felt it wasn't healthy, the amount of time she spent staring at her phone, saturated in the details of other people's lives. Especially as she'd now got a dangerous new reason to scroll at it blindly – she had joined a dating website.

It was Michelle who'd told her about it. Still single, she never seemed to meet anyone she liked enough – though Ellie imagined that being single in LA was different to being single in Newcastle. The dating site was overwhelming, clicking on man after man. Choice after choice. Every single face a different possible life. Marriage, children you might have, with that random man's red hair or this one's freckles. It was intense, and activated deep parts of Ellie's anxiety, but that didn't stop her doing it, of course, because it was also highly addictive.

This one. That one. A fireman in Leeds. A farmer in Shipton. A marketing manager in Durham. Different ages, different backgrounds. Pick and choose the height, the body shape, the education level, the location. But how did you know if you'd made the right choice? With every small swipe of her thumb, she was shutting down a possible future. That face she had briefly glimpsed and discarded, cuddling a dog up a mountain, because she didn't really like dogs and five foot eight was a bit short for her taste – what if he was the love of her life? What if she'd met him in a bar and been entranced by his smile? What if the chemistry between them would have been intense but, reduced to pictures and statistics, she'd overlooked him? She'd never know, but she couldn't match with everyone, either. Even the people you did match with, you had to keep up the chat and arrange to meet and wash your hair and think of interesting things to say to them. It was exhausting. Somehow, over the years that had passed since Paris, Ellie had turned from someone who always had a boyfriend, or at least a love interest to angst over, into someone who was so single she'd forgotten how to be otherwise.

'Where's that tea?' called her mother. 'The running's coming on again.'

Ellie snapped out of her trance – it was so easy for time to slip away while you were online.

'Coming.' She stirred the tea and put the bags into the new compost bin her mother insisted on using, having become very eco-friendly in her retirement. She carried them back in, noticing as she did how her mother put her own phone down sharply, a guilty look on her face. 'What's that?'

'Oh. It's Carol. Wants to maybe meet up tomorrow.'

Carol was her mother's friend from book club.

Ellie frowned. 'I thought she was in Tenerife. Didn't you say they all had food poisoning?' She hadn't particularly wanted to know all the details of Carol and her husband's digestive systems, but the information had stuck.

'Oh. Yes.' Her mother paused. 'Well, I suppose you have to find out eventually, Ellie. I'm meeting Nigel. You know, from the garden centre.'

A silver fox of a gardener, Nigel was always selling her mother extra feed for her roses. It was he who had recommended the compost bin, in fact.

'Oh. Right.'

Ellie sat down, feeling the world shift slightly. Her mother was still married, of course, but did it count if her husband no longer recognised her? So difficult.

'I hope you understand. I know it's hard. I'll always love your dad. But, well – he's not been himself for a long time, has he?'

'No. That makes sense.'

On the TV, blue-clad figures ran and threw and jumped, while Ellie just sat there and drank her tea. If even her mother was dating, she really had to get herself out there.

Not long after, she went to bed in her old room, doing her nightly cleanse and her routine of brush, floss, gargle with mouthwash. Her life had become so regimented. Maybe it was time to shake things up a little. Ellie looked at herself in the mirror with a harsh eye. She was thirty-one. She was single, her last relationship with a French philanderer. No children, one pregnancy she had been right to end, but all the same couldn't help thinking of every July, when her baby might have been born, and life would have changed for ever. Her brother was happy, her mother had found someone, her dad was well enough. Only she was stuck.

She got into bed with her headphones and book and water, and scrolled through some more people on the site. One, two, three, four, five, six. A hypnotic rhythm of faces and names. And then, suddenly, one that she knew. It was a split-second thing, these things. You swiped before your brain could really engage, sometimes, and might even regret it, but there was no way to go back. A lost future, a pang for a life you'd never have. Her finger froze over the screen as her eye suddenly caught on a face she knew. Was it ... yes, she was sure it was him. *Paul, 34, Durham.* The same Paul who'd taken over Steve's room all those years ago, who'd helped Ellie that day when she'd found herself homeless in London. He'd been nice. What was his surname? She'd never found it out.

Her finger hovered over his profile. Was it weird to swipe on someone you actually knew? Would he even remember her? She went to Facebook and searched for Steven Wilmott. She sometimes looked at Steve during her periodic online stalking of old boyfriends. Serge – onto his third child with Claudette, became a music teacher, lost his hair. Steve – working as a marketing manager in Devon, married to a perky blonde woman, also had two kids. Also lost his hair. And Mark – not that Mark had ever been her boyfriend. He was married to Laura, of course, posting lots of outdoorsy shots in Scotland. He had climbed a Munro to raise money to buy prosthetic limbs for landmine victims. He'd founded his own tech company three years before, and although Ellie had no real understanding of what it did, she often found articles in the trade press that mentioned it, on the regular occasions she googled him. When she spoke to Michelle his name usually came up, but she hadn't seen Michelle in over a year, as her friend's career built and built. She was starring in an adaptation of a Wilkie Collins novel at the moment, with Benedict Cumberbatch as her love interest. Ellie saw her on magazine covers or on Graham Norton more often than in real life. Sometimes she ran into her mum at the supermarket, and got the impression Michelle hadn't seen her family for a while, either. The price of fame.

That must be him, in Steve's friend list – Paul Sanderson.

A small picture of a man's silhouette on a mountaintop. What was Paul even doing in the area? There weren't many investment banks in the north. Perhaps he'd changed careers? She was intrigued, she realised. But couldn't she just send him a message on Facebook, mention how funny it was to see his face pop up? Was that too direct?

She could hear her mother in the bathroom, switching the light on and off several times as she forgot to put on her various creams and unguents. Her mum was dating! The man from the garden centre! Ellie would have loved to discuss it with someone, but Alan wouldn't see why it was big news, and Michelle was miles away, and no one else would get it. Mark – Mark would understand, get how mind-boggling it was to think of Judy Warren on a date with a man who made his own compost. But that bridge was burned long ago. So why could she never let it go entirely out, the tiny flame she had in her heart, simmering like a gas burner on low?

Reckless suddenly, she swiped right on Paul and shut the website down, put her phone to one side. It was just a tiny movement of her finger, but it felt exhilarating, to open a small portal to the past like that. If Paul saw it, if he didn't immediately swipe left on her, or worse, not even recognise her, or have his settings put to only women under thirty, then maybe he'd get in touch.

She turned off her light, forcing herself to stop scrolling, since she had to be at the hospital the next day. God, it was so addictive, the little flare of dopamine to the brain. The illusion of connection, of validation. But it wasn't real. The way she'd met Paul, that had been real. He'd helped her, he'd been kind and compassionate both to her and to Steve, who must have been the world's most annoying flatmate. That moment of looking up from her distress and seeing his kind face, his neatly ironed shirt and tie, his fair hair with its severe City cut. Maybe that was how you were supposed to meet people. By serendipity, happenstance, the way she'd walked into that French bakery and met Serge, the way she'd literally fallen over Steve in Leicester Square. Not through the tiny rectangle of your phone.

Just as Ellie was dozing off, her phone vibrated, and she shot her hand out for it, wide awake again and flooded with adrenaline. Message sign. She clicked it open, made clumsy by hurry. *It's a match*, it declared! And there was Paul, 34, in her matches. Dots, to show he was typing a message to her. Ellie waited. The dots stopped. And then started up again. He was typing to her, this man she'd met once ten years ago, suddenly back in her orbit, as if by fate or magic.

Paul was as straightforward as he'd been back then. There was none of the nonsense she'd had from other guys, sending a few messages then going quiet, or chatting for days and never actually arranging a date.

Ellie! he said. *Is this Ellie Warren — we met years ago back in Ladbroke Grove — Steve's Ellie?*

Yep it's me! Though not Steve's any more obvs. She thought about it and added a little smiley face. *Back in my hometown. What brings you north?*

She saw the dots that told her he was typing. *My mum had dementia sadly so I moved back to get her into sheltered housing. Then when she passed I stayed on to renovate her house and hopefully put it on market.*

Oh, my dad has dementia too. Sorry to hear that.

Me too. Sad club to be in 😔

So are you working up here?

Not right now. Took a leave of absence – sort of a career break lol.

Uh oh, he used lol non-ironically. Normally that would be a deal breaker for her, but she already knew him, or at least had met him. He wasn't stupid – he had a high-powered job in finance. He was just . . . straightforward, maybe.

What about you? he added.

I'm at medical school. Took some time out for my dad, and my brother was really ill also. He's fine now.

Oh Ellie. You really have had a time of it. I'm sorry. And with that simple kindness, that empathy, she felt something shift in her heart, and for the first time in years tears were in her throat. She *had* had a time of it! Not just her father and Alan, but Serge and the baby and Mark. She deserved someone to be nice to her. Maybe he'd had the same idea, because next he typed, *I would love to hear more if I could take you out for dinner? There are some great places here in Durham, or I can come to you.*

He was asking her out to dinner. Such a small thing, but none of the men she'd dated since had done that. Her first date with Serge had been at his flat, and they hadn't left for two days. Steve had only ever taken her to the chippie, if she was lucky.

Ellie didn't hesitate over typing back: *I'd love that. Durham would be fine thanks, I have a car now.*

That would mean she couldn't drink too much and get silly; it was a long time since she'd been out on a date. Assuming that's what this was? Or did he just mean a catch-up? They were on a dating site, after all.

Great, said Paul. *Here's my number so we can get off this thing!*

So simple. Ellie went to sleep with a smile playing around the corners of her mouth, a feeling that after years in the doldrums things were maybe going to be OK.

The dinner was soon set for the following Friday – Ellie didn't have much in her diary, a fact she tried to play down as they bandied dates about. He booked it, and she started worrying about what to wear. He hadn't seen her for ten years, and that was during a time when she'd lived off chips and Red Bull and been a size ten, albeit with ashen skin and no muscle tone. She looked at her face critically in the mirror on the morning of the date (was it a date?). Was she more wrinkled? A few bits of grey in her hair that hadn't been there when he last saw her? But he would have aged too. She'd scrutinised his pictures on the site with forensic intensity, but they were too blurry to tell for sure. Had he lost his hair, put on weight? She had definitely put on weight since her days of working in magazines, in a hellscape of disordered eating and size-six sample clothes. But maybe that was for the best. She even went to the gym sometimes now, doing Pilates with her mum or swimming lengths in the pool.

Her other problem was she had absolutely no nice clothes, since she only ever went to university, the hospital or her dad's care home. Back in her flat, she sifted through her sparse wardrobe of jeans, walking trousers and anoraks, one black dress for funerals. How depressing. This was a good excuse to buy something new – and she knew the very person to ask.

It was increasingly hard to keep in contact with Michelle,

seeing as she was always off filming in various parts of the world, but, possessed by a whimsical spirit, Ellie pressed her number. It rang a few times, the single dial-tone that told her Michelle was not in the country. She never was, except for award ceremonies or press junkets. Then, suddenly, the line was picked up. Her old friend's voice, hoarse – 'El?'

'Oh my God! I didn't think you'd answer. Did I wake you up?'

'No, I'm in Hong Kong, it's evening here.'

'What are you doing there?'

Ellie couldn't even imagine what it was like there. Her dreams of travelling the world had gone no further than France. She'd never even been to America, where Michelle now lived when she wasn't jetting to exotic parts. One day, when she had money and time, she'd visit.

'Oh, some Chinese-funded film. I can't understand the plot, but it pays really well. What's up with you?'

'Well. I have a date.'

'Oooh.'

'With this guy Paul. He used to share a flat with Steve, weirdly!'

'Not a stoner slacker?'

'Not at all. The complete opposite.'

'Sounds promising.'

'So I need a new outfit.'

Over the phone, Ellie could hear her friend stir and rustle, as if getting up from a bed or sofa.

'You've called the right person. Get yourself down the shopping centre, and send me lots of pictures. I'll be waiting.'

*

Come Friday night, Ellie was sitting far too early at a table in a Durham restaurant, in the red floral tea dress Michelle had helped her choose. It was nice. Not too stuffy – no tablecloths, just pine wood tables. Flickering candles, soft background music, Italian food. She looked about her nervously. Where was he? What if he didn't turn up? Were people already looking at her pityingly? Didn't you get stood up all the time in internet dating? She'd heard some horror stories from the younger medics at uni.

'Ellie!'

Oh God, there he was. He'd lost weight, and a little hair, but he looked good. Leaner, as if he'd shed some of his softness. Fair hair in a neat short cut. Square, pleasant face. Dressed better too from what she remembered, in an expensive-looking blue suit and cream trousers. She stood up for an awkward hug, his metal-link watch – also expensive-looking – catching in her hair.

'Wow, been a long time,' she said, sitting down again. He smelled really good. Like home baking and lemons.

'I know! What have you been doing with yourself? You were going to work in magazines, I think?'

That life seemed a million years away, an impossibility that she'd ever even been on such a path.

'Well, I went to medical school, finally. I'd always wanted to do that but ended up not studying it at uni. So, I'm hoping to finish this year. It's a bit humbling to be thirty-one and only just graduating, mind you, then of course there's years of training still to go.'

'But you're on the ladder you want to be on. That's better than being at the top of the wrong one, right?' The waitress arrived and offered bread, which he waved away. Perhaps he was low-carb? That would explain his new trimness.

'So tell me about the house renovation?' she said, leaning in, trying to sound bright and interested. A guy like this – solvent, nice, well dressed – he could have anyone. Ellie was acutely aware of her frizzy hair and high-street dress, still beyond her budget. Michelle had tried to cajole her into buying a more expensive brand, but Ellie wasn't earning and had to be careful.

He talked for a while about joists and load-bearing walls and Farrow and Ball, and it wasn't wildly fascinating to someone who'd never owned a home and was years off from doing so, but she liked to listen to him. She felt calm in his presence, like everything was going to be all right. Then she told him about her course, the things she was learning, the rotations she would be on for the next few years.

'Will you specialise in anything?'

'I'm thinking maybe . . . neurology.' She said it a bit shyly, because she was yet to articulate this to anyone, and it was a very competitive area, with a lot of heartache involved. 'After my brother had the tumour, and with Dad's dementia, I guess I've been thinking a lot about brains. How they contain us, all we are, in this hulk of, well, meat I suppose.'

At this exact moment the waitress set down his rare lamb and she laughed, releasing tension. She'd deduced she was right about the carbs – he only ate meat and vegetables, while she nervously chomped her way through the basket of grissini and plate of carbonara, then said no to dessert, though he was most anxious she should have a tiramisu if she wanted one. She felt shamed out of it, however, after hoofing down pasta and bread all night. Didn't want him to think she was greedy. They drank a light fruity red, after he'd made quite a pantomime of going through the wine list and requesting a few to taste. Ellie had always found that a bit cringe, when people went on about nose and vintages – could they really tell the difference? – but perhaps she was just a philistine, immured as she'd been for years in a small provincial town. She'd once had opinions about wine, in a different life, a different country.

Paul had been telling her about his career, depressingly opposite to hers. He'd lived in Hong Kong, Singapore and Munich for a while.

'So then I just thought, there's not a whole lot left to do, so why not take some time to be with Mum? It was always just her and me. I started fixing up the house when she was dying and now she's gone I guess I kind of enjoy it. I'm quite good at wallpapering!'

He was so sweet and modest. And obviously totally minted. He waved away Ellie's debit card, almost embarrassed, once they'd finished their (no dessert) meal. 'Oh please, no, I invited you, let me get it. Anyway you only had one glass of wine.'

She couldn't help but think of all the times she'd had to pay for Steve, as a skint student, or subsidise Serge when he'd spent all his concert fees on Armagnac. It made a nice change.

'How's your course going? You're almost finished, right?'

Four years of studying, and she was on the verge of becoming a doctor. 'It's . . . oh, to be honest it's exhausting. People want so much from you. To save lives, cure their loved ones, have all the answers . . . and I've not even qualified yet, you know? The NHS is so under-funded, it's really a travesty.'

Maybe he wouldn't agree with her politically. But he was nodding politely. 'Yeah. I ended up going private for a lot of Mum's care. It just took too long otherwise.'

They hadn't had that option for Ellie's dad.

'Sometimes I wonder if I'm actually cut out for it.'

She'd never told anyone that before. She certainly wasn't going to admit to her mother that medicine was harder than she'd expected, more heart-breaking, more bewildering. Not after all the years of study and the money spent.

'Being a doctor, that was your dream?' He was touchingly interested in her life.

'One of them. I always wanted – well, when I lived in Paris I started writing a novel.' She ducked her head, embarrassed. 'Kind of a pipe dream, I guess.'

'Why? People do write books. And you must be able to, if you worked in magazines all that time.'

'Not sure it's the same. They hardly ever let me write anything, anyway.'

His brow creased, as if he just desperately wanted her to be happy. 'You can finish it now, can't you?'

'I could. It's hard to find the time, with medicine.'

'I'm sure. That just seems a shame, if you really wanted it all this time.'

Maybe he was right, Ellie thought, as the waitress cleared their plates, hers wiped clean of carbonara sauce. Why hadn't she finished the book? Fear, perhaps, or laziness, or apathy after the shock of Alan's illness. There was no excuse now. Yes, she was busy, but she could find some time each day. Couldn't she?

Then came the awkward moment, the end of the date. Paul walked her to her car, asking solicitously if she'd be all right driving in the dark. She assured him she would be safe.

'So.' She turned to face him. She had always hated this moment, the uncertainty, knowing that every look and breath and word was significant, might influence the rest of your life. Did she want him to kiss her? He was a nice man, handsome with his fair hair and broad, artless face. In good shape. Attentive. That was the trouble with kissing – you couldn't always tell if there was chemistry until you dived in. 'Thanks so much for dinner. It was lovely to see you again. You really helped me that day, back then.'

He looked embarrassed. 'Oh, you don't need to thank me, I didn't do anything. I did wonder about you sometimes. If you were all right.'

'You thought about me?'

'Course I did.' He met her eyes suddenly and a twist ran through her stomach. Oh. She did fancy him, then. 'I'd love to meet up again, Ellie. I had a lovely time.'

'Me too.'

He stepped forward and pressed a kiss onto her lips, firm and quick, tasting of wine, then stood back again.

'I hope that was all right. I'll call you, yeah?'

And she knew he would. That was the thing about Paul. They'd only met twice, but she already knew that, if she chose to walk down this path, a certain life would be waiting for her. Like standing at a door you knew was ajar, your fingers on the handle ready to push.

*

Over the next two months, Ellie and Paul saw each other more and more. They texted throughout the day, soon spreading to good morning and goodnight messages, with one and then two and then three kisses. They met at weekends or when they could, when Ellie wasn't working. He didn't mind driving just to drink terrible coffee with her for an hour in the hospital canteen. It was easy. No misunderstandings, no long gaps without a reply where she'd wonder if she'd done something wrong, or if he'd forgotten all about her. If he might be with someone else. For the first time in her life, Ellie was able to focus on the here and now, not some imaginary future or the decisions of the past. Those were done and behind her, and could not be changed.

Then, towards the end of October that year – as the leaves were turning orange and brown and the night creeping closer every day, a chill in the air that saw Ellie cranking up her car heater in the mornings, dreaming of winter walks with Paul, hand in mittened hand, fires in cosy pubs, maybe even Christmas, who knew! – two things happened.

Ellie was at the hospital one day when she was called down to A & E for a consult – a patient of hers, Mrs Bekingo, had fallen over and broken a hip. It was the third time she'd been in the hospital for dizzy spells, and Ellie had seen her each time, found nothing wrong after multiple tests, so sent her home. She ran down the stairs, realising as she passed a vending machine that she hadn't eaten since her bowl of muesli that morning. It was now 4 p.m. No time now, though. She'd probably end up cramming down a Snickers later – working here had really ruined her diet. Ironically, helping other people was actually making her own health worse, what with so little time to exercise or cook proper meals. Lack of sleep had made her skin pale and sallow, she realised, catching sight of herself in the glass of the door.

'Dr Warren?' Standing in front of her was an irate A & E consultant, in a white coat and scrubs. Dr Singh, his badge read.

'Eh, yeah, hello.'

She still hadn't got used to being called *doctor*. It was so strange, after years of imagining it. It terrified her, the responsibility.

'Come with me.'

He led her to a curtained cubicle, yanking it back so it jangled on its rings. There was Ellie's patient, pale and sweating, her breath jagged, in a hospital gown. This was more than just a fall.

'Hello, Mrs Bekingo, do you remember me?'

Ellie approached her, trying to sound positive. No sign of recognition. Her eyes opened a flicker.

'Where am I?' Her voice was a croak.

Ellie looked at the more senior doctor. 'What's wrong with her?'

'You should be able to tell me, Dr Warren. I gather she's been here three times already?'

'Yes, but we couldn't find anything the matter. We did all the tests, MRI, CT even.'

'Did you think to actually take a history?' he snapped.

'Um – yes?'

Ellie was wracking her brains to think what she'd missed. Clearly, it was something. Her stomach slid down her spine.

Mrs Bekingo was obviously very ill indeed. Dementia? No, not sweating like that. Cancer? Surely not with such a sudden onset. *Think Ellie, think*!

'You're fortunate we have an expert in this area at the hospital today, a colleague of mine who's down for a case conference. I had a hunch and asked her to take a look.'

'So ... what is it?'

'I'll let her explain.'

He stepped over to the curtain and beckoned someone. Ellie heard footsteps. The next minute someone was in the cubicle with them, hands in the pockets of a clean white coat, braids tied back, dark eyes resting on Ellie with instant recognition.

'Um ... hi, Laura,' she said weakly.

Laura was the colleague? That made sense – Glasgow wasn't far away and she and Dr Singh were probably about the same age. Ellie could have been at their level now too if she'd done medicine to start with.

'It's *Dr Carney*,' he said, scandalised by Ellie's informality.

Laura said: 'That's all right. We know each other. Old friends.'

Was that actually true? Ellie hadn't seen her since that terrible day in London, also in a hospital.

Dr Singh looked at his watch. 'I'll leave you to it then. Dr Warren, be sure to listen and fully take in what it was you did wrong. As is it we've hopefully caught it in time, but she easily could have died.'

'How are you, Ellie?' said Laura as the other doctor left. 'Long time, hey?'

'Yeah, yeah, really long time. I'm fine. Um. Working hard.'

'Yeah, I remember these first few years. It gets easier, I promise.'

Laura stepped over to the woman and lightly took her pulse.

'So ... what is it?'

'Hmm? Oh, she'd been to Nigeria several months before. You didn't ask about foreign travel?'

'I ... um, I'm not sure.'

'Well, easy to miss when you don't know tropical diseases. It's malaria – saw it all the time in Sudan.'

'Oh.' How was she supposed to spot a case of that in Newcastle? 'Well, it's good you caught it. Um ... how are things with you?'

Laura laid down the woman's hand and patted her arm gently.

'Oh, fine. We're up in Glasgow now. Mark's set up his own company. Ticking along.'

We. 'Yeah, I saw.' Laura glanced at her. 'Facebook, you know.'

'You were in France?'

'I was. I've been back a while, back in Longton, in fact, and now in Newcastle. My brother was sick, and my dad had some health issues.'

'I'm sorry to hear that.'

Laura put her hands back in her pockets, clearly ready to go. Ellie began to panic. She could not squander this, a chance meeting bringing her back to Mark, or at least to his wife.

'Um, would you tell him hi from me? I ... well, I miss you both.' That was a lie. She never thought about Laura if she could help it.

Laura paused. 'Ellie, can I be honest? He was in bits after what happened. Really dark place, for years. And you just upped and left. Didn't even come to the wedding. That really hurt him, just when he most needed you.'

'I know,' Ellie said, miserably. 'I just felt so bad. It all got too much, you know.'

'Well, I do know, yes, seeing as I had to watch him crawl back from near-death, learn to walk again, get over his PTSD.'

As far as Laura knew, Ellie was a callous cow who'd abandoned her best friend in his hour of need. She could never know the actual truth.

'I can't explain. I'd love to see him, though. Both of you.'

Laura nodded, but didn't say whether she'd tell him or not. 'I have to go. Bye, Ellie, and good luck. It was nice to see you.'

When she went, Ellie bit her lip. Tears were rushing to her eyes – not by a long chalk for the first time in the hospital. Usually she hid in the supply closet to have a good cry. She sat down beside Mrs Bekingo for a moment, devastated. She was no good at this, being a doctor. She had lost Mark, maybe for ever. She'd almost killed someone.

She looked up to realise the patient was staring at her. 'Don't worry, dear,' she said, crisp and alert suddenly. 'I'm sure whoever he is, he is not worth it.'

All week, Ellie brooded over what had happened. Maybe it was a sign that medicine wasn't for her after all – a woman could have died because she'd forgotten to ask a question. Seeing Laura's easy assurance with patients, she wasn't sure she'd ever have that. At least she would meet up with Paul at the weekend. They'd arranged a date in Newcastle, at a bar that Ellie liked, and she was going to show him some of her favourite sights in the city, starting on Saturday afternoon.

All through the week, studying and going to classes and visiting her dad to sit and hold his hand while he watched *Cash in the Attic* and didn't speak, as was increasingly the case, she had a warm glow in her stomach when she thought of it. Saturday came, and she dressed in jeans and a leather jacket, since it was a chilly, bright day. Maybe Paul would take her hand as they walked along the harbourfront. Put it into his own pocket to keep it warm. Cup her face in his hands, kiss her in that way he did, like she was precious and he could hardly believe she was there with him. She walked to meet him at the train station, and there he was where he'd promised to be, exactly on time. He was wearing a tweed coat that again looked pricey, his hair newly cut. He smelled clean and fresh. As she walked to him, a smile breaking over her face, she thought of all the events that had had to take place to bring her here at this exact moment. Her tortured relationship with Steve and its abrupt end. Mark's injury. Serge, the pregnancy. Alan's illness, her dad's dementia. All of it terrible, and all of it suffered through, but perhaps things did happen for a reason, somehow. Perhaps there was a way to forge a positive out of even the worst loss. She melted into his hug – but then she pulled away. Something was wrong. He wasn't smiling.

The same old anxiety stabbed her stomach. *I'm going to be rejected. He's going to leave me. He's only come to dump me.*

235

'What?'

'Ellie, I'm really sorry. I wasn't going to tell you this yet but I saw you and I just . . . I have to.'

'What? You're scaring me now.' She laughed nervously, without humour.

'Um – I didn't tell you last week, but I've been in talks about starting work again.'

Someone at his level did not merely apply for a job. It was all head-hunters and discreet chats and packages.

'Oh?' So maybe he was going back to London. Well, that wasn't the end of the world.

'And I got one.'

'Yeah? Congrat—'

'Ellie, it's in New York. I'm going – I'm moving to New York. Next month.'

She stared at him. That was it then. They'd have a nice month, maybe, go on a few more dates, though he might not even want to see her again if it was all going to end so soon.

'Oh. I see.'

He grasped both her arms, stared intently into her eyes. 'I'm going to say something mad now.'

'OK . . .'

'You could come with me. Why not? It's New York, you'd love it! You can actually finish your book! And it's only a year or two. You can go back to medicine afterwards, if you still want to. They're going to sort everything out – apartment, visas, the lot. Come with me, Ellie.'

Go to New York

Ellie stared out at a skyline she'd seen in films a hundred times. That dream of New York, bookshops and diners and jazz clubs – it was out there beneath her feet. Their apartment was in Brooklyn, a very fancy part, apparently, and looked onto Manhattan in all its glory. She turned away from the dazzling view of the silver river and soaring buildings, every window in every skyscraper a square of gold, to the almost-as-beautiful view behind her. Floor to ceiling windows. Hardwood floors. Pristine, never-used kitchen with the seals still on the equipment. Sofa that could seat ten, beautiful rustic dining table. Master bedroom and a spare, bathroom and en suite. Tastefully chosen art and ornaments and books. It was all wonderful – it was just that none of it was hers. It hadn't seemed sensible to lug her tatty paperbacks and knick-knacks across the ocean, so they were all in her mother's house – for now, anyway. She'd started making noises about selling up – Ellie guessed she wanted to move in with Nigel from the garden centre, who owned a lovely farmhouse out towards Bamburgh.

She'd given up a lot for this view, this amazing flat – apartment – this city so big and buzzing and ever-changing she would never truly know it. For bagels and diners and pastrami and Broadway and department stores and cold-brew coffee. For the man now coming up behind her and kissing her neck, putting solid arms around her. Seeing her father a few times a week, for a start. Alan had promised to rig up a way she could 'video chat' with him on something called FaceTime, but it seemed far fetched and would surely confuse him. She told herself it would not be for ever, only a year or so, that her dad wouldn't realise how long she'd been gone, but she knew there was a very real chance she'd never see him again. She could hardly nip back across the Atlantic if he had a stroke or heart attack.

She'd also given up, yet again, her chance of working as a doctor. The American system was totally different and there was no hope of transferring her degree. She was barely allowed to work here, anyway – she was on a 'partner visa', which tied her residency to Paul's job, and meant she couldn't earn more than him. Not that there was much risk of that. She told herself it was just deferred, that she'd pick it up soon. What difference did one year make when she'd already waited so long to be a doctor? Her mother had been surprisingly keen on this move and hadn't even mentioned the waste of money or how old Ellie would be when she finally got a job. Ellie suspected she worried her daughter would never get married or have children. She was thirty-two now, after all. It wasn't a crazy decision to spend a year in an amazing city, with a man who loved her and would give her that future she wanted. Because that *was* what she wanted. Wasn't it?

Ellie leaned back into Paul's chest, knowing he would hold her up. He dropped a kiss on her neck and she felt a shiver run through her. OK, maybe he didn't make her weak at the knees in the same way Serge had, but how much better this was, how much happier and calmer and more supportive. She had made the right decision. It had been worth it, all the things she had given up, for a chance at love, a relationship that worked. She was almost sure of it.

Stay in the UK

'I can't believe how good you look,' sighed Ellie. 'Like you're air-brushed. But you're actually here.'

Michelle laughed. 'Studio makeup artists may as well be air-brushers, love. It's all paint and feathers.'

When she spoke to Ellie, she shed the mid-Atlantic accent she'd adopted for years now. She did look incredible. Her straight dark hair was piled up above her graceful neck, woven through with white flowers. Her white satin dress, with a halter-neck to show off her toned arms, clung to the gym-honed body she spent hours a day achieving. Her skin was the uniform caramel of the year-round Californian resident. And yet outside the window was the gloomy rain-skidded landscape of the Lake District. The nearby lake, which an hour ago had been deep blue, was now grey and forbidding.

'Sorry the weather's so crap,' said Ellie, wrinkling her nose at it.

'Ah well, it's to be expected.'

'You always said you'd get married in Greece, in some little white church.'

'I know. But it seems a bit *Mamma Mia* now, you know? And we already had to do LA and France and here, so.' Michelle peered in the mirror, adjusting a flower over her ear.

The hotel was wildly excited to be hosting the wedding of someone famous, and there were photographers camped outside the gate, even checked in as guests. Michelle didn't seem to mind, happily answering questions and signing autographs every time she crossed the lobby. This was the third wedding ceremony she'd had, including one in LA and one in the Loire, where her new husband, the film director Thierry Artaud, was from. Michelle had always liked French men, and now she'd landed one with his own vineyard and chateau. It had been a whirlwind romance, barely six months from meeting to marriage. Ellie had first learned about it in the pages of a magazine in the hairdresser's, and that made her a little sad, though she was trying to hide it. Michelle had asked her to be bridesmaid, which meant they were still best friends, despite the distance.

Ellie was relieved she hadn't been expected to go to the other two ceremonies, despite her role as chief bridesmaid. In LA that role had been filled by someone from the Marvel Universe. Money, and time, were tight now she'd finally started her rotation at St Thomas's in London, which she had so often walked past when she'd lived there in her twenties. She barely slept or ate these days, let alone find time for dress fittings or manicures. She had hastily done her own in her hotel room that morning, and the results were less than spectacular. In any case, her hands were red and chafed from endless washing, laying on pulses, giving shots, doing stitches, intubating, all the hundreds of actions she did every day. Some nights she didn't make it home, just collapsed in the on-call room for an hour before starting all over again. She snatched showers in the locker room, stuffed down three-day-old sandwiches from the canteen – Michelle with her strict low-carb diet would be appalled, but there was nothing else on offer. Ellie barely had time to ask herself if it was what she wanted. She was just trying to keep her head above water, get through these tough years of training, make

240

it to the calmer waters of being a senior doctor. It would get better. She had to hold onto that, because she'd given up so much for this job. Social life, hobbies, any hope of cardio-vascular fitness or a healthy diet.

And love. Paul had gone to New York without her, and after a few sad emails their contact had dwindled and died. Time was, Michelle would have understood what Ellie was going through right now. Although she was beautiful and successful, she'd had a string of unsatisfactory romances over the years. No one ever seemed wild enough, or strong enough, to keep her. There was the Hollywood actor, fifteen years older, with so much Botox he couldn't move his face. The hotshot indie producer who'd wanted to be pulled around on a lead like a dog. The banker, insanely rich, who'd wanted her to stop acting and have his babies. But then she'd gone to a film festival and been on a panel with an upcoming French director and here she was, getting married.

Michelle was looking at her.

'What?'

'Nothing. That dress really suits you.'

They'd gone shopping in Selfridge's the week before, on a brief break from work that Ellie couldn't really afford to take. Her friend had guided her as to what would suit her – a floral print maxi with long, bell-like sleeves – and then paid for it, waving away Ellie's protests.

'Shame about my hair, face and nails.'

'Don't worry, Annunziata will fix all that. I set aside an hour for you.'

'Isn't she doing your mum?'

Michelle waved a manicured hand. 'Mum hasn't worn

makeup since they phased out Pan Stik; it would be wasted on her. Do it – enjoy.'

The chance to get fixed up by a Hollywood makeup artist? Ellie could hardly believe it. And yet as she sat in the chair, teased and primped, her scalp burned with rollers, her eyes poked at with false lashes, the sweet, peppy Annunziata trying hard to hide her horror that Ellie had not conditioned, manicured or facialed for many years now, she was just glad this wasn't her life. She held her phone in her lap, sending texts to colleagues checking up on various patients. Although the hotel was beautiful, and the day would be spent drinking champagne, eating Michelin-star food, and mingling with the European film elite, part of her would still rather be in A & E, shining her little torch in people's eyes. Seeing the relief on parents' faces as she told them their child didn't have meningitis, watching husbands hold their wives' hands after they'd collapsed at home. The love and the fear she witnessed every day. It was impossible to not let it consume you.

Ellie sighed, looking at her own unfamiliar face in the mirror. She was going to this wedding by herself, of course. There'd been no chance to meet anyone since she'd turned down Paul's offer to go to New York. Tempting as it had been for a moment, it would have been insane. She barely knew him, she couldn't leave her dad, she was about to finally become a doctor. All the same, it was sad to be at a wedding alone, to sit on the singles table, dance by yourself or with any little kids present. And this wedding, of course, had an even bigger pitfall, which Ellie now encountered on her way to Michelle's suite, coated in makeup and her hair in silky barrel waves. As she was dashing down the corridor, a door suddenly opened and she was face to face with Mark.

Mark. She hadn't seen him in years, but he was the same – nondescript suit, hair damp from the shower.

'Oh,' she said.

He was standing upright, no sign of his prosthesis. Michelle said he did so well with it, it was hardly noticeable, but still the guilt snaked through Ellie.

'El! God, you look . . . '

'Oh, don't, I don't suit all this makeup and primping, I know.'

'I was going to say you look beautiful.'

'Oh.'

Mark had never said that to her before. Or anything about her appearance at all. They'd just been best friends, until they weren't, and she had never got over missing him.

She tried to cover the awkwardness with gushing. 'God, how are you? Where's Laura?'

He stiffened. 'She's – we thought it best if she didn't come.'

'Working?' She knew Laura was a consultant in A & E, but consultants could usually get the weekend off for special occasions.

'Um . . . we're just . . . things aren't . . . I probably shouldn't go into it right now. But no, I'm here alone.'

'Me too,' she blurted.

What did that mean? Was he getting divorced? Were she and Mark finally single at the same moment and in the same place, for the first time since they'd been eighteen?

They stood there staring at each other for a while, not saying a word, then Michelle's door opened. 'There you are, come on . . . Oh. Hi Marko.'

He snapped out of his trance. 'Shell! Looking rough as hell, I see.'

'Shut your face.' She hugged him, still in her silk dressing down.

'You're too gorgeous,' said Mark, kissing her cheek. 'Hope you have the most amazing day.'

'Thanks. Let me just steal our pal Ellie away?'

'See you guys later. Best of luck, you're both stunning.'

He set off down the corridor, slinging his jacket over his shoulder, and Michelle gave Ellie a highly expressive look, arching one expensively shaped eyebrow.

'What? I didn't even know he was here.'

'Uh huh.'

'Come on.' Ellie headed into Michelle's room. 'We better finish up here. You're walking down the aisle in half an hour and the photographer wants some shots first.'

Michelle sighed. 'Urgh, why. I get my picture taken all the time for work.'

'Don't be daft, you need pictures of your wedding.'

'Fine. But no hilarious posed shots, promise? I will actually die.'

'Yeah, yeah.'

Ellie shut the door behind them, heart hammering. Mark was here. Alone. What did it mean? What was going to happen? Had she finally looped back to where she was supposed to be, after all these years?

JUNE 2019

Ellie was back in the car, driving towards her mother's house. Not that it would be hers for much longer. It was already on the market, and the final link with Ellie's childhood would be gone. This was probably the last morning she'd wake up in that poky little room, the last time she could have unearthed the box of childhood memories which had sent her into such a tailspin.

So what was happening? Well, she was getting married. When her fiancé had opened the hotel room door to her, she'd garbled some nonsense about just wanting to talk to him, see his face.

'The wedding's been such a rush, you know? Maybe we've lost sight of us.'

He'd looked baffled. He was a straightforward man, not given to overthinking. He would never obsess over paths not taken, other lives he could have lived. The life he had was the one that mattered.

'Oh. As far as I'm concerned, everything's totally fine. I thought you were happy?'

She had been until that morning, hadn't she?

'I don't know,' she'd said, miserably, perched on the edge of his bed. 'I just feel weird.'

He'd sighed, run his hands over his face. 'You're worrying me now.'

'I'm sorry. I just – I have the jitters, I suppose.'

He took her hands in his, sitting opposite her in the hotel-room chair. 'What can I say to make you feel better?'

'Just ... are we doing the right thing? It's been fast, hasn't it.'

He frowned. His fingers were entwined in hers, soft and well kept. He got manicures, even. 'Not really, if you think about it.'

'No. I suppose that's true. I guess maybe I ... imagined I'd feel differently on my wedding day. Not stressed out, fighting with my mum about false eyelashes, you know.'

He smiled, half exasperated. 'You've been to weddings before! It's a big logistical event, not a romantic dream. It's totally normal to feel stressed, babe.'

Was he right? Was she living in a fantasy world, where she and Mark were meant for each other? Even though they'd never actually been together; had gone years without even speaking. Was she just panicking, self-sabotaging, destroying her chance of marriage with the kind and supportive man sitting opposite her, tie undone? It wasn't as if Mark had ever asked to be with her, or told her he had feelings for her. Not for years, anyway.

She tried, 'I just – is this what you want? To be with me?'

Yes, he was kind, and treated her well, and he cared about her, but sometimes she wasn't sure he understood her. What really made her Ellie, in the deep core of herself. She wasn't convinced she could show him all her cracks and flaws, the mistakes she'd made, the paths she'd walked down, the moments of dark and light that added up to her unique self.

'Of course! We'll have a lovely life together, babe. You know that.'

She knew what kind of life that would be. He would work and earn money and she'd hopefully have a baby in a year or two. She'd go with him on corporate dinners and smile and make small talk. They'd have amazing holidays and maybe a second home somewhere and she'd never have to worry about earning because there would always be enough money. She'd be taken care of, she'd have someone coming home at the end of the day for a hug and glass of wine and chat. She would not be alone. But was that what she wanted? Truly?

'You're sure I'll make you happy?'

He had blinked. 'I don't know what else to tell you. I want this. If you don't, well, I really wish you'd said sooner, but please do tell me now. I'm in. I always have been.'

What could she say to that? The concrete promise of love and support and a family, that could not be thrown away because of some vague doubts and worries, because of a half-overheard conversation between Mark and his wife.

'OK. This is just nerves, isn't it?'

He squeezed her hand. 'I'm sure it is. Now come on, babe. It's all paid for, it would be sad to let people down when they've come all this way. Wouldn't it?'

The very idea of cancelling made Ellie feel sick.

'No. That would be awful.'

'All right. So go and get ready, and I'll see you in two hours?'

'Yes. OK. Sorry! I don't know what's wrong with me.'

'It's all right. Pretty normal, I think.'

Ellie had found herself getting back in the car and starting the engine, driving back. She was on the path home now. Easy just to follow it. Put her dress on. Get married. Dance the steps that were laid out for her. What was the alterative? Burn it all down for the faint hope Mark might be available? When he'd never actually told her he wanted her, and all she had to go on was a drunken conversation fourteen years before? When he was married to another woman? It was stupid. It was time to stop chasing alternative futures and grow up. Make a sensible choice. Get on with her life.

CHOICE 9 – APRIL 2014

'So I'll see you later at the restaurant?'

Paul was knotting his tie at the mirror, watching her over his shoulder as Ellie lay in bed, half-asleep.

'Mm.'

She'd forgotten the name of the restaurant, but it would probably be in the shared online calendar he'd set up for them. She knew without checking it would be expensive, trendy, probably with square plates on which sat tiny dollops of food, shaved and foamed and sprinkled.

When they first moved to New York, Ellie throwing aside her carefully laid plans to become a doctor and abandoning her career and family, she had usually woken up when he did, at five. Jet lag made this easy, and she'd loved the slow creep of the rosy dawn over the river, the way it set fire one by one to the windows of the skyscrapers. While he went to work, she'd wander the streets, popping in and out of interesting little shops, going to museums she'd been dreaming of for years, hunting down the best food in the city. But that had worn off, and nowadays she struggled to find a purpose in New York.

She could get a job, technically, but not in medicine

without a lengthy retraining process. She'd always told herself they might return to the UK after a year or two, though it was coming up to two and Paul showed no signs of wanting to leave. She'd only been back to the UK once in that time, for Christmas, a rushed few days of visits to family. She hadn't even made Michelle's UK wedding ceremony, after a freak snowstorm had grounded all the flights from the Eastern Seaboard. Michelle had been unbothered, and Ellie and Paul had gone to the extremely glamorous LA ceremony instead, sitting next to an actual Oscar winner at the outdoor service in Malibu. She was glad in a way that she'd missed the UK one, because Mark and Laura certainly would have been there, and seeing them would only have stirred up trouble, old memories, hopes for a life that didn't exist. This was her life now. She'd moved to New York instead of taking up her training post at St Thomas's, gambled on a year or two's adventure in a new country, the chance to finish her book. She had chosen this, the opportunity to live in a shining new place, and she just needed to find her feet a little.

It had been a whirlwind time in New York, eating out almost every night, visiting jazz clubs and museums and art openings, weekends upstate, holidays all over the US. New friends, the non-working wives of Paul's colleagues mostly, who only wanted to brunch and go to the gym and complain about their nannies. They hardly hid their discomfort that Ellie and Paul didn't have kids, and weren't even married. It had been strange when they first came out here, tied together by official bureaucracy, despite barely knowing each other. The last month before travelling had been frantic with packing and organising, trips to the American Embassy in London, queuing up to get their paperwork stamped. Then the flight over – first class, which had utterly overwhelmed Ellie, who kept putting the little toiletries and bottles of champagne into her bag, until Paul gently reminded her there would be plenty more when they got there. The limo ride to the new apartment, all her senses frazzled by the smell and noise of the city, the famous skyline burned into her eyes. When they arrived, Paul had unpacked his hand luggage – the rest was being shipped over – showered, then gone straight to sleep on the other side of the giant bed, planting a chaste kiss on her head. Twitchy with jet lag and confusion, Ellie had lain awake wondering if she'd made a terrible mistake. But then, choosing the sizzling passion, as with Serge, had never worked either. Paul was a good man, and a safe choice.

Things between them had now settled into a comfortable routine, and even if they were in no danger of disturbing their neighbours with their chemistry, she knew he thought she was beautiful and smart and funny, and having that after so many years of bad boyfriends and loneliness was like sinking into a warm bath at the end of a cold and rainy day. She was lucky. They got on well, enjoyed the same things for the most part, and even if he wasn't a deep thinker, perhaps that was good for her – someone who didn't obsess and worry about the past and the future and the lives left unlived. Someone who just existed in the moment. In this reality.

Paul had finished getting ready now, his tie tied, jacket on. His car service would be downstairs, and the doorman would hold the door open for him, and once he'd travelled to his office in downtown Manhattan, another doorman would open that door for him. Life could be easy here, if you had money. All the rough edges smoothed away. Ellie was starting to miss those edges, though. Cooking, shopping for food. Mopping the floor. Being on hold for hours trying to sort out prescriptions for her dad. They had top-notch private healthcare here, and it was like going to a spa every time you had a doctor's appointment. She felt an ache in her chest when she thought of her dad, alone in his care home. He'd wonder why she'd stopped visiting.

He picked up his keys. 'What are you going to do today?'

'Oh. I don't know. Gym, I guess.'

She'd been planning a yoga class, even though she found it excruciating, her restless mind turning over and over as the instructor encouraged them to clear their heads and breathe. Like it was so easy.

'Hmm.'

'What?' she snapped, tetchier than she'd meant to be. She hadn't slept well, the endless roar and honking horns of the city penetrating even to their top-floor sanctuary.

'I just think you need something else to do. Not work, necessarily, but – something. What about the book?'

'I'm working on the book. It's not that easy, I can't just churn it out.' But was she really working on it? It had been going so well when she lived in Paris, words flowing out of her. Then she'd fallen for Serge and, somehow, it was as if a vital joist or hinge inside her had snapped, and she'd never been able to find that again. She had tried, since moving here, but somehow the long empty days seemed to suck the motivation out of her. But he was right. If she couldn't finish her book

252

here, it would have been a waste of everything, all the sacrifices she'd made with her family and career. She made an effort to sit up, smile. She was aware that, with his punishingly long hours, he almost always saw her in her pyjamas, with tousled hair and no makeup. 'I'll look into it today.'

'Great! I really think you need a way to fill your time. Maybe that will help you settle a bit.' He leaned over to kiss her sweaty forehead. 'Money's no object, of course. If you want to get help or take a class or something.'

He meant well, saying that. He genuinely didn't mind paying for everything. But all the same, she felt like she was worth less than him, a kept woman. Even her mother, of a very different generation, had always earned her own money.

'Have a good day,' she said, forcing a smile.

Once he'd gone, the apartment felt big and cold, chilled by the constant air conditioning. They were so high up the windows didn't even open, and often she felt sealed off from the city below. She made herself get up and turned on the shower full-blast, scouring herself with American-style water pressure. She picked out an outfit that she imagined a writer in New York might wear – wide-legged jeans, a velvet jacket, a floppy hat she'd never actually worn as she felt silly in it. Sunglasses, a silk scarf Michelle had given her for her last birthday. She put on mascara and blusher – New York women were so groomed she felt like a British scruff next to them. Then she set out into the city, endlessly in motion, full of infinite possibility, to find some kind of path for herself.

With no particular agenda, she decided to head towards NYU, which was in a pretty leafy part of the city called

Greenwich Village. With its red-brick buildings and shaded cafés, it almost felt like Europe. Ellie was constantly shocked by how new everything was in America. Some of the oldest buildings in the city were considerably less old than rooms she had slept in at Oxford, places she'd walked past with barely a second glance. She bought a large iced coffee, too big and too expensive like everything here, and had to throw away half of it, feeling guilty about the plastic and the waste of money. Not that she had to worry about money now, if she stayed with Paul. If she married him, as he had begun to hint, she'd never have to work a day in her life. She'd have staff, cleaners, a nanny if they had a child. A lovely, blessed, glittering life, and with a man who was nice, too, and down to earth despite his great success, who loved nothing more than eating crisps in front of the American version of *The Office*, going to baseball games and drinking beer from plastic cups.

So why did she get a grip of fear in her stomach when she thought about it? Maybe because settling down, having a child, might mean finally giving up on a rewarding career of her own. She was thirty-three. If she didn't get back to medicine soon it might be too late. But writing – you were never too old to write, were you? She stopped at a notice-board outside the door of the college, a flyer pinned down. A man's face, unsmiling in black and white, clearly artistic from the way he rested his head in one hand. *James Diaz*, it said. *Learn writing from the National Book Award finalist. Eight-week course.* Quickly, she scanned the text. It started on the fifteenth. That was – that was tomorrow, wasn't it? Over the years Ellie had often spent chunks of time googling writing courses, never going as far as to sign up for anything. Many times she had just missed the start, or convinced herself it was too late, that she'd need a run up to it. But what if she didn't? What if this was a moment she seized? Paul had even suggested taking a class, and this could be the impetus she needed to get back on track.

She stood there on the sun-dappled pavement, the cool young students moving around her, trying to decide. Every instinct told her to run, that she wasn't ready to show her work to people, let alone an award-nominated author. But where had that attitude ever got her? Her eye was caught by a map of the campus, showing the different buildings. A red circle proclaimed *You Are Here*, and it stirred some memory in Ellie, something Mark had said maybe, years ago. A sign. Almost forcing herself, she went inside to the reception desk. A woman sat behind it, dunking a doughnut into coffee as she studied her computer screen. It would surely be full. Or the sign-up date would have passed.

'Excuse me?' The woman looked up. 'Um – the writing course, the one with the flyer? Is it – would I still be able to join?'

The doughnut was set down, and some slow typing ensued, with sugary fingers.

Finally, the woman said: 'Looks like you're in luck, hon. We just had a drop-out.'

Oh! Like it was meant to be.

'Amazing! Thank you!'

'That'll be eight hundred dollars. And fill in these forms.'

The woman passed over a clipboard with a large bundle of papers, which ordinarily would have been something Ellie would shrink from, but she didn't even mind. Paul would be so happy when she told him she'd already sorted her life out, starting from tomorrow. Once she'd filled in the many, many forms and paid the fee, Ellie set off in search of a stationery shop, filled with buoyant energy and the hope of new beginnings.

The next afternoon, Ellie was at her desk in a small, slightly dingy room in the university, with grey plastic seats and Formica tables arranged around the three sides of the room. At the top, a table for the teacher, an overhead projector, an already obsolete bit of technology. Her enthusiasm had been slightly dented by her mother's reaction, when she'd told her during their dutiful weekly call.

'More study? You're going to be the most qualified unemployed person in the world, Eleanor.'

Ouch. 'It's just an extension class, Mum. No qualifications – just to learn.'

Her mother sniffed, and the sound reached Ellie across miles of ocean. 'Don't think you need to take a class to know how to put pen to paper. Would you not be better just getting on with it?'

Ellie counted to three. It didn't work.

'Can you just be supportive? It isn't easy, leaving everything behind at home, you know. Stepping away from medicine. It feels like so much pressure to finish this book.'

Her mother softened. 'I know. But you'll have the time of your life. New York! I'd be over like a shot if I could.'

'You can! I keep telling you.'

Flights to New York weren't expensive, and Ellie had several times offered to pay for them as a gift. Paul earned so much she never had to think of the price of anything. She was very lucky, she knew that. Luckier than 99 per cent of people on the planet. And yet it was a strange sensation, to move so easily through life, everything paid for and organised and delivered to her door. Without the friction of living, she felt like she was sliding, unmoored. Adrift.

'Oh, I can't leave your dad.'

Ellie's mother was now in a serious relationship with Nigel from the garden centre, and yet she visited her husband every few days, and hadn't divorced him, and wouldn't move in with Nigel despite him asking, despite them having adopted a dog together, an unhinged lurcher called, of all things, Popkin. Was that a different kind of love, from a deep and solid place Ellie couldn't even imagine? She tried to picture how she'd feel if Paul got ill, if she had to take care of him, if he didn't know her any more. If he had an accident or got cancer, or later on, dementia like her dad. She couldn't. The future seemed like a blank to her. He was never cruel to her, never cheated, he held her at night in the vast bed, and brought home flowers and gifts, took her to nice places, but sometimes as they faced each other across a table in a fancy restaurant, she could feel the conversation running dry between them, and a small tick of worry set off in her stomach. Perhaps she wanted too much. She had idealised her relationship with Mark, a teenage friendship, based on all those years when they were kids, and then one night together in her bed. It wasn't enough to know how they would have been together. They'd made each other laugh hysterically at seventeen, yes, but that was almost twenty years ago. Perhaps this was a grown-up relationship, holidays with each other's families, collecting your dry-cleaning, sorting the recycling.

Her mother then went on to say, archly, 'I'd come over if there was a reason!'

Hurriedly, Ellie shut her down. 'Mm. OK, I have to run, need to sort some stuff for tomorrow.'

She knew what her mother meant by a reason. Marriage, or a baby, in either order. And the thought of both those things filled Ellie with utter terror.

She put her worries aside now, as the door to the classroom opened and in came a man she recognised from the poster. He was about forty, with some grey in his beard and dark hair, wearing a tweed jacket, jeans, red Converses and a long woollen scarf, though it was hot outside. He was carrying a man satchel and an old paperback shoved into the pocket of his jacket.

'Hello everyone,' he said, with a soft Boston accent.

Sometimes in life you see a person, and something inside you, a switch you didn't even know was off, snaps into place, and you think – *oh. There you are.* This happened to Ellie as the teacher, James Diaz, presumably, caught her eye – his were hazel, with thick lashes – and a jolt went through her, as if she'd been in a trance and had abruptly come out of it to find the world sharp and bright. Confused, she rummaged in her new notebook and uncapped her pen. The other students were an intimidating mix of trendy New Yorkers, either in suits and designer gear straight from the office, or hipsters in clear-rimmed classes and baseball caps, wearing the same kind of ratty sports gear Ellie had dressed in back in the 1990s, to the despair of her mother.

James Diaz was talking. 'Welcome, everyone. Welcome to the first step in your literary career, which who knows, might end up with a published novel, a major award, a million readers, the *New York Times* bestseller list. That's what's so exciting about fiction. You start with nothing but your paper or pen – or maybe your MacBook' – he nodded to one of the Wall Street guys, who smiled ruefully over the lid of his shiny silver machine – 'and you add in nothing but your imagination, and miracles happen. I've seen it a dozen times, and it can happen for you too. Let's start by hearing about your work.'

He began on the opposite side of the class to Ellie, perching on the desk and nodding as people rambled on haltingly about their ideas. His head was propped on his fist like in the poster. As Ellie switched off from the drawling American accents, she felt something she recognised from years ago in Paris, when her loneliness had alchemised into focus, as the words of her book seemingly fell from the air into her head. Excitement. Hope. It was possible. She could always change her life, switch onto another track like the confusing Subway trains here. She could be a writer.

It was her turn. She felt absurdly nervous, clearing her throat. 'Um, hi, I'm Ellie . . . '

'English!'

'Um, yeah.'

'That's amazing. Land of poets. Welcome, Ellie. What's your idea?'

'Um, well, it's something I wrote a bit of a few years back. About time, and choices, and parallel universes.' She looked him in the eye and something happened to her again, the perspective of the world tilted a few degrees. 'It's a love story,' she said, gazing at him.

And he looked right back and said, 'I can't wait to read it.'

On her way out of class that night, Ellie stopped outside the main entrance, looking surreptitiously around her. The poster was out of date now, surely, since the class had begun. No one would miss it. She ripped it from the railings and stuffed it in her bag, folding away the picture of James Diaz's face to gaze at later on, when she was alone.

The class lasted for eight weeks, and every moment of the three-hour sessions was precious to Ellie. Everything James said was so wise, so hypnotic in his soft buttery voice. He was so inspiring, the way he'd worked himself up from a two-bedroom flat with his four siblings, to become a famous writer and lecturer at NYU. Her brain filled up with ideas and images, characters and lines and scenes. The book was almost writing itself, as if laid on out train tracks stretching into the distance. Ellie spent the rest of her time scribbling in notebooks or on the pink MacBook Paul had bought her, sitting in coffee shops or at the table in their apartment, looking out over the city.

After class, a group of them had started going to the student bar around the corner, a dive with sticky floors and 90s music that Ellie loved, because it reminded her of the Blacksmith's Arms back home in Longton. And Mark. But she was doing well not thinking about him, because her thoughts were filled with James Diaz. She had tracked down all three of his books, even the early one that was out of print, and devoured them, plus the short story he'd had published in the *New Yorker* and all the articles he'd written. Three weeks in a row she had subtly angled to sit beside him in the booth they always took, but been pushed aside by Ilana, a harsh-voiced hipster girl who worked on a 'podcast' – whatever that was – or Jennifer, who was something big in tech and wore men's suits, disturbingly sexy with her long blonde hair. They were both at least six years younger than Ellie, and she'd never felt so frumpy. She had put on weight since moving to America – there was so much food, and the portions so huge, and everything came with bacon or cheese or maple syrup, or all three – and her clothes had become baggier, mumsier. Loose jeans and dresses and floral prints. Consciously, she upped her game. Wore makeup to class. Sought out unusual pieces in vintage shops, 1970s jumpsuits and bell-bottom jeans and gypsy tops. She didn't want to interrogate herself too closely about why she was doing all this. Just a crush. Just fantasy, that was all. Nothing bad. Nothing to hurt Paul.

Then, finally, after the very last class, she managed to hustle her way – without appearing to, of course – to sit by his side. His tweed jacket was brushing her arm as they drank their bottled beers, and under the table she could feel the faint pressure of his thigh in the cramped booth. What was she doing? She had a boyfriend, a serious one. It was just a little infatuation. She admired his writing, that was all. And he was handsome, yes. He had charisma. Her eye fell on his left hand. No ring. Not that this meant anything.

He turned to her suddenly. 'And how did our resident Brit find the course?'

'Oh! Brilliant, really. I've learned so much.'

'Brilliant,' he echoed. 'Such a great word. I really liked your pages, Ellie.'

She had submitted some the week before, as everyone did throughout the course.

'Oh! Really?'

'Really. I can tell you've got some experience with this.'

'I wrote most of the book a few years back, actually.'

'Why didn't you finish?'

'Oh I don't know. I fell in love, gave it up.' It was the second time she'd said the word *love* while looking in his eyes, and it made her dizzy. 'Usual story.'

'I can relate. You should keep going, you really have talent.' Casually, he sipped from his beer. 'You know, I'm going to a literary party next week. A book launch for a friend. You'd be welcome to come with, if you like. Good chance to meet people in the industry.'

Her heart was hammering. 'Really? What day is it?'

Was he asking her out? Was this the time to mention she had a boyfriend, one she lived with and whose job allowed her to be here in New York in the first place?

'Thursday.'

She was supposed to go away with Paul the day after, for a weekend upstate somewhere. Surely there could be no harm in attending one party. Networking, really. In fact, it would almost be irresponsible not to.

'I'd love to. That's so kind of you.'

'Sure thing.' He tipped his beer at her, then turned to talk to Ilana, who'd been straining to hear their conversation with jealous eyes.

Ellie was elated, terrified, jumpy. She told herself it was nothing. She knew it wasn't.

*

The next week moved with agonising slowness. She felt she should spend the time writing so as not to feel such a fraud at the party, so each day she went to a coffee shop and sat in the window, self-conscious with her laptop, but nothing came to her. All she could do was worry about James and the party. Could it really be that he was interested in her? How to drop Paul into the conversation, without it seeming pointed? If she was honest, she didn't really want to. It wasn't right, was it? After her experience with Mark, the all-consuming guilt she'd felt for years now, Ellie knew she wasn't cut out for romantic intrigue. She didn't want to hurt Paul, who'd only ever treated her like a queen, and on a purely practical note, she couldn't even stay in this country if he broke up with her. But on the other hand, this could be her big chance. There'd be agents at the party, James had said. Ellie could hardly let herself dream of that, being signed by a big New York agent. She'd spent so long imagining her own book on the shelf under *W*, and it now felt almost within her grasp.

That morning, she was awake before Paul, sick with nerves. Coming into the living room, he was surprised to find her on the sofa, wrapped in a blanket in the grey morning light.

'You OK?'

'Couldn't sleep.'

He raised his eyebrows. Ellie could always sleep in the mornings, even after years of dragging herself from bed at six for medical school. 'Nothing serious I hope?'

'No. Just having thoughts about the book, I suppose.'

'That's great!' He ambled to the kitchen, scratching his

263

head. She looked him over. Trim body kept in shape with rigorous dieting and daily gym visits. Expensive boxers and T-shirt. Firing up a coffee machine that cost more than Ellie would have earned in a month, had she stuck with medicine. 'You'll be finished soon, then?'

'Um . . . I don't know. It's not really a linear thing.'

'Right, right, of course.'

She blurted: 'I've been invited to this party tonight. A book launch. The teacher from class, he . . . invited some of us.' That was a lie.

Paul was nodding. 'Oh, great. I have that client dinner, so that suits.'

'But – we're going away in the morning. Won't that be a pain?'

'Not unless you're planning to stay out till five doing shots!'

He was joking, but she had no idea what publishing parties were like. Or what James Diaz might expect by her acceptance of the invitation. The thought of it made her whole body jittery with fear, or excitement, or some combination of the two. She told herself firmly it was just a career decision. But looking at the back of Paul's head, where the hair was receding despite his expensive barbershop appointments, she felt a wave of tenderness and guilt. This wasn't just about writing and she knew it.

'I was thinking . . . maybe I shouldn't go, though.'

'Why not?'

'Oh, I don't know. They're all young and hip.'

'El, you're thirty-three. That's hardly an OAP.'

'I know, but . . . I'll feel out of place. And I haven't packed yet.'

He looked baffled, as well he might, when she had the whole day free to pack for a weekend trip.

'Also the book is so nearly done, it might derail me a bit. Maybe I should stay in and just take a run at it?'

'Whatever you decide, I'm sure it will be fine, babe.'

That was Paul all over. He just made decisions, whether big or small, and never agonised over the potential consequences – the idea that even a tiny choice, like going to a party or not, could have profound implications for the rest of your life. Maybe Ellie should try being more like him. It surely wouldn't make a difference whatever she did tonight.

Go to the party

Ellie barely ate all day the day of the party, and by six was jittery. She'd been dressed for hours in what she'd finally settled on, a long 1970s dress with silver jewellery. It might be too much though – she'd never been to a book launch. Perhaps they were casual affairs, or more business wear. God, she had no idea.

She had arranged to meet James at a coffee place on the Lower East Side, near the bookshop where the launch was to be held, and got there far too early. She imagined what he'd see as he approached her, and tried to pose as if deep in thought, writing important words. He was five minutes late, then eight, and she was way too overdressed for this café where everyone was in ripped jeans and sweatshirts from the 1980s, and she was sweating in fear, and then she saw him cross the road. He was in his usual tweed jacket with his leather satchel, and she knew she was really dressed all wrong.

'Hey!' he said.

'Hey.'

'You look nice.'

'Oh, thank you. It's a bit much I guess! I didn't know what people wear to these things.'

'No, no. You'll really stand out. Shall we? It's just round the corner.'

Walking into the launch with him was a high point for Ellie. People turned to wave and blow him kisses, and copies of one of his own books were piled high on a side table, and she was by his side, people glancing at her and wondering who she was. This could be my life, she thought. The writer's wife. It was a thought that stopped her breath, even in the privacy of her own head. So stupid – this was just a party, that was all. He was her teacher. He was just being encouraging.

The night raced by. She was talking to a tall woman with braids about authentic voices in publishing. She joked with an older man in a red suit about whether Henry James was influenced by British literature or vice versa. A very young man in ripped jeans chatted her up over the hummus, not that Ellie was eating anything. She was too excited, and didn't want garlic breath because ... well, not for any particular reason. Instead, she drank: white wine then red and then some champagne that had appeared mysteriously.

From time to time James appeared and grasped her elbow, sending shock waves through her. 'OK?'

'Oh yeah, I'm having a great time.'

He smiled. 'I can see. You fit right in here.'

Ellie had forgotten she was supposed to be networking, until he stopped a thin, elegant woman in a grey trouser suit and old-fashioned glasses, who was passing by.

'Margot! How are you?'

She had a husky Southern accent. 'James! Baby, hi.' They exchanged kisses.

'This is Ellie. One of my students, very promising.'

'Oh, another?' said the woman, lightly. 'Pleased to meet you. What are you working on?'

Thankfully, after his tuition, Ellie could reel off the 'pitch' for her novel.

Margot's groomed eyebrows went up. 'That actually sounds very commercial. Here.' She produced a card seamlessly, as if it had already been in her hand. 'Think of me when you're ready to submit.'

She departed into the crowd, waggling her manicured fingers at James. Ellie stared at the embossed name, speechless. *Margot Dunning, literary agent. DDK.*

'Did that . . . just happen?'

James laughed. 'I know it seems like a magical world you can't get into, but it's just people, and they're always looking for the next big thing. It could be you. Why not? Come with me, I happen to know they have a bottle of brandy hidden behind the literary theory books.'

Later, Ellie was perched on a book ladder as the party wound down. James was saying goodbye to yet another woman, this one curvy and beautiful, with red curls, in a satin blouse and pencil skirt. He was holding her arms, laughing, but a trifle nervously. Ellie couldn't hear what they were saying – the woman kept throwing glances her way. What did it mean? Coupled with Margot's comment earlier: *another*. What did that mean? Was he a womaniser? That was the last thing she needed, after how much Serge had hurt her. He must be, with his looks and talent. Why wouldn't he be, if he was single? It didn't mean he wasn't looking for something more. And it was her he'd brought here, her he was going to leave with.

You have a boyfriend, Ellie, her conscience nudged her. She drowned it out with another gulp of brandy. He came over to her now, the red-haired woman going out the door, her shoulders slightly slumped.

'Sorry. People always drink too much at these things.'

Ellie had drunk too much as well. 'I really need to finish my book, huh.'

He drained his glass of champagne. 'You really do. So. Where now?'

It was after eleven already. Ellie hadn't looked at her phone, but she knew there would be several messages from Paul on it. He'd likely gone to bed already.

'Now? It's late.'

He spread his arms. 'Haven't you heard this is the city that doesn't sleep? There's a great dive bar round the corner.'

She hesitated. Paul wouldn't be happy – they were leaving first thing for their weekend away. But on the other hand she had no friends in the city and she'd not been out for the night in almost two years.

'All right then.'

'Great!' It seemed natural, as they walked, waving good-bye to the cardiganed bookstore owner, who was chucking bottles in the recycling, for him to tuck her hand under his arm, holding her fingers in the other. 'Not far. So tell me more about you, Ellie. Now you're not my student any more.'

Her pulse raced. Did he mean ...? 'Well, I grew up in England, moved here about two years ago.'

'How come?'

'Ummm.' Oh God, this was the moment to say it. Really, she should have mentioned it weeks ago. 'Came with a man.' Why had she phrased it like that, and not 'my boyfriend'? She knew why.

'Ah. And now?'

'He's still ... yeah. We came for his job. Finance, you know.'

'OK.' He didn't let go of her hand, however. 'Happy?'

'Oh God, what a question. Is anyone ever happy?' She forced a laugh. 'What about you?'

'Similar, I suppose. I live with someone. An editor, in fact. High-powered. Older. Discovered me when I was a fledgling author.'

Maybe they were the same then, trapped to some degree in relationships they couldn't leave without upsetting their lives. Not that she felt trapped! She loved Paul. Didn't she? And yet she was here.

'Right, I see.'

'Doesn't actually pay all that much, being a literary ingénu. I had a big book deal, but that was five years ago, and there's tax and agent fees and all that. Something to be aware of.'

She didn't want to talk about money. The fact was, they were both in relationships. Both perhaps vaguely unsatisfied.

'He's lovely,' she said. 'My ... the man.'

269

'Well, so is she.' His smile twisted. 'You can go home to him, Ellie. I won't drag you into something you don't want to do. You've been drinking, and you were my student until last week. So.'

Another decision. She stood on the New York street, the night air warm and clammy, the blare of sirens and roar of the city all around her. It was just a small thing. Another drink. No big deal. Networking, she told herself. That's all it was. For her career. Paul would understand, when she explained. She just had to choose.

'Paul? Wake up.'

'Um?' He rolled over, blinking in the bedside light she'd snapped on. 'Ellie, what time is it? I was asleep!'

He was annoyed and had every right to be. She'd rolled into the apartment at one in the morning. Booze was seeping out of her pores now – beer, wine, spirits, the lot. It was years since she'd drunk that much, and on no dinner, too. Shame seeped out of her as well. She'd made a fool of herself, probably said some stupid things, allowed herself to flirt with another man.

'Look, I'm sorry it's so late,' she burst out. 'It was just – such a good opportunity. An agent gave me her card, even.'

He was fumbling for his phone. 'Well, that's good, but why did you wake me up? I'm seeing my trainer at six.'

That was him all over. Early starts, healthy exercise, low-fat meals. Controlled. Safe. After the trainer he'd drive her out of the city for a romantic weekend. She knew exactly how it would go. Some beautiful location. Michelin-star food. Walks in the woods in their expensive matching hiking boots. Predictable sex. Suddenly she could not bear the idea of it all being set out for her.

'We need to talk,' said Ellie. 'I'm sorry, Paul, but it really can't wait.'

A week later, Ellie was waiting in the lobby of the building, having just packed up all her belongings ready to head to JFK. She had too many cases and was worried about excess baggage. It was terrible how you got used to having money, having the edges of life smoothed away, forgetting that it wasn't even your money to spend. Ever since ending things with Paul, telling him she wasn't happy and had to go back to the UK, to her own life, she'd walked away from that world. He'd been crushed, of course, and the look on his face as he sat up in bed was one that haunted Ellie late at night as she tried to get to sleep.

After that terrible moment, Paul had gone to a hotel for a few days while she organised her trip home. He'd offered to pay for first-class flights, and get her a car to the airport, but Ellie had refused. She had to start standing on her own two feet, so she was getting the AirTrain, but she did need a bit of help lugging her stuff to the station, and here he was, ten minutes late again.

'Hi, James.'

James Diaz shook his head at her. 'Can't believe you're going, just like that.'

'I know. But I have to.'

She had of course turned to James Diaz for help. It wasn't entirely because of him that she'd broken up with Paul, but that had been a factor. After their night out, drunken and

271

foolish as it was, she just knew that this was how she wanted to feel about her partner. Alive, and tingly, and like there wasn't enough time to say everything she wanted to tell him. She'd never felt that about Paul, even at the start. But James Diaz was not the man for her, either, much as she might wish this was her life, in love with another writer in New York. Visions of typing side by side in bed in the mornings. Reading each other's work. Going to launches and lectures together. That could never happen, because for one thing he had a partner. For another, Ellie had no legal right to be in this country. So she was leaving, making a sensible choice for once.

As he lifted one of her big holdalls, she grasped the handle of her wheely suitcase, shouldered her backpack. Not much to show for almost two years in this city. At the train station, he folded her into a hug.

'Um – take care.'

'I bet you'll win the bloody Booker Prize now,' she said, disengaging before she cried.

It took all her strength not to kiss him, press her face into his neck and breathe him in.

'I bet *you* will. Seriously, you are good. Don't let it slide again, OK?'

Like she had with Serge. Falling in love seemed to dry her up creatively. But the book, nestled on the hard drive of her laptop in her backpack, backed up onto several USB sticks and Dropbox and Google docs, was almost done, and no one could take that away from her.

Ellie hauled her cases to the platform and waited for the train. As she headed away towards the airport, the city

272

receding from her, she was thinking about the book. That was the future. Not another man, another failed love affair. It was time to finally focus on herself.

Not go to the party

'Sssh, shh now. It's OK.'

Ellie rocked the baby back and forth, back and forth, but the wailing didn't stop. And why should it? Things were far from OK. Across the Atlantic, her home country had just voted to leave the EU. Thinking of the ease of her time in Paris, able to travel and work as she wanted, Ellie's heart was heavy, and she worried about food shortages, the economy tanking. Her mother had become increasingly panicked as the referendum approached. She'd joined Facebook at last, and seemed to spend all her time reading political threads on it, getting into arguments. Most of her friends were keen on Brexit and, clearly, so were lots of other people in the country. Ellie felt sad for her son, who'd lose all those freedoms associated with a European passport, and her unborn niece or nephew. Katie was due in October, and it was amazing to think Alan would be a father, that their children would have a cousin so close in age. Assuming Ellie moved back to the UK, of course.

The door to the bedroom opened and Paul came out, rubbing his eyes. 'What time is it?'

'Three. They're calling it for Leave.'

'I have a meeting at seven.'

'Well, I can't exactly force him to shut up,' she snapped. A short pause, a space full of hurt between them. 'Sorry.'

'I'm sorry. Here, let me try.' He took the baby from her, rocked the little boy against his chest. 'There, there. Ssssh now, Sam. Shh.' He'd chosen the name, his grandfather's. Sam Sanderson, that was Ellie's son's name. She had picked neither, and sometimes felt she'd given birth to a stranger. Like a medieval queen, married off to produce an heir, non-existent in herself.

Ellie and Paul had got engaged two years before, after the weekend trip to upstate New York had proven to be a proposal. Leading her into the beautiful, luxurious wooden cabin, with the floor to ceiling glass windows over the woods, the hot tub and fire pit on their private deck, the champagne on ice and flowers everywhere, he had dropped to one knee and asked her, snapping open a blue Tiffany box with a giant diamond inside.

Ellie's first reaction had been to panic and cringe – he looked so silly, kneeling on the uneven wooden floor, staring up at her. And it was too soon, she wasn't ready. But how could she say no, when he was so good to her? This was what she wanted, someone to call her own. A husband, a partner. A family. Who could say no to a proposal like that, from a man you loved and had lived with for almost two years? Who offered security, love, happiness? Of course she'd said yes. They'd got married in the Caribbean the year after, Ellie in a white strappy dress, her bare feet burning on the sand. Michelle and her director husband had flown in from a shoot in Fiji, and Ellie's mother and Nigel had come, along with Alan and Katie, married themselves for a year by then. Verity, heavily pregnant in London, sent her apologies, and Camilla had just given birth to twins so was similarly indisposed.

There was no one else she'd wanted at her wedding. Mark of course would not come. It would have been strange to invite him, given they hadn't spoken in years. She was married now – she'd chosen her path. And like clockwork, within a year of marriage, Sam had arrived. Ellie was a mother. It seemed so surreal. Her own mother was surprisingly doting, given what a hands-off parent she'd been herself, and kept hinting that Ellie and Paul should move back to the UK, but Ellie didn't know if they ever would. Paul had friends here, squash buddies, colleagues, and she had their wives, plus the mums she'd met at her antenatal class. She was one of them now, a non-working, rich Upper East Side wife. As pleasant as Paul was, he was the one who set the path of their lives, determined where they'd live.

Her novel had been forgotten as soon as Paul proposed, Ellie's time slowly subsumed into planning the wedding, buying an apartment in a fancy building, then having the baby. Being a writer was just a pipe dream anyway, and likely James Diaz had only encouraged her because he fancied her. She had never contacted him again after returning from the weekend upstate, avoiding the few messages he'd sent until it all petered out. She was relieved she hadn't gone to the launch party after all, because she knew she might have done something she'd have regretted. That was a glimpse of a different life, which now would not happen. She was a wife, she had a baby. She didn't need to work, because Paul paid for the apartment in a doorman building, the car, the maid service, the gym and yoga memberships he'd gently encouraged her into, their regular holidays, their meals out when they could get a babysitter. She should be happy. And she was. She *was* happy.

Paul soon passed the baby back to her and went to bed. On TV, Ellie watched her home country tear itself apart, and wondered how close things had been to going another way. The pundits all said the result had been so narrow, they'd almost called it for the other side before it seemed to swing back. It had rained heavily in London that day, apparently, and that held people back from voting, unable to get home on delayed trains. Or maybe they'd been complacent. Everyone had assumed the Remain side would win, and so perhaps just enough people had decided not to vote, after a longer than usual journey home, or not to bother waiting in the rain, and history went one way rather than another, and here it was. The world had changed for ever. She felt the US going the same way, with the presidential election approaching in November. Radicalisation, the rise of the right, everyone angry and polarised and numb.

Despairing of sleep, she got her laptop and indulged in her favourite pointless pastime, surfing the internet. Twitter, endless spirals of fear and rage. Facebook, people she knew arguing with each other. It was all so grim. What kind of world was this for Sam, now grizzling quietly against her chest? She was about to log off when she saw a red dot that indicated a Facebook message. She clicked on it and had to stare at the name for a few seconds until it sank in. It couldn't be. Mark Grant. Years since he'd been in touch.

Hi. That was all it said. She could see he was online, across the ocean and in a different time zone. Mark was out there, awake, and waiting to talk to her.

*

It was dizzying, how easy it was to fall back into communication with Mark. It was the baby, he said, that had prompted him to get in touch. Despite the years and gulf between them, he couldn't not congratulate her on her first child (though her wedding had passed without a word). After the first message, she stayed up most of the night chatting with him, while Sam slept fretfully against her chest. When Paul got up and left for work at five, Ellie was dozing on the sofa, and hurriedly shut down her laptop so Paul wouldn't see the hours' worth of messages, dissecting Brexit, then moving on to filling each other in on the last nine years or so of life. He didn't mention Laura. She didn't mention Paul.

Ellie felt like a deep-sea diver after weeks of no sleep. Paul never did the night feeds, since he was working and she was breastfeeding, so sleep had to be dribbled out, an hour here, forty minutes there. At lunchtime she took Sam's buggy – stroller – down in the lift – elevator – ignoring the snooty older couple who rolled their eyes at his screaming, and out into the grey day, a chill wind coming off the river. She walked him down the pavement – sidewalk – to the nearby park.

She had no idea what happened next, and no time to wonder about it. Her mind was on Mark, thinking with a warm burn of excitement of the messages they'd sent all night, his words waiting for her when she woke up, across the world in a different time zone. Could it really have happened, she and Mark back in touch at last? So maybe she wasn't paying attention, or she'd forgotten what side of the road they drove on here. Or maybe she was just tired. Whatever the cause, she stepped out into the road, half-dead with tiredness, and knew in an instant she'd made a mistake. There was a squeal of brakes, and every instinct in her made her push the buggy far ahead of her, to the safety of the opposite pavement. But there was no time to do it for herself, and she turned her head to see a blur of yellow taxi, and a terrible noise, and she was lifted up and thrown, all the air out of her, and everything went black, for ever.

JUNE 2019

'Oh, you're ready, are you? Well, you're lucky you can do it so quickly.'

Ellie ignored her mother, who was livid about her disappearing act and the appropriation of her car. None of that mattered, because today was her wedding day. It was going to happen. She'd finally be a bride, after years of attending other people's weddings. Not Mark's, of course, but Verity's, Camilla's, Michelle's in LA that time, even Alan's for goodness' sake. Yet Ellie had never got there. She knew her mother had been very hopeful when Ellie decided on a whim to follow Paul across the Atlantic, and perhaps Ellie had too, if she was totally honest with herself. But she'd still come back alone less than two years later. And now she was going to walk down the aisle like she was walking down the path laid out for her. All her indecision, all her choices, her failed love affairs and jobs and the dreams she hadn't achieved, they were behind her now. From the moment she came back from New York, she had taken control of her life, sorted out her career, made herself happy for once. This – the choice to marry a nice man – had been part of it, hadn't it? Of the new sensible, healthy Ellie. At the end of the day, there was probably no decision on earth that would ever feel totally right to her. There would always be doubts and worries, because she was Ellie Warren, and she would always overthink every move she made. So she was choosing this, firmly stilling the butterflies in her stomach, making a concrete decision instead of dithering. She was getting married. She told herself she was calm, as her mother rammed the flower wreath harder onto her head.

'Ow, Mum!'

'It'll never stay on otherwise. I said you shouldn't wash your hair.'

'I'm not getting married with dirty hair.'

'Here.' Her mother whipped out a can of hairspray and doused Ellie in it.

'Stop,' she choked. 'Stop! Don't gas me before I've even got to the altar.'

'Altar, indeed. Tell me, where's the altar in a hotel?'

Her mother, who hadn't been to church in a decade, was pretending to be miffed about the non-religious ceremony.

Ellie no longer got annoyed at her ways. 'Is Dad en route?'

'Alan's gone to get him.'

'I'm glad he's coming,' said Ellie. 'It won't be weird for Nigel?'

She'd grown fond of her de facto stepfather since returning from New York years before. He wasn't a chatty man, but he knew a lot about gardening, and hiking, and how to fix things round the house. And he seemed to make her mother happy, even if it was sometimes hard to tell.

'Oh, he's very understanding.' Her mother paused. 'He's a good man. Your father was very good too. Is. It's just – sad that he was taken from us.'

'I know.' Ellie squeezed her mother's cold hand.

Her mum took it away, fussed some more with her hair, which was waved and topped with the flowers.

'I don't know what was wrong with a nice tiara.'

'Well, it's not 1986 for one thing.'

'I have a lovely one you could have borrowed. Something borrowed, something blue. Have you got all that?'

'Verity gave me something blue.' Lacy pants edged with ribbon in fact, but she didn't tell her mother that. 'And the dress is new and the shoes are kind of old – well, I've worn them a few days to break them in.'

She loved them, 1940s style in soft leather, the heels not too high, so she wouldn't tower over her intended.

'Here.'

Her mother twisted her fingers, wincing a little, and placed something in Ellie's hand. Her own engagement ring, a modest diamond purchased in the 1970s.

'Oh, Mum.' Ellie was touched.

'Just for today. Anyway, I think Nigel would like to get me another one.' She blushed a little.

'No one would judge, you know.'

It would be sad, divorcing a man who didn't know what was happening. But life went on. She was entitled to happiness.

Her mother wiped briskly at her eyes and Ellie blinked hard several times herself.

'Never mind that now. Are you ready? Finally? It's very rude to keep people waiting.'

'Yeah. Almost. I just – need a minute.' Ellie hesitated. There was still one person she hadn't asked for advice. 'Mum – you do like him, don't you?'

'Of course I do! Lovely man. So generous, very steady. What you need, Ellie – you're so flighty.'

Ellie rolled her eyes. She'd been settled into the same career for five years now, but it was pointless arguing with her mother on her wedding day. 'OK.'

'I'll tell the car we're ready. Don't be long now.'

Ellie stared at herself in the mirror, through the same ghosts of stickers she had contemplated that morning. It had only been a few hours ago, but she felt like she'd been through an emotional wringer since then. Reliving all her past decisions, second-guessing every step that had led her here. Trying to find her way back, feeling for the join, the moments when her life had crossed onto another track. She could see now how pointless that was. She only had this life. The other choices, other paths, other Ellies, just didn't exist. Maybe in other universes, like Mark had once said, but she couldn't access those, so it was meaningless.

A knock at the door.

'All right, Mum, I'm coming.'

She gathered her heavy cream silk skirt, loving the weight of it as it swept her legs, and stood up.

'Sorry. It's just me.'

Mark. It was Mark, standing in the door of her bedroom, in a grey morning suit.

'Oh,' she said.

He stared at her. 'My God, El. You look . . . my God.'

Mark. Why now? Just when she'd made up her mind to go through with this? Mind reeling, Ellie waited to hear what he had to say.

CHOICE 10 – OCTOBER 2017

'Natasha turned to Ben and smiled. Finally, after all the ups and downs, twists and turns of their history, she knew she was exactly where, and when, she was supposed to be.'

Ellie set down the book and looked out at the sea of faces. A storm of applause. She blinked. This was surreal. Here she was, standing at a podium in a bookshop, reading from her just-published novel. She was holding a finished copy in her hand, the pages stiff and white, the hardback embossed in silver, the endpapers (a new term to her) beautifully designed with drawings of world landmarks. The story of two people who kept finding and losing each other, across the globe and different historical time periods. 'A high concept love story with time travel elements', her editor had called it, who was all of twenty-eight and smiling up at Ellie from the audience in a patterned jumpsuit.

This was it, Ellie told herself. A published novel. A launch party, everyone she knew and loved there to celebrate her. Or almost everyone, at least. She had made it. Her dreams had come true. She was the happiest she'd ever been. Wasn't she?

She genuinely was. Since returning from America, she'd

done her best to stop relying on others, stop yearning for love, stop second-guessing everything. She was a working doctor now, training to be a GP and over the first few hellish foundation years of no sleep, and she had also finally managed to finish and sell her book. The agent from the party back in New York, Margot Dunning, had helped her find a UK one, and was representing Ellie in America.

Ellie sometimes got chills thinking how close she'd come to not going to that literary party. She might never have been published. She might still be with Paul, living the vaguely unhappy life of a trophy wife, miles from home. So yes, she was happy. It didn't even matter that she was almost thirty-seven, single and childless. She'd had to stop being haunted by past choices, working as a doctor. When you held someone's fate in your hands, you had to forget about sliding doors, butterfly effects, what-ifs. Otherwise surely it would destroy you, the idea that by taking the stairs instead of the lift, someone died when you could have saved them. Or if you'd just done one thing differently or faster. If you'd not taken a holiday when you did, a parent might have pulled through. If you'd not gone to your mother's birthday dinner, someone's child might have survived. The burden would be terrible.

She was glad her reading was over, so now she could relax and mingle. There was her mum and Nigel, smiling and waving. Alan and Katie had sent their excuses, because she was still breast-feeding Ellie's new niece, Lucy. But Verity had made it, declaring it her first night out since having her second baby, and was getting stuck into the Prosecco with Camilla, who also had kids now – twins who ran her ragged. Michelle had sent apologies from Croatia, where she was filming a fantasy series. But Ellie had made other friends, she was pleased to see, since coming back from America three years before. Old university people, colleagues from the magazine she'd worked on, fellow students from Newcastle, most of them now doctors, wide-eyed with tiredness, staff from St Thomas's, where she'd trained. She wasn't sure if she would keep being a doctor for ever – it was hugely hard work, getting harder every year with cuts and unhappy patients and a failing social-care system that cycled the same elderly and homeless people through A & E. Patching up the drunk and the angry. Children with too many bruises, old people with no one to care for them, desperate teens cutting into their own skin. But even if that was not to be her path for ever, she had another one, her book in her hands, the small span of it representing so much.

Enjoy it, she told herself. *You've made it.* What once had seemed impossible had become reality. She could turn her back on the mistakes of the past, Serge and Steve and Paul and James. And Mark. Work was the answer, not men. Ever since she'd left Paul, she'd been on her own apart from the odd foray into dating apps, quickly becoming disillusioned and deleting them again. Working, building a life for herself. It wasn't bad.

As the applause died down and people turned to each other and began to chat, or joined the queue for the bar, Ellie found herself looking round, feeling oddly deflated. She'd thought he would come, she really had, when she'd recklessly copied him into the email invite list. But of course Mark was not there.

*

The party lasted till nine, when the bookshop closed, and Ellie ended up in a crammed restaurant with her mother and Nigel, various friends and acquaintances swept up from the launch. She kept her book on her knee, stroking the pages like a pet. Her book. It had finally happened. So, the big question was – what now? When you achieve your life's biggest goal, what to do next? Write another book, she supposed, though it wasn't coming easily.

On her way home in an Uber to South London, drunk on Prosecco and buzzing on adrenaline, replaying the night and worrying about the people she hadn't managed to speak to, or if she'd forgotten to thank someone in her speech, Ellie had a short cathartic cry. She was a writer. Her book existed in the world. And yet, terrible as it was to admit this even to herself, she wished there were someone coming home with her. Squeezing her hand, telling her they were proud. Making her a cup of tea when they reached the home they shared. Rubbing her sore feet from the foolishly high heels she'd bought in the Kurt Geiger sale. She was ready to meet someone again – she still wanted that family she'd always dreamed of, though every time it had seemed to come close, things had fallen apart one way or the other. And she was glad. It would have been a huge mistake to have Serge's baby, or stay with Steve, or even with Paul in New York, kind as he was. A life dependent on him was not what she wanted.

Out of the window, she could see the lights of the Oxo Tower, where she'd been supposed to meet Mark all those years ago. Naively, she'd had no idea it was quite a fancy place. And just streets away was that other pub she'd sug-gested they go to, on the night they'd finally kissed. Maybe they wouldn't have, if they'd gone there instead. Who knew? London seemed printed over with different versions of herself, different memories, a silver web of the past and present.

Ellie scrolled through Facebook as the cab stopped at lights. So many congratulatory messages and posts. Without any expectation, she clicked on her messages. And there was one in black, unread. Mark Grant. Mark actual Grant. Her heart rushed up into her mouth. How many years since he'd contacted her? Twelve – the date was imprinted on her memory, the day of the bombs.

Hey, thanks for the invite. Was away with work so just saw it.

With shaking fingers, she typed back. *No worries. Was a fun night.*

She didn't expect a reply right away, or indeed ever, but saw that his avatar had a green dot, and a new message quickly flashed up. *You wrote an actual book!*

I know. Can't quite believe it. She hesitated, then typed, *How are you?*

Same old same old.

Hardly. Saw your company is thriving!

She googled him from time to time, and often read business profiles of him in the trade press. His company did something in AI, which apparently was a real growth area that was probably going to kill them all one day.

Pays the mortgage anyway. But El, you wrote a book!

I did. 😔

That's amazing. And so young for it.

Forty in no time.

Don't remind me, I'm the same age remember.

He was three weeks older than her, and throughout

their childhood they'd often had joint birthday parties, Action Man meets Barbie. Ellie's fingers itched to ask him everything, tell him more. It was Mark. She was talking to Mark, somewhere in the world. A small miracle.

Where are you based? she risked. Too personal? *Scotland still?*

Oh no, moved a while back. London now. Hampstead.

Fancy!!!

He was in the same city as her. For Laura's work, perhaps?

Ah yeah it's nice enough. Got a fixer-upper. He was so modest. Between him and Laura, they must be loaded. *You should come over sometime, see the place.*

Ellie blinked at the words. He wanted to meet? He had forgiven her then, at least – or perhaps he'd never been angry? Perhaps the blame was all in her head?

Sure, she typed. *I would love that. Laura too?* What a stupid thing to ask.

Well she does live here. Doing a fellowship at UCH, that's why we moved. Tried to stick it out but London gets us all in the end.

Of course. That would be amazing, thanks.

Her heart was hammering like she'd just run a race. What did it mean? Could she really face an evening with Mark and his wife, who possibly hated her? Presumably Laura had never passed on the message from the last time she and Ellie had met – or she had and Mark had ignored it. But of course she could. She would do anything to have him back in her life, and that was just the truth of it.

Three days later, Ellie was standing on the steps of an elegant red-brick house holding a bottle of wine she now realised was too cheap. The place was beautiful, easily two million, with stained glass around the door and a turreted roof, neat gravel on the driveway. Even to have a driveway in this part of town was impressive. *This could have been my life,* she thought as she listened to the musical chime of their doorbell. But could it? Maybe, if they'd ever got it together, she and Mark would have realised they weren't right together, and split up, their friendship ruined. Maybe, if she'd had the chance to play it out with him, she could have moved on, fallen for someone else. She could be married too now, perhaps with a child. Or she might have stayed with the nice, rich man who'd actually loved her. Would she have been happier with Paul if it wasn't for the ghost of Mark? Impossible to say.

Ellie's metaphysical ramblings were interrupted by the door opening. Laura, in loose white trousers and a vest top, showing off her toned arms. How did she get time to work out when she was saving lives every day?

'Hi Ellie.' Fractionally warmer than last time Ellie had seen her, but not much. 'Oh, thank you.' She received the bottle Ellie thrust at her. 'That's really kind of you. Come on in. Mark's embroiled in some kind of garlic-based emergency.'

The house was beautiful inside. Teal paint, pictures and mirrors with gilt frames, rosewood furniture. Ellie averted her eyes from some wedding photos, Laura standing straight in a plain white dress, a small unfussy bouquet in one hand. Mark looked pale and ill in the shots, taken so soon after his injury. But there he was now in the kitchen, the picture of health. Ellie couldn't help her gaze rushing to his legs, though she hated herself for it. In jeans, it was impossible to tell.

'El! You made it.' The air was filled with a smell of roasting garlic and herbs. 'Sorry, just had to rescue this. Nothing worse than blackened garlic.'

'Mm, yeah.'

Mark cooked now? Once he'd barely been able to make a Pot Noodle. She recalled him crunching on the dried noodles, wondering what he'd done wrong, and her heart hurt for the time that had been lost.

Laura opened the fridge. 'Wine, Ellie?'

'God, yes please! Definitely need a drink after the week I've had.'

'Oh, did something happen?'

'Not really. Just trying to write book two, and juggling work, you know.'

'Oh, you qualified in the end? I thought you'd quit.'

Ellie bristled at that *in the end*, but put on a smile. 'No, just took a little break. I'll most likely go the GP route.'

Laura uncorked the wine – a different bottle, not the one Ellie had brought.

'You can fit that in with writing?'

'I'll try! How about you, what have you been up to?'

Too late, she remembered who she was talking to.

'Well, I lost three patients today,' said Laura, opening a cupboard.

'Oh my God, I'm so sorry.'

That hadn't happened to Ellie for a while – she tended to see people who weren't so much at crisis point.

Laura shrugged. Her shoulders in her vest top were toned and strong. 'Och, it's just part of the job. I try not to self-medicate with booze, though, it's a slippery slope.'

290

As she poured out three glasses, a tiny one for herself and huge ones for Ellie and Mark, Ellie felt shame course through her. No wonder Mark had chosen Laura. Ellie would simply never be as good as her.

She noticed that Mark did not comfort his wife after what she'd said about losing patients. Perhaps it was such a regular occurrence he didn't feel the need to.

Laura brought Ellie's wine and clinked her own tiny glass off it. 'Cheers. It's lovely to see you again – isn't it, Mark?'

He looked up briefly from the smoking pan. 'Oh. Yeah, of course.'

'So,' said Laura, setting her arms on the rustic wood table. 'What have you been up to? Update us on the last few years.'

How could she, thought Ellie, as she launched into a sanitised version. Every mention of a man, every discussion of France or London or America, it all carried too much weight.

All night, through the meal of delicious tapas and pasta with wild greens and garlic, dessert of crème caramel which Laura didn't touch – 'Sugar's so bad for you, I try to avoid' – Ellie noticed there was in fact no physical contact between her and Mark at all. Just before ten, Laura, who'd stuck to water after her half-glass of red, looked at the clock and sighed.

'Bedtime for me I'm afraid – early shift. Nice to see you again, Ellie.' She hugged her briefly, smelling of herbs and soap. Then she turned to her husband. No hug for him. 'Try not to make noise when you come up, OK?'

Then they were alone. Mark and Ellie. She was struggling to get her head around the fact of being in the same room as him, close enough to reach over and touch his hand. He had

291

changed – expensive watch, soft jumper and jeans that must be designer, good haircut. Glasses that weren't fixed with masking tape. But he was also the same. There was a glass cabinet of Star Wars figurines in the living room, and several framed film posters hung awkwardly alongside modern art, dramatic abstract seascapes.

To fill the silence, Ellie said, 'Seems like Laura works pretty hard.'

He rolled his eyes. 'You've no idea. Evenings, weekends, holidays – hard to argue when she's saving lives.'

'It's very impressive.'

He toyed with the foil from the wine bottle. 'I know. But you don't really feel you can complain, if she missed your mum's birthday because she was saving a three-year-old from meningitis.'

'How is your mum?'

Ellie hadn't really spoken to her since that Christmas long ago, trying to ring Mark, bewildered at the sudden distance between them.

'Oh, full of beans. Zumba, Pilates, book club – she has a better social life than me. Dad, too. They're talking about buying a house in France.'

'Mine's the same. Mum, that is.'

He looked up, his quick blue gaze catching her like it used to. 'Sorry to hear about your dad.'

'Oh, thanks. He's OK. Happy enough, I think.'

'I remember him driving us round to discos when we were kids.'

'Yeah. He was good that way.' She'd forgotten what it was like to have someone in your life like this, who knew you all the way back to when you were small. All the people you'd been in your life. Even Michelle had only known almost-adult Ellie. 'Alan's got a baby, can you believe it? He married this lovely girl.'

'I really can't.' He shook his head. 'Is that something you wanted?'

Such a casual question. Ellie swallowed hard. Her plate was in front of her, smeared with blackberry juice from the dessert. A beautiful colour.

'Um, it never happened I guess.' Not entirely true. She still thought every year about how old her French baby might be. Nine, now. It was hard to believe. 'You?'

It was a rude question, perhaps, given he was married and she was single, but they'd once been able to talk about anything.

Mark sat back in his chair. 'Laura's not keen. It would derail her career, she says, which I suppose is true.'

Ellie had no such excuse. She was just incapable of making a relationship work.

'And you?' she risked.

He looked away. 'Yeah, I guess I assumed I'd have them. But it's her body, her career. I won't force her into it.'

Such a good man. She thought of Paul, how he used to bring up the future in a casual yet not-at-all casual way. A life that could have been there waiting for her.

'It's amazing, what she does. A & E, that's rough. I'm not sure I'll hack it many more years, to be honest.'

'But you're a writer now. The dream! It's amazing!'

It was sad how quickly you got used to things. 'I suppose it is, yeah.'

'It's huge, El. I walked past Waterstones the other day and your hardback was in the window. It's such a nice cover.'

'Isn't it? Thank you.'

'I'm so proud of you. I always knew you could do it, if you just put your mind to it.' He lifted his glass, and they clinked, and Ellie had to look away, because otherwise she might say something she was going to regret.

In doing so, she caught sight of the clock. It was after eleven, and she still had to journey back to south London. 'Oh God, I better go.'

'Let me call you an Uber.'

'Oh, no, honestly I'll be fine. The Tube's still running.'

'It's really no trouble.'

'You're a long way from the Megabus now,' she teased, putting her jacket on. 'And that watch is definitely an upgrade from the Casio with the green paint.'

'That Casio kept great time, you know. This was a present.' He held out his wrist, wiry and strong. 'From an investor who really wanted in on my company.'

'Fancy schmancy.' How quickly they'd fallen back into their old teasing.

'It's probably off a market stall. I wouldn't know the difference to be honest.'

At the door, Ellie paused. She knew she had to say something, however ill advised it was. They'd never be truly close again if there was this weight between them.

'Mark – I've been meaning to say – I've never forgiven myself for ... what happened. Last time.'

Last time they'd talked properly, she meant. July, 2005.

Immediately, he froze. 'It wasn't your fault.'

'No, but you'd never have been on there if it wasn't ... if I hadn't ... '

Mark didn't meet her eyes, as he reached out to straighten a picture that wasn't crooked. 'Look, Ellie. Things happen in life. It's a random universe, full of chaos. We can't blame ourselves for the choices we make or don't make. There's no possible way to know the outcome. So I don't spend time regretting the past. I can't change it, and neither can you. All we can is move on.'

She wanted to ask so much more – are you OK, does it hurt, did you ever tell her about us? – but he had firmly shut the topic down. She stepped out of the warm house into the drizzle of a London night.

Mark hovered in the doorway. 'At least let me get you a cab to the station.'

'Come on, it's one minute away.'

Which was true. The house really must be worth a lot. She made herself leave and walk to the station, where she waited for a Tube going south. She wondered if it had been a mistake to bring up that night they'd spent together – certainly Mark hadn't referred to it in any way. But if they were going to rebuild even a fraction of their previous closeness, it had to be with total honesty.

When she exited the Tube at the other side in Balham, she had a message from him.

Hope you got home safe. M x

A little kiss. It wasn't much, but it sent Ellie to bed with a smile on her face.

Over the next few weeks, life was rosy for Ellie. Her book was out, doing well, hitting number fifteen in the bestseller

295

charts. Several interviews and reviews came out in magazines. And best of all, she messaged with Mark every day, gradually increasing until there was a near-constant chat between them. Part of her, a distant numb part, wondered if this was OK, given that he was married. But they were childhood friends, and Laura knew they were chatting – she even came along once or twice when they met for drinks, though she usually quickly left after a call from the hospital – someone else's life she had to save.

One day, Ellie was in her usual writing spot, at her desk staring out at the trees on the quiet side street her flat was on. Only rented for now, but the advance for the book was enough that she could think about buying soon. Her publishers seemed happy, already talking about contracting her for another two books, which her agent said was a good sign. She was noodling over her next one, with a cooling cup of tea and her MacBook. This was the life she had dreamed of, cosy on a chilly grey day, her feet propped up on the radiator, mind gently turning. Nothing urgent to do and nowhere to be. Then her phone rang. That was weird – no one really called her except for her agent. She didn't recognise the number so punched the answer button, hoping for a new foreign rights deal, or perhaps the Hollywood offer she'd been dreaming of.

'Ellie?'

It was Laura.

'Oh, yeah – hi.'

Why was Laura calling her? And why did her heart start to swoop and stutter with guilt? She hadn't done anything wrong, had she? Just messaged Laura's husband dozens of times a day.

Laura's voice was brisk, her Scottish accent still pronounced. 'I'm in Balham, wondered if you had time for a coffee?'

She lived in Hampstead and worked near Euston – what would she be doing in South London?

'Ummm, sure – not really doing anything right now.'

It was true. She'd written all of one paragraph since lunchtime, entirely wasting her writing day. But why? What was Laura going to say?

'Great. I'm at this place called, let me see, the Brunchery?'

'Oh yeah, that's really close. Give me five minutes.'

'See you.' She rang off.

Ellie sat in shock for a few moments, then ran a brush through her chaotic hair, found her purse, laced up her ankle boots. No makeup – Laura never wore any herself. What was this all about? Maybe it was nothing. She'd better go or she'd be late.

Laura was sitting in the window of the coffee shop, hair up in a loose topknot, leaning her chin on her hand. Such a beautiful, sculpted face. Such quick intelligence in her dark eyes.

'Hey.'

'Hi!' Ellie gushed to cover her nerves. 'What a nice surprise!'

'What would you like?'

Laura already had a cup in front of her – it looked like green tea. Of course.

'OK, I'll just – would you like anything – no – OK! Just a sec!'

Ellie ordered at the counter, a latte, then paid on her card.

No doubt Laura would disapprove of the calories, the dairy, the caffeine. She sat down opposite Mark's wife. Laura was in jeans and a loose patterned top with a leather jacket. Immediately Ellie felt grungy in her hoody. Why hadn't she made more effort? But she'd always been like this – whatever she wore, whether smart or casual, she would inevitably feel it had been the wrong choice.

'So, what brings you to Balham?'

'Oh, you know. Meeting a friend.' Sounded vague. Suspicious.

'Great. What have you been up to?'

Laura shrugged. 'Working. That's usually it, sadly. So it's nice Mark has you to hang out with.' Was that pointed? Laura was sipping her tea, which smelled horrible, and she didn't look angry, but Ellie still worried.

'Oh yeah – I guess – well, it's been great to see him again. And meet you properly.'

'We met before, of course. A good few times.'

She must have been talking about that terrible day.

'Yeah.' Ellie's heart was hammering and she hadn't even drunk the coffee yet.

'That was one of the worst days of my life,' Laura went on.

'Mine too.' Did that sound like she was taking away from Laura's pain? 'I mean, worse for you of course.'

'Hmm.' Laura swilled her tea. Ellie had the feeling she was working up to saying something, but had no idea what it could be. *Stop messaging my husband? I know that you slept with him?* 'You know, Ellie, I'm not religious. Not at all, never have been. But that day – I actually prayed, though I didn't know who to. I made promises, that if he was just alive, I'd take care of him for ever. And he was. A miracle. So we got married. It seemed the least we could do.'

'OK.' What did that mean? The least we could do?

Laura paused. 'This is hard to say, Ellie. Things haven't been easy. The way you see him now, successful, confident, it wasn't always like that. After the bomb he wasn't right for a long time. And it was hard on both of us, on our marriage.'

'I'm sure.' Ellie still didn't know what she was trying to say, but sensed there was something, the edges of it.

'So – you being back in his life, that's lovely, and I can tell he's really missed you all this time.'

'Um . . . yeah, me too.' Ellie could hardly look at her, staring into her coffee instead.

'I just hope it doesn't stir things up again. You know, since he last saw you right before the bomb.' She knew. She had to know. Why else would she say it like that? 'It might . . . bring back old memories. Issues we dealt with a long time ago.'

Ellie tried to make sense of this. 'So . . . you're saying I shouldn't have got in touch?'

'God, no. It was such a shame you fell out. I'm just saying . . . go easy with him. He's not as strong as he looks.'

'Um . . . all right.'

There was a message, but Ellie couldn't quite decode it. *Keep your distance*, that seemed to be the gist.

Laura paused for a moment, then sat back, as if shying away from whatever point she wanted to make. 'So tell me about your books? Must be so exciting, being a writer.'

Weird, thought Ellie, as she sorted through her stock responses to this question. Something was definitely not right, she just couldn't tell what it was.

A strained hour of small talk later, she was walking back to her flat when her phone buzzed. Mark, following up on a long stream of surreal messages they'd been exchanging about dinosaurs. She started typing back, then caught herself. Maybe Laura was right, and it wasn't fair to pop up again and remind him of the past. To be contacting him so much when he was married, when Laura had been the one to piece him back together and Ellie had simply run. She put the phone away in her pocket, message unanswered.

It was very strange how having a book published brought people out of the woodwork. Over the next few weeks, Ellie received messages from old school friends, university acquaintances, and several journalists from her magazine days, with the heavy implication that they wanted to pick her brains about getting their own novels published. Sometimes this was just stated explicitly; she took to cutting and pasting the same bit of advice.

She was also amused to receive a message from Connor Mullins, now bald, married with three kids, and living in the Midlands. He was working in the pharmaceutical industry and Ellie wasn't sure what his motive was in contacting her – surely he didn't harbour writing dreams? Or want to pick up their flirtation where they'd left it, back in 2002? She sent a few brief messages then let it peter out. It was so strange – Connor Mullins, who'd almost played such a small but vital role in her life, and also in Steve's, though Steve didn't know it. She had wondered over the years how different things might have been if she'd gone to his room that night, as she had so desperately wanted to. Would she have got together

300

with him? She'd broken up with Steve anyway, so it hardly made a difference. No sense chasing that old dream.

However, one day Ellie woke up bleary-eyed at eight – perhaps she really was more suited to the life of a writer than that of a doctor – to find a message waiting for her. Sent at 5 a.m. Someone in another time zone, or someone who got up really early? It turned out to be both – Paul.

Ellie stared at the message, alongside the same avatar he'd had for years, him standing on a mountaintop with the sunset behind him. She'd taken that picture.

Hey, picked up a magazine in the airport and there you were! You got your book published – that is brilliant. So so many congratulations.

Her heart hurt somewhere. She'd broken his, left him and fled. At the time she'd known, deep in her gut, that she wasn't happy, despite the affluence and ease of her world. She was so much happier now, in her small flat in Balham, writing under the eaves, swimming at the local baths down the road, shopping in markets, walking in parks, connecting with old friends. Should she ignore this message, let Paul go the way she had Connor Mullins? A path into the past, a door she had already shut. But it was Paul. She owed him more than that.

Hi there, she typed back. *Yeah I did. Finally. How's New York?*

Paul was not much of a social media person, so she was surprised to see him immediately replying.

Not there any more! Accepted a job at Ernst and Young in London.

Oh. He was in London too. Sitting there in her cosy bed, listening to rain tap on the skylight, a cup of tea by her side in her favourite huge mug, the one with the picture of the Statue of Liberty, Ellie had the sense of paths branching out

301

again. What was the point in meeting up with him, assuming he would even want to? What would it achieve? Closure, perhaps. Or just poking at a healed wound?

As she waited, he took the step for her. *Perhaps a drink sometime?*

Ellie sighed. The tides of life kept bringing people to her again and again. Michelle, who was very into tarot and astrology since moving to LA, would say it was the universe acting to pull them back into her orbit. Mark would say it was just the randomness of atoms bouncing about, or the statistical probability that someone like Paul, who worked in international finance, might eventually get a job back in the UK. Or that an ex so serious they'd lived together might get in touch.

Sure, she typed.

It would be rude otherwise. Then she closed down Facebook and made herself get back to her work. The deadline was getting close, and it turned out the second book was much harder than the first, which she had after all been writing on and off for ten years. She'd had no idea then that it would get published. It was always impossible to predict the future, or know which decision was right. You just had to go with whatever seemed best at the time. A year from now, if Ellie had learned anything at all, things were likely to look totally different.

One year later

'Here we are.'

Ellie was absolutely busting for a wee. They'd been driving

for hours out of London, and she'd felt she couldn't ask him to stop at a service station in the beautiful vintage convertible he'd hired (top up, because it was October in England). Finally, they had reached their weekend destination, near the border with Wales. Paul had pulled up by some discreet wooden gates. The surroundings were green and leafy and there were no other cars. She felt peace wash over her.

'Thank you.'

She put her hand on Paul's chino-clad thigh, and he squeezed it. 'I hope you like this place. It was quite hard to get a reservation.'

'I'm sure I will.'

A cabin, he'd said. She'd pictured something rustic, which hopefully would have wi-fi and no spiders. But what they drew up to, after he'd spoken into an intercom and the gates had opened, was something else. It looked like the grounds of a hotel, with several wooden roofs poking out from the dense treeline. Bright green lawns rolled to the edge of the trees, then disappeared into shadow. There were golf buggies, and even the blue flash of a swimming pool.

'All right?' said Paul, killing the engine after parking carefully beside a Jaguar.

'Um ... yes! You said a cabin.'

'It will be a cabin. Just ... part of a larger complex.'

When did this become my life, Ellie wondered, as staff in green polo shirts appeared to take their bags, and they were ushered into the cosy reception, built of logs and with plush rugs underfoot, and offered a choice of champagne or punch. She'd told herself it would be different if she got back together with Paul, that she'd hold her own more, pay her way. For the most part she'd managed, but this was their one-year anniversary, and he'd really gone all in. Then they were loaded into a golf buggy and driven down a forest trail to their cabin. It rose out of the trees – wood and glass, with an uninterrupted view of the trees.

'You might see a beaver!' said the young man, who was all of twenty. 'They've been rewilding the woods nearby.'

'Oh, lovely.'

Ellie was starting to feel uneasy and she wasn't sure why. Yes, Paul was rich, but this time they'd had a sort of tacit agreement they would split most costs, so she didn't feel like a kept woman. This place was seriously nice – way out of her league. She also really needed the loo and the young man was still enthusiastically showing them the room's features, the TV hidden behind a sliding wooden panel, the under-floor heating.

Paul tipped the guy, discreetly, and Ellie wandered round, looking for the bathroom. She'd have to get changed imme-diately – her jeans and walking boots were not going to cut it here. The furniture was rustic but luxurious, tables hewn from tree trunks, quilts on the bed and rugs on the floor, hidden here and there a top-of-the-range hairdryer, coffee maker and sound system. Outside, the deck with a hot tub already steaming away.

'Wow.'

'Do you like it?'

'Of course! It's amazing.'

She felt guilty that Paul had planned such a lovely trip for them and she'd been head down in her third novel all week, puzzling out a particular plot strand which had left her brain fried. Since it dealt with time travel, she'd been sorely tempted to call Mark and ask him for help, but after her weird coffee with Laura a year before, she'd tried hard to keep him at arm's length. They were still friends, but rarely met up alone, usually with Laura and Paul in tow, or with Michelle. It was safer that way, Ellie felt. But he was always so good at talking through knotty issues. Would it really be bad if they had a quick cup of tea just the two of them? He was hardly Mike Pence; it couldn't be dangerous in the daylight hours.

'Um, do you know where's the ...' There were so many doors! Cupboards perhaps? Where was the loo?

'I'm glad you like it.' Paul seemed nervous, fiddling with a carafe of water on a small table. It too was beautiful, shaped like the bulb of a flower, the glasses hand-blown with finger dents along the side. 'I wanted it to be really special.'

'It is.'

She glanced around for her bag, hoping she'd remembered a swimsuit. Quick pee and she'd be straight in that hot tub – assuming she could find the bloody bathroom.

'Because, Ellie ... there's something I want to ask you.'

Oh God. She froze, ice all over despite the warm room. Her overloaded bladder twinged. How had she missed this? The special weekend away, the romantic setting, their one-year anniversary of getting back together. She should have seen it coming. What was she going to say? She didn't know.

'I shouldn't have let you go in New York. I won't make the same mistake again,' said Paul. Ellie looked over and saw him at the top of the stairs, kneeling on the wooden floor, a ring box in his hand. Bright blue. Tiffany. 'I've had this for years – I knew back then, I should have asked you sooner. Eleanor Warren, will you marry me?'

Oh God. The world tilted. This was happening. It was really happening. And she had to answer. She had to make a choice.

JUNE 2019

Mark was in her childhood bedroom, sitting on the stool by the dressing table, picking absently at a My Little Pony sticker which had been there for thirty years or more. He had of course been in there before, playing snakes and ladders or ludo on rainy days in their childhood, but not for about the same amount of time. Neither of them said anything for a long moment. He was in a suit and tie, which looked too tight about his throat. She was in her wedding dress, her veil draped over the bed waiting to be donned right before she left for the hotel, which was supposed to be in the next five minutes. Her mother would rather die than keep people waiting. Mark should be there too, in fact. So why was he here?

'Where's Laura?' Ellie's voice was shaky.

'Um – she left, actually. She's sorry not to be here, she said. Um. But she couldn't.'

'She got paged?' Someone else's life hanging in the balance, maybe. But Laura worked in London. Surely it was too far away to be called in for an emergency?

'No.' He scraped harder at the sticker. Same square fingers she'd once known so well, always covered in marker pen and cuts from coming off his bike and small burns from science experiments in his dad's garage. Mark. 'Listen, El – when we started hanging out together again, I was really pleased. I'd missed you, and it always seemed so stupid we fell out when we were such good friends.'

'Yeah.'

'You didn't even come to my wedding.'

She was staring at the box of her old tattered books. Chalet School, Famous Five. And of course, Choose Your Own Adventure. So many days spent curled up on her bed dreaming of the life she'd have, the places she'd live, babies she'd bring up, books she would write. 'I couldn't. I'm sorry.'

'After the attack, I was ... in a dark place. Barely alive. It was like – it didn't just take my leg, it changed some deep part of me. I was so angry, so lost. And you were gone.'

'I'm sorry.' Ellie's head drooped. Her mascara was going to run before she even got down the aisle. Her mother would be furious. 'I felt so guilty. About what I did.'

He laughed bitterly. 'Ellie, we both did it. And then Laura was there for me, helping me, healing me, and I felt so terrible about what I did to her that it just seemed inevitable we'd get married. Especially after you left.'

What did he mean? Ellie couldn't think over the pounding of her heart. It was her wedding day! Why was he saying all this?

He looked up at her. 'On the day, I kept hoping you'd turn up. I looked out for you in the congregation. I told myself, if she comes, I'll say something, I'll not go through with it ... but you didn't come.'

No, because she had fled her mistakes, made different ones instead, run to Paris, fallen for another unsuitable man.

Turned her back on the path she was meant to be on. And now here she was, about to marry someone else.

Tears were slipping from her eyes, black-stained. 'Mark, why are you here? What is this?'

'We've missed each other too many times, El. It's almost too late, but not quite. So I'm saying what I should have said years ago. I love you. I was going to tell you when we were seventeen, then you kissed that boy, and at uni, but then you met Steve. Then when we were in our twenties, but you went to France instead. So I tried not to, for years, but then you came to the house in Hampstead and you had raindrops in your hair and I just knew I could talk to you all night and all the next day and never stop. That I'd never run out of things to say to you. And I'm sick of thinking about what might have been. I'm here, and you're here, so let's not lose our last chance, Ellie.'

'You're married!'

'Not for much longer. Laura and I, we love each other – well, she's amazing, a truly wonderful person. But it's not the same. It's not right. We've been on the brink for years now – almost split up more times than I can remember. She said she'd come today to keep up appearances, but on the drive up it was just obvious.'

Ellie was bewildered. 'That's why she left?'

'Yeah. She knows what I'm doing here.'

Which was? Ellie still wasn't sure. 'I'm getting married.'

'I know. God, the timing sucks. And he's a nice guy too.' They'd met several times, a few awkward dinners and barbecues over the year Ellie and Paul had been engaged. 'I hate to do this to anyone. But we can't make the same mistake again, Ellie. We've made it too many times already.'

'We need to be very clear here.' Her voice was shaking. She had mascara stains on the bodice of her dress. It was a pretty but uninspired choice, which was how Ellie had felt all the way through her wedding preparations, hen do in a fancy spa hotel in Scotland, dress shopping, venue choosing. Like she was going through the motions, getting ready to walk through a door she wasn't excited about. A life she hadn't wanted, not really. It had been Paul pushing to get married so soon, and sometimes she'd wondered if it was because she'd ended it years before. His hurt pride. His determination to have her, tuck her into his life. If he even wanted her, this new assertive version of her anyway. 'What are you saying, exactly? I can't afford to miss you again.'

'Don't marry him. Be with me. Let's give it a go. I love you.'

He took her hand – the first time they had touched in years. All of their recent meet-ups had been touch free, although Laura had hugged her, as if he couldn't bear to make contact with her skin. His hand was warm, a pulse beating strong in his wrist. The old Casio watch with the green paint. Ellie blinked. It really was there.

'Is that . . . ?'

'Oh. Yeah. The Patek Philippe, it's beautiful but it's not really me. I'm more . . . old and nerdy. Paint stained.'

'From when you tried to make your Teenage Mutant Ninja Turtles glow in the dark.'

'Right. And who else would know that about me?' He was stroking the side of her hand, and Ellie had not let go of his. 'I've thought about you every day since we've been apart.'

'But Mark – we've hardly spent any time together since

310

we were eighteen. We're different people now. We might not get on at all.' What a risk it was, to lose the friendship again, walk away from settled, serious relationships with good people. Upset her mother, waste all the money spent on today, take off her wedding dress unworn. Break Paul's heart for the second time.

He shrugged. 'Eh. I'm willing to risk it. After all, what's life without taking a few wrong paths?'

The room was spinning. Behind Mark, on the dressing table, was the box she'd found that morning, the old books she had once loved to read, making her way through different situations, safe in the knowledge that if she got eaten by a crocodile or crawled through quicksand she could flip back to the beginning and start again. She was older now, and knew life was not like that. Choices had consequences. People got hurt, lives were changed for ever. There was death and loss and pain you could not come back from. But it wasn't too late. She could still go back – not start again, since twenty years had gone by in the meantime. But make a different start instead.

Marry Paul, or leave him at the altar. Be with Mark, and risk all that this entailed, or choose the life that was laid out for her. That was the choice she had to make.

Marry Paul
2022

Ellie looked at the clock. After eight, and still no sign of him. Fidgety, she wandered the kitchen looking for things to tidy, but it was already immaculate. The pasta she'd made, recipe clipped from the *Guardian* weekend supplement, was cold on the hob. The granite surfaces of the worktops and kitchen island were wiped to a high shine. She had already drunk the one glass of wine she allowed herself per night, and was eyeing the bottle.

Upstairs, in her beautifully decorated room, under the hand-painted frieze of zoo animals, Charlotte slept. She was nearly two now, and a good baby in the sense that she slept a lot, went happily to nursery, ate what she was given. She had Paul's placid temperament, though her unruly hair and sharp dark eyes were Ellie's. As for Ellie, she had two days a week childcare so she could supposedly finish her fourth book, and yet she still hadn't. Paul was a bit dubious about sending the little girl to nursery – he'd said several times Ellie didn't have to work if she didn't want to, Charlotte needed her mother, didn't want his child raised by strangers, etc. And maybe he was right. Most days she found herself staring out of the window at their quiet side street in Kensington, the blossoming trees and voices of straw-hatted children being ushered to and from the private school at the end of the road. She could walk to Harrods if she liked, buy up the food hall or a new dress or a vase or set of cutlery. Anything she wanted. Her gym was a ten-minute walk away, with a steam room and pool and all-day classes. She went most days, to keep herself in the kind of shape expected of the non-working wife of a man in high finance. Paul was complimentary, but Ellie couldn't help comparing herself to the wives of his colleagues, noticing when one was ditched for a younger woman. But despite all this luxury, Ellie was numb. She loved her child, yes, and her life was nice, and easy, and safe. Paul was calm and generous and loving, at least when he wasn't working, which was most of the time. They hadn't slept together much since Charlotte was born, but that wasn't so unusual, especially given how Ellie had torn and been stitched back together.

Ellie looked at the clock again and sighed. It was the third time this week she'd sat with a cold dinner, dribbling bits of wine out of the bottle, telling herself it didn't add up to a second or third glass, even though she knew it did. Waiting for him. When he did come home, he'd eat the food, exhausted, then go straight to bed, to be up at five for his personal trainer and the Japanese markets. She didn't think there was someone else. Just his usual mistress – his job. It took so much of him, and she could hardly complain, since it paid for her lifestyle. But she wasn't happy. She could no longer ignore that fact.

A key in the lock. Ellie jumped to attention, scanning the room to make sure everything was ready. Paul had never said he expected a clean house and dinner and a sleeping child, would never dream of it, but what was her job if not this? Not writing. She hadn't really done that in years. Instead, she was trying to be the best wife she could, and if she couldn't connect with him deep down, she could at least make sure the house was tidy and the dinner cooked.

Paul came in, his expensive overcoat draped over his arm, along with the leather satchel she'd bought him for Christmas. With his money.

'You're very late,' she said.

He set down his bag and coat. 'I'm sorry.'

'It's OK, it's just … I was worried. Dinner?'

'Um, no, I ate already. We just got takeaway at the office, it was so crazy today.'

'OK.'

They faced each other across their perfect, tidy kitchen. Like strangers instead of people who'd been together two different times, and eventually married, and had a child. Every single day Ellie wondered if she'd made the right choice in sending Mark away that day in her bedroom, patching up her face as best she could, though her mother had still commented on how blotchy she was, walking to the wedding car and the hotel and down the aisle and marrying Paul. Telling herself she was on this path, and it was too late to get off. She had not spoken to Mark since, though she knew he and Laura had divorced. She had committed fully to her decision. When she stood over Charlotte's crib, and smoothed back her dark curls, it was hard to believe any choice that had led to the child not existing was the right one. But here she was, with her husband, and they were like people who'd never even met before. And suddenly she knew she was going to say something. Something that would change the course of her life for ever.

'Paul,' she said, her voice choked up. 'I'm sorry but I really can't go on like this. We have to talk.'

JUNE 2019

Ellie was in the garden again, pacing around in her wedding dress. She had grass stains on the hem of it and she was already late for her own wedding. Verity, her mother, sister-in-law, niece and brother stared out at her through the kitchen window. Ellie had sent them away with a burst of rage.

'I need a minute! To myself! Just a minute!'

Mark had also disappeared, she didn't know where. *I'll leave you to think*, he'd said, as if he hadn't totally upended her life. Rising to his feet from her dresser stool, walking out of her childhood room.

'Nerves,' her mother had muttered. 'All right, Ellie, but we have to leave in five minutes, it's terribly rude otherwise.'

She knew it was. God, she couldn't do this to Paul, not again. She should never have got engaged, she could see that now. But wouldn't it be worse to marry him with all these doubts in her mind? She could picture their future exactly. A nice house, in a nice part of London, probably Kensington or Chelsea. A child, perhaps, in the next few years. She wouldn't have to work if she didn't want to, there'd be no pressure to finish her next book, and she'd have money for whatever she wanted – gyms and holidays and clothes. A cleaner, a nanny. Whereas the opposite, leaving him at the altar, choosing a different path – she could not picture that at all. She could end up alone. No husband. No kids.

'What's going on, Warren?'

She looked up to see someone standing in her gateway, slim, radiant, sunglasses on despite the dull day, holding up the skirt of a sea-green bridesmaid's dress. Hollywood star Michelle Allenby. Further down the lane, Ellie could see a limo waiting. Michelle would have been at the house that morning, if only she wasn't so high powered and famous that the very idea of staying in Longton was anathema to her. She'd been planning to fly to Newcastle (first class) that morning, check into the Malmaison and meet Ellie at the wedding hotel. Ellie understood – her friend was so famous now she could hardly hang out with them at the house, then walk into the hotel like any other punter. She'd have to be smuggled downstairs in the service lift, and they were praying the press didn't get wind of it. Her bridesmaid's dress had been couriered to her, and Ellie was ashamed to have styled a Bafta nominee in a Coast Empire-line, but Michelle had appeared thrilled with the sea-green crêpe number.

'I thought you weren't coming here?' said Ellie, confused.

'Mark texted.'

'Oh.'

'Jesus, what is it with you two and timing, eh?'

Ellie burst into tears again.

Michelle calmly fished in her tiny clutch bag and passed her a tissue. 'Come on, it's not the end of the world. I've brought you a getaway car, should one be needed.'

'How could he do this? Today of all days?'

'He couldn't let you go again. And he's a decent guy, you know. Once you're married, he'll bow out for good.' Like she had done, or tried to, when he got married himself. 'But he just had to try.'

'What about Laura?'

Michelle shrugged. 'Oh, that's been on the slide for years.'

'It has? Why didn't you tell me?'

'Because. When did you ever let me talk about Mark?'

'Good point.' Ellie sniffed. 'God, this is a total mess. I can't leave Paul at the altar, I just can't.'

'Well, it's not really an altar, is it? It's the function room of a Marriot hotel.'

'Stop taking the piss.'

'I'm not, El. Just putting it into perspective. It will be awkward, yes, and people will gossip for a few months, but it's better than marrying the wrong person. Isn't it?'

Ellie's life stretched before her, two roads branching off, like that stupid poem they'd done at school. If she married Paul, she could picture it so clearly. But a part of her sank at the idea. With Mark, she had no idea what the future held. Could not even imagine it. It could implode within days, or he could leave her like Serge had, break her heart. The affection between them could slowly die, like with Steve all those years ago, Steve whom she'd picked instead of Mark – and what a stupid choice that had been, not that she'd even known she was making it. Or maybe not. Maybe, if they'd been a couple at nineteen, at different universities and with all their mistakes ahead of them, it wouldn't have worked out. There was no way to know. It was all chaos.

She tried to get her breathing under control.

'What do you want to do?' said Michelle. 'I'm here no matter what. We can Thelma and Louise it, even.'

'There's no canyons round here.'

'Well yes, love, I was thinking more in a "nice spa hotel" sense.'

Ellie gulped. 'I want him. I've always wanted him.'

'Right.'

'But – what if it doesn't work out? What if we get hurt or one of us dies or we can't have kids or . . . anything?' Mark had already been so badly injured by her actions. Could she bear to have that in her hands again – his life, his heart? And hers in his?

Michelle shook her head. 'That's life, El. If we could control it, it wouldn't mean so much. Wouldn't you rather walk down a scary ghost-filled path with Mark, than a nice smooth paved one with Paul?'

She would, she realised. And maybe that was what it was all about. Choosing the path you couldn't see down, which could be filled with disaster and loss, because you knew you were walking it with the right person.

'Where is he? Do you know?' She had to talk to him at least. Find out if they were on the same page.

Michelle jerked her head. 'In the limo.'

'What?'

'He called me to pick him up on the road, but I insisted on driving back. You two need to sort this out, once and for all. So. Go.'

Ellie didn't understand. 'Just take your car?'

'It's hired for the day. Go wherever you like. Decide.'

'And – what about you? The wedding? My mother?'

318

'Just let me handle that. She always liked me, Judy.'

Ellie sniffed. 'No she didn't.'

'Yeah, she didn't, did she? Thought I was a bad influence.' Michelle let her skirt down. She looked typically amazing, even in a dress from the high street. 'At least I can take this off now. My Spanx are killing me.'

'Sorry it isn't couture.'

'Huh, those things are like torture. Half the time I have actual pins in me. Anyway, stop making fun of me and go, live your life, get your man. Jesus, do I have to do everything for you two?'

'But Paul . . . '

'You'll talk to him later. Trust me, nothing you can say now will help the situation. Go.'

Ellie poised at her gate, dirty wedding dress bunched in her hands, hair falling down. Her mother in the kitchen, a slow look of horror dawning on her face. Another huge mistake in the process of being made. Another heart she would break, and her own on the line, as well as Mark's. Her future ahead of her, unseen, the clear ordered vision of her life in disarray, the children she might have had vanishing into the ether. But that was OK. Because the best path was the one she hadn't walked down yet. And so she went.

Choose Mark

2022

'Er, what is this?' Ellie tapped her finger on the Scrabble score pad.

'This is me winning.'

'How can you be winning? I was fifty points up just now!'

'But that was before I played "foxy" on a triple word score.'

'Urgh, you're such a cheat, Mark Grant!'

'How dare you!'

The game was interrupted then because Frank, all of two years old, wandered over and calmly put the X tile into his mouth. As Ellie fished it out, to great howls of protest, Mark stood up, pushing his old Casio watch up his arm.

'Anyway – tea break?'

Ellie pulled Frank onto her lap to soothe him. 'Decaf for me.'

She was pregnant again – at the age of forty-one, which had horrified her mother, who was now married to Nigel and living on his farm. Ellie's dad had died two years ago, his name living on in the grandson he'd stayed alive just long enough to meet.

She looked around the modest house in the suburbs of Newcastle. They'd both wanted to be near their remaining parents, in the end, as well as Alan, Katie, Lucy and their new arrival baby Thomas, and Mark had never really been a fan of London in any case. He'd given Laura the Hampstead house, which she'd promptly sold before going to Somalia with Médecins Sans Frontières. She was now engaged to a very handsome Danish doctor, and sent emails detailing a life that was different to Ellie's in every way. Sometimes, Ellie still had a small pang at not working as a doctor any more, but when she caught sight of her five published novels on the bookshelf, surrounded by foreign-language translations, it was hard to regret her choices.

It was a Sunday, the wood burner was lit, a chicken roasting in the oven. Soon, hopefully, Frank would go down for a nap and Ellie and Mark could watch a film. As always, she'd want a romcom and he'd want something set in space. They would argue over it good-naturedly. Later, Michelle would Facetime from LA, on her terrace with the pool overlooking the city, probably dressed in yoga gear and drinking a green juice, her French director husband in the background making her breakfast. Everything was at it should be.

From the kitchen came the sound of cursing.

Ellie covered her son's ears. 'Shhh, Grant! What is it?'

'Carrots are burning.'

'I said the oven was up too high.'

'Yeah, yeah, know it all. Maybe we can scrape the burnt bits off.'

'Yum yum, *carrottes brûlées.*'

'Ooh la la, Frenchy show-off.'

Ellie stood up and heaved her son onto her hip. 'Come on, Frank, let's see what a mess Daddy has made of our dinner.'

Perhaps not everything was perfect, and she had no idea what the road ahead of her held. Sickness and loss and maybe she and Mark would stop loving each other – there was no way to tell. All she knew was that, in this very moment, even with the burning carrots and the toddler dribbling onto her top, she would not change a single step of her journey, because every one of them had led her right to here.

ACKNOWLEDGEMENTS

Thank you to Darcy Nicholson and all at Sphere for an insightful and wise edit, and to Diana Beaumont and all at Marjacq for top-notch editing.

I started writing this book several years ago at Skyros, so thank you to them too for inviting me to teach and giving me inspiration.

Thanks to all my readers also. If you've enjoyed this book, I'd love to hear from you on Instagram, @evawoodsakaclairemcgowan, Twitter (@inkstainsclaire), or via my website, www.ink-stains.co.uk

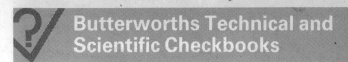

Butterworths Technical and
Scientific Checkbooks

KV-365-626

Engineering Science 3
Checkbook

J O Bird
BSc(Hons), AFIMA, TEng(CEI), MIElecIE
A J C May
BA, CEng, MIMechE, FIElecIE, MBIM

Butterworths
London Boston Durban Singapore Sydney Toronto Wellington

First published 1983

© Butterworth & Co (Publishers) Ltd 1983

British Library Cataloguing in Publication Data

Bird, J.O.
  Engineering science 3 checkbook. — (Butterworths
  technical and scientific checkbooks)
  1. Engineering
  I. Title
  620   TA145

  ISBN 0 408 00695-1
  ISBN 0 408 00624-2 Pbk

Typeset by Scribe Design, Gillingham, Kent
Printed in Scotland by Thomson Litho Ltd., East Kilbride

Contents

Note to Reader

As textbooks become more expensive, authors are often asked to reduce the number of worked and unworked problems, examples and case studies. This may reduce costs, but it can be at the expense of practical work which gives point to the theory.

Checkbooks if anything lean the other way. They let problem-solving establish and exemplify the theory contained in technician syllabuses. The Checkbook reader can gain *real* understanding through seeing problems solved and through solving problems himself.

Checkbooks do not supplant fuller textbooks, but rather supplement them with an alternative emphasis and an ample provision of worked and unworked problems. The brief outline of essential data—definitions, formulae, laws, regulations, codes of practice, standards, conventions, procedures, etc—will be a useful introduction to a course and a valuable aid to revision. Short-answer and multi-choice problems are a valuable feature of many Checkbooks, together with conventional problems and answers.

Checkbook authors are carefully selected. Most are experienced and successful technical writers; all are experts in their own subjects; but a more important qualification still is their ability to demonstrate and teach the solution of problems in their particular branch of technology, mathematics or science.

Authors, General Editors and Publishers are partners in this major low-priced series whose essence is captured by the Checkbook symbol of a question or problem 'checked' by a tick for correct solution.

Preface

This textbook of worked problems provides coverage of the Technician Education Council level 3 unit in Engineering Science (syllabus U80/735, formerly U76/054). However, it can be regarded as a basic textbook in engineering science for a much wider range of courses, such as equivalent Australian TAFE courses.

The aims of the book are to give a basic mechanical and electrical science background for engineering technicians and, more specifically, to introduce the student to a basic range of instrumentation and measurements and so develop the understanding of electrical circuit components, systems, heat, dynamics and energy.

Each topic considered in the text is presented in a way that assumes in the reader only knowledge attained in Engineering Science 2 (syllabus U80/734) and Mathematics 2 (syllabus U80/691). This practical Engineering Science book contains some 111 illustrations and 200 detailed worked problems, followed by some 550 further problems with answers.

The authors would like to express their appreciation for the friendly co-operation and helpful advice given to them by the publishers. Thanks are due to Mrs Elaine Woolley for the excellent typing of the manuscript.

Finally the authors would like to add a word of thanks to their wives, Elizabeth and Juliet, for their continued patience, help and encouragement during the preparation of this book.

J O Bird
A J C May
Highbury College of Technology
Portsmouth

Butterworths Technical and Scientific Checkbooks

General Editors for Science, Engineering and Mathematics titles:
J.O. Bird and A.J.C. May, Highbury College of Technology, Portsmouth.

General Editor for Building, Civil Engineering, Surveying and Architectural titles:
Colin R. Bassett, lately of Guildford County College of Technology.

A comprehensive range of Checkbooks will be available to cover the major syllabus areas of the TEC, SCOTEC and similar examining authorities. A comprehensive list is given below and classified according to levels.

Level 1 (Red covers)
Mathematics
Physical Science
Physics
Construction Drawing
Construction Technology
Microelectronic Systems
Engineering Drawing
Workshop Processes & Materials

Level 2 (Blue covers)
Mathematics
Chemistry
Physics
Building Science and Materials
Construction Technology
Electrical & Electronic Applications
Electrical & Electronic Principles
Electronics
Microelectronic Systems
Engineering Drawing
Engineering Science
Manufacturing Technology
Digital Techniques
Motor Vehicle Science

Level 3 (Yellow covers)
Mathematics
Chemistry
Building Measurement
Construction Technology
Environmental Science
Electrical Principles
Electronics
Microelectronic Systems
Electrical Science
Mechanical Science
Engineering Mathematics & Science
Engineering Science
Engineering Design
Manufacturing Technology
Motor Vehicle Science
Light Current Applications

Level 4 (Green covers)
Mathematics
Building Law
Building Services & Equipment
Construction Technology
Construction Site Studies
Concrete Technology
Economics for the Construction Industry
Geotechnics
Engineering Instrumentation & Control

Level 5
Building Services & Equipment
Construction Technology
Manufacturing Technology

1 The measurement of temperature

A. MAIN POINTS CONCERNED WITH THE MEASUREMENT OF TEMPERATURE

1   A change in temperature of a substance can often result in a change in one or more
of its physical properties. Thus, although temperature cannot be measured directly,
its effects can be measured. Some properties of substances used to determine
changes in temperature include changes in dimensions, electrical resistance, state,
type and volume of radiation and colour.

2   Temperature measuring devices available are many and varied. The following are
most often used in science and industry:

   (i) **Liquid-in-glass thermometer** uses the expansion of a liquid with increase in
temperature as its principle of operation (see *Problems 1 to 3*).

   (ii) **Thermocouples** use the emf set up when the junction of two dissimilar metals
is heated (see *Problems 4 to 8*).

   (iii) **Resistance thermometers** use the change in electrical resistance caused by
temperature change (see *Problems 9 to 13*).

   (iv) **Pyrometers** use the principle that all substances emit radiant energy when hot,
the rate of emission depending on their temperature (see *Problems 14 to 16*).

   (v) **Temperature indicating paints and crayons** change colour with increase in
temperature, or melt (see *Problem 17*).

   (vi) **Bimetallic thermometers** use the expansion of metal strips with increase in
temperature (see *Problem 17*).

   (vii) **Mercury-in-steel thermometer** uses the expansion and contraction of mercury
with change in temperature (see *Problem 18*).

   (viii) **Gas thermometer** uses the variation in the volume of a fixed mass of gas at
constant pressure, or the variation in pressure of a fixed mass of gas at constant
volume, to measure temperature (see *Problem 18*).

B. WORKED PROBLEMS ON THE MEASUREMENT OF TEMPERATURE

Problem 1 Describe briefly (a) the construction, (b) principle of operation,
(c) advantages, (d) disadvantages, of a typical liquid-in-glass thermometer.

   (a) **Construction.** A typical liquid-in-glass thermometer is shown in *Fig 1* and
consists of a sealed stem of uniform small-bore tubing, called a capillary tube,

made of glass, with a cylindrical glass bulb formed at one end. The bulb and part of the stem are filled with a liquid such as mercury or alcohol and the remaining part of the tube is evacuated. A temperature scale is formed by etching graduations on the stem (see (b)). A safety reservoir is usually provided, into which the liquid can expand without bursting the glass if the temperature is raised beyond the upper limit of the scale.

(b) **Principle of operation.** The operation of a liquid-in-glass thermometer depends on the liquid expanding with increase in temperature and contracting with decrease in temperature. The position of the end of the column of liquid in the tube is a measure of the temperature of the liquid in the bulb — shown as 15°C in *Fig 1*, which is about room temperature. Two fixed points are needed

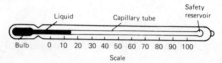

Fig 1

to calibrate the thermometer, with the interval between these points being divided into 'degrees'. In the first thermometer, made by Celsius, the fixed points chosen were the temperature of melting ice (0°C) and that of boiling water at standard atmospheric pressure (100°C), in each case the blank stem being marked at the liquid level. The distance between these two points, called the fundamental interval, was divided into 100 equal parts, each equivalent to 1°C, thus forming the scale.

The **clinical thermometer**, with a limited scale around body temperature, the **maximum and/or minimum thermometer**, recording the maximum day temperature and minimum night temperature, and the **Beckman** thermometer, which is used only in accurate measurement of temperature change and has no fixed points, are particular types of liquid-in-glass thermometer which all operate on the same principle.

(c) **Advantages.** The liquid-in-glass thermometer is simple in construction, relatively inexpensive, easy to use and portable, and is the most widely used method of temperature measurement having industrial, chemical, clinical and meteorological applications.

(d) **Disadvantages.** Liquid-in-glass thermometers tend to be fragile and hence easily broken, can only be used where the liquid column is visible, cannot be used for surface temperature measurements, cannot be read from a distance and are unsuitable for high temperature measurements.

Problem 2 State the advantages and disadvantages of using mercury compared with alcohol as the liquid in a liquid-in-glass thermometer.

The use of mercury in a thermometer has many advantages, for mercury:
(i) is clearly visible; (ii) has a fairly uniform rate of expansion;
(iii) is readily obtainable in the pure state; (iv) does not 'wet' the glass;
(v) is a good conductor of heat.
Mercury has a freezing point of −39°C and cannot be used in a thermometer below this tempeature. Its boiling point is 357°C but before this temperature is reached some distillation of the mercury occurs if the space above the mercury is a vacuum. To prevent this, and to extend the upper temperature limits to over 500°C, an inert gas such as nitrogen under pressure is used to fill the remainder

of the capillary tube. Alcohol, often dyed red to be seen in the capillary tube, is considerably cheaper than mercury and has a freezing point of −113°C, which is considerably lower than for mercury. However it has a low boiling point at about 79°C.

Problem 3 List four possible sources of error inherant in liquid-in-glass thermometers.

Typical errors in liquid in glass thermometers may occur due to:
(i) the slow cooling rate of glass; (ii) incorrect positioning of the thermometer;
(iii) a delay in the thermometer becoming steady (i.e. slow response time);
(iv) non-uniformity of the bore of the capillary tube, which means that equal intervals marked on the stem do not correspond to equal temperature intervals.

Problem 4 Describe the principle of operation of a thermocouple.

At the junction between two different metals, say, copper and constantan, there exists a difference in electrical potential, which varies with the temperature of the junction. This is known as the 'thermo-electric effect'. If the circuit is completed with a second junction at a different temperature, a current will flow round the circuit. This principle is used in the thermocouple. Two different metal conductors having their ends twisted together are shown in *Fig 2*. If the two junctions are at different temperatures, a current I flows round the circuit.

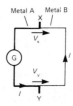

Fig 2

The deflection on the galvanometer G depends on the difference in temperature between junctions X and Y and is caused by the difference between voltages V_X and V_Y. The higher temperature junction is usually called the 'hot junction' and the lower temperature junction the 'cold junction'. If the cold junction is kept at a constant known temperature, the galvanometer can be calibrated to indicate the temperature of the hot junction directly. The cold junction is then known as the reference junction.

In many instrumentation situations, the measuring instrument needs to be located far from the point at which the measurements are to be made. Extension leads are then used, usually made of the same material as the thermocouple but of smaller gauge. The reference junction is then effectively moved to their ends. The thermocouple is used by positioning the hot junction where the temperature is required. The meter will indicate the temperature of the hot junction only if the reference junction is at 0°C for:

(temperature of hot junction) = (temperature of the cold junction)
+ (temperature difference)

In a laboratory the reference junction is often placed in melting ice, but in industry it is often positioned in a thermostatically controlled oven or buried underground where the temperature is constant.

Thermocouple junctions are made by twisting together two wires of dissimilar metals before welding them. The construction of a typical copper-constantan thermocouple for industrial use is shown in *Fig 3*. Apart from the actual junction the two conductors used must be insulated electrically from each other with appropriate insulation and is shown in *Fig 3* as twin-holed tubing. The wires and insulation are usually inserted into a sheath for protection from environments in which they might be damaged or corroded. A copper-constantan thermocouple can measure temperature from $-250°C$ up to about $400°C$, and is used typically with boiler flue gases, food processing and with sub-zero temperature measurement.

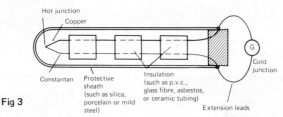

Fig 3

An iron-constantan thermocouple can measure temperature from $-200°C$ to about $850°C$, and is used typically in paper and pulp mills, re-heat and annealing furnaces and in chemical reactors. A chromel-alumel thermocouple can measure temperatures from $-200°C$ to about $1100°C$ and is used typically with blast furnace gases, brick kilns and in glass manufacture.

For the measurement of temperatures above $1100°C$ radiation pyrometers are normally used. However, thermocouples are available made of platinum-platinum/rhodium, capable of measuring temperatures up to $1400°C$, or tungsten-molybedenum which can measure up to $2600°C$.

A thermocouple:
 (i) has a very simple, relatively inexpensive construction;
 (ii) can be made very small and compact; ·
 (iii) is robust;
 (iv) is easily replaced if damaged;
 (v) has a small response time;
 (vi) can be used at a distance from the actual measuring instrument and is thus ideal for use with automatic and remote-control systems.

Sources of error in the thermocouple which are difficult to overcome include:
 (i) voltage drops in leads and junctions;

(ii) possible variations in the temperature of the cold junction;

(iii) stray thermoelectric effects, which are caused by the addition of further metals into the 'ideal' two-metal thermocouple circuit. Additional leads are frequently necessary for extension leads or voltmeter terminal connections.

A thermocouple may be used with a battery- or mains-operated electronic thermometer instead of a millivoltmeter. These devices amplify the small emfs from the thermocouple before feeding them to a multi-range voltmeter calibrated directly with temperature scales. These devices have great accuracy and are almost unaffected by voltage drops in the leads and junctions.

Problem 8 A chromel-alumel thermocouple generates an emf of 5 mV. Determine the temperature of the hot junction if the cold junction is at a temperature of 15°C and the sensitivity of the thermocouple is 0.04 mV/°C.

Temperature difference for 5 mV = $\dfrac{5 \text{ mV}}{0.04 \text{ mV/°C}}$ = 125°C

Temperature of hot junction
  = temperature of cold junction + temperature difference
  = 15°C + 125°C = **140°C**

Problem 9 Describe, with the aid of a diagram, the construction of a typical resistance thermometer. Why is platinum so commonly used in such a thermometer?

Resistance thermometers are made in a variety of sizes, shapes and forms depending on the application for which they are designed. A typical resistance thermometer is shown diagrammatically in *Fig 4*. The most common metal used for the coil in such thermometers is platinum even though its sensitivity is not as high as other metals such as copper and nickel. However, platinum is a very stable metal and provides reproducible results in a resistance thermometer. A platinum resistance thermometer is often used as a calibrating device. Since platinum is expensive, connecting leads of another metal, usually copper, are used with the thermometer to connect it to a measuring circuit.

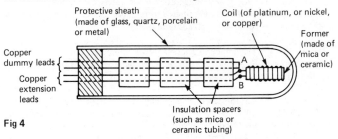

Fig 4

The platinum and the connecting leads are shown joined at A and B in *Fig 4*, although sometimes this junction may be made outside of the sheath. However, these leads often come into close contact with the heat source which can introduce errors into the measurements. These may be eliminated by including a pair of identical leads, called dummy leads, which experience the same temperature change as the extension leads (see *Problem 10*).

With most metals a rise in temperature causes an increase in electrical resistance, and since resistance can be measured accurately this property can be used to measure temperature. If the resistance of a length of wire at $0°C$ is R_0, and its resistance at $θ°C$ is $R_θ$, then $R_θ = R_0 (1 + αθ)$, where $α$ is the temperature coefficient of resistance of the material.

Rearranging gives: temperature $θ = \dfrac{R_θ - R_0}{αR_0}$

Values of R_0 and $α$ may be determined experimentally or obtained from existing data. Thus, if $R_θ$ can be measured, temperature $θ$ can be calculated. This is the principle of operation of a resistance thermometer. Although a sensitive ohmmeter can be used to measure $R_θ$, for more accurate determinations a Wheatstone bridge circuit is used as shown in *Fig 5*. This circuit compares an unknown resistance $R_θ$ with others of known values, R_1 and R_2 being fixed values and R_3 being variable. Galvanometer G is a sensitive centre-zero micro-ammeter. R_3 is varied until zero deflection is obtained on the galvanometer, i.e. no current flows through G and the bridge is said to be 'balanced'.

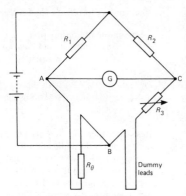

At balance: $R_2R_θ = R_1R_3$, from which

$$R_θ = \frac{R_1R_3}{R_2},$$

and if R_1 and R_2 are of equal value, then $R_θ = R_3$.

Fig 5

A resistance thermometer may be connected between points A and B in *Fig 5* and its resistance $R_θ$ at any temperature $θ$ accurately measured. Dummy leads included in arm BC help to eliminate errors caused by the extension leads which are normally necessary in such a thermometer.

(a) Resistance thermometers using a nickel coil are used mainly in the range $-100°C$ to $300°C$, whereas platinum resistance thermometers are capable of measuring with greater accuracy temperatures in the range $-200°C$ to about $800°C$. This upper range may be extended to about $1500°C$ if high melting point materials are used for the sheath and coil construction.

(b) Platinum is commonly used in resistance thermometers since it is chemically inert, i.e. unreactive, resists corrosion and oxidation and has a high melting point of $1769°C$. A disadvantage of platinum is its slow response to temperature variation.

(c) Platinum resistance thermometers may be used as calibrating devices or in applications such as heat treating and annealing processes and can be adapted easily for use with automatic recording or control systems. Resistance thermometers tend to be fragile and easily damaged especially when subjected to excessive vibration or shock.

Problem 12 A platinum resistance thermometer has a resistance of 25Ω at 0°C. When measuring the temperature of an annealing process a resistance value of 60 Ω is recorded. To what temperature does this correspond? Take the temperature coefficient of resistance of platinum as 0.0038/°C.

$R_\theta = R_0(1 + \alpha\theta)$, where $R_0 = 25\ \Omega$, $R_\theta = 60\ \Omega$ and $\alpha = 0.0038/°C$.

Rearranging gives **temperature** $\theta = \dfrac{R_\theta - R_0}{\alpha R_0} = \dfrac{60 - 25}{(0.0038)(25)} = \mathbf{368.4°C}$

Problem 13 (a) What is a thermistor? (b) What advantage does a thermistor possess over platinum when used in a resistance thermometer?

(a) A thermistor is a semiconducting material — such as mixtures of oxides of copper, manganese, cobalt, etc. — in the form of a fused bead connected to two leads. As its temperature is increased its resistance rapidly decreases. Typical resistance/ temperature curves for a thermistor and common metals are shown in *Fig 6*. The resistance of a typical thermistor can vary from 400 Ω at 0°C to 100 Ω at 140°C.

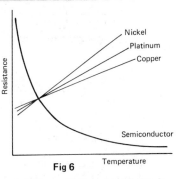

Fig 6

(b) The main advantages of a thermistor are its high sensitivity and small size. It provides an inexpensive method of measuring and detecting small changes in temperature.

Problem 14 What is a pyrometer? In what applications it is used?

A pyrometer is a device for measuring very high temperatures and uses the principle that all substances emit radiant energy when hot, the rate of emission depending on their temperature. The measurement of thermal radiation is therefore a convenient method of determining the temperature of hot sources and is particularly useful in industrial processes. There are two main types of pyrometer, namely the total radiation pyrometer and the optical pyrometer.

Pyrometers are very convenient instruments since they can be used at a safe and comfortable distance from the hot source. Thus applications of pyrometers are found in measuring the temperature of molten metals, the interiors of furnaces or the interiors of volcanoes. Total radiation pyrometers can also be used in conjunction with devices which record and control temperature continuously.

7

Problem 15 Explain briefly, with appropriate sketches, the basic principle of operation of (a) a total radiation pyrometer; (b) an optical pyrometer.

(a) A typical arrangement of a **total radiation pyrometer** is shown in *Fig 7*. Radiant energy from a hot source, such as a furnace, is focused on to the hot junction of a thermocouple after reflection from a concave mirror. The temperature rise recorded by the thermocouple depends on the amount of radiant energy received, which in turn depends on the temperature of the hot source. The galvanometer G shown connected to the thermocouple records the current which results from the emf developed and may be calibrated to give a direct reading of the temperature of the hot source. The thermocouple is protected

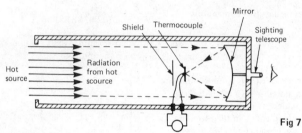

Fig 7

from direct radiation by a shield as shown and the hot source may be viewed through the sighting telescope. For greater sensitivity, a thermopile may be used, a thermopile being a number of thermocouples connected in series. Total radiation pyrometers are used to measure temperature in the range 700°C to 2000°C.

(b) **Optical pyrometer.** When the temperature of an object is raised sufficiently two visual effects occur; the object appears brighter and that there is a change in colour of the light emitted. These effects are used in the optical pyrometer where a comparison or matching is made between the brightness of the glowing hot source and the light from a filament of known temperature.

The most frequently used optical pyrometer is the disappearing filament pyrometer and a typical arrangement is shown in *Fig 8*. A filament lamp is built into a telescope arrangement which receives radiation from a hot source, an image of which is seen through an eyepiece. A red filter is incorporated as

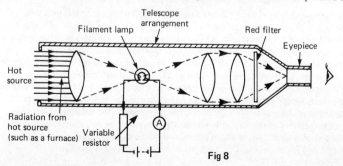

Fig 8

a protection to the eye. The current flowing through the lamp is controlled by a variable resistor. As the current is increased the temperature of the filament increases and its colour changes. When viewed through the eyepiece the filament of the lamp appears superimposed on the image of the radiant energy from the hot source. The current is varied until the filament glows as brightly as the background. It will then merge into the background and seem to disappear. The current required to achieve this is a measure of the temperature of the hot source and the ammeter can be calibrated to read the temperature directly. Optical pyrometers may be used to measure temperatures up to, and even in excess of, 3000°C.

Problem 16 State five advantages and five disadvantages of pyrometers compared with other temperature measuring devices.

Advantages of pyrometers

(i) There is no practical limit to the temperature that a pyrometer can measure.
(ii) A pyrometer need not be brought directly into the hot zone and so is free from the effects of heat and chemical attack that can often cause other measuring devices to deteriorate in use.
(iii) Very fast rates of change of temperature can be followed by a pyrometer.
(iv) The temperature of moving bodies can be measured.
(v) The lens system makes the pyrometer virtually independent of its distance from the source.

Disadvantages of pyrometers

(i) A pyrometer is often more expensive than other temperaturing measuring devices.
(ii) A direct view of the heat process is necessary.
(iii) Manual adjustment is necessary.
(iv) A reasonable amount of skill and care is required in calibrating and using a pyrometer. For each new measuring situation the pyrometer must be re-calibrated.
(v) The temperature of the surroundings may affect the reading of the pyrometer and such errors are difficult to eliminate.

Problem 17 Briefly explain the principle of operation and the main uses of:
(a) temperature indicating paints and temperature sensitive crayons;
(b) bimetallic thermometers.

(a) **Temperature indicating paints** contain substances which change their colour when heated to certain temperatures. This change is usually due to chemical decomposition, such as loss of water, in which the change in colour of the paint after having reached the particular temperature will be a permanent one. However in some types, the original colour returns after cooling. Temperature indicating paints are used where the temperature of inaccessible parts of apparatus and machines is required. They are particularly useful in heat-treatment processes where the temperature of the component needs to be known before a quenching operation. There are several such paints available and most have only a small temperature range so that different paints have to be used for different temperatures. The usual range of temperatures covered by these paints is from about 30°C to 700°C.

Temperature sensitive crayons consist of fusible solids compressed into the form of a stick. The melting point of such crayons is used to determine when a given temperature has been reached. The crayons are simple to use but indicate a single temperature only, i.e. its melting point temperature. There are over a hundred different crayons available, each covering a particular range of temperature. Crayons are available for temperatures within the range of 50°C to 1400°C. Such crayons are used in metallurgical applications such as preheating before welding, hardening, annealling or tempering, or in monitoring the temperature of critical parts of machines or for checking mould temperatures in the rubber and plastics industries.

(b) **Bimetallic thermometers** depend on the expansion of metal strips which operate an indicating pointer. Two thin metal strips of differing thermal expansion are welded or riveted together and the curvature of the bimetallic strip changes with temperature change. For greater sensitivity the strips may be coiled into a flat spiral or helix, one end being fixed and the other being made to rotate a pointer over a scale. Bimetallic thermometers are useful for alarm and overtemperature applications where extreme accuracy is not essential. If the whole is placed in a sheath, protection from corrosive environments is achieved but with a reduction in response characteristics. The normal upper limit of temperature measurement by this thermometer is about 200°C, although with special metals the range can be extended to about 400°C.

Problem 18 Explain briefly the principle of operation and the main uses of the: (a) mercury-in-steel thermometer; (b) gas thermometer.

(a) The **mercury-in-steel thermometer** is an extension of the principle of the mercury-in-glass thermometer. Mercury in a steel bulb expands via a small bore capillary tube into a pressure indicating device, say a Bourdon gauge, the position of the pointer indicating the amount of expansion and thus the temperature. The advantages of this instrument are that it is robust and, by increasing the length of the capillary tube, the gauge can be placed some distance from the bulb and can thus be used to monitor temperatures in positions which are inaccessible to the liquid in glass thermometer. Such thermometers may be used to measure temperatures up to 600°C.

(b) The **gas thermometer** consists of a flexible U-tube of mercury connected by a capillary tube to a vessel containing gas. The change in the volume of a fixed mass of gas at constant pressure, or the change in pressure of a fixed mass of gas at constant volume, may be used to measure temperature. This thermometer is cumbersome and rarely used to measure temperature directly, but it is often used as a standard with which to calibrate other types of thermometer. With pure hydrogen the range of the instrument extends from −240°C to 1500°C and measurements can be made with extreme accuracy.

Problem 19 State which device would be most suitable to measure the following:
(a) metal in a furnace, in the range 50°C to 1600°C;
(b) the air in an office in the range 0°C to 40°C;
(c) boiler flue gas in the range 15°C to 300°C;
(d) a metal surface, where a visual indication is required when it reaches 425°C;
(e) materials in a high-temperature furnace in the range 2000°C to 2800°C;

(f) to calibrate a thermocouple in the range $-100°C$ to $500°C$;
(g) brick in a kiln up to $900°C$;
(h) an inexpensive method for food processing applications in the range $-25°C$ to $-75°C$.

(a) Radiation pyrometer;
(b) Mercury-in-glass thermometer;
(c) Copper-constantan thermocouple;
(d) Temperature-sensitive crayon;
(e) Optical pyrometer;
(f) Platinum resistance therometer or gas thermometer;
(g) Chromel-alumel thermocouple;
(h) Alcohol-in-glass thermometer.

C. FURTHER PROBLEMS ON THE MEASUREMENT OF TEMPERATURE

(a) SHORT ANSWER PROBLEMS

For each of the temperature measuring devices listed in 1 to 10, state very briefly its principle of operation and the range of temperatures that it is capable of measuring.

1 Mercury-in-glass thermometer.
2 Alcohol-in-glass thermometer.
3 Thermocouple.
4 Platinum resistance thermometer.
5 Total radiation pyrometer.
6 Optical pyrometer.
7 Temperature sensitive crayons.
8 Bimetallic thermometer.
9 Mercury in steel thermometer.
10 Gas thermometer.

(b) MULTI-CHOICE PROBLEMS (Answers on page 156)

1 The most suitable device for measuring very small temperature changes is a
   (a) thermopile; (b) thermocouple; (c) thermistor.
2 When two wires of different metals are twisted together and heat applied to the junction, an emf is produced. This effect is used in a thermocouple to measure:
   (a) emf; (b) temperature; (c) expansion; (d) heat.
3 A cold junction of a thermocouple is at room temperature of $15°C$. A voltmeter connected to the thermocouple circuit indicates 10 mV. If the voltmeter is calibrated as $20°C/mV$, the temperature of the hot source is:
   (a) $185°C$; (b) $200°C$; (c) $35°C$; (d) $215°C$.
4 The emf generated by a copper-constantan thermometer is 15 mV. If the cold junction is at a temperature of $20°C$, the temperature of the hot junction when the sensitivity of the thermocouple is 0.03 mV/$°C$ is:
   (a) $480°C$; (b) $520°C$; (c) $20.45°C$; (d) $500°C$.

11

In *Problems 5 to 12,* select the most appropriate temperature measuring device from this list.

(a) copper-constantan thermocouple; (b) thermistor;
(c) mercury-in-glass thermometer; (d) total radiation pyrometer;
(e) platinum resistance thermometer; (f) gas thermometer;
(g) temperature sensitive crayon; (h) alcohol-in-glass thermometer;
(i) bimetallic thermometer; (j) mercury-in-steel thermometer;
(k) optical pyrometer.

5 Overtemperature alarm at about 180°C.
6 Food processing plant in the range −250°C to +250°C.
7 Automatic recording system for a heat treating process in the range 90°C to 250°C.
8 Surface of molten metals in the range 1000°C to 1800°C.
9 To calibrate accurately a mercury-in-glass thermometer.
10 Furnace up to 3000°C.
11 Inexpensive method of measuring very small changes in temperature.
12 Metal surface where a visual indication is required when the temperature reaches 520°C.

(c) CONVENTIONAL PROBLEMS

For each of the temperature measuring devices listed in *Problems 1 to 10,*
(a) describe, with appropriate sketches, their construction and state how they operate; (b) state their characteristics and range; (c) discuss their limitations, advantages and disadvantages; (d) state typical applications where they may be used.

1 Thermocouple.
2 Mercury-in-glass thermometer.
3 Optical pyrometer.
4 Platinum resistance thermometer.
5 Alcohol-in-glass thermometer.
6 Gas thermometer.
7 Total radiation pyrometer.
8 Temperature indicating paints and temperature sensitive crayons.
9 Mercury-in-steel thermometer.
10 Bimetallic thermometer.
11 A platinum-platinum/rhodium thermocouple generates an emf of 7.5 mV. If the cold junction is at a temperature of 20°C, determine the temperature of the hot junction. Assume the sensitivity of the thermocouple to be 6 μV/°C.   [1270°C]
12 Explain how temperature is measured using a resistance thermometer incorporating a Wheatstone bridge circuit. Explain why dummy leads are used in such a circuit. Why is platinum most often used in a resistance thermometer?
13 A platinum resistance thermometer has a resistance of 100Ω at 0°C. When measuring the temperature of a heat process a resistance value of 177Ω is measured using a Wheatstone bridge. Given that the temperature coefficient of resistance of platinum is 0.0038/°C, determine the temperature of the heat process correct to the nearest degree.   [203°C]

2 The measurement of fluid flow

A MAIN POINTS CONCERNED WITH THE MEASUREMENT OF FLUID FLOW

1   The measurement of fluid flow is of great importance in many industrial processes, some examples including air flow in the ventilating ducts of a coal mine, the flow rate of water in a condenser at a power station, the flow rate of liquids in chemical processes, the control and monitoring of the fuel, lubricating and cooling fluids of ships and aircraft engines, and so on. Fluid flow is one of the most difficult of industrial measurements to carry out, since flow behaviour depends on a great many variables concerning the physical properties of a fluid.

2   There are available a large number of fluid flow measuring instruments generally called **flowmeters**, which can measure the flow rate of liquids (in m^3/s) or the mass flow rate of gaseous fluids (in kg/s). The two main categories of flowmeters are differential pressure flowmeters and mechanical flowmeters.

3   (i) When certain flowmeters are installed in pipelines they often cause an obstruction to the fluid flowing in the pipe by reducing the cross-sectional area of the pipeline. This causes a change in the velocity of the fluid, with a related change in pressure. *Fig 1* shows a section through a pipeline into which a flowmeter has been inserted. The flow rate of the fluid may be determined from a measurement of the difference between the pressures on the walls of the pipe at specified distances upstream and downstream of the flowmeter. Such devices are known as **differential pressure flowmeters**.

(ii) The pressure difference in *Fig 1* is measured using a manometer connected to appropriate pressure tapping points. The pressure is seen to be greater upstream of the flowmeter than downstream, the pressure difference being shown as h.

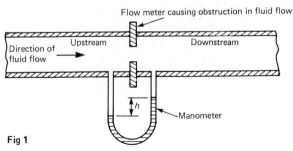

Flow meter causing obstruction in fluid flow

Upstream   Downstream

Direction of
fluid flow →

h

Manometer

Fig 1

Calibration of the manometer depends on the shape of the obstruction, the positions of the pressure tapping points and the physical properties of the fluid.

(iii) Examples of differential pressure flowmeters commonly used include:
   (a) Orifice plate (see *Problems 1 and 2*).
   (b) Venturi tube (see *Problems 3 and 4*).
   (c) Flow nozzles (see *Problem 5*).
   (d) Pitot-static tube (see *Problems 6 to 8*).
(iv) British Standard reference BS 1042: Part 1: 1964 and Part 2A: 1973 'Methods for the measurement of fluid flow in pipes' gives specifications for measurement, manufacture, tolerances, accuracy, sizes, choice, and so on, of differential flowmeters.

4 (i) With mechanical flowmeters a sensing element situated in a pipeline is displaced by the fluid flowing past it.
   (ii) Examples of mechanical flowmeters commonly used include:
      (a) Deflecting vane flowmeter (see *Problem 9*).
      (b) Turbine type meters (see *Problem 10*).

5 Other flowmeters available include:
   (a) Float and tapered-tube meter (see *Problems 11 and 12*),
   (b) Electromagnetic flowmeter (see *Problem 13*),
   (c) Hot wire anemometers (see *Problem 14*).

B. WORKED PROBLEMS ON THE MEASUREMENT OF FLUID FLOW

Problem 1 Describe with an appropriate sketch the construction of a typical orifice plate and state how it is used to measure fluid flow rate.

An orifice plate consists of a circular, thin, flat plate with a hole (or orifice) machined through its centre to fine limits of accuracy. The orifice has a

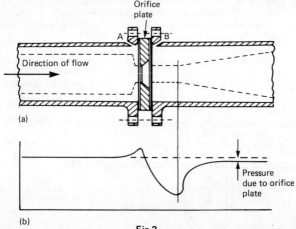

Fig 2

diameter less than the pipeline into which the plate is installed and a typical section of an installation is shown in *Fig 2(a)*. Orifice plates are manufactured in stainless steel, monel metal, polyester glass fibre, and for large pipes, such as sewers or hot gas mains, in brick and concrete.

When a fluid moves through a restriction in a pipe, the fluid accelerates and a reduction in pressure occurs, the magnitude of which is related to the flow rate of the fluid. The variation of pressure near an orifice plate is shown in *Fig 2(b)*. The position of minimum pressure is located downstream from the orifice plate where the flow stream is narrowest. This point of minimum cross-sectional area of the jet is called the 'vena contracta'. Beyond this point the pressure rises but does not return to the original upstream value and there is a permanent pressure loss. This loss depends on the size and type of orifice plate, the positions of the upstream and downstream pressure tappings and the change in fluid velocity between the pressure tappings which depends on the flow rate and the dimensions of the orifice plate.

In *Fig 2(a)* corner pressure tappings are shown at A and B. Alternatively, with an orifice plate inserted into a pipeline of diameter d, pressure tappings are often located at distances of d and $d/2$ from the plate respectively upstream and down-stream. At distance d upstream the flow pattern is not influenced by the presence of the orifice plate and distance $d/2$ coincides with the vena contracts.

Problem 2 (a) List two advantages and three disadvantages of using orifice plates to measure flow rate. (b) State in which applications orifice plates are likely to be used.

(a) *Advantages of orifice plates:*
   (i) they are relatively inexpensive;
   (ii) they are usually thin enough to fit between an existing pair of pipe flanges.

   Disadvantages of orifice plates:
   (i) the sharpness of the edge of the orifice can become worn with use, causing calibration errors;
   (ii) the possible build-up of matter against the plate;
   (iii) a considerable loss in the pumping efficiency due to the pressure loss down-stream of the plate.
(b) Orifice plates are usually used in medium and large pipes and are best suited to the indication and control of essentially constant flow rates. Several applications are found in the general process industries.

Problem 3 Explain, with the aid of a diagram, the construction of a Venturi tube.

The Venturi tube or venturimeter is an instrument for measuring with accuracy the flow rate of fluids in pipes. A typical arrangement of a section through such a device is shown in *Fig 3*, and consists of a short converging conical tube called the inlet or upstream cone, leading to a cylindrical portion called the throat. This is followed by a diverging section called the outlet or recovery cone. The entrance and exit diameter is the same as that of the pipeline into which it is installed. Angle β is usually a maximum of 21°, giving a taper of $\beta/2$ or 10½°. The length of the throat is made equal to the diameter of the throat. Angle α is about 5° to 7° to ensure a minimum loss of energy but where this is unimportant α can be as large as 14° to 15°.

15

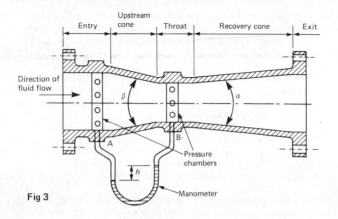

Fig 3

Pressure tappings are made at the entry (at A) and at the throat (at B) and the pressure difference h which is measured using a manometer or similar gauge, is dependent on the flow rate through the meter. Usually pressure chambers are fitted around the entrance pipe and the throat circumference with a series of tapping holes made in the chamber to which the manometer is connected. This ensures that an average pressure is recorded. The loss of energy due to turbulence which occurs just downstream with an orifice plate is largely avoided in the venturimeter due to the gradual divergence beyond the throat.

Venturimeters are usually made a permanent installation in a pipeline and are manufactured usually from stainless steel, cast iron, monel metal or polyester glass fibre.

Problem 4 State three advantages and two disadvantages of venturimeters as a method of determining flow rate in pipelines.

Advantages of venturimeters:

(i)   High accuracy results are possible.
(ii) There is a low pressure loss in the tube (typically only 2% to 3% in a well proportioned tube).
(iii) Venturimeters are unlikely to trap any matter from the fluid being metered.

Disadvantages of venturimeters:

(i) High manufacturing cost.
(ii) The installation tends to be rather long (typically 120 mm for a pipe of internal diameter 50 mm).

Problem 5 How does a flow nozzle compare with an orifice plate and a venturimeter for measuring fluid flow rates?

The flow nozzle lies between the orifice plate and the venturimeter both in performance and cost. A typical section through a flow nozzle is shown in *Fig 4*

16

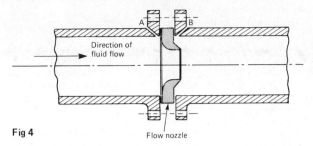

Fig 4

Flow nozzle

where pressure tapping are located immediately adjacent to the upstream and downstream faces of the nozzle (i.e. at points A and B). The fluid flow does not contract any further as it leaves the nozzle and the pressure loss created is considerably less than that occurring with orifice plates. Flow nozzles are suitable for use with high velocity flows for they do not suffer the wear that occurs in orifice plate edges during such flows.

Problem 6 Explain briefly the principle of a Pitot-static tube and show how this principle is used in a practical device.

A Pitot-static tube is a device for measuring the velocity of moving fluids or of the velocity of bodies moving through fluids. It consists of one tube, called the Pitot tube, with an open end facing the direction of the fluid motion, shown as pipe R in *Fig 5*, and a second tube, called the static tube, with the opening at 90° to the fluid flow, shown as T in *Fig 5*. Pressure recorded by a pressure gauge moving with the flow, i.e. static or stationary relative to the fluid, is called static pressure and connecting a pressure gauge to a small hole in the wall of a pipe, such as point T in *Fig 5*, is the easiest method of recording this pressure. The difference in pressure $(p_R - p_T)$, shown as h in the manometer of *Fig 5*, is an indication of the speed of the fluid in the pipe.

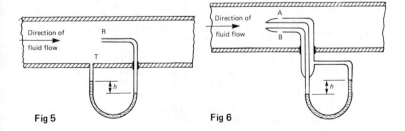

Fig 5

Fig 6

Fig 6 shows a practical Pitot-static tube consisting of a pair of concentric tubes. The centre tube is the impact probe which has an open end which faces 'head-on' into the flow. The outer tube has a series of holes around its circumference located at right angles to the flow, as shown by A B in *Fig 6*. The manometer, showing a pressure difference of h, may be calibrated to indicate the velocity of flow directly.

17

A Pitot-static tube may be used for both turbulent and non-turbulent flow. The tubes can be made very small compared with the size of the pipeline and the monitoring of flow velocity at particular points in the cross-section of a duct can be achieved. The device is generally unsuitable for routine measurements and in industry is often used for making preliminary tests of flow rate in order to specify permanent flow measuring equipment for a pipeline. The main use of Pitot tubes is to measure the velocity of solid bodies moving through fluids, such as the velocity of ships. In these cases, the tube is connected to a Bourdon pressure gauge which can be calibrated to read velocity directly. A development of the Pitot tube, a pitometer, tests the flow of water in water mains and detects leakages.

Problem 8 State four advantages and three disadvantages of Pitot-static tubes.

Advantages of Pitot-static tubes:
(i)   They are inexpensive devices.   (ii)   They are easy to install.
(iii) They produce only a small pressure loss in the tube.
(iv) They do not interrupt the flow.

Disadvantages of Pitot-static tubes:
(i)   Due to the small pressure difference, they are only suitable for high velocity fluids.
(ii) They can measure the flow rate only at a particular position in the cross-section of the pipe.
(iii) They easily become blocked when used with fluids carrying particles.

Problem 9 Describe briefly the construction and principle of operation of a deflecting vane flowmeter.

The deflecting vane flowmeter consists basically of a pivoted vane suspended in the fluid flow stream as shown in *Fig 7*. When a jet of fluid impinges on the vane it deflects from its normal position by an amount proportional to the flow rate.

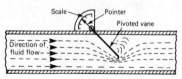

Fig 7

The movement of the vane is indicated on a scale which may be calibrated in flow units. This type of meter is normally used for measuring liquid flow rates in open channels or for measuring the velocity of air in ventilation ducts. The main disadvantages of this device is that it restricts the flow rate and it needs to be recalibrated for fluids of differing densities.

Problem 10 Name three turbine-type flowmeters and describe briefly for each, their construction, principle of operation and main applications.

Turbine-type flowmeters are those which use some form of multi-vane rotor and are driven by the fluid being investigated. Three such devices are the cup anemo-meter, the rotary vane positive displacement meter and the turbine flowmeter.

(a) **Cup anemometer.** An anemometer is an instrument which measures the velocity of moving gases and is most often used for the measurement of wind speed. The cup anemometer has three or four cups of hemispherical shape mounted at the end of arms radiating horizontally from a fixed point. The cup system spins round the vertical axis with a speed approximately proportional to the velocity of the wind. With the aid of a mechanical and/or electrical counter the wind speed can be determined and the device is easily adapted for automatic recording.

(b) **Rotary vane positive displacement meters** measure the flow rate by indicating the quantity of liquid flowing through the meter in a given time. A typical such device is shown in section in *Fig 8* and consists of a cylindrical chamber into which is placed a rotor containing a number

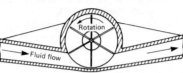

Fig 8

of vanes (six in this case). Liquid entering the chamber turns the rotor and a known amount of liquid is trapped and carried round to the outlet. If x is the volume displaced by one blade then for each revolution of the rotor in *Fig 8*, the total volume displaced is $6x$. The rotor shaft may be coupled to a mechanical counter and electrical devices which may be calibrated to give flow volume. This type of meter in its various forms is used widely for the measurement of domestic and industrial water consumption, for the accurate measurement of petrol in petrol pumps and for the consumption and batch control measurements in the general process and food industries for measuring flows as varied as solvents, tar and mollases (i.e. thickish treacle).

(c) A **turbine flowmeter** contains in its construction a rotor to which blades are attached which spin at a velocity proportional to the velocity of the fluid which flows through the meter. A typical section through such a meter is shown in *Fig 9*. The number of revolutions made by the turbine blades may be determined by a mechanical or electrical device enabling the flow rate or total flow to be

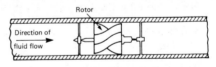

Fig 9

determined. Advantages of turbine flowmeters include a compact durable form, high accuracy, wide temperature and pressure capability and good response characteristics. Applications include the volumetric measurement of both crude and refined petroleum products in pipelines up to 600 mm bore, and in the water, power, aerospace, process and food industries, and with modification may be used for natural, industrial and liquid gas measurements. Turbine flowmeters require periodic inspection and cleaning of the working parts.

Problem 11 Describe briefly the principle of operation of a float and tapered tube flowmeter.

With orifice plates and venturimeters the area of the opening in the obstruction is fixed and any change in the flowrate produces a corresponding change in pressure. With the float and tapered tube meter the area of the restriction may be varied so as to maintain a steady pressure differential. A typical meter of this type is shown diagrammatically in *Fig 10* where a vertical tapered tube contains a 'float' which has a density greater than the fluid. The float in the tapered tube produces a restriction to the fluid flow. The fluid can only pass in the annular area between the float and the walls of the tube. This reduction in area produces an increase in velocity and hence a pressure difference, which causes the float to rise. The greater the flow rate, the greater is the rise in the float position, and vice-versa. The position of the float is a measure of the flow rate of the fluid and this is shown on a vertical scale engraved on a transparent tube of plastic or glass. For air, a small sphere is used for the float but for liquids there is a tendency to instability and the float is then designed with vanes

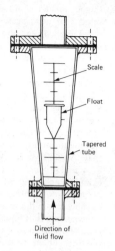

Fig 10

which cause it to spin and thus stabilise itself as the liquid flows past. Such meters are often called 'rotameters'. Calibration of float and tapered tube flow meters can be achieved using a Pitot-static tube or by installing an orifice plate or venturimeter in the pipeline.

Problem 12 State three advantages and four disadvantages of float and tapered tube flowmeters and suggest possible practical applications of the device.

Advantages of float and tapered tube flowmeters:
(i)   Have a very simple design.
(ii) Can be made direct reading.
(iii) Can measure very low flow rates.

Disadvantages of float and tapered tube flowmeters:
(i)   They are prone to errors, such as those caused by temperature fluctuations.
(ii) They can only be installed vertically in a pipeline.
(iii) They cannot be used with liquids containing large amounts of solids in suspension.
(iv) They need to be recalibrated for fluids of different densities.

Practical applications of float and tapered tube meters are found in the medical field, in instrument purging, in mechanical engineering test rigs and in simple process applications, in particular for very low flow rates. Many corrosive fluids can be handled with this device without complications.

Problem 13 Explain the principle of operation of an electromagnetic flowmeter, stating its main advantages and applications.

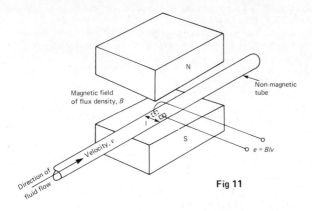

Fig 11

The flow rate of fluids which conduct electricity, such as water or molten metal, can be measured using an electromagnetic flow meter whose principle of operation is based on the laws of electromagnetic induction. When a conductor of length l moves at right angles to a magnetic field of density B at a velocity v, an induced emf e is generated, given by $e = B\,l\,v$, (see *Engineering Science 2 Checkbook*, chapter 3). With the electromagnetic flowmeter arrangement shown in *Fig 11*, the fluid is the conductor and the emf is detected by two electrodes placed across the diameter of the non-magnetic tube. Rearranging $e = B\,l\,v$ gives

velocity $v = \dfrac{e}{Bl}$

Thus with B and l known, when e is measured, the velocity of the fluid can be calculated.

Main advantages of electromagnetic flowmeters:
(i) Unlike other methods, there is nothing to directly impede the fluid flow.
(ii) There is a linear relationship between the fluid flow and the induced emf.
(iii) Flow can be metered in either direction by using a centre-zero measuring instrument.

Applications of electromagnetic flowmeters are found in the measurement of speeds of slurries, pastes and viscous liquids, and they are also widely used in the water production, supply and treatment industry.

Problem 14 What is a hot-wire anemometer? State two advantages of the device.

A simple hot-wire anemometer consists of a small piece of wire which is heated by an electric current and positioned in the air or gas stream whose velocity is to be measured. The stream passing the wire cools it, the rate of cooling being dependant on the flow velocity. In practice there are various ways in which this is achieved:
(i) If a constant current is passed through the wire, variation in flow results in a change of temperature of the wire and hence a change in resistance which may be measured by a Wheatstone bridge arrangement. The change in resistance may be related to fluid flow.
(ii) If the wire's resistance, and hence temperature, is kept constant, a change in

fluid flow results in a corresponding change in current which can be calibrated as an indication of the flow rate.

(iii) A thermocouple may be incorporated in the assembly, monitoring the hot wire and recording the temperature which is an indication of the air or gas velocity.

Advantages of the hot-wire anemometer:
(a) Its size is small; (b) it has great sensitivity.

Problem 15 Choose the most appropriate fluid flow measuring device for the following circumstances:
(a) The most accurate, permanent installation for measuring liquid flow rate.
(b) To determine the velocity of low-speed aircraft and ships.
(c) Accurate continuous volumetric measurement of crude petroleum products in a duct of 500 mm bore.
(d) To give a reasonable indication of the mean flow velocity, while maintaining a steady pressure difference on a hydraulic test rig.
(e) For an essentially constant flow rate with reasonable accuracy in a large pipe bore, with a cheap and simple installation.

(a) Venturimeter.
(b) Pitot-static tube.
(c) Turbine flow meter.
(d) Float and tapered-tube flow meter.
(e) Orifice plate.

C. FURTHER PROBLEMS ON THE MEASUREMENT OF FLUID FLOW

(a) SHORT ANSWER PROBLEMS

In the flowmeters listed 1 to 10, state typical practical applications of each.

1 Orifice plate.	2 Venturimeter.
3 Float and tapered-tube meter.	4 Electromagnetic flowmeter.
5 Pitot-static tube.	6 Hot-wire anemometer.
7 Turbine flowmeter.	8 Deflecting vane flowmeter.
9 Flow nozzles.	10 Rotary vane positive displacement meter.

(b) MULTI-CHOICE PROBLEMS (Answers on page 156)

1 The term 'flow rate' usually refers to:
(a) mass flow rate; (b) velocity of flow; (c) volumetric flow rate.

2 The most suitable device for determining the velocity of solid bodies moving through fluids is:
(a) venturimeter; (b) orifice plate; (c) pitot-static tube; (d) float and tapered-tube meter.

3 Which of the following statements is false?
When a fluid moves through a restriction in a pipe:
(a) the fluid accelerates and the pressure increases;

22

(b) the fluid decelerates and the pressure decreases;

(c) the fluid decelerates and the pressure increases;

(d) the fluid accelerates and the pressure decreases.

4 With an orifice plate in a pipeline the vena contracta is situated:

    (a) downstream at the position of minimum cross-sectional area of flow;

    (b) upstream at the position of minimum cross-sectional area of flow;

    (c) downstream at the position of maximum cross-sectional area of flow;

    (d) upstream at the position of maximum cross-sectional area of flow.

In *Problems 5 to 14*, select the most appropriate device for the particular requirements from the following list:

(a) orifice plate;   (b) turbine flowmeter; (c) flow nozzle;

(d) pitometer;   (e) venturimeter;   (f) cup anemometer;

(g) electromagnetic flowmeter;   (h) pitot-static tube;

(i) float and tapered-tube meter;   (j) hot-wire anemometer;

(k) deflecting vane flow meter.

5 Easy to install, reasonably inexpensive, for high-velocity flows.

6 To measure the flow rate of gas, incorporating a Wheatstone bridge circuit.

7 Very low flow rate of corrosive liquid in a chemical process.

8 To detect leakages from water mains.

9 To determine the flow rate of liquid metals without impeding its flow.

10 To measure the velocity of wind.

11 Constant flow rate, large bore pipe, in the general process industry.

12 To make a preliminary test of flow rate in order to specify permanent flow measuring equipment.

13 To determine the flow rate of fluid very accurately with low pressure loss.

14 To measure the flow rate of air in a ventilating duct.

(c) CONVENTIONAL PROBLEMS

For the flow measurement devices listed 1 to 5, (a) describe briefly their construction; (b) state their principle of operation; (c) state their characteristics and limitations; (d) state typical practical applications; (e) discuss their advantages and disadvantages.

1 Orifice plate. 2 Venturimeter. 3 Pitot-static tube.

4 Float and tapered-tube meter. 5 Turbine flowmeter.

3 Tensile testing

A. MAIN POINTS CONCERNED WITH TENSILE TESTING

1   Forces acting on a material cause a change in dimensions and the material is said
    to be in a state of **stress**. Stress is the ratio of the applied force F to cross-sectional
    area A of the material. The symbol used for tensile and compressive stress is σ
    (Greek letter sigma). The unit of stress is the Pascal Pa, where 1 Pa $= 1$ N/m^2.

Hence

$$\sigma = \frac{F}{A} \text{ Pa}$$

where F is the force in newtons and A is the cross-sectional area in square meters.
For tensile and compressive forces, the cross-sectional area is that which is at right
angles to the direction of the force. For a shear force the shear stress is equal to
F/A, where the cross-sectional area A is that which is parallel to the direction of
the force.
The symbol used for shear stress is the Greek letter tau, τ.

2   The fractional change in a dimension of a material produced by a force is called
    the **strain**.
    For a tensile or compressive force, strain is the ratio of the change of length to the
    original length. The symbol used for strain is ϵ (Greek epsilon). For a material of
    length l metres which changes in length by an amount x metres when subjected to
    stress,

$$\epsilon = \frac{x}{l}$$

Strain is dimensionless and is often expressed as a percentage,

i.e.

$$\text{Percentage strain} = \frac{x}{l} \times 100$$

For a shear force, strain is denoted
by the symbol γ (Greek letter gamma)
and, with reference to *Fig 1*, is given
by:

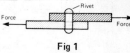

Fig 1

$$\gamma = \frac{x}{l}$$

3   (i) **Elasticity** is the ability of a material to return to its original shape and size on
        the removal of external forces.
    (ii) **Plasticity** is the property of a material of being permanently deformed by a
        force without breaking. Thus if a material does not return to the original shape,
        it is said to be plastic.

24

(iii) Within certain load limits, mild steel, copper, polythene and rubber are examples of elastic materials. lead and plasticine are examples of plastic materials.

4 If a tensile force applied to a uniform bar of mild steel is gradually increased and the corresponding extension of the bar is measured, then provided the applied force is not too large, a graph depicting these results is likely to be as shown in *Fig 2*. Since the graph is a straight line, **extension is directly proportional to the applied force.**

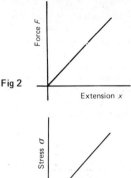

5 If the applied force is large, it is found that the material no longer returns to its original length when the force is removed. The material is then said to have passed its **elastic limit** and the resulting graph of force/extension is no longer a straight line (see para. 9).

Fig 2

Stress $\sigma = F/A$, from para. 1, and since, for a particular bar, A can be considered as constant, then $F \propto \sigma$.

Strain $\epsilon = x/l$, from para 2, and since for a particular bar l is constant, then $x \propto \epsilon$.

Hence for stress applied to a material below the elastic limit a graph of stress/strain will be as shown in *Fig 3*, and is a shape similar to the force/extension graph of *Fig 2*.

Fig 3

6 **Hooke's law** states:
  'Within the elastic limit, the extension of a material is proportional to the applied force.'
  It follows from para. 5 that:
  'Within the elastic limit of a material, the strain produced is directly proportional to the stress producing it.'

7 Within the elastic limit, stress α strain, hence stress = (a constant) × strain
  This constant of proportionality is called **Young's Modulus of Elasticity** and is given the symbol E. The value of E may be determined from the gradient of the straight line portion of the stress/strain graph. The dimensions of E are pascals (the same as for stress, since strain is dimensionless).

$$E = \frac{\sigma}{\epsilon} \text{ Pa}$$

Some typical values for Young's modulus of elasticity, E, include:
  Aluminium 70 GPa (i.e. 70 × 10^9 Pa); brass 100 GPa; copper 110 GPa; diamond 1200 GPa; mild steel 210 GPa; lead 18 GPa; tungsten 410 GPa; cast iron 110 GPa; zinc 110 GPa.

8 A material having a large value of Young's modulus is said to have a high value of stiffness, where stiffness is defined as:

$$\text{Stiffness} = \frac{\text{force } F}{\text{extension } x}$$

For example, mild steel is much stiffer than lead.

Since $E = \dfrac{\sigma}{\epsilon}$ and $\sigma = \dfrac{F}{A}$ and $\epsilon = \dfrac{x}{l}$

then $E = \dfrac{F/A}{x/l} = \dfrac{Fl}{Ax} = \left(\dfrac{F}{x}\right)\left(\dfrac{l}{A}\right)$

i.e. $E = \text{(stiffness)} \times \dfrac{l}{A}$

Stiffness (F/x) is also the gradient of the force/extension graph,

hence $E = \text{(gradient of force/extension graph)} \left(\dfrac{l}{A}\right)$

Since l and A for a particular specimen are constant, the greater Young's modulus the greater the stiffness.

9   A **tensile test** is one in which a force is applied to a specimen of a material in increments and the corresponding extension of the specimen noted. The process may be continued until the specimen breaks into two parts and this is called **testing to destruction**. The testing is usually carried out using a universal testing machine which can apply either tensile or compressive forces to a specimen in small, accurately measured steps. **British Standard 18** gives the standard procedure for such a test. Test specimens of a material are made to standard shapes and sizes and

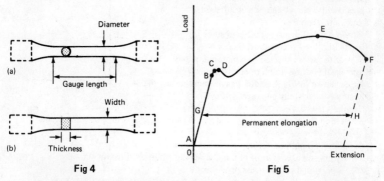

| Fig 4 | Fig 5 |

two typical test pieces are shown in *Fig 4*. The results of a tensile test may be plotted on a load/extension graph and a typical graph for a mild steel specimen is shown in *Fig 5.*

(i)   Between A and B is the region in which Hooke's law applies and stress is directly proportional to strain. The gradient of AB is used when determining Young's modulus of elasticity (see para. 8).

(ii)   Point B is the **limit of proportionality** and is the point at which stress is no longer proportional to strain when a further load is applied.

(iii)   Point C is the **elastic limit** and a specimen loaded to this point will effectively return to its original length when the load is remove, i.e. there is negligible permanent extension.

(iv)   Point D is called the **yield point** and at this point there is a sudden extension with no increase in load.

The yield stress of the material is given by:

Yield stress = $\dfrac{\text{load where yield begins to take place}}{\text{original cross-sectional area}}$

The yield stress gives an indication of the ductility of the material (see para. 10).

(v) Between points D and E extension takes place over the whole gauge length of the specimen.

(vi) Point E gives the maximum load which can be applied to the specimen and is used to determine the ultimate tensile strength (UTS) of the specimen (often just called the tensile strength).

$$\text{UTS} = \frac{\text{maximum load}}{\text{original cross-sectional area}}$$

(vi) Between points E and F the cross-sectional area of the specimen decreases, usually about half way between the ends, and a **waist or neck** is formed before fracture.

Percentage reduction in area

$$= \frac{(\text{original cross-sectional area}) - (\text{final cross-section area})}{\text{original cross-sectional area}} \times 100\%$$

The percentage reduction in area provides information about the malleability of the material (see para. 10). The value of stress at point F is greater than at point E since although the load on the specimen is decreasing as the extension increases, the cross-sectional area is also reducing.

(viii) At point F the specimen fractures.

(ix) Distance GH is called the **permanent elongation** and

$$\text{Percentage elongation} = \frac{\text{increase in length during test to destruction}}{\text{original length}} \times 100\%$$

10 (i) **Ductility** is the ability of a material to be plastically deformed by elongation, without fracture. This is a property which enables a material to be drawn out into wires. For ductile materials such as mild steel, copper and gold, large extensions can result before fracture occurs with increasing tensile force. Ductile materials usually have a percentage elongation value of about 15% or more.

(ii) **Brittleness** is the property of a material manifested by fracture without appreciable prior plastic deformation. Brittleness is a lack of ductility, and brittle materials such as cast iron, glass, concrete, brick and ceramics, have virtually no plastic stage, the elastic stage being followed by immediate fracture. Little or no 'waist' occurs before fracture in a brittle material undergoing a tensile test and there is no noticeable yield point.

(iii) **Malleability** is the property of a material whereby it can be shaped when cold by hammering or rolling. A malleable material is capable of undergoing plastic deformation without fracture.

B. WORKED PROBLEMS ON TENSILE TESTING

Problem 1 A rectangular bar having a cross-sectional area of 75 mm² has a tensile force of 15 kN applied to it. Determine the stress in the bar.

Cross sectional area $A = 75 \text{ mm}^2 = 75 \times 10^{-6} \text{ m}^2$; Force $F = 15 \text{ kN} = 15 \times 10^3 \text{ N}$

Stress in bar, $\sigma = \dfrac{F}{A} = \dfrac{15 \times 10^3 \text{ N}}{75 \times 10^{-6} \text{ m}^2} = 0.2 \times 10^9 \text{ Pa} = \textbf{200 MPa}$

Problem 2 A circular wire has a tensile force of 60.0 N applied to it and this force produces a stress of 3.06 MPa in the wire. Determine the diameter of the wire.

Force F = 60.0 N; Stress σ = 3.06 MPa = 3.06 $\times$ 10^6 Pa

Since $\sigma = \dfrac{F}{A}$, area $A = \dfrac{F}{\sigma} = \dfrac{60.0 \text{ N}}{3.06 \times 10^6 \text{ Pa}}$ = 19.61 $\times$ 10^{-6} m^2 = 19.61 mm^2

Cross-sectional area $A = \dfrac{\pi d^2}{4}$, hence 19.61 = $\dfrac{\pi d^2}{4}$

from which $d^2 = \dfrac{4 \times 19.61}{\pi}$ and $d = \sqrt{\left(\dfrac{4 \times 19.61}{\pi}\right)}$

i.e. **diameter of wire = 5.0 mm**

Problem 3 A bar 1.60 m long contracts by 0.1 mm when a compressive load is applied to it. Determine the strain and the percentage strain.

Strain $\epsilon = \dfrac{\text{extension}}{\text{original length}} = \dfrac{0.1 \text{ mm}}{1.60 \times 10^3 \text{ mm}} = \dfrac{0.1}{1600}$ **= 0.0000625**

Percentage strain = 0.0000625 $\times$ 100 = **0.00625 %**

Problem 4 A wire of length 2.50 m has a percentage strain of 0.012% when loaded with a tensile force. Determine the extension in the wire.

Original length of wire = 2.50 m = 2500 mm; strain = $\dfrac{0.012}{100}$ = 0.00012

Strain $\epsilon = \dfrac{\text{extension } x}{\text{original length } l}$, hence extension $x = \epsilon l$ = (0.00012)(2500) = **0.3 mm**

Problem 5 (a) A rectangular metal bar has a width of 10 mm and can support a maximum compressive stress of 20 MPa. Determine the minimum breadth of the bar when loaded with a force of 3 kN.
(b) If the bar in (a) is 2 m long and decreases in length by 0.25 mm when the force is applied, determine the strain and the percentage strain.

(a) Since stress $\sigma = \dfrac{\text{force } F}{\text{area } A}$, then area $A = \dfrac{F}{\sigma} = \dfrac{3000 \text{ N}}{20 \times 10^6 \text{ Pa}}$ = 150 $\times$ 10^{-6} m^2

= 150 mm^2

Cross-sectional area = width $\times$ breadth, hence **breadth** = $\dfrac{\text{area}}{\text{width}} = \dfrac{150}{10}$ = **15 mm**

(b) Strain $\epsilon = \dfrac{\text{contraction}}{\text{original length}} = \dfrac{0.25}{2000}$ = **0.000125**

Percentage strain = 0.000125 $\times$ 100 = **0.0125%**

Problem 6 A pipe has an outside diameter of 25 mm, an inside diameter of 15 mm and length 0.40 m and it supports a compressive load of 40 kN. The pipe shortens by 0.5 mm when the load is applied. Determine (a) the compressive stress; (b) the compressive strain in the pipe when supporting this load.

Compressive force, F = 40 kN = 40 000 N.

Cross-sectional area of pipe, $A = \dfrac{\pi D^2}{4} - \dfrac{\pi d^2}{4}$, where D = outside diameter = 25 mm and d = inside diameter = 15 mm.

i.e. $A = \dfrac{\pi}{4}(25^2 - 15^2)$ mm$^2 = \dfrac{\pi}{4}(25^2 - 15^2) \times 10^{-6}$ m^2 = 3.142 × 10^{-4} m^2

(a) Compressive stress, $\sigma = \dfrac{F}{A} = \dfrac{40\,000 \text{ N}}{3.142 \times 10^{-4} \text{ m}^2}$ = 12.73 × 10^7 Pa = **127.3 MPa**

(b) Contraction of pipe when loaded, x = 0.5 mm = 0.0005 m.

Original length of pipe, l = 0.4 m.

Hence compressive strain $\epsilon = \dfrac{x}{l} = \dfrac{0.0005}{0.4}$ = **0.00125** (or 0.125%)

Problem 7 A circular hole of diameter 50 mm is to be punched out of a 2 mm thick metal plate. The shear stress needed to cause fracture is 500 MPa. Determine (a) the minimum force to be applied to the punch; (b) the compressive stress in the punch at this value.

(a) Area of metal to be sheared, A = perimeter of hole × thickness of plate.

Perimeter of hole = $\pi d = \pi(0.050)$ = 0.1571 m.

Hence shear area A = 0.1571 × 0.002 = 314.2 × 10^{-6} m^2

Since shear stress = $\dfrac{\text{force}}{\text{area}}$, shear force = shear stress × area

i.e. Shear force = 500 × 10^6 Pa × 314.2 × 10^{-6} N = **157.1 kN**, which is the minimum force to be applied to the punch.

(b) Area of punch = $\dfrac{\pi d^2}{4} = \dfrac{\pi(0.050)^2}{4}$ = 0.001963 m^2

Compressive stress = $\dfrac{\text{force}}{\text{area}} = \dfrac{157.1 \times 10^3 \text{ N}}{0.001963 \text{ m}^2}$ = 8.003 × 10^7 Pa

= **80.03 MPa**, which is the compressive stress in the punch.

Problem 8 A rectangular block of plastic material 500 mm long by 20 mm wide by 300 mm high has its lower face glued to a bench and a force of 200 N is applied to the upper face and in line with it. The upper face moves 15 mm relative to the lower face. Determine (a) the shear stress; (b) the shear strain in the upper face, assuming the deformation is uniform.

(a) Shear stress $\tau = \dfrac{\text{force}}{\text{area parallel to the force}}$

Area of any face parallel to the force = 500 mm × 20 mm = (0.5 × 0.02) m^2
= 0.01 m^2.

Hence shear stress $\tau = \dfrac{200 \text{ N}}{0.01 \text{ m}^2}$ = **20 000 Pa or 20 kPa**

(b) Shear strain $\gamma = \dfrac{x}{l}$ (see side view in *Fig 6*).

$= \dfrac{15}{300}$ = **0.05 (or 5%)**

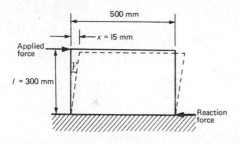

500 mm

x = 15 mm

Applied force

l = 300 mm

Reaction force

Fig 6

Problem 9 A wire is stretched 2 mm by a force of 250 N. Determine the force that would stretch the wire 5 mm, assuming that the elastic limit is not exceeded.

Hooke's law states that extension x is proportional to force F, provided that the elastic limit is not exceeded, i.e. $x \propto F$, or $x = kF$, where k is a constant.

When $x = 2$ mm, $F = 250$ N, thus $2 = k(250)$, or constant $k = \dfrac{2}{250} = \dfrac{1}{125}$

When $x = 5$ mm, then $5 = kF$, i.e. $5 = \left(\dfrac{1}{125}\right) F$, or force $F = 5(125) = 625$ N

Thus to stretch the wire 5 mm a force of 625 N is required

Problem 10 A force of 10 kN applied to a component produces an extension of 0.1 mm. Determine (a) the force needed to produce an extension of 0.12 mm; (b) the extension when the applied force is 6 kN, assuming in each case that the elastic limit is not exceeded.

From Hooke's law, extension x is proportional to force F within the elastic limit, i.e. $x \propto F$, or $x = kF$, where k is a constant.

If a force of 10 kN produces an extension of 0.1 mm, then $0.1 = k(10)$

from which, constant $k = \dfrac{0.1}{10} = 0.01$

(a) When extension $x = 0.12$ mm, then $0.12 = k(F)$, i.e. $0.12 = 0.01 F$

from which, force $F = \dfrac{0.12}{0.01} = $ **12 kN**

(b) When force $F = 6$ kN, then **extension $x = k(6) = (0.01)(6) = $ 0.06 mm**

Problem 11 A copper rod of diameter 20 mm and length 2.0 m has a tensile force of 5 kN applied to it. Determine (a) the stress in the rod; (b) by how much the rod extends when the load is applied. Take the modulus of elasticity for copper as 96 GPa.

(a) Force $F = 5$ kN $= 5000$ N

Cross-sectional area, $A = \dfrac{\pi d^2}{4} = \dfrac{\pi (0.020)^2}{4} = 0.000\,314$ m²

Stress $\sigma = \dfrac{F}{A} = \dfrac{5000 \text{ N}}{0.000\,314 \text{ m}^2} = 15.92 \times 10^6$ Pa $= $ **15.92 MPa**

(b) Since strain $E = \dfrac{\sigma}{\epsilon}$, then strain $\epsilon = \dfrac{\sigma}{E} = \dfrac{15.92 \times 10^6 \text{ Pa}}{96 \times 10^9 \text{ Pa}} = 0.000\,166$

Since $\epsilon = \dfrac{x}{l}$, then extension, $x = \epsilon l = (0.000\,166)(2.0) = 0.000\,332$ m

i.e. **extension of rod is 0.332 mm**

Problem 12 A bar of thickness 15 mm and having a rectangular cross-section carries a load of 120 kN. Determine the minimum width of the bar to limit the maximum stress to 200 MPa. The bar which is 1.0 m long extends by 2.5 mm when carrying a load of 120 kN. Determine the modulus of elasticity of the material of the bar.

Force $F = 120$ kN $= 120\,000$ N.

Cross-sectional area, $A = (15x)10^{-6}$ m^2, where x is the width of the rectangular bar in millimetres.

Stress $\sigma = \dfrac{F}{A}$, from which

$$A = \frac{F}{\sigma} = \frac{120\,000\ \text{N}}{200 \times 10^6\ \text{Pa}} = 6 \times 10^{-4}\ \text{m}^2 = 6 \times 10^2\ \text{mm}^2 = 600\ \text{mm}^2$$

Hence $600 = 15x$, from which, width of bar $x = \dfrac{600}{15} =$ **40 mm**

Extension of bar $= 2.5$ mm $= 0.0025$ m.

Strain $\epsilon = \dfrac{x}{l} = \dfrac{0.0025}{1.0} = 0.0025$

Modulus of elasticity $E = \dfrac{\text{stress}}{\text{strain}} = \dfrac{200 \times 10^6}{0.0025} = 80 \times 10^9 =$ **80 GPa**

Problem 13 An aluminium rod has a length of 200 mm and a diameter of 10 mm. When subjected to a compressive force the length of the rod is 199.6 m. Determine (a) the stress in the rod when loaded; (b) the magnitude of the force. Take the modulus of elasticity for aluminium as 70 GPa.

(a) Original length of rod, $l = 200$ mm; final length of rod $= 199.6$ mm. Hence contraction, $x = 0.4$ mm.

Thus strain $\epsilon = \dfrac{x}{l} = \dfrac{0.4}{200} = 0.002$

Modulus of elasticity, $E = \dfrac{\text{stress } \sigma}{\text{strain } \epsilon}$

Hence stress $\sigma = E\epsilon = 70 \times 10^9 \times 0.002 = 140 \times 10^6$ Pa $=$ **140 MPa**

(b) Since stress, $\sigma = \dfrac{\text{force } F}{\text{area } A}$, then force $F = \sigma A$.

Cross-sectional area, $A = \dfrac{\pi d^2}{4} = \dfrac{\pi (0.010)^2}{4} = 7.854 \times 10^{-5}$ m^2

Hence compressive force $F = \sigma A = 140 \times 10^6 \times 7.854 \times 10^{-5} =$ **11.0 kN**

Problem 14 A brass tube has an internal diameter of 120 mm and an outside diameter of 150 mm and is used to support a load of 5 kN. The tube is 500 mm long before the load is applied. Determine by how much the tube contracts when loaded, taking the modulus of elasticity for brass as 90 GPa.

31

Force in tube $F = 5$ kN = 5000 N.

Cross-sectional area of tube,

$$A = \frac{\pi}{4}(D^2 - d^2) = \frac{\pi}{4}(0.150^2 - 0.120^2) = 0.006\,362 \text{ m}^2$$

Stress in tube, $\sigma = \dfrac{F}{A} = \dfrac{5000 \text{ N}}{0.006\,362 \text{ m}^2} = 0.7859 \times 10^6$ Pa

Since the modulus of elasticity, $E = \dfrac{\text{stress } \sigma}{\text{strain } \epsilon}$

Then, strain $\epsilon = \dfrac{\sigma}{E} = \dfrac{0.7859 \times 10^6 \text{ Pa}}{90 \times 10^9 \text{ Pa}} = 8.732 \times 10^{-6}$

Strain $\epsilon = \dfrac{\text{contraction } x}{\text{original length } l}$

Hence contraction $x = \epsilon l = 8.732 \times 10^{-6} \times 0.500 = 4.37 \times 10^{-6}$ m
Thus, when loaded, the tube contracts by 4.37 μm or 4.37 microns.

Problem 15 In an experiment to determine the modulus of elasticity of a sample of mild steel, a wire is loaded and the corresponding extension noted. The results of the experiment are:

Load (N)	0	40	110	160	200	250	290	340
Extension (mm)	0	1.2	3.3	4.8	6.0	7.5	10.0	16.2

Draw the load/extension graph. The mean diameter of the wire is 1.3 mm and its length is 8.0 m. Determine the modulus of elasticity of the sample, and the stress at the limit of proportionality.

A graph of load/extension is shown in *Fig 7*.

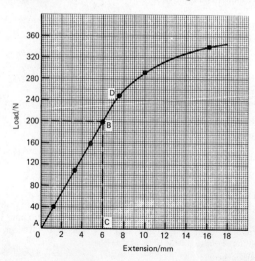

Fig 7

From para. 13, $E = \dfrac{\sigma}{\epsilon} = \dfrac{F/A}{x/l} = \left(\dfrac{F}{x}\right)\left(\dfrac{l}{A}\right)$

F/x is the gradient of the straight line part of the load/extension graph.

Gradient, $\dfrac{F}{x} = \dfrac{BC}{AC} = \dfrac{200 \text{ N}}{6 \times 10^{-3} \text{ m}} = 33.33 \times 10^3 \text{ N/m}$

Modulus of elasticity, E = (gradient of graph)$\left(\dfrac{l}{A}\right)$

Length of specimen, $l = 8.0$ m

Cross-sectional area, $A = \dfrac{\pi d^2}{4} = \dfrac{\pi (0.0013)^2}{4} = 1.327 \times 10^{-6} \text{ m}^2$

Hence modulus of elasticity = $(33.33 \times 10^3)\left(\dfrac{8.0}{1.327 \times 10^{-6}}\right)$ = **201 GPa**

The limit of proportionality is at point D in *Fig 7* where the graph no longer follows a straight line. This point corresponds to a load of 250 N as shown.

Stress at limit of proportionality = $\dfrac{\text{force}}{\text{area}} = \dfrac{250}{1.327 \times 10^{-6}}$

$= 188.4 \times 10^6$ Pa = **188.4 MPa**

Problem 16 A tensile test is carried out on a mild steel specimen of gauge length 40 mm and cross-sectional area 100 mm². The results obtained from the specimen up to its yield point are:

Load (kN)	0	8	19	29	36
Extension (mm)	0	0.015	0.038	0.060	0.072

The maximum load carried by the specimen is 50 kN and its length after fracture is 52 mm. Determine (a) the modulus of elasticity; (b) the ultimate tensile strength; (c) the percentage elongation of the mild steel.

The load/extension graph is shown in *Fig 8*.

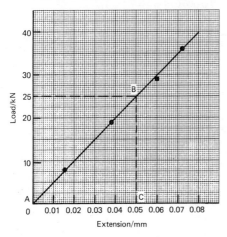

Fig 8

(a) Gradient of straight line = $\dfrac{BC}{AB}$ = $\dfrac{25\,000}{0.05 \times 10^{-3}}$ = 500×10^6 N/m

Young's modulus of elasticity = (gradient of graph)$\left(\dfrac{l}{A}\right)$

l = 40 mm (gauge length) = 0.040 m; area, A = 100 mm^2 = 100×10^{-6} m^2

Young's modulus of elasticity = $(50 \times 10^6)\left(\dfrac{0.040}{100 \times 10^{-6}}\right)$= 200×10^9 Pa

= **200 GPa**

(b) Ultimate tensile strength = $\dfrac{\text{maximum load}}{\text{original cross-sectional area}}$

= $\dfrac{50\,000\text{ N}}{100 \times 10^{-6}\text{ m}^2}$ = 500×10^6 Pa = **500 MPa**

(c) Percentage elongation = $\dfrac{\text{increase in length}}{\text{original length}}$ × 100

= $\left(\dfrac{52 - 40}{40}\right)$ × 100 = $\dfrac{12}{40}$ × 100 = **30%**

Problem 17 The results of a tensile test are:
Diameter of specimen 15 mm; gauge length 40 mm; load at limit of proportionality 85 kN; extension at limit of proportionality 0.075 mm; maximum load 120 kN; final length at point of fracture 55 mm.
Determine (a) Young's modulus of elasticity; (b) the ultimate tensile strength; (c) the stress at the limit of proportionality; (d) the percentage elongation.

(a) Young's modulus of elasticity $E = \dfrac{\text{stress}}{\text{strain}} = \dfrac{F/A}{x/l} = \dfrac{Fl}{Ax}$

where the load at the limit of proportionality, F = 85 kN = 85 000 N,
l = gauge length = 40 mm = 0.040 m,

A = cross-sectional area = $\dfrac{\pi d^2}{4}$ = $\dfrac{\pi(0.015)^2}{4}$ = 0.000 176 7 m^2,

x = extension = 0.075 mm = 0.000 075 m.

Hence Young's modulus of elasticity $E = \dfrac{Fl}{Ax}$ = $\dfrac{(85\,000)(0.040)}{(0.000\,176\,7)(0.000\,075)}$

= 256.6×10^9 Pa = **256.6 GPa**

(b) Ultimate tensile strength = $\dfrac{\text{maximum load}}{\text{original cross-sectional area}}$

= $\dfrac{120\,000}{0.000\,176\,7}$ = 679×10^6 Pa = **679 MPa**

(c) Stress at limit of proportionality = $\dfrac{\text{load at limit of proportionality}}{\text{cross-sectional area}}$

= $\dfrac{85\,000}{0.000\,176\,7}$ = 481.0×10^6 Pa = **481.0 MPa**

(d) Percentage elongation = $\dfrac{\text{increase in length}}{\text{original length}}$ × 100

= $\dfrac{(55 - 40)\text{ mm}}{40\text{ mm}}$ × 100 = **37.5%**

Problem 18 A rectangular zinc specimen is subjected to a tensile test and the data from the test is shown below.

Width of specimen 40 mm; breadth of specimen 2.5 mm; gauge length 120 mm.

Load (kN)	10	17	25	30	35	37.5	38.5	37	34	32
Extension (mm)	0.15	0.25	0.35	0.55	1.0	1.50	2.50	3.50	4.50	5.0

Fracture occurs when the extension is 5.0 mm and the maximum load recorded is 38.5 kN.

Plot the load/extension graph and hence determine (a) the stress at the limit of proportionality; (b) Young's modulus of elasticity; (c) the ultimate tensile strength; (d) the percentage elongation; (e) the stress at a strain of 0.01; (f) the extension at a stress of 200 MPa.

A load/extension graph is shown in *Fig 9*.

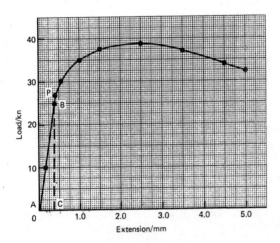

Fig 9

(a) The limit of proportionality occurs at point P on the graph, where the initial gradient of the graph starts to change. This point has a load value of 26.5 kN.

Cross-sectional area of specimen = 40 mm × 2.5 mm = 100 mm²
$$= 100 \times 10^{-6} \text{ m}^2$$

Stress at the limit of proportionality,

$$\sigma = \frac{\text{force}}{\text{area}} = \frac{26.5 \times 10^3 \text{ N}}{100 \times 10^{-6} \text{ m}^2} = 265 \times 10^6 \text{ Pa} = \textbf{265 MPa}$$

(b) Gradient of straight line portion of graph $= \dfrac{\text{BC}}{\text{AC}} = \dfrac{25\,000 \text{ N}}{0.35 \times 10^{-3} \text{ m}}$
$$= 71.43 \times 10^6 \text{ N/m}.$$

Young's modulus of elasticity = (gradient of graph) $\dfrac{1}{A}$

$$= (71.43 \times 10^6)\left(\dfrac{120 \times 10^{-3}}{100 \times 10^{-6}}\right)$$

$$= 85.72 \times 10^9 \text{ Pa} = \textbf{85.72 GPa}$$

(c) Ultimate tensile strength $= \dfrac{\text{maximum load}}{\text{original cross-sectional area}}$

$$= \dfrac{38.5 \times 10^3 \text{ N}}{100 \times 10^{-6} \text{ m}^2}$$

$$= 385 \times 10^6 \text{ Pa} = \textbf{385 MPa}$$

(d) Percentage elongation $= \dfrac{\text{extension at fracture point}}{\text{original length}} \times 100$

$$= \dfrac{5.0 \text{ mm}}{120 \text{ mm}} \times 100 = \textbf{4.17\%}$$

(e) Strain $\epsilon = \dfrac{\text{extension } x}{\text{original length } l}$, from which

Extension $x = \epsilon l = 0.01 \times 120 = 1.20$ mm
From the graph, the load corresponding to an extension of 1.20 mm is 36 kN.

Stress at a strain of 0.01, $\sigma = \dfrac{\text{force}}{\text{area}} = \dfrac{36\,000 \text{ N}}{100 \times 10^{-6} \text{ m}^2}$

$$= 360 \times 10^6 \text{ Pa} = \textbf{360 MPa}$$

(f) When the stress is 200 MPa, then force = area × stress

$$= (100 \times 10^{-6})(200 \times 10^6) = 20 \text{ kN}$$

From the graph, the corresponding extension is **0.30 mm**

Problem 19 A mild steel specimen of cross-sectional area 250 mm² and gauge length 100 mm is subjected to a tensile test and the following data is obtained: Within the limit of proportionality, a load of 75 kN produced an extension of 0.143 mm; load at yield point = 80 kN; maximum load on specimen = 120 kN; final cross-sectional area of waist at fracture = 90 mm² ; the gauge length had increased to 135 mm at fracture.

Determine for the specimen: (a) Young's modulus of elasticity; (b) the yield stress; (c) the tensile strength; (d) the percentage elongation; (e) the percentage reduction in area.

(a) Force $F = 75$ kN = 75 000 N; gauge length $l = 100$ mm = 0.1 m; cross-sectional area $A = 250$ mm² = 250×10^{-6} m² ; extension $x = 0.143$ mm = 0.143×10^{-3} m

Young's modulus of elasticity, $E = \dfrac{\text{stress}}{\text{strain}} = \dfrac{F/A}{x/l} = \dfrac{Fl}{Ax}$

$$= \dfrac{(75\,000)(0.1)}{(250 \times 10^{-6})(0.143 \times 10^{-3})}$$

$$= 210 \times 10^9 \text{ Pa} = \textbf{210 GPa}$$

(b) Yield stress $= \dfrac{\text{load when yield begins to take place}}{\text{original cross-sectional area}}$

$$= \dfrac{80\,000 \text{ N}}{250 \times 10^{-6} \text{ m}^2}$$

$$= 320 \times 10^6 \text{ Pa} = \textbf{320 MPa}$$

(c) Tensile strength = $\dfrac{\text{maximum load}}{\text{original cross-sectional area}}$

$= \dfrac{120\,000 \text{ N}}{250 \times 10^{-6} \text{ m}^2} = 480 \times 10^6 \text{ Pa} = \textbf{480 MPa}$

(d) Percentage elongation $= \left(\dfrac{\text{increase in length during test to destruction}}{\text{original length}}\right) \times 100$

$= \left(\dfrac{135 - 100}{100}\right) \times 100 = \textbf{35\%}$

(e) Percentage reduction in area

$= \dfrac{(\text{original cross-sectional area}) - (\text{final cross-sectional area})}{\text{original cross-sectional area}} \times 100$

$= \left(\dfrac{250 - 90}{250}\right) \times 100 = \left(\dfrac{160}{250}\right) 100 = \textbf{64\%}$

C. FURTHER PROBLEMS ON TENSILE TESTING

(a) SHORT ANSWER PROBLEMS

1 Define stress. What is the symbol used for (a) a tensile stress; (b) a shear stress?
2 Strain is the ratio . . . .
3 Define elasticity and state two examples of elastic materials.
4 Define plasticity and state two examples of plastic materials.
5 State Hooke's law.
6 What is the difference between a ductile and a brittle material?
7 The ratio $\dfrac{\text{stress}}{\text{strain}}$ is called . . . .
8 State the units of (a) stress; (b) strain; (c) Young's modulus of elasticity.
9 Stiffness is the ratio . . . .
10 What is a tensile test?
11 Which British Standard gives the standard procedure for a tensile test?
12 With reference to a load/extension graph for mild steel, state the meaning of (a) the limit of proportionality; (b) the elastic limit; (c) the yield point; (d) the percentage elongation.
13 Ultimate tensile strength is the ratio . . . .
14 Yield stress is the ratio . . . .
15 Define 'percentage reduction in area'.
16 Define (a) ductility; (b) brittleness; (c) malleability.

(b) MULTI-CHOICE PROBLEMS (Answers on page 156)

1 A wire is stretched 3 mm by a force of 150 N. Assuming the elastic limit is not exceeded, the force that will stretch the wire 5 mm is:
(a) 150 N; (b) 250 N; (c) 90 N.
2 For the wire in *Problem 1*, the extension when the applied force is 450 N is:
(a) 1 mm; (b) 3 mm; (c) 9 mm.
3 Which of the following statements is false?
(a) Elasticity is the ability of a material to return to its original dimensions after deformation by a load.

(b) Plasticity is the ability of a material to retain any deformation produced in it by a load.

(c) Ductility is the ability to be permanently stretched without fracturing.

(d) Brittleness is a lack of ductility and a brittle material has a long plastic stage.

4 A circular rod of cross-sectional area 100 mm² has a tensile force of 100 kN applied to it. The stress in the rod is:
(a) 1 MPa; (b) 1 GPa; (c) 1 kPa; (d) 100 MPa.

5 A metal bar 5.0 m long extends by 0.05 mm when a tensile load is applied to it. The percentage strain is:
(a) 0.1; (b) 0.01; (c) 0.001; (d) 0.0001.

An aluminium rod of length 1.0 m and cross-sectional area 500 mm² is used to support a load of 5 kN which causes the rod to contract by 100 μm. For *Problems 6 to 8*, select the correct answer from the following list:
(a) 100 MPa; (b) 0.001; (c) 10 kPa; (d) 100 GPa; (e) 0.01; (f) 10 MPa;
(g) 10 GPa; (h) 0.0001; (i) 10 Pa.

6 The stress in the rod.

7 The strain in the rod.

8 Young's modulus of elasticity.

A brass specimen having a cross-sectional area of 100 mm² and gauge length 100 mm is subjected to a tensile test from which the following information is obtained:
Load at yield point = 45 kN; Maximum load = 52.5 kN; final cross-sectional area of waist at fracture = 75 mm² ; gauge length at fracture = 110 mm.
For *Problems 9 to 12*, select the correct answer from the following list:
(a) 600 MPa; (b) 525 MPa; (c) $33\frac{1}{3}$%; (d) 10%; (e) 9.09%;

(f) 450 MPa; (g) 25%; (h) 700 MPa.

9 The yield stress.

10 The percentage elongation.

11 The percentage reduction in area.

12 The ultimate tensile strength.

(c) CONVENTIONAL PROBLEMS

1 A rectangular bar having a cross-sectional area of 80 mm² has a tensile force of 20 kN applied to it. Determine the stress in the bar.

[250 MPa]

2 A circular cable has a tensile force of 1 kN applied to it and the force produces a stress of 7.8 MPa in the cable. Calculate the diameter of the cable.

[12.78 mm]

3 A square-sectioned support of side 12 mm is loaded with a compressive force of 10 kN. Determine the compressive stress in the support.

[69.44 MPa]

4 A bolt having a diameter of 5 mm is loaded so that the shear stress in it is 120 MPa. Determine the value of the shear force on the bolt.

[2.356 kN]

5 A split pin requires a force of 400 N to shear it. The maximum shear stress before shear occurs is 120 MPa. Determine the minimum diameter of the pin.

[2.06 mm]

6   A wire of length 4.5 m has a percentage strain of 0.050% when loaded with a tensile force. Determine the extension in the wire.

[2.25 mm]

7   A tube of outside diameter 60 mm and inside diameter 40 mm is subjected to a load of 60 kN. Determine the stress in the tube.

[38.2 MPa]

8   A metal bar 2.5 m long extends by 0.05 mm when a tensile load is applied to it. Determine (a) the strain; (b) the percentage strain.

[(a) 0.00002; (b) 0.002%]

9   (a) State Hooke's law.
    (b) A wire is stretched 1.5 mm by a force of 300 N. Determine the force that would stretch the wire 4 mm, assuming the elastic limit of the wire is not exceeded.

[800 N]

10 A rubber band extends 50 mm when a force of 300 N is applied to it. Assuming the band is within the elastic limit, determine the extension produced by a force of 60 N.

[10 mm]

11 A force of 25 kN applied to a piece of steel produces an extension of 2 mm. Assuming the elastic limit is not exceeded, determine (a) the force required to produce an extension of 3.5 mm; (b) the extension when the applied force is 15 kN.

[(a) 43.75 N; (b) 1.2 mm]

12 A coil spring 300 mm long when unloaded, extends to a length of 500 mm when a load of 40 N is applied. Determine the length of the spring when a load of 15 kN is applied.

[375 mm]

13 Sketch on the same axes typical load extension graphs for (a) a strong, ductile material; (b) a brittle material.

14 Define (a) tensile stress; (b) shear stress; (c) strain; (d) shear strain; (e) Young's modulus of elasticity.

15 A circular bar is 2.5 m long and has a diameter of 60 mm. When subjected to a compressive load of 30 kN it shortens by 0.20 mm. Determine Young's modulus of elasticity for the material of the bar.

[132.6 GPa]

16 A bar of thickness 20 mm and having a rectangular cross-section carries a load of 82.5 kN. Determine (a) the minimum width of the bar to limit the maximum stress to 150 MPa; (b) the modulus of elasticity of the material of the bar if the 150 mm long bar extends by 0.8 mm when carrying a load of 200 kN.

[(a) 27.5 mm; (b) 68.2 GPa]

17 A metal rod of cross-sectional area 100 mm^2 carries a maximum tensile load of 20 kN. The modulus of elasticity for the material of the rod is 200 GPa. Determine the percentage strain when the rod is carrying its maximum load.

[0.1%]

18 A metal tube 1.75 m long carries a tensile load and the maximum stress in the tube must not exceed 50 MPa. Determine the extension of the tube when loaded if the modulus of elasticity for the material is 70 GPa.

[1.25 mm]

19 A piece of aluminium wire 5 m long has a cross-sectional area of 100 mm^2. It is subjected to increasing loads, the extension being recorded for each load applied. The results are:

Load (kN)	0	1.12	2.94	4.76	7.00	9.10
Extension (mm)	0	0.8	2.1	3.4	5.0	6.5

Draw the load/extension graph and hence determine the modulus of elasticity for the material of the wire.

[70 GPa]

20 In an experiment to determine the modulus of elasticity of a sample of copper, a wire is loaded and the corresponding extension noted. The results are:

Load (kN)	0	20	34	72	94	120
Extension (mm)	0	0.7	1.2	2.5	3.3	4.2

Draw the load/extension graph and determine the modulus of elasticity of the sample if the mean diameter of the wire is 1.151 mm and its length is 4.0 m.

[110 GPa]

21 A tensile test is carried out on a specimen of mild steel of gauge length 40 mm and diameter 7.35 mm. The results are:

Load (kN)	0	10	17	25	30	34	37.5	38.5	36
Extension (mm)	0	0.05	0.08	0.11	0.14	0.20	0.40	0.60	0.90

At fracture the final length of the specimen is 40.90 mm. Plot the load/extension graph and determine (a) the modulus of elasticity for mild steel; (b) the stress at the limit of proportionality; (c) the ultimate tensile strength; (d) the percentage elongation.

[(a) 202 GPa; (b) 707 MPa; (c) 907 MPa; (d) 2.25%]

22 In a tensile test on a zinc specimen of gauge length 100 mm and diameter 15 mm a load of 100 kN produced an extension of 0.666 mm. Determine (a) the stress induced; (b) the strain; (c) Young's modulus of elasticity.

[(a) 566 MPa; (b) 0.00666; (c) 85 GPa]

23 The results of a tensile test are: the diameter of a specimen is 20 mm; gauge length 50 mm; load at limit of proportionality 80 kN.
Extension at limit of proportionality 0.075 mm; maximum load 100 kN; final length at point of fracture 60 mm.
Determine (a) Young's modulus of elasticity; (b) the ultimate tensile strength; (c) the stress at the limit of proportionality; (d) the percentage elongation.

[(a) 169.8 GPa; (b) 318.3 MPa; (c) 254.6 MPa; (d) 20%]

24 What is a tensile test? Make a sketch of a typical load/extension graph for a mild steel specimen to the point of fracture and mark on the sketch the following: (a) the limit of proportionality; (b) the elastic limit; (c) the yield point.

25 An aluminium alloy specimen of gauge length 75 mm and diameter 11.28 mm is subjected to a tensile test with these results:

Load (kN)	0	2.0	6.5	11.5	13.6	16.0	18.0	19.0	20.5	19.0
Extension (mm)	0	0.012	0.039	0.069	0.080	0.107	0.133	0.158	0.225	0.310

The specimen fractured at a load of 19.0 kN. Determine (a) the modulus of elasticity of the alloy; (b) the percentage elongation.

[(a) 125 GPa; (b) 0.413%]

26 An aluminium test piece 10 mm in diameter and gauge length 50 mᵐ
following results when tested to destruction:
Load at yield point 4.0 kN; maximum load 6.3 kN; extension at y
0.036 mm; diameter at fracture 7.7 mm.
Determine (a) the yield stress; (b) Young's modulus of elasticity
tensile strength; (d) the percentage reduction in area.

[(a) 50.93 MPa; (b) 70.7 GPa; (c) 80.2 MPa; (d) 4ᵥ

4 Hardness and impact tests

A. MAIN POINTS CONCERNING HARDNESS AND IMPACT TESTS

1   The **hardness** of a material may be defined in terms of the resistance the material offers to indentation by another body. Hardness tests are based on pressing a hard substance, such as a diamond or a steel sphere having known dimensions, into the material under test. The hardness can be determined from the size of indentation made for a known load. The three principal hardness tests are:
(a) the Brinell test; (b) the Vickers test; (c) the Rockwell test.

2   In a standard **Brinell test**, a hardened steel ball having a diameter of 10 mm is squeezed into the material under a load of 3000 kg. The diameter of the indentation produced is measured using a microscope. The Brinell hardness number, H_B is given by:

$$H_B = \frac{\text{load}}{\text{spherical area of indent}} = \frac{F}{\frac{\pi D}{2}[D - \sqrt{(D^2 - d^2)}]}$$

where F is the load in kilograms (usually 3000 kg), D is the diameter of the steel ball in millimetres (usually 10 mm), and d is the diameter of the indentation in millimetres.

Variations on the standard test include smaller loads used for soft materials, balls of different diameters (usually restricted to 1, 2 and 5 mm) and the steel ball being replaced by one made of tungsten carbide for use with very hard materials.

Values of Brinell hardness number vary from about 900 for very hard materials having an equivalent tensile strength for steel of 3000 MPa, down to about 100 for materials having an equivalent tensile strength for steel of about 350 MPa. The approximate relationship between tensile strength and hardness is discussed in para. 5 (see *Problems 1 to 4*).

3   In a **Vickers diamond pyramid hardness test**, a square-based diamond pyramid is pressed into the material under test. The angle between opposite faces of the diamond is 136° and the load applied is one of the values 5, 10, 30, 50 or 120 kg, depending on the hardness of the material. The Vickers diamond hardness number, H_V, is given by

$$H_V = \frac{\text{load}}{\text{surface area of indentation}} = \frac{F}{d^2/1.854}$$

where F is the load in kilograms and d is the length of the diagonal of the square of indentation in millimetres (see *Problems 5 to 7*).

42

4   The **Rockwell hardness test** is used mainly for rapid routine testing of finished material, the hardness number being indicated directly on a dial. The value of hardness is based directly on the depth of indentation of either a steel ball or a cone shaped diamond with a sperically rounded tip, called a 'brale'. Whether the steel ball or brale is selected for use depends on the hardness of the material under test, the steel ball being used for materials having a hardness up to that of medium carbon steels.

   Several different scales are shown on the dial, and can include Rockwell A to H scales together with Rockwell K, N and T scales. Examples of the scale used are:

   Scale A : using a brale and a 60 kg load

   Scale B : using a brale and a 150 kg load

   Scale C : using a $\frac{1}{16}$ inch steel ball and a 100 kg load, and so on.

   (See *Problem 8*).

5   For materials of the same quality and for families of materials, an approximate direct proportion relationship seems to exist between tensile strength and Brinell hardness number. For example, a nickel-chrome steel which is hardened and then tempered to various temperatures has tensile strengths varying from 1900 MPa to 1070 MPa as the Brinell hardness number varies from 530 to 300. A constant of proportionality k for: tensile strength = ($k \times$ hardness) in this case is 3.57 for all tempering temperatures. Similarly, for a family of carbon steels, the tensile strength varies from 380 MPa to 790 MPa as the carbon content increases. The Brinell hardness number varies from 115 to 230 over the same range of carbon values and the constant of proportionality in this case is 3.35.

   Because of the general approximate relationship between tensile strength and hardness, tables exist relating these quantities, the tables usually being based on a constant of proportionality of about 3.35.

6   To give an indication of the toughness of a material, that is, the energy needed to fracture it, **impact tests** are carried out. Two such tests are the Izod test, used principally in Great Britain and the Charpy test which is used widely on the continent of Europe.

7   In an **Izod test**, a square test piece of side 10 mm and having a vee-notch of angle 45° machined along one side, is clamped firmly in a vice in the base of the Izod test machine. A heavy pendulum swings down to strike the specimen and fractures it. The difference between the release angle of the pendulum measured to the vertical and the overswing angle after fracturing the specimen is proportional to the energy expended in fracturing the specimen, and can be read from a scale on the testing machine.

   An Izod test is basically an acceptance test, that is, the value of impact energy absorbed is either acceptable or is not acceptable. The results of an Izod test cannot be used to determine impact strength under other conditions (see *Problem 9*).

8   A **Charpy test** is similar to an Izod test, the only major difference being the method of mounting the test specimen and a capability of varying the mass of the pendulum. In the Izod test, the specimen is gripped at one end and is supported as a cantilever, compared with the specimen being supported at each end as a beam, in the Charpy test. One other difference is that the notch is at the centre of the supported beam and faces away from the striker (see *Problem 10*).

B. WORKED PROBLEMS ON HARDNESS AND IMPACT TESTS

Problem 1 Describe briefly machines used when a Brinell hardness test is performed.

Two principal types of specialist machine are used to perform Brinell hardness tests. One is based on hydraulic pressure, the load applied being measured by the hydraulic pressure indicated on a gauge. The other is based on the use of a powerful screw, which, as it advances on rotation, causes two arms carrying weights to be elevated, these weights being connected by levers to the table of the machine. In both cases, a microscope is used to measure the diameter of the indentation. Most universal testing machines may be used for Brinell hardness tests.

Problem 2 List six precautions normally taken when performing a Brinell hardness test.

(a) Although the standard ball diameter is 10 mm, ball sizes of 1, 2 and 5 mm are also available. The ideal value for the ratio of indentation diameter to ball diameter, (d/D), is 0.375 for a realistic hardness number to be obtained and should not be outside the range 0.25 to 0.5. To achieve an acceptable value of d/D, the BSI recommends using the relationship load/(ball diameter)^2 and some of the recommended F/D^2 values for various materials are in kg mm^2 units:

steel	30
copper and aluminium alloys	10
copper and aluminium	5
lead	1

For example, when testing copper using a 10 mm diameter ball, F/D^2 is equal to 5, that is, a load of 500 kg is applied. Thus one precaution is to use a reasonably sized ball and load to give a d/D ratio of approximately 0.375.
(b) The material must have a reasonable thickness. In general, it is desirable to have a thickness of at least ten times the depth of indentation for hard materials and fifteen times for soft materials. The depth of indentation is given by $F/(\pi D H_B)$.
(c) The material must have a reasonable width. The centre of indentation should be not less than two and a half times the diameter of indentation from any edge.
(d) The test surface of the material should be flat and polished.
(e) The load should be held for fifteen seconds.
(f) Two tests should be made and the mean indentation diameter used in subsequent calculations.

Problem 3 In a Brinell hardness test on a specimen of steel, the diameter of indentation is 4.25 mm when using a 10 mm diameter ball and a load of 300 kg. Calculate the Brinell hardness number.

From para 2, the Brinell hardness number, H_B is given by

$$H_B = \frac{F}{\frac{\pi D}{2}[D - \sqrt{(D^2 - d^2)}]}, \text{ where}$$

F is the load, i.e. 3000 kg, D is the ball diameter, i.e. 10 mm, and d is the indentation diameter, i.e. 4.25 mm.

Thus, $H_B = \dfrac{3000}{\dfrac{\pi \times 10}{2}[10 - \sqrt{(10^2 - 4.25^2)}]}$

$= \dfrac{3000}{5\pi[10 - \sqrt{(100 - 18.06)}]}$

$= \dfrac{600}{\pi[10 - 9.052]} = 201$

That is, **the Brinell hardness number is 201**

Problem 4 A Brinell hardness test is to be carried out on an aluminium alloy specimen. Determine the approximate load to be applied to a 5 mm ball. The diameter of the indentation when the test has been carried out is 1.82 mm. Calculate the Brinell hardness number.

From *Problem 2*, the value of load/(ball diameter)^2 for copper and aluminium alloys should be 10, and since the ball diameter is 5 mm, the load F is given by:
$F = 10D^2 = 10 \times 5^2 = $ **250 kg**

From para 2, $H_B = \dfrac{F}{\dfrac{\pi D}{2}[D - \sqrt{(D^2 - d^2)}]}$

$= \dfrac{250}{\dfrac{5\pi}{2}[5 - \sqrt{(5^2 - 1.82^2)}]} = \dfrac{100}{\pi[5 - 4.657]} = 93$

That is, **the Brinell hardness number is 93**

Problem 5 Give four advantages that a Vickers hardness test has when compared with a Brinell hardness test.

(a) The diagonal of the square of indentation obtained in a Vickers hardness test can usually be measured more accurately than the diameter of the circle of indentation resulting from a Brinell hardness test.
(b) The Vickers test usually gives a more accurate result when used to determine the hardness of very hard materials, since the diamond cannot be pressed out of shape so readily as a steel or tungsten carbide ball.
(c) The Vickers test can be used on thin materials, since the load applied is usually much less than those associated with a Brinell test.
(d) No preliminary tests on the ratio d/D or F/D^2 have to be made in a Vickers test, thus a Vickers test is usually more easily performed.

Problem 6 In a Vickers diamond pyramid hardness test on a material, a load of 10 kg produces an indentation having a length of diagonal of 0.215 mm. Calculate the Vickers hardness number.

From para. 3, the Vickers diamond pyramid hardness number, H_V is given by:
$$H_V = \frac{F}{d^2/1.854} = \frac{1.854\,F}{d^2}$$
where F is the load, i.e. 10 kg and d is the length of the diagonal of the square of indentation, i.e. 0.215 mm.

45

Thus, $H_V = \dfrac{1.854 \times 10}{0.215^2} = 401$

Problem 7 If a Brinell test using a 10 mm ball had been carried out on the material used in *Problem 6,* determine the likely diameter of the impression to give the same hardness number.

The hardness values obtained for a material by the Vickers and Brinell tests are the same when the Brinell ratio of indentation to ball diameters, d/D is 0.375. Since the ball diameter is 10 mm, then the diameter of the indentation, d, is given by:

$\dfrac{d}{10} = 0.375$ mm, that is, $d = 3.75$ **mm**

Problem 8 Briefly describe how a Rockwell hardness test is carried out and state one of its disadvantages.

The material to be tested requires no other preparation than the removal of scale and dirt from the surface. The material is placed on the table of the Rockwell testing machine and the indenting tool is brought into contact with the surface under a light load of 10 kg. The scale is adjusted to zero. If, for example, a scale B test is being done, an additional load of 140 kg is applied for a short time, the timing being automatic. The 140 kg load is removed and the hardness value is read directly from the scale under the 10 kg load condition.

The Rockwell hardness test which was devised in the USA is well suited to production-line testing and routine testing of stock. However, one disadvantage is that the BSI require hardness numbers to be based on the surface area of indentation and not on the depth of indentation.

Problem 9 Describe how a specimen is prepared for an Izod test and briefly how the test is performed.

The square specimen of 10 mm side is prepared, having the dimensions shown in *Fig 1*. Four two millimetre deep notches are machined in the specimen, one on each side, being separated from one another by a distance of 28 mm. This allows for up to four tests to be carried out on each specimen.

Fig 1

The specimen is mounted in the vice at the base of the testing machine as shown in *Fig 2*, the centre of the vee-notch being level with the vice jaws. The pendulum of the machine is released from angle θ, strikes the specimen, fractures it and swings past the centre line to angle θ_1. The difference, $\theta - \theta_1$, is a measure of the energy expanded in fracturing the specimen.

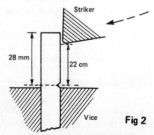

Fig 2

46

As for an Izod test, a square-sectioned test-piece of side 10 mm is prepared, having a single vee-notch, 2 mm deep, machined across one side, as shown in *Fig 3*.

A Charpy test is similar to an Izod test, the principal difference between them being the way in which the specimen is mounted. In the Charpy test, it is supported at each end with the notch at the centre, facing away from the striker.

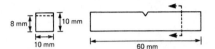

8 mm   10 mm   10 mm   60 mm   **Fig 3**

The load on the pendulum is adjusted to give an impact energy of either 150 or 300 J. The striker of the pendulum is wedge shaped and the length between the pendulum pivot and centre of the striker is such that it strikes the test piece directly behind the notch.

C. FURTHER PROBLEMS ON HARDNESS AND IMPACT TESTS

(a) SHORT ANSWER PROBLEMS

1 State what is meant by the hardness of a material.
2 State the usual ball diameter and load used on steel when carrying out a Brinell hardness test.
3 Write down a formula in terms of load and ball and indentation diameters for determining the Brinell hardness number of a material.
4 List three precautions normally taken when performing a Brinell hardness test.
5 To obtain a reasonably accurate result from a Brinell test, the ratio of indentation to ball diameter should lie within a given range of values. State the range and also the ideal value.
6 List three advantages that a Vickers hardness test has when compared with a Brinell test.
7 State the condition under which the values of hardness obtained by Vickers and Brinell tests are likely to be the same.
8 State the principal advantage and principle disadvantage of a Rockwell hardness test.
9 State briefly the relationship between Brinell hardness number and tensile strength for materials of the same quality.
10 State two differences between an Izod and a Charpy test.

(b) MULTI-CHOICE PROBLEMS (Answers on page 156)

1 When performing a Brinell hardness test, which of the following statements is false?
   (a) The surface of the material should be flat and polished before the test commences.

(b) The load should be held for fifteen seconds.

(c) The usual load is 3000 kg and a ball of 10 mm diameter is used when testing a steel specimen.

(d) A tungsten carbide ball is used when testing aluminium alloys.

2　When using a 10 mm ball in a Brinell test, the ideal indentation diameter is:

(a) 6.25 mm;　(b) 3.75 mm;　(c) 5 mm;　(d) 10 mm.

3　The ratio $\dfrac{\text{load in kg}}{(\text{ball diameter})^2 \text{ in mm}^2}$ should be 5 for copper. The ball diameter when a load of 20 kg is applied to copper is:

(a) 2 mm;　(b) 1 mm;　(c) 5 mm;　(d) 10 mm.

4　Which of the following statements is true when referring to a Brinell test?

(a) The indentation surface area is greater on steel than on aluminium for the same load and ball diameter.

(b) The ratio F/D^2 is ideally 30 for steel where F is the load in kg and D the ball diameter.

(c) A square-based pyramid of steel is used to make the indentation.

(d) This test is a much quicker test than a Rockwell test.

5　In a Vickers hardness test, $H_V = \dfrac{F}{d^2/1.854}$. Which of the following statements are false?

(a) F is the load in kg.

(b) F is the force in newtons.

(c) d is the length of the side of indentation in mm.

(d) d is the length of the diagonal of the square of indentation in mm.

6　The following statements refer to a Rockwell hardness test. Which statement is false?

(a) The surface to be tested should be flat and polished.

(b) The test is well suited to production-line testing.

(c) The scale reading on the dial is related directly to the depth of indentation.

(d) It is not suitable for hardness tests as specified by the BSI.

7　The following statements refer to an Izod test. Which statement is false?

(a) The results cannot be used to determine impact strength under other conditions.

(b) The energy expended in fracturing the test-piece is measured.

(c) The test-piece is supported as a beam, the notch facing away from the striker.

(d) A standard notch, 2 mm deep, is used when preparing the specimen.

8　The following statements refer to a Charpy test. Which is false?

(a) A beam-supported test specimen is used.

(b) The notch faces the striker.

(c) The pendulum load can be varied.

(d) The energy expended in fracturing the specimen is measured.

(c) CONVENTIONAL PROBLEMS

1　A ball of 10 mm diameter is loaded to 3000 kg when testing a certain grade of steel. If the diameter of the indentation is 3.65 mm, determine the Brinell hardness number.

[277]

2　The Brinell hardness number of a duralumin specimen is found to be 110 when using a 5 mm diameter ball and assuming an F/D^2 value of 10. Calculate the diameter of the indentation made during the test.

[1.676 mm]

3   Discuss five precautions taken when carrying out a Brinell hardness test in order that the results obtained shall be reasonably accurate.

4   Explain why it is necessary to vary both the load and the ball diameter in a Brinell test when measuring the hardness of a variety of materials from lead to steel. Discuss such factors as d/D and F/D^2 in your answer.

5   In a Brinell test, a material was found to have a hardness of 410 when a load of 750 kg gave an indentation diameter of 1.508 mm. Determine the likely size of ball diameter used.

[5 mm]

6   Discuss the principal advantages claimed for a Vickers hardness test when compared with a Brinell test.

7   In a Vickers hardness test, the following data was obtained:
Load 30 kg; length of diagonal of indentation 0.415 mm. Determine the Vickers hardness number.

[323]

8   A load of 50 kg is applied during a Vickers hardness test and the Vickers hardness number of the material is 450. Determine the length of the diagonal of the indentation produced during the test.

[0.454 mm]

9   Briefly describe the procedure for carrying out a Rockwell hardness test. What are the principal advantages and disadvantages of this test when compared with a Brinell hardness test?

10 Briefly describe the methods of carrying out:
(a) an Izod impact test; (b) a Charpy impact test. Discuss the basic differences between these two tests.

5 Capacitors and their effects in electric circuits

A. MAIN POINTS CONCERNED WITH CAPACITORS AND THEIR EFFECTS IN ELECTRIC CIRCUITS

1 **Electrostatics** is the branch of electricity which is concerned with the study of electrical charges at rest. An electrostatic field accompanies a static charge and this is utilised in the capacitor.

2 Charged bodies attract or repel each other, depending on the nature of the charge. The rule is: **like charges repel, unlike charges attract.**

3 A **capacitor** is a device capable of storing electrical energy. *Fig 1* shows a capacitor consisting of a pair of parallel metal plates X and Y separated by an insulator, which could be air. Since the plates are electrical conductors each will contain a large number of mobile electrons. Because the plates are connected to a d.c. supply the electrons on plate X, which have a small negative charge, will be attracted to the positive pole of the supply and will be repelled from the negative pole of the supply on to plate Y. X will become positively charged due to its shortage of electrons whereas Y will have a negative charge due to its surplus of electrons.

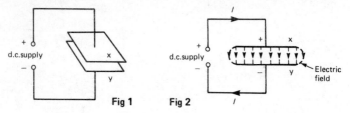

Fig 1   **Fig 2**

The difference in charge between the plates results in a p.d. existing between them, the flow of electrons dying away and ceasing when the p.d. between the plates equals the supply voltage. The plates are then said to be **charged** and there exists an **electric field** between them. *Fig 2* shows a side view of the plates with the field represented by 'lines of electrical flux'. If the plates are disconnected from the supply and connected together through a resistor the surplus of electrons on the negative plate will flow through the resistor to the positive plate. This is called **discharging**. The current flow decreases to zero as the charges on the plates reduce. The current flowing in the resistor causes it to liberate heat showing that **energy is stored in the electric field.**

50

4   From *Engineering Science 2 Checkbook*, chapter 1, charge Q is given by:

$$\boxed{Q = I \times t \text{ coulombs}}$$

where I is the current in amperes, and t the time in seconds.

5   A **dielectric** is an insulating medium separating charged surfaces.

6   Electric field strength, electric force, or voltage gradient,

$$E = \frac{\text{p.d. across dielectric}}{\text{thickness of dielectric}} \text{ , i.e. } \boxed{E = \frac{V}{d} \text{ volts/m.}}$$

7   Charge density, $\sigma = \dfrac{\text{charge}}{\text{area of one plate}} = \dfrac{Q}{A} \text{ C/m}^2$,

8   Charge Q on a capacitor is proportional to the applied voltage V, i.e. $Q \propto V$.

9   $\boxed{Q = CV} \text{ or } \boxed{C = \dfrac{Q}{V}}$

where the constant of proportionality, C, is the **capacitance**.

10 The unit of capacitance is the farad F (or more usually $\mu F = 10^{-6}$ F or pf $= 10^{-12}$ F), which is defined as the capacitance of a capacitor when a p.d. of one volt appears across the plates when charged with one coulomb.

11 Every system of electrical conductors possess capacitance. For example, there is capacitance between the conductors of overhead transmission lines and also between the wires of a telephone cable. In these examples the capacitance is undesirable but has to be accepted, minimised or compensated for. There are other situations, such as in capacitors, where capacitance is a desirable property.

12 The ratio of charge density, σ, to electric field strength, E, is called absolute permittivity, ϵ, of a dielectric.

Thus $\dfrac{\sigma}{E} = \epsilon$

13 Permittivity of free space is a constant, given by $\epsilon_o = 8.85 \times 10^{-12}$ F/m.

14 Relative permittivity, $\epsilon_r = \dfrac{\text{flux density of the field in the dielectric}}{\text{flux density of the field in vacuum}}$

(ϵ_r has no units.)
Examples of the values of ϵ_r include: air = 1, polythene = 2.3,
mica = 3 − 7, glass = 5 − 10, ceramics = 6 − 1000.

15 Absolute permittivity, $\epsilon = \epsilon_o \epsilon_r$. Thus $\boxed{\dfrac{\sigma}{E} = \epsilon_o \epsilon_r.}$

16 For a parallel plate capacitor, capacitance is proportional to area A, inversely proportional to the plate spacing (or dielectric thickness) d, and depends on the nature of the dielectric and the number of plates, n.

Capacitance $\boxed{C = \dfrac{\epsilon_o \epsilon_r A(n-1)}{d} F}$

17 For n capacitors connected **in parallel**, the equivalent capacitance C_T is given by:
$C_T = C_1 + C_2 + C_3 + \ldots\ldots\ldots + C_n$ (similar to resistors connected in series)
Also total charge, $Q_T = Q_1 + Q_2 + Q_3 + \ldots\ldots\ldots + Q_n$

18 For n capacitors connected **in series**, the equivalent capacitance C_T is given by:
$\dfrac{1}{C_T} = \dfrac{1}{C_1} + \dfrac{1}{C_2} + \dfrac{1}{C_3} + \ldots\ldots\ldots + \dfrac{1}{C_n}$ (similar to resistors connected in parallel)
The charge on each capacitor is the same when connected in series.

19 The maximum amount of field strength that a dielectric can withstand is called the dielectric strength of the material.

Dielectric strength, $E_{MAX} = \dfrac{V_{MAX}}{d}$ and $V_{MAX} = d \times E_{MAX}$.

(See *Problems 1 to 15*)

20 The **energy**, W, stored by a capacitor is given by $\boxed{W = \dfrac{1}{2} C V^2 \text{ joules}}$
(See *Problems 16 to 18*.)

21 Practical types of capacitor are characterised by the material used for their dielectric. The main types include: variable air, mica, paper, ceramics, plastic and electrolytic (see *Problem 19*).

22 When a d.c. voltage is applied to a capacitor C and resistor R connected in series, there is a short period of time immediately after the voltage is connected during which the current flowing in the circuit and the voltage across C and R are changing. These changing values are called transients.

Charging a capacitor

23 *Fig 3* shows a capacitor, initially having no charge on its plates, connected in series with resistor R across a d.c. supply. When the switch is closed:
(i) the initial current flowing, i, is given by

$i = \dfrac{V}{R}$, and the capacitor acts as if it is a

short-circuit when $v_c = 0$,

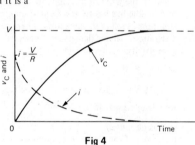

Fig 3   Fig 4

(ii) the current then begins to charge the capacitor so that v_c builds up rapidly across the plates,
(iii) v_R falls to $V - v_c$ (since $V = v_c + v_R$ at all times) and the charging current i reduces to $\dfrac{V - v_c}{R}$,
(iv) eventually the capacitor is charged to the full supply voltage, V, current $i = 0$ and the capacitor acts as an open-circuit. Curves of v_c and i against time are shown in *Fig 4* and are natural or exponential curves of growth and decay.

24 (i) The **time constant** τ of the CR circuit shown in *Fig 3* is defined as: 'the time taken for a transient to reach its final state if the initial rate of change is maintained'.
The time constant τ for any series-connected $C - R$ circuit (as in *Fig 3*) is given by:
time constant $\boxed{\tau = CR \text{ seconds}}$
(ii) In the time $\tau = CR$ seconds, v_C rises to 63.2% of its final value V and, in practical situations, v_C rises to within 1% of its final value V in a time equal to $5\,\tau$ seconds.

Discharging a capacitor

25 *Fig 5* shows a capacitor C fully charged to voltage V, as described above, connected in series with a resistor R. When the switch is closed the initial discharge current is given by $i = \dfrac{V}{R}$. As the capacitor loses its charge, v_C falls and hence i falls. The result is the natural decay curves shown in *Fig 6*. In the time $\tau = CR$ seconds, v_C falls to 36.8% of its initial voltage V and, in practical situations, v_C falls to less than 1% of its initial value in a time 5τ seconds. (See *Problems 20 and 21*.)

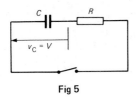

Fig 5

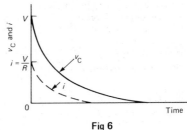

Fig 6

26 When a capacitor has been disconnected from the supply it may still be charged and it may retain this charge for some considerable time. Thus precautions must be taken to ensure that the capacitor is automatically discharged after the supply is switched off. This is done by connecting a high value resistor across the capacitor terminals.

27 (i) In a **d.c. circuit**, a capacitor blocks the current except during the times there are changes in the supply voltage.

(ii) In an **a.c. circuit**, a capacitor provides opposition to current flow which results in the voltage and current waveforms being 90° out of phase. This opposition is called **capacitive reactance X_C** and is given by:

$$X_C = \frac{1}{2\pi f C} \text{ ohms}$$

A typical graph showing the variation of capacitive reactance with frequency is shown in *Fig 7*. In a purely capacitive a.c. circuit current I is given by:

$$I = \frac{V}{X_C} \text{ amperes}$$

(See *Problems 22 to 25*.)

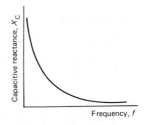

Fig 7

B. WORKED PROBLEMS ON CAPACITORS AND THEIR EFFECTS IN ELECTRIC CIRCUITS

Problem 1 Two parallel rectangular plates measuring 20 cm by 40 cm carry an electric charge of 0.2 μC. Calculate the charge density on the plates. If the plates are spaced 5 mm apart and the voltage between them is 0.25 kV, determine the electric field strength.

Charge, $Q = 0.2 \mu C = 0.2 \times 10^{-6}$ C; Area $A = 20$ cm $\times$ 40 cm $= 800$ cm^2
$$= 800 \times 10^{-4} \text{ m}^2$$

Charge density, $\sigma = \dfrac{Q}{A} = \dfrac{0.2 \times 10^{-6}}{800 \times 10^{-4}} = \dfrac{0.2 \times 10^4}{800 \times 10^6} = \dfrac{2000}{800} \times 10^{-6}$
$$= 2.5 \ \mu C/m^2$$

Voltage $V = 0.25$ kV $= 250$ V; plate spacing, $d = 5$ mm $= 5 \times 10^{-3}$ m

Electric field strength, $E = \dfrac{V}{d} = \dfrac{250}{5 \times 10^{-3}} = $ **50 kV/m.**

Problem 2 The charge density on two plates separated by mica of relative permittivity 5 is $2\mu C/m^2$. Find the voltage gradient between the plates.

Charge density, $\sigma = 2 \mu C/m^2 = 2 \times 10^{-6}$ C/m^2; $\epsilon_0 = 8.85 \times 10^{-12}$ F/m; $\epsilon_r = 5$.

$\dfrac{\sigma}{E} = \epsilon_0 \epsilon_r$. Hence **voltage gradient**, $E = \dfrac{\sigma}{\epsilon_0 \epsilon_r}$

$$= \dfrac{2 \times 10^{-6}}{8.85 \times 10^{-12} \times 5} \text{ V/m}$$
$$= \textbf{45.2 kV/m.}$$

Problem 3 Two parallel plates having a p.d. of 200 V between them are spaced 0.8 mm apart. What is the electric field strength? Find also the charge density when the dielectric between the plates is (a) air and (b) polythene of relative permittivity 2.3.

Electric field strength, $E = \dfrac{V}{d} = \dfrac{200}{0.8 \times 10^{-3}} = $ **250 kV/m.**

(a) For air: $\epsilon_r = 1$

$\dfrac{\sigma}{E} = \epsilon_0 \epsilon_r$, hence **charge density**, $\sigma = E\epsilon_0 \epsilon_r$

$$= 250 \times 10^3 \times 8.85 \times 10^{-12} \times 1 \text{ C/m}^2$$
$$= \textbf{2.213 } \mu C/m^2.$$

(b) For polythene: $\epsilon_r = 2.3$

Charge density, $\sigma = E\epsilon_0 \epsilon_r = 250 \times 10^3 \times 8.85 \times 10^{-12} \times 2.3 \text{ C/m}^2$
$$= \textbf{5.089 } \mu C/m^2.$$

Problem 4 (a) Determine the p.d. across a 4 μF capacitor when charged with 5 mC. (b) Find the charge on a 50 pF capacitor when the voltage applied to it is 2 kV.

(a) $C = 4 \mu F = 4 \times 10^{-6}$ F; $Q = 5$ mC $= 5 \times 10^{-3}$ C

Since $C = \dfrac{Q}{V}$ then $V = \dfrac{Q}{C} = \dfrac{5 \times 10^{-3}}{4 \times 10^{-6}} = \dfrac{5 \times 10^6}{4 \times 10^3} = \dfrac{5000}{4}$

Hence p.d. = **1250 V or 1.25 kV**

(b) $C = 50$ pF $= 50 \times 10^{-12}$ F; $V = 2$ kV $= 2000$ V

$$Q = CV = 50 \times 10^{-12} \times 2000 = \frac{5 \times 2}{10^8} = 0.1 \times 10^{-6}$$

Hence charge = **0.1 μC.**

Problem 5 A direct current of 4 A flows into a previously uncharged 20 μF capacitor for 3 ms. Determine the p.d. between the plates.

$I = 4$ A; $C = 20$ μF $= 20 \times 10^{-6}$ F; $t = 3$ ms $= 3 \times 10^{-3}$ s

$Q = It = 4 \times 3 \times 10^{-3}$ C

$$V = \frac{Q}{C} = \frac{4 \times 3 \times 10^{-3}}{20 \times 10^{-6}} = \frac{12 \times 10^6}{20 \times 10^3} = 0.6 \times 10^3 = 600 \text{ V}$$

Hence the p.d. between the plates is **600 volts.**

Problem 6 A 5 μF capacitor is charged so that the p.d. between its plates is 800 V. Calculate how long the capacitor can provide an average discharge current of 2 mA.

$C = 5$ μF $= 5 \times 10^{-6}$ F; $V = 800$ V; $I = 2$ mA $= 2 \times 10^{-3}$ A

$Q = CV = 5 \times 10^{-6} \times 800 = 4 \times 10^{-3}$ C

Also, $Q = It$, thus $t = \dfrac{Q}{I} = \dfrac{4 \times 10^{-3}}{2 \times 10^{-3}} = 2$ s

Hence the capacitor can provide an average discharge current of 2 mA for **2 seconds.**

Problem 7 (a) A ceramic capacitor has an effective plate area of 4 cm^2 separated by 0.1 mm of ceramic of relative permittivity 100. Calculate the capacitance of the capacitor in picofarads. (b) If the capacitor in part (a) is given a charge of 1.2 μC, what will be the p.d. between the plates?

(a) Area $A = 4$ cm^2 $= 4 \times 10^{-4}$ m^2; $d = 0.1$ mm $= 0.1 \times 10^{-3}$ m;
$\epsilon_o = 8.85 \times 10^{-12}$ F/m; $\epsilon_r = 100$

$$\text{Capacitance, } C = \frac{\epsilon_o \epsilon_r A}{d} \text{ farads} = \frac{8.85 \times 10^{-12} \times 100 \times 4 \times 10^{-4}}{0.1 \times 10^{-3}} \text{ F}$$

$$= \frac{8.85 \times 4}{10^{10}} \text{F} = \frac{8.85 \times 4 \times 10^{12}}{10^{10}} \text{ pF} = \textbf{3540 pF.}$$

(b) $Q = CV$ thus $V = \dfrac{Q}{C} = \dfrac{1.2 \times 10^{-6}}{3540 \times 10^{-12}}$ volts = **339 volts.**

Problem 8 A waxed paper capacitor has two parallel plates, each of effective area 800 cm^2. If the capacitance of the capacitor is 4425 pF, determine the effective thickness of the paper if its relative permittivity is 2.5.

$A = 800$ cm^2 $= 800 \times 10^{-4}$ m^2 $= 0.08$ m^2; $C = 4425$ pF $= 4425 \times 10^{-12}$ F;
$\epsilon_o = 8.85 \times 10^{-12}$ F/m; $\epsilon_r = 2.5$

Since $C = \dfrac{\epsilon_o \epsilon_r A}{d}$ then $d = \dfrac{\epsilon_o \epsilon_r A}{C}$

Hence $d = \dfrac{8.85 \times 10^{-12} \times 2.5 \times 0.08}{4425 \times 10^{-12}} = 0.0004$ m

Hence the thickness of the paper is **0.4 mm.**

Problem 9 A parallel plate capacitor has 19 interleaved plates, each 75 mm by 75 mm and separated by mica sheets 0.2 mm thick. Assuming the relative permittivity of the mica is 5, calculate the capacitance of the capacitor.

$n = 19$; $n - 1 = 18$; $A = 75 \times 75 = 5625$ mm^2 $= 5625 \times 10^{-6}$ m^2;
$\epsilon_r = 5$; $\epsilon_o = 8.85 \times 10^{-12}$ F/m; $d = 0.2$ mm $= 0.2 \times 10^{-3}$ m

Capacitance $C = \dfrac{\epsilon_o \epsilon_r A (n-1)}{d} = \dfrac{8.85 \times 10^{-12} \times 5 \times 5625 \times 10^{-6} \times 18}{0.2 \times 10^{-3}}$ F

$$= 0.0224 \; \mu\text{F or } 22.4 \text{ nF}.$$

Problem 10 A capacitor is to be constructed so that its capacitance is $0.2 \, \mu$F and to take a p.d. of 1.25 kV across its terminals. The dielectric is to be mica which, after allowing a safety factor of 2, has a dielectric strength of 50 MV/m. Find (a) the thickness of the mica needed, and (b) the area of a plate assuming a two-plate construction. (Assume ϵ_r for mica to be 6.)

(a) **Dielectric strength**, $E = \dfrac{V}{d}$, i.e. $d = \dfrac{V}{E} = \dfrac{1.25 \times 10^3}{50 \times 10^6}$ m $= \mathbf{0.025 \; mm}$.

(b) **Capacitance**, $C = \dfrac{\epsilon_o \epsilon_r A}{d}$, hence area $A = \dfrac{Cd}{\epsilon_o \epsilon_r}$

$$= \dfrac{0.2 \times 10^{-6} \times 0.025 \times 10^{-3}}{8.85 \times 10^{-12} \times 6} \; \text{m}^2$$

$$= 0.09416 \; \text{m}^2 = \mathbf{941.6 \; cm^2}.$$

Problem 11 Calculate the equivalent capacitance of two capacitors of 6 μF and 4 μF connected (a) in parallel, and (b) in series.

(a) In parallel, equivalent capacitance $C = C_1 + C_2 = 6\mu\text{F} + 4 \, \mu\text{F} = \mathbf{10 \; \mu F}$.

(b) In series, equivalent capacitance C is given by: $\dfrac{1}{C} = \dfrac{1}{C_1} + \dfrac{1}{C_2} = \dfrac{C_2 + C_1}{C_1 C_2}$

i.e. $C = \dfrac{C_1 C_2}{C_1 + C_2}$ (i.e. $\dfrac{\text{product}}{\text{sum}}$)

This formula is used for the special case of two capacitors in series (which is similar to two resistors in parallel).

Thus $C = \dfrac{6 \times 4}{6 + 4} = \dfrac{24}{10} = \mathbf{2.4 \; \mu F}$.

Problem 12 What capacitance must be connected in series with a 30 μF capacitor for the equivalent capacitance to be 12 μF?

Let $C = 12 \, \mu$F (the equivalent capacitance), $C_1 = 30 \, \mu$F and C_2 be the unknown capacitance.

For two capacitors in series $\dfrac{1}{C} = \dfrac{1}{C_1} + \dfrac{1}{C_2}$

Hence $\dfrac{1}{C_2} = \dfrac{1}{C} - \dfrac{1}{C_1} = \dfrac{C_1 - C}{C C_1}$

$C_2 = \dfrac{C C_1}{C_1 - C} = \dfrac{12 \times 30}{30 - 12} = \dfrac{360}{18} = \mathbf{20 \; \mu F}$.

Problem 13 Capacitances of 1 μF, 3 μF, 5 μF and 6 μF are connected in parallel to a direct voltage supply of 100 V. Determine (a) the equivalent circuit capacitance, (b) the total charge, and (c) the charge on each capcitor.

(a) The equivalent capacitance C for four capacitors in parallel is given by:
$$C = C_1 + C_2 + C_3 + C_4$$
   i.e. $C = 1 + 3 + 5 + 6 = \mathbf{15\ \mu F}$.

(b) Total charge $Q_T = CV$, where C is the equivalent circuit capacitance.
   i.e. $Q_T = 15 \times 10^{-6} \times 100 = 1.5 \times 10^{-3}$ C = **1.5 mC.**

(c) The charge on the 1 μF capacitor $Q_1 = C_1\ V = 1 \times 10^{-6} \times 100 = $ **0.1 mC.**
   The charge on the 3 μF capacitor $Q_2 = C_2\ V = 3 \times 10^{-6} \times 100 = $ **0.3 mC.**
   The charge on the 5 μF capacitor $Q_3 = C_3\ V = 5 \times 10^{-6} \times 100 = $ **0.5 mC.**
   The charge on the 6 μF capacitor $Q_4 = C_4\ V = 6 \times 10^{-6} \times 100 = $ **0.6 mC.**
   [Check: In a parallel circuit $Q_T = Q_1 + Q_2 + Q_3 + Q_4$
   $\qquad Q_1 + Q_2 + Q_3 + Q_4 = 0.1 + 0.3 + 0.5 + 0.6 = 1.5$ mC $= Q_T$]

Problem 14 Capacitances of 3 μF, 6 μF and 12 μF are connected in series across a 350 V supply. Calculate (a) the equivalent circuit capacitance, (b) the charge on each capacitor, and (c) the p.d. across each capacitor.

The circuit diagram is shown in *Fig 8*.

(a) The equivalent circuit capacitance C for three capacitors in series is given by:

$$\frac{1}{C} = \frac{1}{C_1} + \frac{1}{C_2} + \frac{1}{C_3}$$

i.e. $\dfrac{1}{C} = \dfrac{1}{3} + \dfrac{1}{6} + \dfrac{1}{12} = \dfrac{4 + 2 + 1}{12} = \dfrac{7}{12}$

Hence the equivalent circuit capacitance

$C = \dfrac{12}{7} = 1\dfrac{5}{7}\ \mu F.$

(b) Total charge $Q_T = CV$

Hence $\qquad Q_T = \dfrac{12}{7} \times 10^{-6} \times 350 = 600\ \mu C$ or 0.6 mC

Since the capacitors are connected in series 0.6 mC is the charge on each of them.

(c) The voltage across the 3 μF capacitor, $V_1 = \dfrac{Q}{C_1} = \dfrac{0.6 \times 10^{-3}}{3 \times 10^{-6}} = $ **200 V.**

The voltage across the 6 μF capacitor, $V_2 = \dfrac{Q}{C_2} = \dfrac{0.6 \times 10^{-3}}{6 \times 10^{-6}} = $ **100 V.**

The voltage across the 12 μF capacitor, $V_3 = \dfrac{Q}{C_3} = \dfrac{0.6 \times 10^{-3}}{12 \times 10^{-6}} = $ **50 V.**

   [Check: In a series circuit $V = V_1 + V_2 + V_3$
   $\qquad V_1 + V_2 + V_3 = 200 + 100 + 50 = 350$V = supply voltage.]

In practice capacitors are rarely connected in series unless they are of the same capacitance. The reason for this can be seen from the above problem where the lowest valued capacitor (i.e. 3 μF) has the highest p.d. across it (i.e. 200 V) which means that if all the capacitors have an identical construction they must all be rated at the highest voltage.

Problem 15 For the arrangement shown in *Fig 9* find (a) the equivalent capacitance of the circuit, (b) the voltage across QR, and (c) the charge on each capacitor.

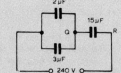

Fig 9

(a) 2 μF in parallel with 3 μF gives an equivalent capacitance of
$2\mu F + 3\mu F = 5\mu F$.
The circuit is now as shown in *Fig 10*.
The equivalent capacitance of 5μF in series with 15μF is given by
$\dfrac{5 \times 15}{5 + 15}$ μF, i.e. $\dfrac{75}{20}$ or **3.75 μF**.

(b) The charge on each of the capacitors shown in *Fig 10* will be the same since they are connected in series. Let this charge be Q coulombs.

Then $Q = C_1 V_1 = C_2 V_2$
i.e. $5 V_1 = 15 V_2$
$V_1 = 3 V_2$
Also $V_1 + V_2 = 240$ V
Hence $3V_2 + V_2 = 240$ V from (1)
Thus $V_2 = 60$ V and $V_1 = 180$ V
Hence the voltage across QR is 60 V.

Fig 10

$C_1 = 5\mu F$ $C_2 = 15\mu F$

(c) The charge on the 15 μF capacitor is $C_2 V_2 = 15 \times 10^{-6} \times 60 = $ **0.9 mC.**
The charge on the 2 μF capacitor is $2 \times 10^{-6} \times 180 = $ **0.36 mC.**
The charge on the 3 μF capacitor is $3 \times 10^{-6} \times 180 = $ **0.54 mC.**

Problem 16 (a) Determine the energy stored in a 3 μF capacitor when charged to 400 V. (b) Find also the average power developed if this energy is dissipated in a time of 10 μs.

(a) Energy stored $W = \dfrac{1}{2} C V^2$ joules
$= \dfrac{1}{2} \times 3 \times 10^{-6} \times 400^2 = \dfrac{3}{2} \times 16 \times 10^{-2} = $ **0.24 J.**

(b) Power $= \dfrac{\text{Energy}}{\text{time}} = \dfrac{0.24}{10 \times 10^{-6}}$ watts $= $ **24 kW.**

Problem 17 A 12 μF capacitor is required to store 4 J of energy. Find the p.d. to which the capacitor must be charged.

Energy stored $W = \dfrac{1}{2}C V^2$ hence $V^2 = \dfrac{2W}{C}$
and $V = \sqrt{\left(\dfrac{2W}{C}\right)} = \sqrt{\left(\dfrac{2 \times 4}{12 \times 10^{-6}}\right)} = \sqrt{\left(\dfrac{2 \times 10^6}{3}\right)}$
$= $ **816.5 volts**

Energy stored $W = \frac{1}{2}C\,V^2$ and $C = \frac{Q}{V}$

Hence $\quad W = \frac{1}{2}\left(\frac{Q}{V}\right)V^2 = \frac{1}{2}QV$

from which $V = \frac{2W}{Q}$

$Q = 10$ mC $= 10 \times 10^{-3}$ C and $W = 1.2$ J

(a) **Voltage,** $V = \dfrac{2W}{Q} = \dfrac{2 \times 1.2}{10 \times 10^{-3}} =$ **0.24 kV or 240 volts**

(b) **Capacitance,** $C = \dfrac{Q}{V} = \dfrac{10 \times 10^{-3}}{240}$ F $= \dfrac{10 \times 10^{6}}{240 \times 10^{3}}\mu$F $=$ **41.67μF.**

1   **Variable air capacitors.** Usually consists of two sets of metal plates (such as
    aluminium) one fixed, the other variable. The set of moving plates rotates on
    a spindle as shown by the end view
    in *Fig 11*. As the moving plates are
    rotated through half a revolution,
    the meshing, and therefore the
    capacitance, varies from a minimum
    to a maximum value. Variable air
    capacitors are used in radio and
    electronic circuits where very low
    losses are required, or where a
    variable capacitance is needed. The maximum value of such capacitors is between
    500 pF and 1000 pF.

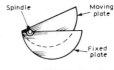

Fig 11

2   **Mica capacitors.** A typical older type construction is shown in *Fig 12*. Usually
    the whole capacitor is impregnated
    with wax and placed in a bakelite
    case. Mica is easily obtained in thin
    sheets and is a good insulator.
    However, mica is expensive and
    is not used in capacitors above
    about 0.1 μF. A modified form
    of mica capacitor is the silvered
    mica type. The mica is coated on
    both sides with a thin layer of
    silver which forms the plates.
    Capacitance is stable and less likely
    to change with age. Such capacitors
    have a constant capacitance with change of temperature, a high working voltage
    rating and a long service life and are used in high frequency circuits with fixed
    values of capacitance up to about 1000 pF.

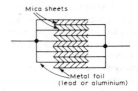

Fig 12

3   **Paper capacitors.** A typical paper capacitor is shown in *Fig 13* where the length
    of the roll corresponds to the capacitance required. The whole is usually

impregnated with oil or wax to
exclude moisture, and then placed
in a plastic or aluminium container
for protection. Paper capacitors
up to about 1 μF are made in
various working voltages. Disadvantages of paper capacitors
include variation in capacitance
with temperature change and a
shorter service life than most other
types of capacitor.

Fig 13

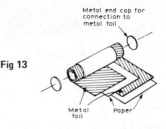

4 **Ceramic capacitors**. These are made in various forms, each type of construction
depending on the value of capacitance required. For high values, a tube of ceramic
material is used as shown in the cross section of *Fig 14*. For smaller values the cup

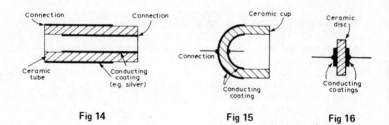

Fig 14   **Fig 15**   **Fig 16**

construction is used as shown in *Fig 15*, and for still smaller values the disc
construction shown in *Fig 16* is used.

Certain ceramic materials have a very high permittivity and this enables capacitors
of high capacitance to be made which are of small physical size with a high
working voltage rating. Ceramic capacitors are available in the range 1 pF to
0.1 μF and may be used in high frequency electronic circuits subject to a wide
range of temperature.

5 **Plastic capacitors**. Some plastic materials, such as polystyrene and Teflon, can be
used as dielectrics. Construction is similar to the paper capacitor but using a
plastic film instead of paper. Plastic capacitors operate well under conditions of
high temperature, provide a precise value of capacitance, a very long service life
and high reliability.

6 **Electrolytic capacitors**. Construction is similar to the paper capacitor with
aluminium foil used for the plates and with a thick absorbent material, such as
paper, impregnated with an electrolyte (ammonium borate), separating the plates.
The finished capacitor is usually assembled in an aluminium container and
hermetically sealed. Its operation depends on the formation of a thin aluminium
oxide layer on the positive plate by electrolytic action when a suitable direct
potential is maintained between the plates. This oxide layer is very thin and forms
the dielectric. (The absorbent paper between the plates is a conductor and does
not act as a dielectric). Such capacitors must only be used on d.c. and must be
connected with the correct polarity; if this is not done the capacitor will be
destroyed since the oxide layer will be destroyed. Electrolytic capacitors are
manufactured with working voltage from 6 V to 500 V, although accuracy is

generally not very high. These capacitors possess a much larger capacitance than other types of capacitors of similar dimensions due to the oxide film being only a few microns thick. The fact that they can be used only on d.c. supplies limits their usefulness.

Problem 20 A 20 μF capacitor is to be charged through a 100 kΩ resistor by a constant d.c. supply. Determine (a) the time constant for the circuit, and (b) the additional resistance required to increase the time constant to 5 s.

(a) **Time constant,** $\tau = CR$ = 20 $\times$ 10^{-6} $\times$ 100 $\times$ 10^3 = **2s.**
(b) When the time constant τ = 5 s, then 5 = CR

i.e. 5 = 20 $\times$ 10^{-6} $\times$ R

from which resistance, $R = \dfrac{5}{20 \times 10^{-6}} = \dfrac{5 \times 10^6}{20}$ = 250 000Ω or 250 kΩ

Thus the additional resistance needed is 250 kΩ – 100 kΩ = **150 kΩ.**

Problem 21 A 0.1 μF capacitor is charged to 200 V before being connected across a 4 kΩ resistor. Determine (a) the initial discharge current, (b) the time constant of the circuit, and (c) the minimum time required for the voltage across the capacitor to fall to less than 2 V.

(a) Initial discharge current, $i = \dfrac{V}{R} = \dfrac{200}{4 \times 10^3}$ = **0.05 A or 50 mA.**

(b) Time constant $\tau = CR$ = 0.1 $\times$ 10^{-6} $\times$ 4 $\times$ 10^3 = **0.0004s or 0.4 ms.**
(c) The minimum time for the capacitor voltage to fall to less than 2 V,

i.e. less than $\dfrac{2}{200}$ or 1% of the initial value is given by 5τ.

5τ = 5 $\times$ 0.4 = **2 ms.**

Problem 22 Describe how a pure capacitance in an a.c. circuit causes voltage and current waveforms to be 90° out of phase.

When a capacitor is connected to an a.c. supply its effects are present at all times since the voltage is continually changing.
   Let the instantaneous values of voltage and charge be v volts and q coulombs respectively. If the voltage increases from zero to v in t seconds and the increase in charge is q coulombs, then $q = Cv$ (from para. 9)
and $q = it$ (from para. 4)

Hence $\dfrac{dq}{dt} = C\dfrac{dr}{dt}$

where $\dfrac{dq}{dt}$ and $\dfrac{dr}{dt}$ are the rates of change of charge and voltage respectively.

Therefore $\boxed{i = C\dfrac{dv}{dt}}$ (since current $i = \dfrac{dq}{dt}$)

Let voltage v be sinusoidal as shown in *Fig 17*.
At point A, the voltage waveform is at its steepest,
i.e. $\dfrac{dv}{dt}$ is a maximum. Hence $i = C\dfrac{dv}{dt}$ is a maximum value and is shown by the

point A'. As v increases, the gradient of the curve decreases (i.e. $\dfrac{dv}{dt}$ decreases)

61

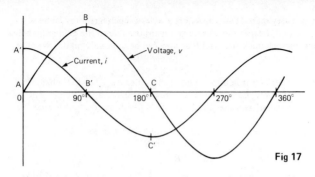

Fig 17

until at point B the gradient is zero. Hence the current is zero, shown by point B'.

Between B and C the gradient of the curve (i.e. $\frac{dv}{dt}$) is negative and hence the current value is negative. At point C the gradient is a maximum negative and thus i is shown by the point C'. The remaining half of the cycle varies in a similar manner to the first half cycle and the resulting current waveform is seen to be sinusoidal but out of phase. The peak of the current waveform A' occurs $90°$ before the peak of the voltage waveform B and the current is said to lead the voltage by $90°$.

Problem 23 Determine the capacitive reactance of a capacitor of 10 μF when connected to a circuit of frequency (a) 50 Hz, (b) 20 kHz.

(a) Capacitive reactance $X_C = \frac{1}{2\pi f C} = \frac{1}{2\pi (50)(10 \times 10^{-6})} = \frac{10^6}{2\pi (50)(10)}$

$= 318.3 \ \Omega$.

(b) $X_C = \frac{1}{2\pi f C} = \frac{1}{2\pi (20 \times 10^3)(10 \times 10^{-6})} = \frac{10^6}{2\pi (20 \times 10^3)(10)} = 0.796 \ \Omega$.

Hence as the frequency is increased from 50 Hz to 20 kHz, X_C decreases from 318.3 Ω to 0.796 Ω. (See *Fig 7*.)

Problem 24 A capacitor has a reactance of 40 Ω when operated on a 50 Hz supply. Determine the value of its capacitance.

Since capacitive reactance $X_C = \frac{1}{2\pi f C}$, **capacitance, $C = \frac{1}{2\pi f X_C} = \frac{1}{2\pi (50)(40)}$ F**

$= \frac{10^6}{2\pi (50)(40)} \ \mu F = \textbf{79.58} \ \pmb{\mu} \textbf{F}.$

Problem 25 Calculate the current taken by a 23 μF capacitor when connected to a 240 V, 50 Hz supply.

Current, $I = \frac{V}{X_C} = \frac{V}{\frac{1}{2\pi f C}} = 2\pi f C V = 2\pi (50)(23 \times 10^{-6})(240) = \textbf{1.73 A}.$

C. FURTHER PROBLEMS ON CAPACITORS AND THEIR EFFECTS IN ELECTRIC CIRCUITS

(a) SHORT ANSWER PROBLEMS

1 Explain the term 'electrostatics'.

2 Complete the statements: Like charges . . . . ; unlike charges
. . . .

3 How can an 'electric field' be established between two parallel metal plates?

4 What is capacitance?

5 State the unit of capacitance.

6 Complete the statement: Capacitance = $\dfrac{\text{. . . . .}}{\text{. . . . .}}$.

7 Complete the statements: (a) 1 μF = ... F.
   (b) 1 pF = ... F.

8 Complete the statement: Electric field strength, E = $\dfrac{\text{. . . . .}}{\text{. . . . .}}$.

9 Complete the statement: Charge density, σ = $\dfrac{\text{. . . . .}}{\text{. . . . .}}$.

10 Draw the electrical circuit diagram symbol for a capacitor.

11 Name two practical examples where capacitance is present, although undesirable.

12 The insulating material separating the plates of a capacitor is called the . . . .
. . . .

13 10 volts applied to a capacitor results in a charge of 5 coulombs. What is the capacitance of the capacitor?

14 Three 3 μF capacitors are connected in parallel. The equivalent capacitance is
. . . .

15 Three 3 μF capacitors are connected in series. The equivalent capacitance is
. . . .

16 State an advantage of series connected capacitors.

17 Name three factors upon which capacitance depends.

18 What does 'relative permittivity' mean?

19 Define 'permittivity of free space'.

20 Name five types of capacitor commonly used.

21 Sketch a typical rolled paper capacitor.

22 Explain briefly the construction of a variable air capacitor.

23 State three advantages and one disadvantage of mica capacitors.

24 Name two disadvantages of paper capacitors.

25 Between what values of capacitance are ceramic capacitors normally available?

26 What main advantages do plastic capacitors possess?

27 Explain briefly the construction of an electrolytic capacitor.

28 What is the main disadvantage of electrolytic capacitors?

29 Name an important advantage of electrolytic capacitors.

30 What safety precautions should be taken when a capacitor is disconnected from a supply?

31 What is meant by the 'dielectric strength' of a material?

32 State the formula used to determine the energy stored by a capacitor.

33 State the effects of a capacitor on the current in a d.c. circuit.

34 State the effects of a capacitor on the current in an a.c. circuit.

35 Sketch typical graphs of capacitor voltage against time for the charge and discharge of a capacitor.

(b) MULTI-CHOICE PROBLEMS (Answers on page 156)

1 Electrostatics is a branch of electricity concerned with:
   (a) energy flowing across a gap between conductors;
   (b) charges at rest;
   (c) charges in motion;
   (d) energy in the form of charges.
2 The capacitance of a capacitor is the ratio:
   (a) charge to p.d. between plates;
   (b) p.d. between plates to plate spacing;
   (c) p.d. between plates to thickness of dielectric;
   (d) p.d. between plates to charge.
3 The p.d. across a 10 μF capacitor to charge it with 10 mC is:
   (a) 100 V; (b) 1 kV; (c) 1 V; (d) 10 V.
4 The charge on a 10 pF capacitor when the voltage applied to it is 10 kV is:
   (a) 100 μC; (b) 0.1 C; (c) 0.1 μC; (d) 0.01 μC.
5 Four 2 μF capacitors are connected in parallel. The equivalent capacitance is:
   (a) 8 μF; (b) 0.5 μF.
6 Four 2 μF capacitors are connected in series. The equivalent capacitance is:
   (a) 8 μF; (b) 0.5 μF.
7 State which of the following is false. The capacitance of a capacitor:
   (a) is proportional to the cross-sectional area of the plates;
   (b) is proportional to the distance between the plates;
   (c) depends on the number of plates;
   (d) is proportional to the relative permittivity of the dielectric.
8 Which of the following statements is false?
   (a) An air capacitor is normally a variable type.
   (b) A paper capacitor generally has a shorter service life than most other types of capacitor.
   (c) An electrolytic capacitor must be used only on a.c. supplies.
   (d) Plastic capacitors generally operate satisfactorily under conditions of high temperature.
9 The energy stored in a 10μF capacitor when charged to 500 V is:
   (a) 1.25 mJ. (b) 0.025 μJ; (c) 1.25 J; (d) 1.25 C.

10 The capacitance of a variable air capacitor is a maximum when:
    (a) the movable plates half overlap the fixed plates;
    (b) the movable plates are most widely separated from the fixed plates;
    (c) both sets of plates are exactly meshed;
    (d) the movable plates are closer to one side of the fixed plate than to the other.
11 A capacitor of 1 μF is connected to a 50 Hz supply. The capacitive reactance is:

(a) 50 MΩ; (b) $\dfrac{10}{\pi}$ kΩ; (c) $\dfrac{\pi}{10^4}\Omega$; (d) $\dfrac{10}{\pi}$ Ω.

12 When a capacitor is connected to an a.c. supply the current:
    (a) leads the voltage by $180°$;
    (b) is in phase with the voltage;

    (c) leads the voltage by $\dfrac{\pi}{2}$ rad;

    (d) lags the voltage by $90°$·

13 In a circuit consisting of a 1 μF capacitor and a 100 kΩ resistor connected in
    series the time constant of the circuit is:
    (a) 10 ms; (b) 100 ms; (c) 1 s; (d) 10 s.

14 The current taken by a 10 μF capacitor when connected to a 1 kV, $\dfrac{500}{\pi}$ Hz

    supply is:

(a) $\dfrac{5}{\pi}$A; (b) 10^5 A; (c) 10 A; (d) 10μA.

(c) CONVENTIONAL PROBLEMS

(Where appropriate take ϵ_o as 8.85×10^{-12} F/m)

Charge density and electric field strength

1   A capacitor uses a dielectric 0.04 mm thick and operates at 30 V. What is the
    electric field strength across the dielectric at this voltage?
                                                                    [750 kV/m]
2   A two-plate capacitor has a charge of 25 C. If the effective area of each plate is
    5 cm² find the charge density of the electric field.
                                                                    [50 kC/m²]
3   A charge of 1.5 μC is carried on two parallel rectangular plates each measuring
    60 mm by 80 mm. Calculate the charge density on the plates. If the plates are
    spaced 10 mm apart and the voltage between them is 0.5 kV, determine the
    electric field strength.
                                                    [312.5 μC/m²; 50 kV/m]
4   Two parallel plates are separated by a dielectric and charged with 10μC. Given
    that the area of each plate is 50 cm², calculate the charge density in the dielectric
    separating the plates.
                                                                    [2 mC/m²]
5   The charge density between two plates separated by polystyrene of relative
    permittivity 2.5 is 5 μC/m². Find the voltage gradient between the plates.
                                                                    [226 kV/m]
6   Two parallel plates having a p.d. of 250 V between them are spaced 1 mm apart.
    Determine the electric field strength. Find also the charge density when the

                                                                              65

dielectric between the plates is (a) air, and (b) mica of relative permittivity 5.

[250 kV/m; (a) 2.213 μC/m^2; (b) 11.063 μC/m^2]

Q = CV problems

7   Find the charge on a 10μF capacitor when the applied voltage is 250 V.

[2.5 mC]

8   Determine the voltage across a 1000 pF capacitor to charge it with 2 μC.

[2 kV]

9   The charge on the plates of a capacitor is 6 mC when the potential between them is 2.4 kV. Determine the capacitance of the capacitor.

[2.5 μF]

10 For how long must a charging current of 2 A be fed to a 5 μF capacitor to raise the p.d. between its plates by 500 V.

[1.25 ms]

11 A direct current of 10 A flows into a previously uncharged 5 μF capacitor for 1 ms. Determine the p.d. between the plates.

[2 kV]

12 A 16 μF capacitor is charged at the constant current of 4 μA for 2 minutes. Calculate the final p.d. across the capacitor and the corresponding charge in coulombs.

[30 V, 480 μC]

13 A steady current of 10 A flows into a previously uncharged capacitor for 1.5 ms when the p.d. between the plates is 2 kV. Find the capacitance of the capacitor.

[7.5 μF]

Parallel plate capacitor

14 A capacitor consists of two parallel plates each of area 0.1 m^2, spaced 0.01 mm in air. Calculate the capacitance in picofarads.

[885 pF]

15 A waxed paper capacitor has two parallel plates, each of effective area 0.2 m^2. If the capacitance is 4000 pF, determine the effective thickness of the paper if its relative permittivity is 2.

[0.885 mm]

16 Calculate the capacitance of a parallel plate capacitor having five plates, each 30 mm by 20 mm and separated by a dielectric 0.75 mm thick having a relative permittivity of 2.3.

[65.14 pF]

17 How many plates has a parallel plate capacitor having a capacitance of 0.005 μF, if each plate is 40 mm square and each dielectric is 0.102 mm thick with a relative permittivity of 6.

[7]

18 A parallel plate capacitors is made from 25 plates, each 70 mm by 120 mm interleaved with mica of relative permittivity 5. If the capacitance of the capacitor is 3000 pF determine the thickness of the mica sheet.

[2.97 mm]

19 A capacitor is constructed with parallel plates and has a value of 50 pF. What would be the capacitance of the capacitor if the plate area is doubled and the plate spacing is halved?

[200 pF]

20 The capacitance of a parallel plate capacitor is 1000 pF. It has 19 plates, each 50 mm by 30 mm separated by a dielectric of thickness 0.40 mm. Determine the relative permittivity of the dielectric.

[1.67]

21 The charge on the square plates of a multiplate capacitor is 80 μC when the potential between them is 5 kV. If the capacitor has 25 plates separated by a dielectric of thickness 0.102 mm and relative permittivity 4.8, determine the width of a plate.

[40 mm]

22 A capacitor is to be constructed so that its capacitance is 4250 pF and to operate at a p.d. of 100 V across its terminals. The dielectric is to be polythene (ϵ_r = 2.3) which, after allowing a safety factor, has a dielectric strength of 20 MV/m. Find (a) the thickness of the polythene needed, and (b) the area of a plate.

[(a) 0.005 mm; (b) 10.44 cm^2]

Capacitors connected in parallel and in series

23 Capacitors of 2μF and 6 μF are connected (a) in parallel, and (b) in series. Determine the equivalent capacitance in each case.

[(a) 8 μF; (b) 1.5 μF]

24 Find the capacitance to be connected in series with a 10 μF capacitor for the equivalent capacitance to be 6 μF.

[15 μF]

25 What value of capacitance would be obtained if capacitors of 0.15 μF and 0.1 μF are connected (a) in series, and (b) in parallel.

[(a) 0.06 μF; (b) 0.25 μF]

26 Two 6 μF capacitors are connected in series with one having a capacitance of 12 μF. Find the total equivalent circuit capacitance. What capacitance must be added in series to obtain a capacitance of 1.2 μF?

[2.4 μF; 2.4 μF]

27 Determine the equivalent capacitance when the following capacitors are connected (a) in parallel, and (b) in series:

(i) 2 μF, 4 μF and 8 μF;
(ii) 0.02 μF, 0.05 μF and 0.1 μF;
(iii) 50 pF and 450 pF;
(iv) 0.01 μF and 200 pF.

$$\begin{bmatrix} \text{(a) (i) } 14\ \mu F, \text{(ii) } 0.17\ \mu F, \text{(iii) } 500\ pF, \text{(iv) } 0.0102\ \mu F \\ \text{(b) (i) } 1\tfrac{1}{7}\ \mu F, \text{(ii) } 0.0125\ \mu F, \text{(iii) } 45\ pF, \text{(iv) } 196.1\ pF \end{bmatrix}$$

28 For the arrangement shown in *Fig 18* find (a) the equivalent circuit capacitance, and (b) the voltage across a 4.5 μF capacitor.   [(a) 1.2 μF; (b) 100 V]

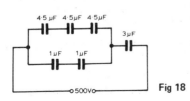

Fig 18

Fig 19

67

29 Three 12 μF capacitors are connected in series across a 750 V supply. Calculate
(a) the equivalent capacitance, (b) the charge on each capacitor, and (c) the p.d.
across each capacitor.

[(a) 4 μF; (b) 3 mC; (c) 250 V]

30 If two capacitors having capacitances of 3 μF and 5 μF respectively are connected
in series across a 240 V supply determine (a) the p.d. across each capacitor, and
(b) the charge on each capacitor.

[(a) 150 V, 90 V; (b) 0.45 mC on each]

31 In *Fig 19* capacitors P, Q and R are identical and the total equivalent capacitance
of the circuit is 3 μF. Determine the values of P, Q and R.

[4.2 μF each]

32 Capacitances of 4 μF, 8 μF and 16 μF are connected in parallel across a 200 V
supply. Determine (a) the equivalent capacitance, (b) the total charge, and (c) the
charge on each capacitor.

[(a) 28 μF; (b) 5.6 mC; (c) 0.8 mC, 1.6 mC, 3.2 mC]

33 A circuit consists of two capacitors P and Q in parallel, connected in series with
another capacitor R. The capacitances of P, Q and R are 4 μF, 12 μF and 8 μF
respectively. When the circuit is connected across a 300 V d.c. supply find (a) the
total capacitance of the circuit, (b) the p.d. across each capacitor, and (c) the
charge on each capacitor.

$$\left[\text{(a) } 5\frac{1}{3}\mu F; \text{(b) } 100 \text{ V across P, } 100 \text{ V across Q, } 200 \text{ V across R;} \atop \text{(c) } 0.4 \text{ mC on P, } 1.2 \text{ mC on Q, } 1.6 \text{ mC on R}\right]$$

Energy stored in capacitors

34 When a capacitor is connected across a 200 V supply the charge is 4 μC. Find
(a) the capacitance, and (b) the energy stored.

[(a) 0.02 μF; (b) 0.4 mJ]

35 Find the energy stored in a 10 μF capacitor when charged to 2 kV.

[20 J]

36 A 3300 pF capacitor is required to store 0.5 mJ of energy. Find the p.d. to which
the capacitor must be charged.

[550 V]

37 A capacitor is charged with 8 mC. If the energy stored is 0.4 J find (a) the voltage,
and (c) the capacitance.

[(a) 100 V; (b) 80 μF]

38 A capacitor, consisting of two metal plates each of area 50 cm^2 and spaced
0.2 mm apart in air, is connected across a 120 V supply. Calculate (a) the energy
stored, (b) the charge density, and (c) the potential gradient.

[(a) 1.593 μJ; (b) 5.31 μC/m^2; (c) 600 kV/m]

39 A bakelite capacitor is to be constructed to have a capacitance of 0.04 F and to
have a steady working potential of 1 kV maximum. Allowing a safe value of field
stress of 25 mV/m find (a) the thickness of bakelite required, (b) the area of plate
required if the relative permittivity of bakelite is 5, (c) the maximum energy
stored by the capacitor, and (d) the average power developed if this energy is
dissipated in a time of 20 μs.

[(a) 0.04 mm; (b) 361.6 cm^2; (c) 0.02 J; (d) 1 kW]

Charging and discharging of capacitors

40 A 15 μF capacitor is to be charged through a 300 kΩ resistor by a constant d.c.

supply. Determine (a) the time constant of the circuit, and (b) the additional resistance needed to increase the time constant to 7.5 s.

[(a) 4.5 s; (b) 200 kΩ]

41 Explain the charging and discharging of a capacitor through a resistor with reference to a graph of capacitor voltage against time.

42 An electrical circuit is controlled by a time switch which depends on the charging of an 8 μF capacitor. If the circuit time constant is to be variable between 0.4 s and 2.4 s determine the limits of the value of the resistance required in series with the capacitor.

[50 kΩ to 300 kΩ]

43 A 6 nF capacitor is charged to 600 V before being connected across a 2 kΩ resistor. Determine (a) the initial discharge current, (b) the time constant of the circuit, and (c) the minimum probable time required for the voltage to fall to less than 1% of its initial value.

[(a) 0.3 A; (b) 12 μs; (c) 60 μs]

Capacitors in a.c. circuits

44 Calculate the capacitive reactance of a 20 μF capacitor when connected to an a.c. circuit of frequency (a) 20 Hz, (b) 500 Hz, (c) 4 kHz.

[(a) 397.9Ω; (b) 15.92 Ω; (c) 1.989 Ω]

45 A capacitor has a reactance of 80 Ω when connected to a 50 Hz supply. Calculate the value of its capacitance.

[39.79 μF]

46 Calculate the current taken by a 10 μF capacitor when connected to a 200 V, 100 Hz supply.

[1.257 A]

47 A capacitor has a capacitive reactance of 400 Ω when connected to a 100 V, 25 Hz supply. Determine its capacitance and the current taken from the supply.

[15.92 μF, 0.25 A]

48 Two similar capacitors are connected in parallel to a 200 V, 1 kHz supply. Find the value of each capacitor if the supply current is 0.628 A.

[0.25 μF]

6 Inductors and their effects in electric circuits

A. MAIN POINTS CONCERNED WITH INDUCTORS AND THEIR EFFECTS IN ELECTRIC CIRCUITS.

1   **Inductance** is the property of a circuit whereby there is an emf induced into the circuit by the change of flux linkages produced by a current change. When the emf is induced in the same circuit as that in which the current is changing, the property is called **self-inductance** L.

2   The **unit of inductance** is the **henry**, **H**.
    'A circuit has an inductance of one henry when an emf of one volt is induced in it by a current changing at the rate of one ampere per second.'

3   A component called an **inductor** is used when the property of inductance is required in a circuit. The basic form of an inductor is simply a coil of wire. (See *Problem 1*.)

4   Two examples of practical inductors are shown in *Fig 1*, and the standard electrical circuit diagram symbols for air-cored and iron-cored inductors are shown in *Fig 2*.

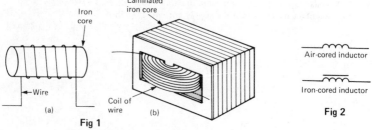

Iron core

Laminated iron core

◄—Wire

Coil of wire

(a)

(b)

Fig 1

Air-cored inductor

Iron-cored inductor

Fig 2

An iron-cored inductor is often called a **choke** since, when used in a.c. circuits, it has a choking effect, limiting the current flowing through it.

5   Inductance is often undesirable in a circuit. To reduce inductance to a minimum the wire may be bent back on itself, as shown in *Fig 3*, so that the magnetising effect of one conductor is neutralised by that of the adjacent conductor. The wire may be coiled around an insulator, as shown, without

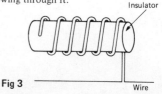

Insulator

Fig 3

Wire

increasing the inductance. Standard resistors may be non-inductively wound in this manner.

6 An inductor possesses an ability to store energy. The energy stored, W, in the magnetic field of an inductor is given by:

$$W = \frac{1}{2} L I^2 \text{ joules.}$$

(See *Problems 2 and 3*.)

Effect of inductance on the current in a d.c. circuit

7 A coil of wire possesses both inductance and resistance, each turn of the coil contributing to both its self-inductance and its resistance. It is not possible to obtain pure inductance. An inductive circuit is usually represented as resistance and inductance connected in series.

8 When a d.c. voltage is connected to a circuit having inductance L and resistance R there is a short period of time immediately after the voltage is connected, during which the current flowing in the circuit and the voltages across L and R are changing. These changing values are called **transients**.

9 **Current growth.**

(a) When the switch S shown in *Fig 4* is closed then $V = v_L + v_R$ (1)

(b) The battery voltage V is constant,

$$v_L = L \times \frac{\text{change of current}}{\text{change of time}},$$

i.e. $v_L = L\left(\dfrac{\Delta I}{t}\right)$, and $v_R = iR$. (2)

Hence at all times $V = L\left(\dfrac{\Delta I}{t}\right) + iR$

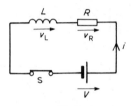

Fig 4

(c) At the instant of closing the switch, the rate of change of current is such that it induces an emf in the inductance which is equal and opposite to V. Hence $V = v_L + 0$, i.e. $v_L = V$. From equation (1), $v_R = 0$ and $i = 0$.

(d) A short time later at time t_1 seconds after closing S, current i_1 is flowing, since there is a rate of change of current initially, resulting in a voltage drop of $i_1 R$ across the resistor. Since V, which is constant, is given by $V = v_L + v_R$, the induced emf v_L is reduced and equation (2) becomes

$$V = L\left(\frac{\Delta I_1}{t_1}\right) + i_1 R.$$

(e) A short time later still, say at time t_2 seconds after closing the switch, the current flowing is i_2, and the voltage drop across the resistor increases to $i_2 R$. Since v_R increases v_L decreases.

(f) Ultimately, some time after closing S, the current flow is entirely limited by R, the rate of change of current is zero and hence v_L is zero. Thus $V = iR$. Under these conditions, steady state current flows, usually signified by I.

Thus $I = \dfrac{V}{R}$, $v_R = IR$ and $v_L = 0$ at steady state conditions.

(g) Curves showing the changes in v_L, v_R and i with time are shown in *Fig 5* and show that v_L is a maximum value initially (i.e. equal to V), decaying

71

exponentially to zero, whereas v_R and i grow from zero to their steady state values of V and $I = \dfrac{V}{R}$ respectively.

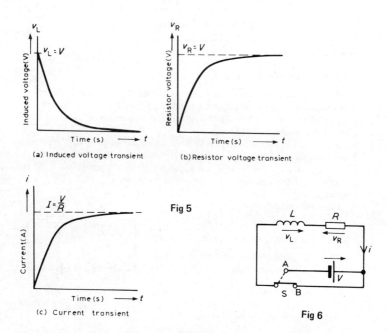

(a) Induced voltage transient

(b) Resistor voltage transient

Fig 5

(c) Current transient

Fig 6

10 The time taken for the current in an inductive circuit to reach its final value depends on the values of L and R. The ratio $\dfrac{L}{R}$ is called the **time constant** τ of the circuit, i.e. $\boxed{\tau = \dfrac{L}{R} \text{ seconds}}$ In the time τ seconds the current rises to 63.2% of its final value I and in practical situations the current rises to within 1% of its final value in a time equal to 5τ seconds.

11 **Current decay**.
When a series $L - R$ circuit is connected to a d.c. supply, as shown in *Fig 6*, with S in position A, a current $I = \dfrac{V}{R}$ flows after a short time, creating a magnetic field ($\Phi \propto I$) associated with the inductor. When S is moved to position B, the current decreases, causing a decrease in the strength of the magnetic field. Flux linkages occur generating a voltage v_L, equal to $L\left(\dfrac{\Delta I}{t}\right)$. By Lenz's law, this voltage keeps current i flowing in the circuit, its value being limited by R. Since $V = V_L + V_R$, $0 = v_L + v_R$ and $v_L = -v_R$, i.e. v_L and v_R are equal in magnitude but opposite in direction. The current decays exponentially to zero and since v_R is proportional to the current flowing, v_R decays exponentially to zero. Since

72

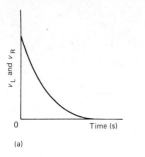
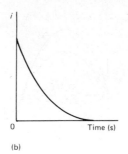

(a)   (b)

Fig 7

$v_L = v_R$, v_L also decays exponentially to zero. The curves representing these transients are shown in *Fig 7*.

12 Summarising, in a d.c. circuit, inductance has no effect on the current except during the time when there are **changes** in the supply current (i.e. immediately following switching on or switching off). (See *Problems 4 to 7*.)

Effects of inductance on the current in an a.c. circuit

13 In an a.c. circuit containing inductance, induced emf $\left[e = L\left(\dfrac{\Delta I}{t}\right)\right]$ is present at nearly all times. The higher the frequency the greater the induced emf. The opposition offered by the induced emf to an applied voltage tends to limit the current in an a.c. circuit. This opposition is called **inductive reactance**, X_L and is given by:

$$X_L = 2\pi f L \text{ ohms}$$

where f = frequency in hertz and L = inductance in henrys.

A graph of inductive resistance against frequency is shown in *Fig 8* and shows that a linear relationship exists between X_L and f.

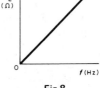

Fig 8

(See *Problems 8 to 10*.)

14 (i) If a sinusoidal voltage is applied to a purely resistive circuit the resulting current is also sinusoidal and 'in-phase' with the voltage, i.e. voltage and current waveforms pass through their zero values at the same instant and attain their maximum values at the same instant, as shown in *Fig 9*.

(ii) Let an a.c. circuit be purely inductive, i.e. the resistance is zero (which is a theoretical condition), and the applied current be sinusoidal, as shown in *Fig 10*. The magnitude of the induced emf $\left[e = L\left(\dfrac{\Delta I}{t}\right)\right]$ is directly proportional to the rate of change of current $\left(\dfrac{\Delta I}{t}\right)$, which is given by the gradient of the tangent to the current curve.

At point A, in *Fig 10(b)*, the rate of change of current is a maximum positive value and thus e is a maximum value but acts in opposition to the applied

73

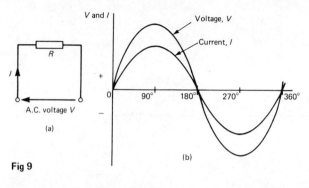

Fig 9

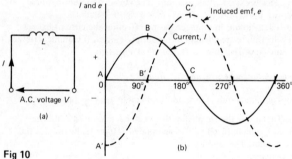

Fig 10

voltage from Lenz's law. This is shown as point A'.

At point B, the rate of change of current (i.e. the gradient of the curve) is zero and hence $e = 0$, shown as point B'.

At point C, the rate of change of current is a maximum negative value and thus e is a maximum positive value shown as point C'.

With similar reasoning applied to the second half of the cycle the induced emf e is seen to be a sine wave. The induced emf, e, has a polarity that is always opposite to the applied voltage V, i.e. e and V are 180° out of phase. The current I and applied voltage V are shown in *Fig 11* and are seen to be 90° out of phase. The maximum value of I, shown as point P occurs 90° after the maximum value of V, shown as point Q and thus the current is said to lag the voltage by 90°

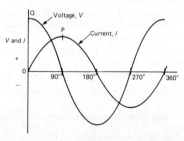

Fig 11

(iii) In practice, both resistance and inductance are present in an inductive circuit which results in current lagging voltage by an angle which is greater than $0°$ and less than $90°$.
15 Summarising, in an a.c. circuit, pure inductance introduces opposition to current flow, called inductive reactance X_L ($= 2\pi fL$), and also causes the current to lag the voltage by $90°$.

B WORKED PROBLEMS ON INDUCTORS AND THEIR EFFECTS IN ELECTRIC CIRCUITS

Problem 1 State four factors which can affect the inductance of an inductor.

An inductor consists of a coil of wire.
Factors which affect the inductance of an inductor include:
(i) the number of turns of wire – the more turns the higher the inductance;
(ii) the cross-sectional area of the coil of wire – the greater the cross-sectional area the higher the inductance;
(iii) the presence of a magnetic core – when the coil is wound on an iron core the same current sets up a more concentrated magnetic field and the inductance is increased;
(iv) the way the turns are arranged – a short thick coil of wire has a higher inductance than a long thin one.

Problem 2 An 8 H inductor has a current of 3 A flowing through it. How much energy is stored in the magnetic field of the inductor?

Energy stored, $W = \dfrac{1}{2} L I^2 = \dfrac{1}{2} (8) (3)^2 = $ **36 joules.**

Problem 3 A flux of 25 mWb links with a 1500 turn coil when a current of 3 A passes through the coil. Calculate (a) the inductance of the coil, (b) the energy stored in the magnetic field, and (c) the average emf induced if the current falls to zero in 150 ms.

(a) **Inductance,** $L = \dfrac{N\Phi}{I} = \dfrac{(1500)(25 \times 10^{-3})}{3} = $ **12.5 H**

(b) **Energy stored in field,** $W = \dfrac{1}{2} L I^2 = \dfrac{1}{2}(12.5)(3)^2 = $ **56.25 J.**

(c) **Induced emf,** $E = N \left(\dfrac{\Delta\Phi}{t}\right) = (1500) \left(\dfrac{25 \times 10^{-3}}{150 \times 10^{-3}}\right) = $ **250 V.**

Problem 4 What difficulties can be experienced when switching inductive circuits?

Energy stored in the magnetic field of an inductor exists because a current provides the magnetic field. When the d.c. supply is switched off the current falls rapidly, the magnetic field collapses causing a large induced emf which will either cause an arc across the switch contacts or will break down the insulation between adjacent turns of the coil. The high induced emf acts in a direction which tends to keep the current flowing, i.e. in the same direction as the applied voltage. The energy from the magnetic field will thus be aided by the supply voltage in maintaining an arc, which could cause severe damage to the switch. To reduce the induced emf when the supply switch is opened, a discharge resistor R_D is connected in parallel with the inductor as shown in *Fig 12*. The magnetic field energy is dissipated as heat in R_D and R and arcing at the switch contacts is avoided.

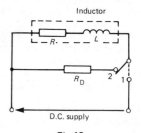

Fig 12

Problem 5 A coil of inductance 0.04 H and resistance 10Ω is connected to a 120 V, d.c. supply. Determine (a) the final value of current, (b) the time constant of the circuit, (c) the value of current after a time equal to the time constant from the instant the supply voltage is connected, (d) the expected time for the current to rise to within 1% of its final value.

(a) Final steady current, $I = \dfrac{V}{R} = \dfrac{120}{10} = $ **12 A**

(b) Time constant of the circuit, $\tau = \dfrac{L}{R} = \dfrac{0.04}{10} = $ **0.004 s or 4 ms.**

(c) In the time τ s the current rises to 63.2% of its final value of 12 A, i.e. in 4 ms the current rises to 0.632 × 12 = **7.58 A.**

(d) The expected time for the current to rise to within 1% of its final value is given by 5τ s, i.e. 5 × 4 = **20 ms.**

Problem 6 A coil of inductance 0.5 H and resistance 6 Ω is connected in parallel with a resistance of 15 Ω to a 120 V d.c. supply. Determine (a) the current in the 15 Ω resistance, (b) the steady state current in the coil, and (c) the current in the 15 Ω resistance at the instant the supply is switched off.

The circuit diagram is shown in *Fig 13*.
(a) Current flowing in 15Ω resistor $I_R = \dfrac{V}{R_2} = \dfrac{120}{15} = $ **8 A.**

(b) The steady state current flowing in coil, $I_{COIL} = \dfrac{V}{R_1} = \dfrac{120}{6} = $ **20 A.**

(c) At the instant the supply is switched off the current flowing in R_2 is the same as the current flowing in the coil, i.e. **20 A** (see *Fig 14*).

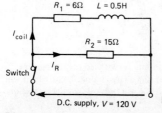

Fig 13

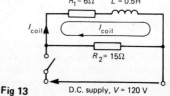

Fig 14

Problem 7 A coil of resistance 20 Ω and inductance 0.8 H is to be discharged from a steady current of 3 A through a parallel resistance of 40 Ω. Determine (a) the induced emf at the instant the current begins to fall, and (b) the initial rate of change of current.

(a) The instant when current begins to fall is when the supply is switched off. The circuit is shown in *Fig 15*.
Total resistance of the closed loop,
$R = R_1 + R_2 = 20 + 40 = 60 \Omega$
Emf induced,
$e = I_{COIL} R = (3)(60) = \textbf{180 V}.$

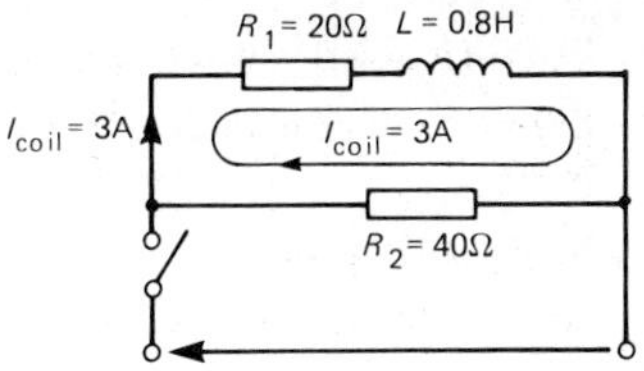

(b) Induced emf $e = L\left(\dfrac{\Delta I}{t}\right)$

Hence initial rate of change of current,

$\left(\dfrac{\Delta I}{t}\right) = \dfrac{e}{L} = \dfrac{180}{0.8} = \textbf{225 A/s}.$

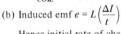

$R_1 = 20\Omega \quad L = 0.8\text{H}$

$I_{coil} = 3\text{A}$

$I_{coil} = 3\text{A}$

$R_2 = 40\Omega$

Fig 15

Problem 8 (a) Calculate the reactance of a coil of inductance 0.32 H when it is connected to a 50 Hz supply. (b) A coil has a reactance of 124 Ω in a circuit with a supply of frequency 5 kHz. Determine the inductance of the coil.

(a) Inductive reactance $X_L = 2\pi f L = 2\pi(50)(0.32) = \textbf{100.5 } \Omega.$

(b) Since $X_L = 2\pi f L$, inductance $L = \dfrac{X_L}{2\pi f} = \dfrac{124}{2\pi(5000)}$ H = **3.95 mH**.

Problem 9 A coil of inductance 0.2 H has an inductive reactance of 754 Ω when connected to an a.c. supply. Calculate the frequency of the supply.

$L = 0.2$ H; $X_L = 754 \Omega$

Since $X_L = 2\pi f L$, frequency, $f = \dfrac{X_L}{2\pi L} = \dfrac{754}{2\pi(0.2)} = \textbf{600 Hz}.$

Problem 10 A coil has an inductance of 40 mH and negligible resistance. Calculate its inductive reactance and the resulting current if connected to (a) a 240 V; 50 Hz supply, and (b) a 100 V, 1 kHz supply.

(a) Inductive reactance, $X_L = 2\pi f L = 2\pi(50)(40 \times 10^{-3}) = \textbf{12.57}\Omega$

Current, $I = \dfrac{V}{X_L} = \dfrac{240}{12.57} = \textbf{19.09 A}.$

(b) Inductive reactance, $X_L = 2\pi(1000)(40 \times 10^{-3}) = \textbf{251.3 } \Omega$

Current, $I = \dfrac{V}{X_L} = \dfrac{100}{251.3} = \textbf{0.398 A}.$

C. FURTHER PROBLEMS ON INDUCTORS AND THEIR EFFECTS IN ELECTRIC CIRCUITS

(a) SHORT ANSWER PROBLEMS

1 Define inductance and name its unit.

2 What is an inductor? Sketch a typical practical inductor.

3 Explain how a standard resistor may be non-inductively wound.

4 Energy W stored in the magnetic field of an inductor is given by
$W = \dots\dots\dots\dots\dots$.

5 What is a transient?

6 State briefly the effects of inductance on the current in a d.c. circuit.

7 The opposition to current in a purely inductive a.c. circuit is called $\dots\dots\dots\dots$
and is calculated using the formula $\dots\dots\dots\dots\dots$.

8 In an a.c. circuit, what effect does pure inductance have on the phase angle between current and voltage?

(b) MULTI-CHOICE PROBLEMS (Answers on page 156)

1 The effect of inductance occurs in an electrical circuit when:
(a) the resistance is changing; (b) the flux is changing; (c) the current is changing.

2 Which of the following statements is false?
The inductance of an inductor increases: (a) with a short, thick, coil: (b) when wound on an iron core; (c) as the number of turns increases: (d) as the cross-sectional area of the coil decreases.

3 The time constant for a d.c. circuit containing resistance R and inductance L is given by: (a) $\dfrac{R}{L}$ s; (b) $\dfrac{L}{R}$ s; (c) $L R$ s.

An inductor of inductance 0.1 H and negligible resistance is connected in series with a 50 Ω resistor to a 20 V, d.c. supply. In *Problems 4 to 8,* use this data to determine the value required, selecting your answers from those given below.

(a) 5 ms;   (b) 12.6 V;   (c) 0.4 A;   (d) 500 ms;   (e) 7.4 V;
(f) 2.5 A;   (g) 2 ms;   (h) 0 V;   (i) 0A;   (j) 20 V.

4 The value of the time constant of the circuit.

5 The approximate value of the voltage across the resistor at a time equal to the time constant after being connected to the supply.

6 The final value of current flowing in the circuit.

7 The initial value of voltage across the inductor.

8 The final value of the steady-state voltage across the inductor.

9 A circuit comprising a 12 Ω resistor and a 4 H inductance connected across a 60 V d.c. supply has a steady current flowing of:
(a)   5 A;   (b)   15 A;   (c)   3¾ A;   (d)   3 A.

10 An inductance of 10 mH connected across a 100 V, 50 Hz supply has an inductive reactance of:
(a) $10\pi\ \Omega$;   (b) $1000\pi\ \Omega$;   (c) $\pi\ \Omega$;   (d) π H.

78

11 When the frequency of an a.c. circuit containing resistance and inductance connected in series is increased (the voltage remaining constant), the current: (a) decreases; (b) increases; (c) stays the same.

12 Pure inductance in an a.c. circuit results in a current that:
(a) leads the voltage by 90°; (b) is in phase with the voltage; (c) leads the voltage by π rad; (d) lags the voltage by $\frac{\pi}{2}$ rad.

(c) CONVENTIONAL PROBLEMS

1 Describe the basic form of an inductor and state the factors which affect inductance.

2 Describe the effect of an inductor on the current in a d.c. circuit. Explain how difficulties encountered in switching inductive circuits can be overcome.

3 An inductor of 20 H has a current of 2.5 A flowing in it. Find the energy stored in the magnetic field of the inductor.

[62.5 J]

4 Calculate the value of the energy stored when a current of 30 mA is flowing in a coil of inductance 400 mH.

[0.18 mJ]

5 The energy stored in the magnetic field of an inductor is 80 J when the current flowing in the inductor is 2 A. Calculate the inductance of the coil.

[40 H]

6 A flux of 30 mWb links with a 1200 turn coil when a current of 5 A is passing through the coil. Calculate (a) the inductance of the coil, (b) the energy stored in the magnetic field, and (c) the average emf induced if the current is reduced to zero in 0.20 seconds.

[(a) 7.2 H; (b) 90 J; (c) 180 V]

7 A coil of resistance 20Ω and inductance 500 mH is connected to a d.c. supply of 160 V. Determine (a) the final value of current, (b) the time constant, (c) the current after a time equal to the time constant from the instant the supply voltage is connected, and (d) the expected time for the current to rise to within 1% of its final value.

[(a) 8A; (b) 25 ms; (c) 5.06 A; (d) 0.125 s]

8 An inductive circuit has a time constant of 50 ms. If the steady value of current flowing through the circuit is 2 A when connected to a 200 V d.c. supply, calculate the value of resistance and the value of inductance.

[R = 100Ω; L = 5 H]

9 A coil of inductance 0.3 H and resistance 10Ω is connected in parallel with a resistance of 25 Ω to a 100 V d.c. supply. Determine (a) the current in the 25 Ω resistor, (b) the steady state current in the coil, and (c) the current in the 25 Ω resistance at the instant the supply is switched off.

[(a) 4A; (b) 10 A; (c) 10 A]

10 A coil of resistance 15 Ω and inductance 0.3 H is to be discharged from a steady current of 5 A through a parallel resistance of 30 Ω. Determine (a) the induced emf at the instant the current begins to fall, and (b) the initial rate of change of current.

[(a) 225 V; (b) 750 A/s]

11 Calculate the inductive reactance of a coil of inductance 0.2 H when it is connected to (a) a 50 Hz, (b) a 600 Hz, and (c) a 4 kHz supply.

[(a) 62.83 Ω; (b) 754 Ω; (c) 5.027 kΩ]

12 A coil has an inductive reactance of 120 Ω in a circuit with a supply frequency of 4 kHz. Calculate the inductance of the coil.

[(4.77 mH]

13 A supply of 240 V, 50 Hz is connected across a pure inductance and the resulting current is 1.2 A. Calculate the inductance of the coil.

[0.637 H]

14 An emf of 200 V at a frequency of 2 kHz is applied to a coil of pure inductance 50 mH. Determine (a) the reactance of the coil, and (b) the current flowing in the coil.

[(a) 628 Ω; (b) 0.318 A]

15 A 120 mH inductor has a 50 mA, 1 kHz alternating current flowing through it. Find the p.d. across the inductor.

[37.7 V]

16 Describe the effects of an inductor on the current in an a.c. circuit.

7 Block diagrams and logic gates

A. MAIN POINTS CONCERNING BLOCK DIAGRAMS AND LOGIC GATES

Block diagrams

1 In mechanical and electrical work, a **system** may be defined as an arrangement of interdependent components which give a definite output for a specified input. Systems are usually represented as shown in *Fig 1* by a boundary line (often a rectangular block), together with one or more inputs and one or more outputs.

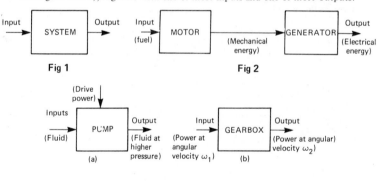

Fig 1

Fig 2

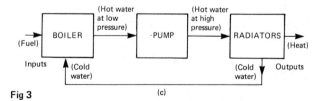

Fig 3

2 A mechanical system comprising a motor-generator set is represented by a simple **block diagram** as shown in *Fig 2*.

Other systems – a pump, a gearbox and a simple heating system – are shown in block diagram form in *Fig 3*.

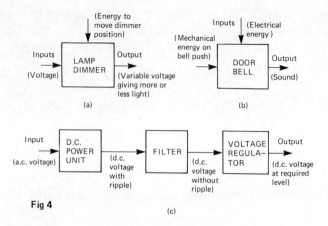

Fig 4

3 Some electrical systems representing a lamp dimmer, a door bell and a rectifier are shown in block diagram form in *Fig 4*.

4 An important electrical system is an **amplifier,** in which the output from the system is an enlarged version of the input to the system. An amplifier which enlarges the input signal by a factor of two is shown in *Fig 5*.

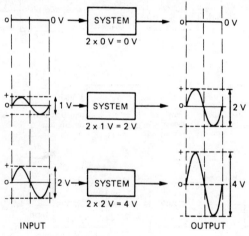

Fig 5

Amplifiers are used in nearly all communication systems; for example, a small signal gathered by the stylus and cartridge of a record player is amplified before being fed to the loudspeaker. The ratio of the output quantity to the input quantity for an amplifier is called the **gain** of the amplifier. Thus, if the input signal to an amplifier is 5 volts and the output signal is 100 volts, the voltage gain is 100/5, that is 20 (see *Problems 1 to 3*).

Logic systems

5   Logic systems are based on two-state devices and use a special kind of algebra, called Boolean algebra to represent the input to and output from the system. A **two-state device** is one whose basic elements can only have one of two conditions. Thus, two-way switches, which can be either on or off, and the binary numbering system, having the digits 0 and 1 only, are two-state devices. In Boolean algebra, if A represents one state, then $\overline{A}$, called 'not-A', represents the second state. In logic systems, the basic building blocks used are the **or**-function, the **and**-function and the **not**-function, together with combinations of these.

6   *The or-function.* In Boolean algebra, the or-function for two elements A and B is written as $A + B$, and is defined as 'A, or B, or both A and B'. The equivalent electrical circuit for a two-input **or**-function is given by two switches connected in parallel. With reference to *Fig 6(a)*, the lamp will be on when A is on, when B is on, or when both A and B are on. In the table shown in *Fig 6(b)*, all the possible

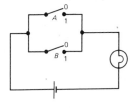

1	2	3
Input (switches)		Output (lamp)
A	B	$Z = A + B$
0	0	0
0	1	1
1	0	1
1	1	1

(a) Switching circuit for **or** – function   (b) Truth table for **or** – function   **Fig 6**

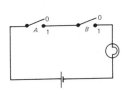

Input (switches)		Output (lamp)
A	B	$Z = A.B$
0	0	0
0	1	0
1	0	0
1	1	1

(a) Switching circuit for **and** – function   (b) Truth table for **and** – function   **Fig 7**

switch combinations are shown in columns 1 and 2, in which a 0 represents a switch being off and a 1 represents the switch being on, these columns being called the input. Column 3 is called the output and a 0 represents the lamp being off and a 1 represents the lamp being on. Such a table is called a **truth table**.

7   *The and-function.* In Boolean algebra, the **and**-function for two elements A and B is written as $A.B$ and is defined as 'both A and B'. The equivalent electrical circuit for a two-input **and**-function is given by two switches connected in series. With reference to *Fig 7(a)* the lamp will be on only when both A and B are on. The truth table for a two-input **and**-function is shown in *Fig 7(b)*.

8   *The not-function.* In Boolean algebra, the **not**-function for element A is written as $\overline{A}$, and is defined as 'the opposite to A'. Thus if A means switch A is on, $\overline{A}$ means

that switch A is off. The truth table for the **not**-function is shown in *Table 1*.

9 In paras 6, 7 and 8 above, the Boolean expressions, equivalent switching circuits and truth tables for the three functions used in Boolean algebra are given for a two-input system. A system may have more than two inputs and the Boolean expression for a three-input **or**-function having elements A, B and C is $A + B + C$. Similarly, a three-input **and**-function is written as $A.B.C$.

TABLE 1

Input A	Output $Z = \overline{A}$
0	1
1	0

The equivalent electrical circuits and truth tables for three-input **or** and **and**-functions are shown in *Fig 8(a)* and *(b)* respectively.

10 In practice, logic gates are used to perform the **and**, **or** and **not** functions. Logic gates can be made from switches, magnetic devices or fluidic devices but most

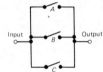

Input A B C	Output $Z = A + B + C$
0 0 0	0
0 0 1	1
0 1 0	1
0 1 1	1
1 0 0	1
1 0 1	1
1 1 0	1
1 1 1	1

Input A B C	Output $Z = A. B. C$
0 0 0	0
0 0 1	0
0 1 0	0
0 1 1	0
1 0 0	0
1 0 1	0
1 1 0	0
1 1 1	1

(a) The **or** — function electrical circuit and truth table

(b) The **and** — function electrical circuit and truth table

Fig 8

logic gates in use are electronic devices. Various logic gates are available. For example, the Boolean expression $(A. B. C)$ can be produced using a three-input, **and**-gate and $(C + D)$ by using a two-input **or**-gate. The principal gates in common use are introduced in paras 11 to 15. The term 'gate' is used in the same sense as a normal gate, the open state being indicated by a binary '1' and the closed state by a binary '0'. A gate will open only when the requirements of the gate are met and, for example, there will only be a '1' output on a two-input **and**-gate when both the inputs to the gate are at a '1' state.

11 *The* **and**-*gate.* Two different symbols used for a three input **and**-gate are shown in *Fig 9* and the truth table is shown in *Fig 8(b)*. This shows that there will only be a '1' output when A is 1 and B is 1 and C is 1, written as: $Z = A.B.C.$

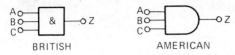

BRITISH   AMERICAN

Fig 9

12 *The* **or**-*gate.* Two different symbols used for a three-input **or**-gate are shown in *Fig 10* and the truth table is shown in *Fig 8(a)*. This shows that there will be a '1' output when A is 1, or B is 1, or C is 1, or any combinations of A, B or C is 1, written as: $Z = A + B + C$

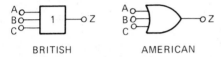

BRITISH   AMERICAN

Fig 10

13 *The* **invert**-*gate or* **not**-*gate.* Two different symbols used for an **invert** gate are shown in *Fig 11*, and the truth table is shown in *Table 1*. This shows that a '0' input gives a '1' output and vice-versa, i.e. it is an 'opposite to' function. The invert of A is written $\overline{A}$ and is called 'not-A'.

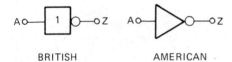

BRITISH   AMERICAN

Fig 11

14 *The* **nand**-*gate.* Two different symbols used for a a **nand**-gate are shown in *Fig 12(a)* and the truth table is shown in *Fig 12(b)*. This gate is equivalent to an **and**-gate and an **invert**-gate in series (not-and = nand) and the output is written as: $Z = \overline{A.B.C.}$

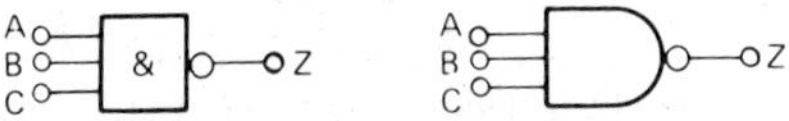

| INPUTS | | | | OUTPUT |
A	B	C	A.B.C.	$Z = \overline{A.B.C.}$
0	0	0	0	1
0	0	1	0	1
0	1	0	0	1
0	1	1	0	1
1	0	0	0	1
1	0	1	0	1
1	1	0	0	1
1	1	1	1	0

Fig 12(b)

A B & Z   A B & Z

BRITISH   AMERICAN

Fig 12(a)

15 *The nor-gate.* Two different symbols used for a **nor**gate are shown in *Fig 13(a)* and the truth table is shown in *Fig 13(b)*. This gate is equivalent to an **or**-gate and an **invert**-gate in series, (nor-or = nor), and the output is written as:

$$Z = \overline{A + B + C}$$

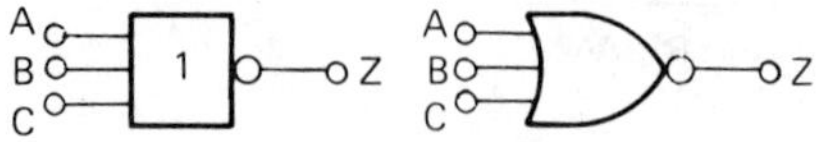

INPUTS				OUTPUT
A	B	C	A+B+C	$Z=\overline{A+B+C}$
0	0	0	0	1
0	0	1	1	0
0	1	0	1	0
0	1	1	1	0
1	0	0	1	0
1	0	1	1	0
1	1	0	1	0
1	1	1	1	0

BRITISH · AMERICAN

Fig 13(a)

Fig 13(b)

Combinational logic networks

16 In most logic circuits, more than one gate is needed to give the required output. Except for the **invert**-gate, logic gates generally have two, three or four inputs and are confined to one function only; thus, for example, a two-input **or**-gate or a four-input **and**-gate can be used when designing a logic circuit. The way in which logic gates are used to generate a given output is shown in *Problems 4 to 8.*

B. WORKED PROBLEMS ON BLOCK DIAGRAMS AND LOGIC GATES

Problem 1 Draw a block diagram, showing the inputs and outputs of a simple public address system, the main components being a microphone, a voltage amplifier to amplify the input soundwave signal and a power amplifier to supply the power to drive the loudspeakers.

The block diagram is shown in *Fig 14.* The input to the microphone is soundwaves, which are altered into a small electrical voltage by the microphone and form the input to the voltage amplifier. The enlarged voltage from the voltage amplifier contains insufficient power to drive the loudspeakers, and is fed to a power

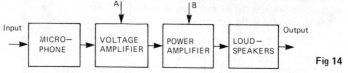

Fig 14

amplifier. Both the voltage and power amplifiers require additional electrical energy to drive them, hence two additional inputs, A and B, are shown for these blocks. The output from the power amplifier drives the loudspeakers, giving a final output of amplified sound waves.

Problem 2 A pressure recording system consists of a transducer to convert pressure energy to an electrical voltage, a voltage amplifier and a chart recorder. Draw the block diagram of this system.

The block diagram is shown in *Fig 15*. All three of the devices require an electrical energy input in addition to the signal being fed in, hence two inputs are shown to each block. The voltage output from the pressure transducer is amplified, giving a

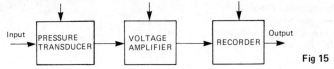

Fig 15

larger voltage input to the recorder. The output from the recorder is a visual indication of the pressure.

Problem 3 For the amplifiers shown in *Fig 16*, determine (a) the voltage gain; (b) the current gain; (c) the power gain.

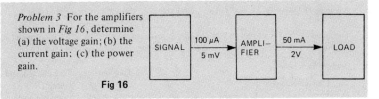

Fig 16

(a) The voltage gain A_V is given by the ratio of the output voltage from the amplifier to the voltage input to the amplifier. From *Fig 16*,

$$A_V = \frac{2}{0.005} = 400$$

(b) The current gain, A_I is the ratio of output to the input current.

Thus $A_I = \frac{0.050}{0.0001} = 500$

(c) The power input is given by the product of the voltage and current, thus $P_i = 0.005 \times 0.0001 = 0.5 \times 10^{-6}$ W

The output power, $P_o = 2 \times 0.050 = 0.1$ W

Thus power gain, $A_p = \frac{0.1}{0.5 \times 10^{-6}} = 200\,000$

It can be seen from this result that $A_p = A_v \times A_I$

Problem 4 Devise a logic circuit to meet the requirements of the Boolean expression: $Z = A . (B + C)$

The equation given indicates that there are three input variables, *A*, *B* and *C*. The term $(B + C)$ can be produced using a two-input **or**-gate and the output of this gate can be combined with *A* by an **and**-function using a two-input **and**-gate. Hence the required logic circuit is as shown in *Fig 17*.

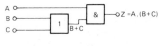

Fig 17

Problem 5 Devise a logic system to meet the requirements of:
$Z = A.\bar{B} + C$

With reference to *Fig 18* an
invert-gate, shown as (1),
gives $\bar{B}$. The **and**-gate shown
as (2), has input of A and
$\bar{B}$, giving $A.\bar{B}$. The **or**-gate,
shown as (3), has inputs of
$A.\bar{B}$ and C, giving
$Z = A.\bar{B} + C$

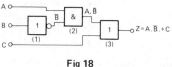

Fig 18

Problem 6 Devise a logic system to meet the requirements of $(P + \bar{Q}) . (\bar{R} + S)$

The logic system is shown in *Fig 19*. The given expression shows that two **invert**-
functions are needed to give $\bar{Q}$ and $\bar{R}$ and these are shown as gates (1) and (2).

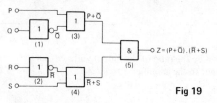

Fig 19

Two **or**-gates shown as (3) and
(4), give $(P + \bar{Q})$ and $(\bar{R} + S)$
respectively. Finally an **and**-
gate shown as (5), gives the
required output, $Z = (P + \bar{Q}) .$
$(\bar{R} + S)$

Problem 7 A system has four inputs, P, Q, R and S. An output is required from
the system of: [not R and {not-P or (not-Q and not-S)}]
Devise a logic circuit to meet the required output.

The Boolean equation is $Z = \bar{R}.(\bar{P} + \bar{Q}.\bar{S})$. The logic circuit to produce this output
is shown in *Fig 20*.

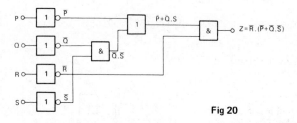

Fig 20

Problem 8 An alarm indicator in a grinding mill complex should be activated if
(a) the power supply to all mills is off; (b) the hopper feeding the mills is less
than 10% full; (c) if less than two of the three grinding mills are in action. Devise
a logic system to meet these requirements.

Let variable A represent the power supply not being on to all the mills. Let B represent the hopper feeding the mills being less than 10% full and let C, D and E represent the three mills not being in action. The required equation to activate the alarm is $Z = A.B.(C + D + E)$. A three-input or-gate gives $(C + D + E)$ and a two-input and-gate gives $A.B$. A second two-input and-gate is used to give the required output, as shown in *Fig 21*.

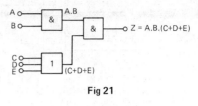

Fig 21

C. FURTHER PROBLEMS ON BLOCK DIAGRAMS AND LOGIC GATES

(a) SHORT ANSWER PROBLEMS

1 Describe what is meant by a 'system'.
2 Describe the usual way of representing a system.
3 What is the purpose of an amplifier?
4 State the meaning of the term 'two-state device'.
5 Write the Boolean expression for A and B and C.
6 Write the Boolean expression for A or B or C.
7 Write the Boolean expression for not-A.
8 Draw a truth table for a two-input or-function.
9 Draw a truth table for a two-input and-function.
10 Draw a truth table for a not-function.
11 Draw the logic gate symbols for the or and nor-gates.
12 Draw the logic gate symbols for the and and nand-gates.

(b) MULTI-CHOICE PROBLEMS (Answers on page 156)

1 The following statements refer to systems. Which statement is false?
   (a) They have an input. (b) They have an output.
   (c) They have boundaries, represented usually by rectangular blocks.
   (d) A complete system can be represented by blocks which are not inter-connected.
2 Which of the following statements is false?
   (a) Mechanical and electrical devices may be represented by block diagrams.
   (b) An amplifier is a system which provides an input quantity which is larger than the output quantity.
   (c) The ratio of output quantity to input quantity is called the gain of an amplifier.
   (d) A system has a definite output for a specified input.

In *Problems 3 to 6*, use the logic circuit shown in *Fig 22*, selecting the correct answers from this list:
   (a) $\overline{A}.B$; (b) $\overline{A} + B$; (c) A; (d) $\overline{A}$; (e) $B.C$; (f) $B + C$;
   (g) $\overline{A}.B + (B + C)$; (h) $(\overline{A} + B).(B.C)$; (i) $\overline{A}.B.(B + C)$; (j) $(\overline{A} + B) + (B.C)$.

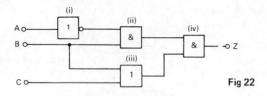

Fig 22

3 The output from gate (i).
4 The output from gate (ii).
5 The output from gate (iii).
6 The output from gate (iv).

The logic gates shown in *Fig 23* have not been specified. In *Problems 7 to 10* select from the list below the type of gate used to give the output specified.

(a) **and**-gate; (b) **or**-gate; (c) **not**-gate; (d) **nand**-gate; (e) **nor**-gate.

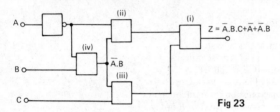

$Z = \overline{A}.B.C + \overline{A} + \overline{A}.B$

Fig 23

7 From logic gate (i).
8 From logic gate (ii).
9 From logic gate (iii).
10 From logic gate (iv).

(c) CONVENTIONAL PROBLEMS

1 List the main components of a refrigerator and draw a block diagram showing how they are interconnected, giving the inputs and output of each block.
2 Draw a block diagram showing the main systems found on a motorcylce, giving the inputs and outputs of each block.
3 A power station has the following principal systems: a boiler for generating steam, a steam turbine for converting heat energy to mechanical energy, an alternator and a transformer to deliver the electrical energy at the correct voltage to the National Grid. Draw and fully label, a block diagram depicting these systems.
4 Describe the basic function of an amplifier and state what is meant by (a) voltage gain; (b) current gain; (c) power gain.
5 An amplifier has an input signal of 250 μA at 10 mV and this is amplified to 5 mA at 1V. Determine the current, voltage and power gains of the amplifier.

[20; 100; 2000]

6 The current and voltage gains of an amplifier are 30 and 50 respectively. The input signal to the amplifier is 3 mA at 7 mV. Determine the output current and voltage.

[90 mA; 350 mV]

90

In *Problems 7 to 15* devise logic systems to meet the requirements of the Boolean equations given.

7   $Z = \overline{A} + B.C$ [See *Fig 24(a)*]
8   $Z = A.\overline{B} + B.\overline{C}$ [See *Fig 24(b)*]
9   $Z = A.B.\overline{C} + \overline{A}.\overline{B}.C$ [See *Fig 24(c)*]
10 $Z = (\overline{A} + B).(\overline{C} + D)$ [See *Fig 24(d)*]
11 $Z = A.\overline{B} + B.\overline{C} + C.\overline{D}$ [See *Fig 24(e)*]
12 $Z = \overline{R}.(P + \overline{Q})$ [See *Fig 25(a)*]
13 $Z = \overline{P}.\overline{Q}.R + P.(Q + R)$ [See *Fig 25(b)*]
14 $Z = \overline{D}.(\overline{A}.C + \overline{B})$ [See *Fig 26(a)*]
15 $Z = \overline{A}.\overline{B}.C.\overline{D} + B.D$ [See *Fig 26(b)*]

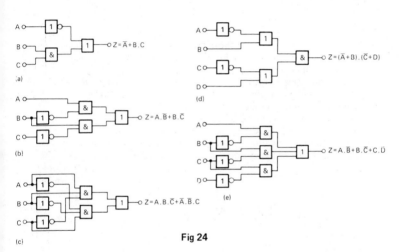

Fig 24

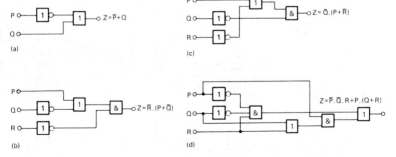

Fig 25

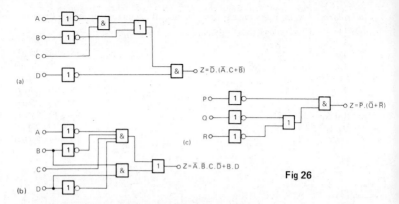

(a)

$Z = \overline{D}.(\overline{A}.C + \overline{B})$

(c)

$Z = \overline{P}.(\overline{Q} + R)$

(b)

$Z = \overline{A}.B.C.\overline{D} + B.D$

Fig 26

16 In a chemical process, three of the transducers used are *P, Q* and *R*, giving output signals of either 0 or 1. Devise a logic system to give a 1 output when:
    (a) *P* and *Q* and *R* all have 0 outputs, or when:
    (b) *P* is 0 and (*Q* is 1 or *R* is 0). $[\overline{P}.(Q + R),$ see *Fig 27(a)*]

17 Lift doors should close, if:
    (a) the master switch, (*A*), is on and either
    (b) a call, (*B*), is received from any other floor, or
    (c) the doors, (*C*), have been open for more than 10 seconds, or
    (d) the selector push within the lift (*D*), is pressed for another floor.
    Devise a logic circuit to meet these requirements.

$[Z = A.(B + C + D)],$
see *Fig 27(b)*

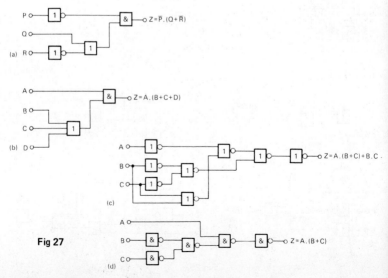

(a) $Z = \overline{P}.(Q + \overline{R})$

(b) $Z = A.(B + C + D)$

(c) $Z = A.(B + C) + B.C.$

(d) $Z = A.(B + C)$

Fig 27

92

18 A water tank feeds three separate processes, *A, B* and *C*. When any two of the processes are in operation at the same time, a signal is required to start a pump to maintain the head of water in the tank. Devise a logic circuit to give the required signal.

$$[Z = A.(B + C) + B.C, \text{ see } Fig\ 28(a)]$$

19 A logic signal is required to give an indication when:
(a) the supply to an oven is on, (*A*), and
(b) the temperature of the oven exceeds 210°C, (*B*) or
(c) the temperature of the oven is less than 190°C, (*C*).
Devise a logic circuit to meet these requirements.

$$[Z = A.(B + C), \text{ see } Fig\ 28(b).]$$

(a)   (b)

Fig 28

8 Ideal gas laws

A. MAIN POINTS CONCERNED WITH IDEAL GAS LAWS

1   The relationships which exist between pressure, volume and temperature in a gas are given in a set of laws called **the gas laws.**

2   (i) **Boyle's law** states:
    'the volume V of a fixed mass of gas is inversely proportional to its absolute pressure p at constant temperature'.

    i.e. $p \propto \dfrac{1}{V}$ or $p = \dfrac{k}{V}$ or $pV = k$, at constant temperature,

    where p = absolute pressure in pascals (Pa),
    V = volume in m^3, and
    k = a constant.

   (ii) Changes which occur at constant temperature are called **isothermal** changes.

   (iii) When a fixed mass of gas at constant temperature changes from pressure p_1 and volume V_1 to pressure p_2 and volume V_2 then:
   $p_1 V_1 = p_2 V_2$

3   (i) **Charles' law** states:
    'for a given mass of gas at constant pressure, the volume V is directly proportional to its thermodynamic temperature T'.

    i.e. $V \propto T$ or $V = kT$ or $\dfrac{V}{T} = k$, at constant pressure,

    where T = thermodynamic temperature in kelvin (K).

   (ii) A process which takes place at constant pressure is called an **isobaric** process.

   (iii) The relationship between the Celsius scale of temperature and the thermodynamic or absolute scale is given by:
   kelvin = degrees Celsius + 273
   i.e. **K = °C + 273** or °C = K − 273

   (iv) If a given mass of gas at constant pressure occupies a volume V_1 at a temperature T_1 and a volume V_2 at temperature T_2, then
   $$\frac{V_1}{T_1} = \frac{V_2}{T_2}$$

4   (i) The **Pressure law** states:
    'the pressure p of a fixed mass of gas is directly proportional to its thermodynamic temperature T at constant volume'.
    i.e. $p \propto T$ or $p = kT$ or $\dfrac{P}{T} = k.$

(ii) When a fixed mass of gas at constant volume changes from pressure p_1 and temperature T_1, to pressure p_2 and temperature T_2 then:

$$\frac{p_1}{T_1} = \frac{p_2}{T_2}$$

5 (i) **Dalton's law of partial pressure** states:
'the total pressure of a mixture of gases occupying a given volume is equal to the sum of the pressures of each gas, considered separately, at constant temperature'.

(ii) The pressure of each constituent gas when occupying a fixed volume alone is known as the **partial pressure** of that gas.

6 An **ideal gas** is one which completely obeys the gas laws given in paras. 2 to 5. In practice no gas is an ideal gas, although air is very close to being one. For calculation purposes the difference between an ideal and an actual gas is very small.

7 (i) Frequently, when a gas is undergoing some change, the pressure, temperature and volume all vary simultaneously. Provided there is no change in the mass of a gas, the above gas laws can be combined, giving:

$$\boxed{\frac{p_1 V_1}{T_1} = \frac{p_2 V_2}{T_2} = k}$$ where k is a constant.

(ii) For an ideal gas, constant $k = mR$, where m is the mass of the gas in kg, and R is the **characteristic gas constant**,

i.e. $\dfrac{pV}{T} = mR$ or $\boxed{pV = mR\,T}$

This is called the **characteristic gas equation**.
In this equation, p = absolute pressure in pascals, V = volume in m^3, m = mass in kg, R = characteristic gas constant in J/(kg K) and T = thermodynamic temperature in kelvin.

(iii) Some typical values of the characteristic gas constant R include: air, 287 J/(kg K), hydrogen 4160 J/(kg K), oxygen 260 J/(kg K) and carbon dioxide 184 J/(kg K).

8 **Standard temperature and pressure (i.e. STP)** refers to a temperature of 0°C, i.e. 273 K, and normal atmospheric pressure of 101.325 kPa. (See *Problems 1 to 16*.)

9 It may be shown that for a gas occupying a volume V at pressure p and containing n molecules each of mass m moving at an average velocity of c,

$$\boxed{pV = \frac{1}{3}\,m\,n\,c^2}$$

Also, the kinetic energy of the molecules of a gas is proportional to its thermodynamic temperature. (See *Problems 17 and 18*.)

10 When a liquid evaporates, molecules with sufficient kinetic energy escape from the liquid's surface. The higher the temperature of the liquid the greater the average kinetic energy of the molecules and the greater the number of molecules which are able to escape. Since it is the molecules with the highest kinetic energy which escape, the average kinetic energy of the remaining molecules decreases and thus the liquid cools.

11 If a liquid evaporates a **vapour** is formed. When a vapour exists in the presence of its own liquid a **saturated vapour** is formed. If all the liquid evaporates an **unsaturated vapour** is produced. The higher the temperature the greater the number of molecules which escape to form the vapour. These molecules bombard the walls of the container and thus exert a pressure.

The **saturated vapour pressure** depends only on the temperature of the vapour.

TABLE 1

Temperature (°C)	Saturated vapour pressure of water (10^3 Pa)
0	0.61
10	1.23
20	2.33
30	4.23
40	7.35
50	12.3
60	19.9
70	31.2
80	47.4
90	70.2
100	101
150	476
200	1550

The saturated vapour pressure of water at various temperatures is shown in *Table 1*.

A liquid boils at a temperature when its saturated vapour pressure is equal to the atmospheric pressure. Thus water will boil at a temperature greater than 100°C if the atmospheric pressure is increased. This is the principle of the pressure cooker.

12 A saturated vapour does not obey the gas laws since its pressure depends only on temperature. An unsaturated vapour will obey the gas laws fairly closely as long as it remains unsaturated. If an unsaturated vapour at a particular

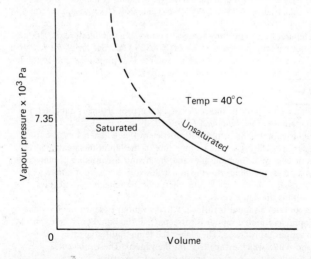

Fig 1

temperature is decreased in volume its pressure will rise in accordance with Boyle's law until it reaches the saturated vapour pressure at that particular temperature (see *Fig 1*). When the vapour pressure at 40°C reaches 7.35×10^3 Pa the vapour becomes saturated as it starts to liquefy. (See *Problems 19 and 20.*)

B. WORKED PROBLEMS ON IDEAL GAS LAWS

Problem 1 A gas occupies a volume of 0.10 m³ at a pressure of 1.8 MPa. Determine (a) the pressure if the volume is changed to 0.06 m³ at constant temperature, and (b) the volume if the pressure is changed to 2.4 MPa at constant temperature.

(a) Since the change occurs at constant temperature (i.e. an isothermal change), Boyle's law applies, i.e. $p_1 V_1 = p_2 V_2$, where p_1 = 1.8 MPa, V_1 = 0.10 m³ and V_2 = 0.06 m³.
Hence $(1.8)(0.10) = p_2 \ (0.06)$
from which, **pressure** $p_2 = \dfrac{1.8 \times 0.10}{0.06}$ = **3 MPa.**

(b) $p_1 V_1 = p_2 V_2$ where p_1 = 1.8 MPa, V_1 = 0.10 m³ and p_2 = 2.4 MPa.
Hence $(1.8)(0.10) = (2.4) \ V_2$
from which, **volume** $V_2 = \dfrac{(1.8)(0.10)}{2.4}$ = **0.075 m³.**

Problem 2 In an isothermal process, a mass of gas has its volume reduced from 3200 mm³ to 2000 mm³. If the initial pressure of the gas is 110 kPa, determine the final pressure.

Since the process is isothermal, it takes place at constant temperature and hence Boyle's law applies, i.e. $p_1 V_1 = p_2 V_2$, where p_1 = 110kPa, V_1 = 3200 mm³ and V_2 = 2000 mm³.
Hence $(110)(3200) = p_2 \ (2000)$,
from which, **final pressure,** $p_2 = \dfrac{(110)(3200)}{2000}$ = **176kPa.**

Problem 3 Some gas occupies a volume of 1.5 m³ in a cylinder at a pressure of 250 kPa. A piston, sliding in the cylinder, compresses the gas isothermally until the volume is 0.5 m³. If the area of the piston is 300 cm², calculate the force on the piston when the gas is compressed.

An isothermal process means constant temperature and thus Boyle's law applies, i.e. $p_1 V_1 = p_2 V_2$, where V_1 = 1.5 m³, V_2 = 0.5 m³ and p_1 = 250 kPa.

Hence $(250)(1.5) = p_2 \ (0.5)$, from which, pressure, $p_2 = \dfrac{(250)(1.5)}{(0.5)}$ = 750kPa

Pressure = $\dfrac{\text{force}}{\text{area}}$, from which, force = pressure × area

Hence **force on the piston** = $(750 \times 10^3 \text{ Pa}) (300 \times 10^{-4} \text{ m}^2)$ = **22.5 kN.**

Problem 4 A gas occupies a volume of 1.2 litres at 20°C. Determine the volume it occupies at 130°C if the pressure is kept constant.

Since the change occurs at constant pressure (i.e. an isobaric process), Charles' law applies, i.e. $\dfrac{V_1}{T_1} = \dfrac{V_2}{T_2}$ where $V_1 = 1.2$ l, $T_1 = 20°C = (20 + 273)K = 293$ K, and $T_2 = (130 + 273)K = 403$ K.

Hence $\dfrac{1.2}{293} = \dfrac{V_2}{403}$

from which, **volume at 130°C, $V_2 = \dfrac{(1.2)(403)}{293}$ = 1.65 litres.**

Problem 5 Gas at a temperature of 150°C has its volume reduced by one third in an isobaric process. Calculate the final temperature of the gas.

Since the process is isobaric it takes place at constant pressure and hence Charles' law applies, i.e. $\dfrac{V_1}{T_1} = \dfrac{V_2}{T_2}$ where $T_1 = (150 + 273)K = 423$ K and $V_2 = \dfrac{2}{3}V_1$.

Hence $\dfrac{V_1}{423} = \dfrac{\frac{2}{3}V_1}{T_2}$

from which, **final temperature, $T_2 = \dfrac{2}{3}(423)$ = 282 K** or $(282 - 273)°C$, i.e. **9°C.**

Problem 6 Gas initially at a temperature of 17°C and pressure 150 kPa is heated at constant volume until its temperature is 124°C. Determine the final pressure of the gas, assuming no loss of gas.

Since the gas is at constant volume, the pressure law applies,

i.e. $\dfrac{p_1}{T_1} = \dfrac{p_2}{T_2}$, where $T_1 = (17 + 273)K = 290$ K, $T_2 = (124 + 273)K = 397K$ and $p_1 = 150$ kPa.

Hence $\dfrac{150}{290} = \dfrac{p_2}{397}$

from which, **final pressure, $p_2 = \dfrac{(150)(397)}{290}$ = 205.3kPa.**

Problem 7 A gas R in a container exerts a pressure of 200 kPa at a temperature of 18°C. Gas Q is added to the container and the pressure increases to 320 kPa at the same temperature. Determine the pressure that gas Q alone exerts at the same temperature.

Initial pressure $p_R = 200$ kPa and pressure of gases R and Q together, $p = p_R + p_Q = 320$ kPa.
By Dalton's law of partial pressure, the pressure of gas Q alone is $p_Q = p - p_R = 320 - 200 = $ **120 kPa.**

Problem 8 A gas occupies a volume of 2.0 m³ when at a pressure of 100 kPa and a temperature of 120°C. Determine the volume of the gas at 15°C if the pressure is increased to 250 kPa.

Using the combined gas law, $\dfrac{p_1 V_1}{T_1} = \dfrac{p_2 V_2}{T_2}$, where $V_1 = 2.0$ m³, $p_1 = 100$ kPa,
$p_2 = 250$ kPa,
$T_1 = (120 + 273)$K = 393 K and
$T_2 = (15 + 273)$K = 288 K

gives: $\dfrac{(100)(2.0)}{393} = \dfrac{(250)\,V_2}{288}$

from which, **volume at 15°C**, $V_2 = \dfrac{(100)(2.0)(288)}{(393)(250)} = $ **0.586 m³**.

Problem 9 20000 mm³ of air initially at a pressure of 600 kPa and temperature 180°C is expanded to a volume of 70000 mm³ at a pressure of 120 kPa. Determine the final temperature of the air, assuming no losses during the process.

Using the combined gas law, $\dfrac{p_1 V_1}{T_1} = \dfrac{p_2 V_2}{T_2}$, where $V_1 = 20000$ mm³
$V_2 = 70000$ mm³
$p_1 = 600$ kPa, $p_2 = 120$ kPa and
$T_1 = (180 + 273)$K = 453 K

gives: $\dfrac{(600)(20000)}{453} = \dfrac{(120)(70000)}{T_2}$

from which, **final temperature,** $T_2 = \dfrac{(120)(70000)(453)}{(600)(20000)} = $ **317 K or 44°C.**

Problem 10 Some air at a temperature of 40°C and pressure 4 bar occupies a volume of 0.05 m³. Determine the mass of the air assuming the characteristic gas constant for air to be 287 J/(kg K).

From para. 7(ii), $pV = mRT$, where $p = 4$ bar $= 4 \times 10^5$ Pa (since 1 bar $= 10^5$ Pa),
$V = 0.05$ m³, $T = (40 + 273)$K = 313 K and
$R = 287$ J/(kg K)

Hence $(4 \times 10^5)(0.05) = m\,(287)(313)$

from which, **mass of air,** $m = \dfrac{(4 \times 10^5)(0.05)}{(287)(313)} = $ **0.223 kg or 223 g.**

Problem 11 A cylinder of helium has a volume of 600 cm³. The cylinder contains 200 g of helium at a temperature of 25°C. Determine the pressure of the helium if the characteristic gas constant for helium is 2080 J/(kg K).

From the characteristic gas equation, $pV = mRT$, where $V = 600$ cm³
$= 600 \times 10^{-6}$ m³,
$m = 200$ g $= 0.2$ kg,
$T = (25 + 273)$K = 298 K
and $R = 2080$ J/(kg K)

Hence $(p)(600 \times 10^{-6}) = (0.2)(2080)(298)$

from which, **pressure** $p = \dfrac{(0.2)(2080)(298)}{(600 \times 10^{-6})} = 206\,600\,000$ Pa = **206.6 MPa.**

Problem 12 A spherical vessel has a diameter of 1.2 m and contains oxygen at a pressure of 2 bar and a temperature of -20°C. Determine the mass of oxygen in the vessel. Take the characteristic gas constant for oxygen to be $0.260\,\text{kJ/(kg K)}$.

From the characteristic gas equation, $pV = m\,R\,T$,

where V = volume of spherical vessel = $\dfrac{4}{3}\pi r^3 = \dfrac{4}{3}\pi\left(\dfrac{1.2}{2}\right)^3 = 0.905$ m³

$p = 2\ \text{bar} = 2 \times 10^5$ Pa, $T = (-20 + 273)$K = 253 K and
$R = 0.260\ \text{kJ/(kg K)} = 260\ \text{J/(kg K)}$.

Hence $(2 \times 10^5)(0.905) = m\,(260)(253)$

from which, **mass of oxygen,** $m = \dfrac{(2 \times 10^5)(0.905)}{(260)(253)} = $ **2.75 kg.**

Problem 13 Determine the characteristic gas constant of a gas which has a specific volume of 0.5 m³/kg at a temperature of 20°C and pressure 150 kPa.

From the characteristic gas equation, $pV = m\,R\,T$

from which, $R = \dfrac{pV}{mT}$, where $p = 150 \times 10^3$ Pa

$T = (20 + 273)$K = 293 K and

specific volume, $\dfrac{V}{m} = 0.5$ m³/kg

Hence the **characteristic gas constant,**

$R = \left(\dfrac{p}{T}\right)\left(\dfrac{V}{m}\right) = \left(\dfrac{150 \times 10^3}{293}\right)(0.5) = $ **256 J/(kg K).**

Problem 14 A vessel has a volume of 0.80 m³ and contains a mixture of helium and hydrogen at a pressure of 450 kPa and a temperature of 17°C. If the mass of helium present is 0.40 kg determine (a) the partial pressure of each gas, and (b) the mass of hydrogen present. Assume the characteristic gas constant for helium to be 2080 J/(kg K) and for hydrogen 4160 J/(kg K).

(a) $V = 0.80$ m³, $p = 450$ kPa, $T = (17 + 273)$K = 290 K, $m_{He} = 0.40$ kg, $R_{He} = 2080$ J/(kg K).

If p_{He} is the partial pressure of the helium, then using the characteristic gas equation, $p_{He}V = m_{He}R_{He}T$
gives $(p_{He})(0.80) = (0.40)(2080)\,(290)$

from which, **the partial pressure of the helium,** $p_{He} = \dfrac{(0.40)(2080)(290)}{(0.80)}$

$= $ **301.6 kPa.**

By Dalton's law of partial pressure the total pressure p is given by the sum of the partial pressures, i.e. $p = p_H + p_{He}$,

from which, **the partial pressure of the hydrogen,** $p_H = p - p_{He} = 450 - 301.6$

$= $ **148.4 kPa.**

(b) From the characteristic gas equation, $p_H V = m_H R_H T$

Hence $(148.4 \times 10^3)(0.8) = m_H (4160)(290)$

from which, **mass of hydrogen, $m_H = \dfrac{(148.4 \times 10^3)(0.8)}{(4160)(290)}$ = 0.098 kg or 98g.**

Problem 15 A compressed air cylinder has a volume of 1.2 m³ and contains air at a pressure of 1 MPa and a temperature of 25°C. Air is released from the cylinder until the pressure falls to 300 kPa and the temperature is 15°C. Determine (a) the mass of air released from the container, and (b) the volume it would occupy at STP. Assume the characteristic gas constant for air to be 287 J/(kg K).

$V_1 = 1.2 \text{ m}^3 \ (= V_2), p_1 = 1 \text{ MPa} = 10^6 \text{ Pa}, T_1 = (25 + 273)\text{K} = 298 \text{ K},$
$T_2 = (15 + 273)\text{K} = 288 \text{ K}, p_2 = 300 \text{ kPa} = 300 \times 10^3 \text{ Pa and } R = 287 \text{ J/(kg K)}.$

(a) Using the characteristic gas equation, $p_1 V_1 = m_1 R T_1$, to find the initial mass of air in the cylinder gives: $(10^6)(1.2) = m_1 (287)(298)$

from which, mass $m_1 = \dfrac{(10^6)(1.2)}{(287)(298)}$ = 14.03 kg

Similarly, using $p_2 V_2 = m_2 R T_2$ to find the final mass of air in the cylinder gives $(300 \times 10^3)(1.2) = m_2 (287)(288)$

from which, mass $m_2 = \dfrac{(300 \times 10^3)(1.2)}{(287)(288)}$ = 4.36 kg

Mass of air released from cylinder = $m_1 - m_2$ = 14.03 − 4.36 = **9.67 kg.**

(b) At STP, $t = 273$ K and $p = 101.325$ kPa.

Using the characteristic gas equation $pV = m R T$

volume, $V = \dfrac{mRT}{p} = \dfrac{(9.67)(287)(273)}{101325}$ = 7.48 m³.

Problem 16 A vessel X contains gas at a pressure of 750 kPa at a temperature of 27°C. It is connected via a valve to vessel Y which is filled with a similar gas at a pressure of 1.2 MPa and a temperature of 27°C. The volume of vessel X is 2.0 m³ and that of vessel Y is 3.0 m³. Determine the final pressure at 27°C when the valve is opened and the gases are allowed to mix. Assume R for the gas to be 300 J/(kg K).

For vessel X: $p_X = 750 \times 10^3 \text{ Pa}, T_X = (27 + 273)\text{K} = 300 \text{ K}, V_X = 2.0 \text{ m}^3,$
$R = 300 \text{ J/(kg K)}.$

From the characteristic gas equation, $p_X V_X = m_X R T_X$

Hence $(750 \times 10^3)(2.0) = m_X (300)(300)$

from which, mass of gas in vessel X, $m_X = \dfrac{(750 \times 10^3)(2.0)}{(300)(300)}$ = 16.67 kg.

For vessel Y: $p_Y = 1.2 \times 10^6 \text{ Pa}, T_Y = (27 + 273)\text{K} = 300 \text{ K}, V_Y = 3.0 \text{ m}^3,$
$R = 300 \text{ J/(kg K)}.$

From the characteristic gas equation, $p_Y V_Y = m_Y R T_Y$

Hence $(1.2 \times 10^6)(3.0) = m_Y (300)(300)$

from which, mass of gas in vessel Y, $m_Y = \dfrac{(1.2 \times 10^6)(3.0)}{(300)(300)}$ = 40 kg.

When the valve is opened, mass of mixture, $m = m_X + m_Y$ = 16.67 + 40 = 56.67 kg.

Total volume, $V = V_X + V_Y$ = 2.0 + 3.0 = 5.0 m³, R = 300 J/(kg K), T = 300 K.

From the characteristic gas equation, $pV = mRT$

$$p(5.0) = (56.67)(300)(300)$$

from which, **final pressure, p** $= \dfrac{(56.67)(300)(300)}{(5.0)} = 1.02$ MPa

Problem 17 Briefly explain what is meant by the kinetic theory of gases.

The kinetic theory of gases suggests that gases are composed of particles in motion. The continual bombardment of any surface by the gas causes a pressure to be exerted; the greater the density of a gas, the more frequent the number of collisions between molecules and the surface and the greater the pressure exerted. Hence the pressure increases either when the colume of a certain mass of gas is reduced, or when more gas is pumped into a vessel. When the temperature of a gas is increased, the speed of the molecules increases, causing an increase in both the number and the momentum imparted by each collision. This accounts for the increase in pressure of a gas with increase in temperature.

Maxwell (in 1860) explained some of the properties of a gas by assuming that the molecules of a gas make elastic collisions, spend negligible time actually in collision, and themselves occupy a negligible part of the volume of the gas. Also, the attractive forces between molecules are assumed negligible.

Problem 18 A gas molecule of mass m bounces back and forth between the walls of a rectangular container, hitting the end walls (of area A) along the normal to the walls and moving between the walls at a constant speed c. The distance between the walls is l. If the gas contains a total of n molecules derive (a) the relation $pV = \dfrac{1}{3}nmc^2$, where p is the pressure on the wall and V is the volume of the container, and (b) the relationship between the kinetic energy of the molecules and the thermodynamic temperature.

Distance travelled in time t is ct

The number of collisions in time t is $\dfrac{ct}{2l}$ (since the molecules travel a distance $2l$ between collisions at one wall)

The momentum of a molecule changes from $+mc$ to $-mc$, i.e. a change of $2mc$, when it collides with a wall

The total change in momentum in time t is $(2mc)\left(\dfrac{ct}{2l}\right) = mc^2\left(\dfrac{t}{l}\right)$

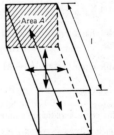

Fig 2

The velocities of all the molecules can be resolved into three mutually perpendicular directions (see *Fig 2*), and of the total number of molecules n, $\dfrac{1}{3}n$ can be considered to be moving towards the wall of area A of the container

Total change in momentum in time t due to all the molecules in the container

$= \dfrac{1}{3}n\left(mc^2\dfrac{t}{l}\right)$

102

Average force on wall in time t = rate of change of momentum

$$= \frac{\frac{1}{3}n\left(mc^2\,\frac{t}{l}\right)}{t} = \frac{1}{3}n\,m\,\frac{c^2}{l}$$

Pressure on wall = $\dfrac{\text{force}}{\text{area } A} = \dfrac{\frac{1}{3}n\,m\,\frac{c^2}{l}}{A} = \dfrac{1}{3}\dfrac{n\,m\,c^2}{A\,l}$

Volume of box = $A\,l$, hence pressure $p = \dfrac{1}{3}\dfrac{n\,m\,c^2}{V}$

or $\qquad pV = \dfrac{1}{3}n\,m\,c^2$.

(b) Density of gas molecules $\rho = \dfrac{n\,m}{V}$

Hence $p = \dfrac{1}{3}\rho\,c^2$

Also, since density $\rho = \dfrac{\text{total mass of gas } M}{\text{volume } V}$

then $p = \dfrac{1}{3}\dfrac{M}{V}c^2$ or $pV = \dfrac{1}{3}M\,c^2 = \dfrac{2}{3}\left(\dfrac{1}{2}M\,c^2\right)$

Thus $pV = \dfrac{2}{3} \times$ (kinetic energy of molecules)

However, from para 7(ii), $pV = M\,R\,T$ or $pV = kT$

Hence the kinetic energy of the molecules of a gas is directly proportional to its thermodynamic temperature T.

Problem 19 1.0 m³ of an unsaturated water vapour at a pressure of 1.5×10^3 Pa and a temperature of 20°C is compressed at constant temperature. What is the volume of the vapour when it starts to liquefy?

When the vapour starts to liquefy the vapour becomes saturated. At 20°C the saturated vapour pressure is 2.33×10^3 Pa (see *Table 1*). Until the pressure reaches this value we can assume Boyle's law is applicable.

Thus $p_1 V_1 = p_2 V_2$,

where $p_1 = 1.5 \times 10^3$ Pa ; $V_1 = 1.0$ m³ ; $p_2 = 2.33 \times 10^3$ Pa

Therefore $1.5 \times 10^3 \times 1.0 = 2.33 \times 10^3 \, V_2$

thus **the volume of the vapour when it starts to liquefy,**

$V_2 = \dfrac{1.5 \times 10^3}{2.33 \times 10^3} = $ **0.64 m³**.

Problem 20 A closed vessel contains a mixture of air and saturated water vapour. The pressure in the vessel is 9.52×10^4 Pa when the temperature is 30°C. Calculate the pressure in the vessel when the temperature is 70°C, assuming that the water vapour remains saturated.

The saturated vapour pressure of water at 30°C is 4.23×10^3 Pa (from *Table 1*). According to Dalton's law of partial pressures the pressure of a mixture of gases is the sum of the partial pressures of its constituents.

Thus the pressure of the air = $(9.52 \times 10^4 - 4.23 \times 10^3)$ Pa

$= 9.097 \times 10^4$ Pa

The pressure of air is proportional to its absolute temperature.

Thus $\dfrac{p_1}{T_1} = \dfrac{p_2}{T_2}$

In this example $p_1 = 9.097 \times 10^4$ Pa; $T_1 = 273 + 30 = 303$ K; $T_2 = 273 + 70 = 343$ K

p_2 is the pressure of the air at 70°C

Thus $\dfrac{9.097 \times 10^4}{303} = \dfrac{p_2}{343}$

and $\qquad p_2 = \dfrac{343 \times 9.097 \times 10^4}{303}$

$\qquad\qquad = 1.03 \times 10^5$ Pa

The saturated vapour pressure of water at 70°C = 31.2×10^3 Pa (from *Table 1*)

Thus the pressure in the vessel at 70°C $\quad = 1.03 \times 10^5 + 31.2 \times 10^3$

$\qquad\qquad\qquad\qquad\qquad\qquad = \mathbf{134\,200\ Pa}$

$\qquad\qquad\qquad\qquad\qquad\qquad$ or $\mathbf{1.34 \times 10^5\ Pa.}$

C. FURTHER PROBLEMS ON IDEAL GAS LAWS

(a) SHORT ANSWER PROBLEMS

1 State Boyle's law.
2 State Charles' law.
3 State the Pressure law.
4 State Dalton's law of partial pressures.
5 State the relationship between the Celsius and the thermodynamic scale of temperature.
6 What is (a) an isothermal change, and (b) an isobaric change?
7 Define an ideal gas.
8 State the characteristic gas equation.
9 What is meant by STP?
10 How is the kinetic energy of the molecules of a gas related to its absolute temperature?
11 Define saturated vapour.
12 Complete the following statement. The pressure of a saturated vapour depends only on its . . . .

(b) MULTI-CHOICE PROBLEMS (Answers on page 156)

1 Which of the following statements is false?
   (a) At constant temperature, Charles' law applies.
   (b) The pressure of a given mass of gas decreases as the volume is increased at constant temperature.
   (c) Isobaric changes are those which occur at constant pressure.
   (d) Boyle's law applies at constant temperature.
2 A gas occupies a volume of 4 m³ at a pressure of 400 kPa. At constant temperature, the pressure is increased to 500 kPa. The new volume occupied by the gas is:
   (a) 5 m³; (b) 0.3 m³; (c) 0.2 m³; (d) 3.2 m³.
3 A gas at a temperature of 27°C occupies a volume of 5 m³. The volume of the same mass of gas at the same pressure but at a temperature of 57°C is:
   (a) 10.56 m³; (b) 5.50 m³; (c) 4.55 m³; (d) 2.37 m³.

4 Which of the following statements is false?
  (a) The kinetic energy of the molecules of a gas is proportional to the absolute temperature of the gas.
  (b) Isothermal changes are those which occur at constant volume.
  (c) The volume of a gas increases when the temperature increases at constant pressure.
  (d) Changes which occur at constant pressure are called isobaric changes.

A gas has a volume of 0.4 m³ when its pressure is 250 kPa and its temperature is 400 K. Use this data in *Problems 5 and 6*.

5 The temperature when the pressure is increased to 400 kPa and the volume is increased to 0.8 m³ is:
  (a) 400 K; (b) 80 K; (c) 1280 K; (d) 320 K.
6 The pressure when the temperature is raised to 600 K and the volume is reduced to 0.2 m³ is:
  (a) 187.5 kPa; (b) 250 kPa; (c) 333.3 kPa; (d) 750 kPa.
7 A gas has a volume of 3 m³ at a temperature of 546 K and a pressure of 101.325 kPa. The volume it occupies at STP is:
  (a) 3 m³; (b) 1.5 m³; (c) 6 m³.
8 Which of the following statements is false?
  (a) A characteristic gas constant has units of J/(kg K).
  (b) STP conditions are 273 K and 101.325 kPa.
  (c) All gases are ideal gases.
  (d) An ideal gas is one which obeys the gas laws.

A mass of 5 kg of air is pumped into a container of volume 2.87 m³. The characteristic gas constant for air is 287 J/(kg K). Use this data in *Problems 9 and 10*.

9 The pressure when the temperature is 27°C is:
  (a) 1.6 kPa; (b) 6 kPa; (c) 150 kPa; (d) 15 kPa.
10 The temperature when the pressure is 200 kPa is:
  (a) 400°C; (b) 127°C; (c) 127 K; (d) 283 K.
11 The saturation vapour pressure of water:
  (a) is independent of temperature;
  (b) decreases with increasing temperature;
  (c) increases with increasing temperature;
  (d) doubles when the volume is halved.
12 When molecules evaporate from the surface of a liquid:
  (a) the average kinetic energy of the remaining molecules increases;
  (b) the temperature of the remaining liquid remains unchanged;
  (c) an unsaturated vapour is produced;
  (d) the average kinetic energy of the remaining molecules decreases.

(c) CONVENTIONAL PROBLEMS

1 The pressure of a mass of gas is increased from 150 kPa to 750 kPa at constant temperature. Determine the final volume of the gas, if its initial volume is 1.5 m³.
                                                              [0.3 m³]

2   Some gas initially at 16°C is heated to 96°C at constant pressure. If the initial volume of the gas is 0.80 m³, determine the final volume of the gas.

[1.02 m³]

3   In an isothermal process, a mass of gas has its volume reduced from 50 cm³ to 32 cm³. If the initial pressure of the gas is 80 kPa, determine its final pressure.

[125 kPa]

4   The piston of an air compressor compresses air to $\frac{1}{4}$ of its original volume during its stroke. Determine the final pressure of the air if the original pressure is 100 kPa, assuming an isothermal change.

[400 kPa]

5   A gas is contained in a vessel of volume 0.02 m³ at a pressure of 300 kPa and a temperature of 15°C. The gas is passed into a vessel of volume 0.015 m³. Determine to what temperature the gas must be cooled for the pressure to remain the same.

[−57°C]

6   In an isobaric process gas at a temperature of 120°C has its volume reduced by a sixth. Determine the final temperature of the gas.

[54.5°C]

7   Gas, initially at a temperature of 27°C and pressure 100 kPa, is heated at constant volume until its temperature is 150°C. Assuming no loss of gas, determine the final pressure of the gas.

[141 kPa]

8   A gas A in a container exerts a pressure of 120 kPa at a temperature of 20°C. Gas B is added to the container and the pressure increases to 300 kPa at the same temperature. Determine the pressure which gas B alone exerts at the same temperature.

[180 kPa]

9   A quantity of gas in a cylinder occupies a volume of 2 m³ at a pressure of 300 kPa. A piston slides in the cylinder and compresses the gas, according to Boyle's law, until the volume is 0.5 m³. If the area of the piston is 0.02 m², calculate the force on the piston when the gas is compressed.

[24 kN]

10 A given mass of air occupies a volume of 0.5 m³ at a pressure of 500 kPa and a temperature of 20°C. Find the volume of the air at STP.

[2.30 m³]

11 A spherical vessel has a diameter of 2.0 m and contains hydrogen at a pressure of 300 kPa and a temperature of −30°C. Determine the mass of hydrogen in the vessel. Assume the characteristic gas constant R for hydrogen is 4160 J/(kg K).

[1.24 kg]

12 A gas occupies a volume of 1.20 m³ when at a pressure of 120 kPa and a temperature of 90°C. Determine the volume of the gas at 20°C if the pressure is increased to 320 kPa.

[0.363 m³]

13 A cylinder 200 mm in diameter and 1.5 m long contains oxygen at a pressure of 2 MPa and a temperature of 20°C. Determine the mass of oxygen in the cylinder. Assume the characteristic gas constant for oxygen is 260 J/(kg K).

[1.24 kg]

14 A gas is pumped into an empty cylinder of volume 0.1 m³ until the pressure is 5 MPa. The temperature of the gas is 40°C. If the cylinder mass increases by

5.32 kg when the gas has been added, determine the value of the characteristic gas constant.
[300 J/(kg K)]

15 The mass of a gas is 1.2 kg and it occupies a volume of 13.45 m³ at STP. Determine its characteristic gas constant.
[4160 J/(kg K)]

16 A vessel P contains gas at a pressure of 800 kPa at a temperature of 25°C. It is connected via a value to vessel Q which is filled with similar gas at a pressure of 1.5 MPa and a temperature of 25°C. The volume of vessel P is 1.5 m³ and that of vessel R is 2.5 m³. Determine the final pressure at 25°C when the valve is opened and the gases are allowed to mix. Assume R for the gas to be 297 J/(kg K).
[1.24 MPa]

17 30 cm³ of air initially at a pressure of 500 kPa and temperature 150°C is expanded to a volume of 100 cm³ at a pressure of 200 kPa. Determine the final temperature of the air, assuming no losses during the process.
[291°C]

18 A vessel contains 4 kg of air at a pressure of 600 kPa and a temperature of 40°C. The vessel is connected to another by a short pipe and the air exhausts into it. The final pressure in both vessels is 250 kPa and the temperature in both is 15°C. If the pressure in the second vessel before the air entered was zero, determine the volume of each vessel. Assume R for air is 287 J/(kg K).
[0.60 m³; 0.72 m³]

19 A quantity of gas in a cylinder occupies a volume of 0.5 m³ at a pressure of 400 kPa and a temperature of 27°C. It is compressed according to Boyle's law until its pressure is 1 MPa, and then expanded according to Charles' law until its volume is 0.03 m³. Determine the final temperature of the gas.
[177°C]

20 Some air at a temperature of 35°C and pressure 2 bar occupies a volume of 0.08 m³. Determine the mass of the air assuming the characteristic gas constant for air to be 287 J/(kg K).
[0.181 kg]

21 Determine the characteristic gas constant R of a gas which has a specific volume of 0.267 m³/kg at a temperature of 17°C and pressure 200 kPa.
[184 J/(kg K)]

22 A vessel has a volume of 0.75 m³ and contains a mixture of air and carbon dioxide at a pressure of 200 kPa and a temperature of 27°C. If the mass of air present is 0.5 kg determine (a) the partial pressure of each gas, and (b) the mass of carbon dioxide. Assume the characteristic gas constant for air to be 287 J(kg K) and for carbon dioxide 184 J/(kg K).
[(a) 57.4 kPa, 142.6 kPa; (b) 1.94 kg]

23 A cylinder contains 20 kg of air at a pressure of 2.5 MPa and a temperature of 27°C. Oxygen is now pumped into the cylinder until the pressure is increased to 4 MPa, the temperature remaining at 27°C. Calculate (a) the mass of oxygen pumped into the cylinder, and (b) the temperature to which the mixture must rise in order to increase the pressure to 5 MPa. Take R for air as 287 J/(kg K) and R for oxygen as 260 J/(kg K).
[(a) 13.25 kg; (b) 102°C]

24 A mass of gas occupies a volume of 0.02 m³ when its pressure is 150 kPa and its temperature is 17°C. If the gas is compressed until its pressure is 500 kPa and its temperature is 57°C, determine (a) the volume it will occupy and (b) its mass, if the characteristic gas constant for the gas is 205 J/(kg K).
[(a) 0.0068 m³; (b) 0.052 kg]

25 A compressed air cylinder has a volume of 0.6 m³ and contains air at a pressure of 1.2 MPa absolute and a temperature of 37°C. After use the pressure is 800 kPa absolute and the temperature is 17°C. Calculate (a) the mass of air removed from the cylinder, and (b) the volume the mass of air removed would occupy at STP conditions. Take R for air as 287 J/(kg K) and atmospheric pressure as 100 kPa.

[(a) 2.33 kg; (b) 1.826 m³]

26 An unsaturated water vapour is compressed at a constant temperature of 40°C. It is found that when the volume has decreased to 40% of its original value the vapour starts to liquefy. Calculate the initial pressure. The saturated vapour pressure of water at 40°C is 7.35×10^3 Pa.

[2.94×10^3 Pa]

27 A closed vessel contains a mixture of air and saturated ethyl ether vapour at 10°C. The pressure at this temperature is 1.05×10^5 Pa. Calculate the pressure in the vessel when the temperature is 20°C, assuming that the vapour remains saturated. The saturated vapour pressure of ethyl ether is 3.9×10^4 Pa at 10°C and 5.9×10^4 Pa at 20°C.

[1.27×10^5 Pa]

9 Properties of water and steam

A. MAIN POINTS CONCERNING THE PROPERTIES OF WATER AND STEAM

1 When two systems are at different temperatures, the transfer of energy from one system to the other is called **heat transfer**. For a block of hot metal cooling in air, heat is transferred from the hot metal to the cool air. The **principle of conservation of energy** may be stated as

'energy cannot be created nor can it be destroyed',

and since heat is a form of energy, this law applies to heat transfer problems.

A more convenient way of expressing this law when referring to heat transfer problems is:

$$\left(\begin{array}{c}\text{Initial energy of the system}\end{array}\right) + \left(\begin{array}{c}\text{energy entering}\\\text{the system}\end{array}\right) = \left(\begin{array}{c}\text{final energy of}\\\text{the system}\end{array}\right) + \left(\begin{array}{c}\text{energy leaving}\\\text{the system}\end{array}\right)$$

or, $$\left(\begin{array}{c}\text{Energy entering}\\\text{the system}\end{array}\right) = \left(\begin{array}{c}\text{change of}\\\text{energy within}\\\text{the system}\end{array}\right) + \left(\begin{array}{c}\text{energy leaving}\\\text{the system}\end{array}\right)$$

(see *Problem 1*.)

2 Fluids consist of a very large number of molecules moving in random directions within the fluid. When the fluid is heated, the speeds of the molecules are increased, increasing the kinetic energy of the molecules. There is also an increase in volume due to an increase in the average distance between molecules, causing the potential energy of the fluid to increase. The **internal energy**, U of a fluid, is the sum of the internal kinetic and potential energies of the molecules of a fluid, measuring in joules. It is not usual to state the internal energy of a fluid as a particular value in heat transfer problems, since it is normally only the **change** in internal energy which is required (see *Problem 2*).

3 The sum of the internal energy and the pressure energy of a fluid is called the **enthalpy** of the fluid, denoted by the symbol H and measured in joules. The pressure energy, or work done, is given by the product of pressure, p, and volume V, that is: pressure energy = pV joules.

Thus, enthalpy = internal energy + pressure energy (or work done),

i.e. $H = U + pV$.

As for internal energy, the actual value of enthalpy is usually unimportant and it is the **change** in enthalpy which is usually required. In heat transfer problems involving steam and water, water is considered to have zero enthalpy at a standard pressure of 101 kPa and a temperature of 0°C. The word 'specific' associated with

quantities indicates 'per unit mass'. Thus the **specific enthalpy** is obtained by
dividing the enthalpy by the mass and is denoted by the symbol h. Thus:

Specific enthalpy = $\dfrac{\text{enthalpy}}{\text{mass}} = \dfrac{H}{m} = h$

The units of specific enthalpy are joules per kilogram, (J/kg).

4   The specific enthalpy of water, h_f, at temperature $\theta°C$ is the quantity of heat
needed to raise 1 kg of water from $0°C$ to $\theta°C$, and is called the **sensible heat** of the
water. Its value is given by:
specific heat capacity of water, (c) × temperature change (θ)
that is, $h_f = c\theta$
The specific heat capacity of water varies with temperature and pressure but is
normally taken as 4.2 kJ/kg, thus
$h_f = 4.2\ \theta$ **kJ/kg**

5   When water is heated at a uniform rate, a stage is reached (at 100°C at standard
atmospheric pressure), where the addition of more heat does not result in a
corresponding increase in temperature. The temperature at which this occurs is
called the **saturation temperature**, t_{SAT}, and the water is called **saturated water**.
As heat is added to saturated water, it is turned into **saturated steam**. The amount
of heat required to turn 1 kg of saturated water into saturated steam is called the
specific latent heat of vaporisation, and is given the symbol, h_{fg}. The total specific
enthalpy of steam at saturation temperature h_g is given by:
the specific sensible heat + the specific latent heat of vaporisation,
i.e. $h_g = h_f + h_{fg}$

6   If the amount of heat added to saturated water is insufficient to turn all the water
into steam, then the ratio

$\dfrac{\text{mass of saturated steam}}{\text{total mass of steam and water}}$ is called the **dryness fraction** of the steam, denoted

by the symbol q. The steam is called **wet steam** and its total enthalpy is given by:
enthalpy of saturated water + (dryness fraction) × (enthalpy of latent heat of
vaporisation)
that is, $h_f + q\,h_{fg}$.

7   When the amount of heat added to water at saturation temperature is sufficient to
turn all the water into steam, it is called either saturated vapour or **dry saturated
steam**. The addition of further heat results in the temperature of the steam rising
and it is then called **superheated steam**. The specific enthalpy of superheated steam
above that of dry saturated steam is given by $c(t_{SUP} - t_{SAT})$, where c is the
specific heat capacity of the steam and t_{SUP} is the temperature of the superheated
steam. The total specific enthalpy of the superheated steam is given by:
$h_f + h_{fg} + c(t_{SUP} - t_{SAT})$, or $h_g + c\,(t_{SUP} - t_{SAT})$

8   The relationship between temperature
and specific enthalpy can be shown
graphically and a typical temperature-
specific enthalpy diagram is shown in
Fig 1. In this figure, AB represents
the sensible heat region where any
increase in enthalpy results in a
corresponding increase in
temperature. BC is called the
evaporation line and points between
B and C represent the wet steam

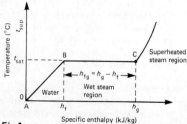

Fig 1

110

region, point C representing dry saturated steam. Points to the right of C represent the superheated steam region.

9   The boiling point of water, t_{SAT} and the various specific enthalpies associated with water and steam [h_f, h_{fg}, h_g and $c(t_{SUP} - t_{SAT})$], all vary with pressure. These values at various pressures have been tabulated in **steam tables**, extracts from these being shown in *Tables 1 and 2*.

TABLE 1

Pressure		Saturation temperature t_{SAT} (°C)	Specific enthalpy (kJ/kg)		
(bar)	(kPa)		Saturated Water h_f	Latent heat h_{fg}	Saturated Vapour h_g
1	100	99.6	417	2258	2675
1.5	150	111.4	467	2226	2693
2	200	120.2	505	2202	2707
3	300	133.5	561	2164	2725
4	400	143.6	605	2134	2739
5	500	151.8	640	2109	2749
6	600	158.8	670	2087	2757
7	700	165.0	697	2067	2764
8	800	170.4	721	2048	2769
9	900	175.4	743	2031	2774
10	1000	179.9	763	2015	2778
15	1500	198.3	845	1947	2792
20	2000	212.4	909	1890	2799
30	3000	233.8	1008	1795	2803
40	4000	250.3	1087	1714	2801

TABLE 2

Pressure		Saturation temperature t_{SAT}(°C)	Saturated vapour h_g	Specific enthalpy (kJ/kg) Superheated steam at				
(bar)	(kPa)			200°C	250°C	300°C	350°C	400°C
1	100	99.6	2675	2876	2975	3075	3176	3278
1.5	150	111.4	2693	2873	2973	3073	3175	3277
2	200	120.2	2707	2871	2971	3072	3174	3277
3	300	133.5	2725	2866	2968	3070	3172	3275
4	400	143.6	2739	2862	2965	3067	3170	3274
5	500	151.8	2749	2857	2962	3065	3168	3272
6	600	158.8	2757	2851	2958	3062	3166	3270
7	700	165.0	2764	2846	2955	3060	3164	3269
8	800	170.4	2769	2840	2951	3057	3162	3267
9	900	175.4	2774	2835	2948	3055	3160	3266
10	1000	179.9	2778	2829	2944	3052	3158	3264
15	1500	198.3	2792	2796	2925	3039	3148	3256
20	2000	212.4	2799		2904	3025	3138	3248
30	3000	233.8	2803		2858	2995	3117	3231
40	4000	250.3	2801			2963	3094	3214

In *Table 1*, the pressure in both bar and kilopascals, and saturated water temperature, are shown in columns on the left. The columns on the right give the corresponding specific enthalpies of water, (h_f) and dry saturated steam (h_g), together with the specific enthalpy of the latent heat of vaporisation, (h_{fg}).

The columns on the right of *Table 2* give the specific enthalpies of dry saturated steam, (h_g) and superheated steam at various temperatures. The values stated refer to zero enthalpy. However, if the degree of superheat is given, this refers to the saturation temperature. Thus at a pressure of 100 kPa, the column headed, say, 250°C has a degree of superheat of $(250 - 99.6)$°C, that is 150.4°C (see *Problems 3 to 9*).

10 Superheated steam behaves very nearly as if it is an ideal gas and the gas laws introduced in Chapter 8 may be used to determine the relationship between pressure, volume and temperature (see *Problem 10*).

B. WORKED PROBLEMS ON THE PROPERTIES OF WATER AND STEAM

Problem 1 Apply the principle of conservation of energy to a lamp connected to an electrical supply.

If the lamp is considered to be a system, then the enrgy entering the system is the electrical energy (watt seconds or joules). The change of energy of the system is an increase in the kinetic and potential energies of the molecules of the lamp. The energy leaving the system is in the form of light and heat energies. Thus

(electrical energy entering = (change of internal + (light and heat energy
  the system)   energy)   leaving the system)

Problem 2 Discuss three factors affecting the internal energy of a fluid.

The amount of internal energy of a fluid depends on:
(a) The type of fluid; in gases the molecules are well separated and move with high velocities, thus a gaseous fluid has a higher internal energy than the same mass of a liquid.
(b) The mass of a fluid; the greater the mass, the greater the number of molecules and hence the greater the internal energy.
(c) The temperature; the higher the temperature the greater the velocity of the molecules.

Problem 3 In a closed system, that is, a system in which the mass of fluid remains a constant, the internal energy changes from 25 kJ to 50 kJ and the work done by the system is 55 kJ. Determine the heat transferred to the system to effect this change.

From para 3, $H = U + pV$, where H is the enthalpy, (often taken as the heat energy added or taken from a system), U is the change of internal energy and pV is the pressure energy or work done.
Thus $H = [(50 - 25) + 55]$ kJ = $(25 + 55)$ kJ = 80 kJ
That is, **heat transferred to the system is 80 kJ**

Problem 4 A system raising plant generates dry saturated steam at a pressure of 1.5 MPa. Use steam tables to find (a) the saturation temperature; (b) the specific enthalpy of the dry saturated steam; (c) the enthalpy of 1t of the steam.

(a) From *Table 1*, at a pressure of 1.5 MPa (that is 1500 kPa), the saturation temperature, t_{SAT} is **198.3°C**. That is, at a pressure of 1.5 MPa, the water boils at 198.3°C.
(b) The specific enthalpy of the dry saturated steam is also given in *Table 1*, (column 6), showing that h_g is **2792 kJ/kg**.
(c) The enthalpy is the total heat content of the steam and since, from part (b), 1 kg contains 2792 kJ, then 1 tonne (that is 1000 kg), contains 1000 × 2792 kJ or **2792 MJ**.

Problem 5 Dry saturated steam at a pressure of 1.0 MPa is cooled at constant pressure until it has a dryness fraction of 0.6. Determine the change in the specific enthalpy of the steam.

From *Table 1*, the specific enthalpy of dry saturated steam h_g, at a pressure of 1.0 MPa (1000 kPa), is 2778 kJ/kg.
From para 6, the specific enthalpy of wet steam is $h_f + q\,h_{fg}$.
At a pressure of 1.0 MPa, h_f is 763 kJ/kg and h_{fg} is 2015 kJ/kg.
Thus, the specific enthalpy of the wet steam = 763 + (0.6 × 2015) = 1972 kJ/kg.
The change in the specific enthalpy is (initial value minus the final value), that is
Change in specific enthalpy = 2778 − 1972 = **806 kJ/kg**

Problem 6 The condenser of a turbine converts wet steam at the outlet of the turbine into water at the base of the condenser. The pressure in a condenser is 100 kPa and the dryness fraction of the steam entering the condenser is 0.7. The water is pumped from the condenser at a temperature of 27°C. Find the heat removed by the condenser cooling water per hour, if the mass of steam condensed is 120 t/h. Take the specific heat capacity of water as 4.2 kJ/kg.

From para. 6, the specific enthalpy of wet steam is $h_f + q\,h_{fg}$.
From *Table 1*, h_f at 100 kPa is 417 kJ/kg and h_{fg} is 2258 kJ/kg. Thus the specific enthalpy of the wet steam is 417 + (0.7 × 2258), i.e. 1997.6 kJ/kg. The specific enthalpy of the water leaving the condenser is given by 4.2 θ kJ/kg, (see para 4), i.e. 4.2 × 27 = 113.4 kJ/kg. Thus specific heat removed by the cooling water is 1997.6 − 113.4, that is 1884.2 kJ/kg.
The total heat removed per hour is: mass × (specific heat removed by the cooling water) that is, 120 000 kg × 1884.2 kJ/kg, or **226.1 GJ/h**.

Problem 7 Determine the degree of superheat and the specific enthalpy of steam leaving a boiler at a pressure of 3.0 MPa and a temperature of 400°C.

Details of the specific enthalpies of superheated steam are given in *Table 2*. At a pressure of 3.0 MPa, i.e. 3000 kPa, the saturation temperature is 233.8°C, hence the degree of superheat is 400 − 233.8, or **166.2°C**.

The specific enthalpy of superheated steam at 3.0 MPa and 400°C is given in *Table 2* as **3231 kJ/kg.**

Problem 8 Feed water is pumped into a boiler at a temperature of 30°C and steam leaves the boiler at a pressure of 2.0 MPa and having 87.6°C of superheat. Determine the heat supplied by the boiler for each kilogram of steam produced.

With reference to *Table 2*, at a pressure of 2.0 MPa, the saturation temperature is 212.4°C. Thus the temperature of the superheated steam is (212.4 + 87.6)°C, that is 300°C.

At a pressure of 2.0 MPa and temperature of 300°C, the specific enthalpy of the steam leaving the boiler is 3025 kJ/kg.

The specific enthalpy of the feed water is 4.2 × 30, that is 126 kJ/kg, (see para 4). Thus the heat supplied by the boiler is 3025 − 126, i.e. **2899 kJ/kg.**

Problem 9 Draw the temperature-enthalpy diagram for 1 kg of water or steam at a pressure of 2 MPa when heated from 30°C to 400°C.

From para 4, the specific enthalpy of water at 30°C is 4.2 × 30, or 126 kJ/kg, shown as point A in *Fig 2*. The saturation temperature at 2 MPa is given in *Table 1* and is 212.4°C, the corresponding specific enthalpy, h_f being 909 kJ/kg. This is shown as point B in *Fig 2*. AB represents the sensible heat region. The specific enthalpy h_g of the saturated vapour (dry saturated steam), is 2799 kJ/kg

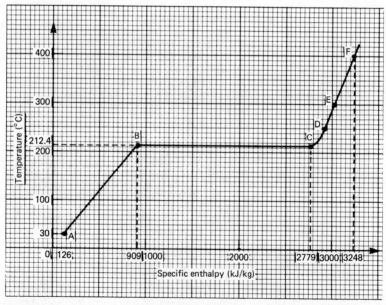

Fig 2

114

at 212.4°C, shown as point C in *Fig 2*. Thus BC represents the specific latent heat of vaporisation region.

From *Table 2*, the specific enthalpies of superheated steam are:

2094 kJ/kg at 250°C; 3025 kJ/kg at 300°C; 3248 kJ/kg at 400°C,

shown as points D, E and F respectively in *Fig 2*. Thus CF represents the super-heated steam region.

Problem 10 From complete steam tables for superheated steam the following data for superheated steam at a pressure of 1 MPa and a temperature of 400°C is determined:

Specific volume $= 0.3065$ m^3/kg. Specific gas constant, $R = 0.4562$ kJ/(kg K). Determine the percentage difference in volume, if it is assumed that superheated steam is an ideal gas.

The relationship between pressure, volume and temperature, assuming an ideal gas, is $pV = mRT$ (see *chapter 8*). For the superheated steam $p = 1$ MPa $= 10^6$ Pa, $m = 1$ kg, $R = 456.2$ J/(kg K) and $T = (273 + 400)$K $= 673$ K.

Since $pV = mRT$, then $V = \dfrac{mRT}{p}$

$$= \frac{1 \times 456.2 \times 673}{10^6} = 0.3070 \text{ m}^3$$

Since 0.3065 m^3 is the true value, the percentage difference is given by

$$\frac{0.3065 - 0.3070}{0.3065} \times 100 = \mathbf{0.16\%}$$

If this principle is extended to other temperatures and pressures it may be shown that superheated steam does approximate closely to an ideal gas.

C. FURTHER PROBLEMS ON THE PROPERTIES OF WATER AND STEAM

(a) SHORT ANSWER PROBLEMS

1 State briefly the law of conservation of energy and how it is applied to heat transfer problems.

2 What is meant by the internal energy of a fluid?

3 What is meant by the enthalpy of a fluid? State its units.

4 Write down the relationships between enthalpy, internal energy and pressure energy.

5 State the values of pressure and temperature corresponding to zero enthalpy of water.

6 What is meant by specific enthalpy? State its units.

7 Write down the relationship for the specific enthalpy of water at a temperature of θ°C.

8 Define the dryness fraction of steam.

9 What are steam tables and why are they necessary?

10 State the relationship between superheated steam and an ideal gas.

In *Problems 1 to 3*, which of the statements are false?

1 The internal energy of a fluid:
   (a) is the sum of the kinetic and potential energies of the fluid;
   (b) is a constant;
   (c) depends on the mass of the fluid;
   (d) depends on the temperature of the fluid.

2 (a) The unit of specific enthalpy is the kilojoule.
   (b) Enthalpy = internal energy + pressure energy.
   (c) It is the change of enthalpy which is normally required in heat transfer problems.
   (d) Zero enthalpy is taken as 0°C and 101 kPa in heat transfer problems.

3 (a) A change of enthalpy causes a change of temperature for water in the sensible heat region.
   (b) A change of enthalpy causes no change of temperature in the latent heat of vaporisation region.
   (c) A change of enthalpy causes a change of temperature for superheated steam.
   (d) The specific enthalpy of dry saturated steam is given by $h_f + h_g$.

In a steam raising plant operating at a pressure of 1.5 MPa, water is fed to a boiler at 30°C and steam leaves the boiler at 300°C. Use steam tables to find the quantities stated in *Problems 4 to 8*, selecting the correct answer from those given here. Take the specific heat capacity of water as 4.2 kJ/kg.
   (a) 2792 kJ/kg; (b) 420 kJ/kg; (c) 1102 kJ/kg; (d) 100°C; (e) 198.3°C;
   (f) 845 kJ/kg; (g) 126 kJ/kg; (h) 1947 kJ/kg; (i) 5584 kJ/kg; (j) 3039 kJ/kg;

4 The specific enthalpy of the feed water.
5 The specific enthalpy of the saturated water.
6 The specific latent heat of vaporisation.
7 The specific enthalpy of the steam when dry saturated.
8 The specific enthalpy of the steam leaving the boiler.

5 kg of wet steam at a pressure of 150 kPa and having a dryness fraction of 0.8 is condensed into water and cooled to a temperature of 50°C. Use steam tables to find the quantities stated in *Problems 9 and 10*, selecting the correct answers from those given below.
   (a) 111.4 kJ; (b) 467 kJ/kg; (c) 1050 kJ; (d) 2226 kJ/kg; (e) 11130 kJ;
   (f) 11239 kJ; (g) 2247.8 kJ/kg; (h) 9989 kJ; (i) 1997.8 kJ/kg.

9 The enthalpy of the steam before being cooled.
10 The enthalpy of the water after cooling has taken place.

(c) CONVENTIONAL PROBLEMS

(Use steam tables as necessary. Take the specific heat capacity of water as 4.2 kJ/kg.)

1 In a closed system the internal energy is increased from 10 kJ to 70 kJ and the work done by the system is 120 kJ. Find the energy entering the system.

[180 kJ]

2 When the energy entering a closed system is 3 MJ, the work done by the sytem is 2.7 MJ. Determine the change in the internal energy of the system.

[300 kJ]

3   Find the saturation temperature and specific enthalpy of saturated water at a
    pressure of 700 kPa. What will be the enthalpy of 100 kg of saturated water at this
    pressure?

                                              [165°C; 697 kJ/kg; 69.7 MJ]

4   50 kg of water is heated from a temperature of 15°C to its boiling point at a
    pressure of 150 kPa. Determine the increase in the enthalpy of the water.

                                              [20.2 MJ]

5   Saturated water at a pressure of 400 kPa is heated until its dryness fraction is
    0.75. Determine the change of specific enthalpy.

                                              [995.5 kJ/kg]

6   Water enters a steam raising plant at a pressure of 1 MPa and at a temperature of
    30°C. If its specific enthalpy is increased by 2450.5 kJ/kg, determine the dryness
    fraction of the wet steam produced.

                                              [0.9]

7   100 kg of dry saturated steam at a pressure of 2 MPa is superheated to a
    temperature of 400°C. Determine the increase in enthalpy of the steam.

                                              [44.9 MJ]

8   Wet steam, having a dryness fraction of 0.6 is heated to a temperature of 250°C
    at a pressure of 3.0 MPa. Determine the increase in the specific enthalpy.

                                              [773 kJ/kg]

9   2 tonnes of steam at a pressure of 200 kPa and having a dryness fraction of 0.75,
    is cooled in a condenser to 27°C. Determine the amount of heat removed from the
    steam.

                                              [4086 MJ]

10 A small boiler is used to convert 25 kg of water at 48°C to wet steam having a
    dryness fraction of 0.92, at a pressure of 600 kPa. Find the amount of heat added
    to the water by the boiler.

                                              [59.71 MJ]

11 A boiler delivers 200 t of steam per hour to a turbine at a pressure of 1.5 MPa and
    with 201.7°C of superheat. After passing through the turbine it has a dryness
    fraction of 0.3 at a pressure of 150 kPa. Find the amount of heat taken from the
    steam by the turbine.

                                              [424.2 GJ]

12 Draw a temperature-enthalpy diagram for 1 kg of water/steam at a pressure of
    1 MPa, when heated from 50°C to 300°C.

$$\left[\begin{array}{l}\text{The specific enthalpy/temperature coordinates are}\\(201, 50);(763, 179.9);(2778; 179.9);(3052, 300)\end{array}\right]$$

13 Water at a temperature of 40°C and at a pressure of 700 kPa is heated until it
    becomes superheated steam at a temperature of 400°C. Draw a temperature-
    specific enthalpy diagram for the water/steam.

$$\left[\begin{array}{l}\text{The specific enthalpy/temperature coordinates are}\\(168, 40);(697, 165);(2764, 165);(3269, 400)\end{array}\right]$$

14 From steam tables, superheated steam at a pressure of 2 MPa and a temperature
    of 350°C has a specific volume of 0.1386 m³/kg. Determine the volume of the
    superheated steam using the gas laws and comment on the result obtained. The
    specific gas constant of steam at this temperature and pressure is 0.4446 kJ/(kg K).

                                              [0.1385 m³/kg; superheated steam approximates to an ideal gas]

15 Assuming superheated steam is an ideal gas, determine the pressure of 5 kg of
    superheated steam, if it occupies a volume of 2.613 m³ at a temperature of 300°C.
    Take R at this temperature and pressure as 0.455 kJ/(kg K).

                                              [499 kPa]

10 Linear momentum and impulse

A. MAIN POINTS CONCERNED WITH LINEAR MOMENTUM AND IMPULSE

1 (i) The **momentum** of a body is defined as the product of its mass and its velocity, i.e. **momentum** = mu, where m = mass (in kg) and u = velocity (in m/s). The unit of momentum is kg m/s.

   (ii) Since velocity is a vector quantity, **momentum is a vector quantity**, i.e. it has both magnitude and direction.

2 (i) **Newton's first law of motion** states:
   'a body continues in a state of rest or in a state of uniform motion in a straight line unless acted on by some external force'.
   Hence the momentum of a body remains the same provided no external forces act on it.

   (ii) **The principle of conservation of momentum** for a closed system (i.e. one on which no external forces act) may be stated as:
   'the total linear momentum of a system is a constant'.

   (iii) The total momentum of a system before collision in a given direction is equal to the total momentum of the system after collision in the same direction. In *Fig 1*, masses m_1 and m_2 are travelling in the same direction with velocity $u_1 > u_2$. A collision will occur, and applying the principle of conservation of momentum:
   total momentum before impact = total momentum after impact
   i.e. $m_1 u_1 + m_2 u_2 = m_1 v_1 + m_2 v_2$,
   where v_1 and v_2 are the velocities of m_1 and m_2 after impact.
   (See *Problems 1 to 7*.)

   Mass m_1 Mass m_2

   Fig 1

3 (i) **Newton's second law of motion** states:
   'the rate of change of momentum is directly proportional to the applied force producing the change, and takes place in the direction of this force'.
   In the SI system, the units are such that:
   the applied force = rate of change of momentum
   $$= \frac{\text{change of momentum}}{\text{time taken}} \qquad (1)$$

   (ii) When a force is suddenly applied to a body due to either a collision with another body or being hit by an object such as a hammer, the time taken in equation (1) is very small and difficult to measure. In such cases, the total effect of the force is measured by the change of momentum it produces.

(iii) Forces which act for very short periods of time are called **impulsive forces**. The product of the impulsive force and the time during which it acts is called the **impulse** of the force and is equal to the change of momentum produced by the impulsive force.

i.e. **impulse = applied force × time = change in linear momentum.**

(iv) Examples where impulsive forces occur include when a gun recoils and when a free-falling mass hits the ground. Solving problems associated with such occurrences often requires the use of the equation of motion: $v^2 = u^2 + 2as$.

4   When a pile is being hammered into the ground, the ground resists the movement of the pile and this resistance is called a **resistive force. Newton's third law of motion** may be stated as:

'for every force there is an equal and opposite force'.

The force applied to the pile is the resistive force. The pile exerts an equal and opposite force on the ground.

5   In practice, when impulsive forces occur, energy is not entirely conserved and some energy is changed into heat, noise, and so on.

B. WORKED PROBLEMS ON LINEAR MOMENTUM AND IMPULSE

Problem 1 Determine the momentum of a pile driver of mass 400 kg when it is moving downwards with a speed of 12 m/s.

Momentum = mass × velocity = 400 kg × 12 m/s
                                               = **4800 kg m/s downwards.**

Problem 2 A cricket ball of mass 150 g has a momentum of 4.5 kg m/s. Determine the velocity of the ball in km/h.

Momentum = mass × velocity

Hence velocity = $\dfrac{\text{momentum}}{\text{mass}}$ = $\dfrac{4.5 \text{ kg m/s}}{150 \times 10^{-3} \text{ kg}}$ = 30 m/s

30 m/s = 30 × 3.6 km/h = **108 km/h = velocity of cricket ball.**

Problem 3 Determine the momentum of a railway wagon of mass 50 tonnes moving at a velocity of 72 km/h.

Momentum = mass × velocity

Mass = 50 t = 50 000 kg (since 1 t = 1000 kg);

velocity = 72 km/h = $\dfrac{72}{3.6}$ m/s = 20 m/s

Hence **momentum** = 50 000 kg × 20 m/s = 1 000 000 kg m/s
                                                       = 10^6 **kg m/s.**

Problem 4 A wagon of mass 10 t is moving at a speed of 6 m/s and collides with another wagon of mass 15 t, which is stationary. After impact, the wagons are coupled together. Determine the common velocity of the wagons after impact.

Mass $m_1 = 10$ t $= 10\,000$ kg, $m_2 = 15\,000$ kg
Velocity $u_1 = 6$ m/s, $u_2 = 0$.
Total momentum before impact $= m_1\,u_1 + m_2\,u_2$
$$= (10\,000 \times 6) + (15\,000 \times 0) = 60\,000 \text{ kg m/s}$$
Let the common velocity of the wagons after impact be v m/s.
Since total momentum before impact = total momentum after impact
$$60\,000 = m_1\,v + m_2\,v$$
$$= v(m_1 + m_2) = v(25\,000)$$
$$\text{Hence } v = \frac{60\,000}{25\,000} = 2.4 \text{ m/s}$$
i.e. **the common velocity after impact is 2.4 m/s in the direction in which the 10 t wagon is initially travelling.**

Problem 5 A body has a mass of 30 g and is moving with a velocity of 20 m/s. It collides with a second body which has a mass of 20 g and which is moving with a velocity of 15 m/s. Assuming that the bodies both have the same velocity after impact, determine this common velocity, (a) when the initial velocities have the same line of action and the same sense, and (b) when the initial velocities have the same line of action but are opposite in sense.

Mass $m_1 = 30$ g $= 0.030$ kg, $m_2 = 20$ g $= 0.020$ kg, velocity $u_1 = 20$ m/s, $u_2 = 15$ m/s.
(a) When the velocities have the same line of action and the same sense, both u_1 and u_2 are considered as positive values.
Total momentum before impact $= m_1\,u_1 + m_2 u_2$
$$= (0.030 \times 20) + (0.020 \times 15) = 0.60 + 0.30$$
$$= 0.90 \text{ kg m/s.}$$
Let the common velocity after impact be v m/s.
Total momentum before impact = total momentum after impact
i.e. $\qquad\qquad 0.90 = m_1\,v + m_2\,v = v(m_1 + m_2)$
$\qquad\qquad 0.90 = v(0.030 + 0.020)$
from which, **common velocity**, $v = \dfrac{0.90}{0.050} = $ **18 m/s in the direction in which the bodies are initially travelling.**
(b) When the velocities have the same line of action but are opposite in sense, one is considered as positive and the other negative. Taking the direction of mass m_1 as positive gives:
velocity $u_1 = +20$ m/s and $u_2 = -15$ m/s.
Total momentum before impact $= m_1 u_1 + m_2 u_2$
$$= (0.030 \times 20) + (0.020 \times -15) = 0.60 - 0.30$$
$$= +0.30 \text{ kg m/s,}$$
and since it is positive this indicates a momentum in the same direction as that of mass m_1.
If the common velocity after impact is v m/s then
$$0.30 = v(m_1 + m_2) = v(0.050)$$
from which, **common velocity**, $v = \dfrac{0.30}{0.050} = $ **6 m/s in the direction that the 30 g mass is initially travelling.**

Problem 6 A ball of mass 50 g is moving with a velocity of 4 m/s when it strikes a stationary ball of mass 25 g. The velocity of the 50 g ball after impact is 2.5 m/s in the same direction as before impact. Determine the velocity of the 25 g ball after impact.

Mass m_1 = 50 g = 0.050 kg, m_2 = 25 g = 0.025 kg.
Initial velocity u_1 = 4 m/s, u_2 = 0; final velocity v_1 = 2.5 m/s, v_2 is unknown.
Total momentum before impact = $m_1 u_1 + m_2 u_2$
$$= (0.050 \times 4) + (0.025 \times 0) = 0.20 \text{ kg m/s}$$
Total momentum after impact = $m_1 v_1 + m_2 v_2$
$$= (0.050 \times 2.5) + (0.025 v_2)$$
$$= 0.125 + 0.025 v_2$$

Total momentum before impact = total momentum after impact
Hence $0.20 = 0.125 + 0.025 v_2$

from which, **velocity of 25 g ball after impact**, $v_2 = \dfrac{0.20 - 0.125}{0.025} = \textbf{3 m/s}$.

Problem 7 Three masses, P, Q and R lie in a straight line. P has a mass of 5 kg and is moving towards Q at 8 m/s. Q has a mass of 7 kg and a velocity of 4 m/s, and is moving towards R. Mass R is stationary. P collides with Q, and P and Q then collide with R. Determine the mass of R assuming all three masses have a common velocity of 2 m/s after the collision of P and Q with R.

Mass m_P = 5 kg, m_Q = 7 kg; Velocity u_P = 8 m/s, u_Q = 4 m/s.
Total momentum before P collides with Q = $m_P u_P + m_Q u_Q$
$$= (5 \times 8) + (7 \times 4) = 68 \text{ kg m/s}$$
Let P and Q have a common velocity of v_1 m/s after impact.
Total momentum after P and Q collide = $m_P v_1 + m_Q v_1$
$$= v_1 (m_P + m_Q) = 12 v_1$$
Total momentum before impact = total momentum after impact
i.e. $68 = 12 v_1$

from which, common velocity of P and Q, $v_1 = \dfrac{68}{72} = 5\dfrac{2}{3}$ m/s

Total momentum after P and Q collide with R = $(m_{P+Q} \times 2) + (m_R \times 2)$, since the common velocity after impact = 2 m/s
$$= (12 \times 2) + (2 m_R)$$
Total momentum before P and Q collide with R = total momentum after P and Q collide with R

i.e. $(m_{P+Q} \times 5\dfrac{2}{3}) = (12 \times 2) + 2m_R$

i.e. $12 \times 5\dfrac{2}{3} = 24 + 2m_R$

$68 - 24 = 2m_R$

from which, **mass of R**, $m_R = \dfrac{44}{2} = \textbf{22 kg}$.

121

Problem 8 The average force exerted on the workpiece of a press-tool operation is 150 kN, and the tool is in contact with the workpiece for 50 ms. Determine the change in momentum.

From para. 3(iii), change of linear momentum = applied force × time (= impulse)
Hence **change in momentum of workpiece** $= 150 \times 10^3 \text{N} \times 50 \times 10^{-3} \text{s}$
$$= 7500 \text{ kg m/s (since 1 N} = 1 \text{ kg m/s}^2)$$

Problem 9 A force of 15 N acts on a body of mass 4 kg for 0.2 s. Determine the change in velocity.

Impulse = applied force × time = change in linear momentum
    i.e. 15 N × 0.2 s   = mass × change in velocity
                             = 4 kg × change in velocity
from which, **change in velocity** $= \dfrac{15 \text{ N} \times 0.2 \text{ s}}{4 \text{ kg}} = $ **0.75 m/s**
                             (since 1 N = 1 kg m/s^2).

Problem 10 A mass of 8 kg is dropped vertically on to a fixed horizontal plane and has an impact velocity of 10 m/s. The mass rebounds with a velocity of 6 m/s. If the mass-plane contact time is 40 ms, calculate (a) the impulse, and (b) the average value of the impulsive force on the plane.

(a) **Impulse** = change in momentum
            $= m(u_1 - v_1)$, where u_1 = impact velocity = 10 m/s and
                         v_1 = rebound velocity = −6 m/s
                         (v_1 is negative since it acts in the opposite
                         direction to u_1)
            = 8 kg (10 − −6) m/s
            = 8 × 16 = **128 kg m/s**
(b) Impulsive force $= \dfrac{\text{impulse}}{\text{time}} = \dfrac{128 \text{ kg m/s}^2}{40 \times 10^{-3} \text{ s}} = $ **3200 N or 3.2 kN.**

Problem 11 The hammer of a pile driver of mass 1 t falls a distance of 1.5 m on to a pile. The blow takes place in 25 ms and the hammer does not rebound. Determine the average applied force exerted on the pile by the hammer.

Initial velocity $u = 0$, acceleration due to gravity, $g = 9.81$ m/s^2 and distance, $s = 1.5$ m.
Using the equation of motion $v^2 = u^2 + 2gs$
            then $v^2 = 0^2 + 2(9.81)(1.5)$
from which impact velocity, $v = \sqrt{[2(9.81)(1.5)]} = 5.425$ m/s
Neglecting the small distance moved by the pile and hammer after impact,
momentum lost by hammer = the change of momentum
                        $= mv = 1000$ kg × 5.425 m/s
Rate of change of momentum $= \dfrac{\text{change of momentum}}{\text{change of time}} = \dfrac{1000 \times 5.425}{25 \times 10^{-3}} = 217\,000$ N

Since the impulsive force is the rate of change of momentum, **the average force exerted on the pile is 217 kN.**

122

Problem 12 A mass of 40 g having a velocity of 15 m/s collides with a rigid surface and rebounds with a velocity of 5 m/s. The duration of the impact is 0.30 ms. Determine (a) the impulse, and (b) the impulsive force at the surface.

Mass m = 40 g = 0.040 kg, initial velocity, u = 15 m/s, final velocity v = −5 m/s (negative since the rebound is in the opposite direction to velocity u).

(a) Momentum before impact = mu = 0.040 × 15 = 0.6 kg m/s
    Momentum after impact = mv = 0.040 × −5 = −0.2 kg m/s
    Impulse = change of momentum = 0.6 − −0.2 = **0.8 kg m/s.**

(b) Impulsive force = $\dfrac{\text{change of momentum}}{\text{change of time}}$ = $\dfrac{0.8 \text{ kg m/s}}{0.20 \times 10^{-3}\text{s}}$ = **4000 N or 4 kN**

Problem 13 A gun of mass 1.5 t fires a shell of mass 15 kg horizontally with a velocity of 500 m/s. Determine (a) the initial velocity of recoil, and (b) the uniform force necessary to stop the recoil of the gun in 200 mm.

Mass of gun m_g = 1.5 t = 1500 kg; mass of shell m_s = 15 kg;
initial velocity of shell, u_s = 500 m/s.

(a) Momentum of shell = $m_s u_s$ = 15 × 500 = 7500 kg m/s
    Momentum of gun = $m_g\, v$ = 1500 v, where v = initial velocity of recoil of the gun
    By the principle of conservation of momentum,
    initial momentum = final momentum,
    i.e. 0 = 7500 + 1500 v
    from which, velocity v = $\dfrac{-7500}{1500}$ = −5 m/s (the negative sign indicating recoil velocity)
    i.e. **the initial velocity of recoil = 5 m/s.**

(b) The retardation of the recoil, a, may be determined using $v^2 = u^2 + 2\,as$, where v, the final velocity is zero, u, the initial velocity is 5 m/s and s, the distance, is 200 mm, i.e. 0.2 m
    Rearranging $v^2 = u^2 + 2\,as$ for a gives:
    $a = \dfrac{v^2 - u^2}{2\,s} = \dfrac{0^2 - 5^2}{2(0.2)} = \dfrac{-25}{0.4} = -62.5 \text{ m/s}^2$
    Force necessary to stop recoil in 200 mm = mass × acceleration
    $= 1500 \text{ kg} \times 62.5 \text{ m/s}^2$
    = **93750 N or 93.75 kN.**

Problem 14 A vertical pile of mass 100 kg is driven 200 mm into the ground by the blow of a 1 t hammer which falls through 750 mm. Determine (a) the velocity of the hammer just before impact, (b) the velocity immediately after impact (assuming the hammer does not bounce), and (c) the resistive force of the ground assuming it to be uniform.

(a) For the hammer, $v^2 = u^2 + 2\,gs$,
    where v = final velocity, u = initial velocity = 0, g = 9.81 m/s^2 and
          s = distance = 750 mm = 0.75 m
    Hence $v^2 = 0^2 + 2(9.81)(0.75)$,
    from which, **velocity of hammer just before impact,** $v = \sqrt{[2(9.81)(0.75)]}$
    = **3.84 m/s.**

(b) Momentum of hammer just before impact = mass × velocity

$$= 1000 \text{ kg} \times 3.84 \text{ m/s} = 3840 \text{ kg m/s}$$

Momentum of hammer and pile after impact = momentum of hammer before impact

Hence 3840 kg m/s = (mass of hammer and pile)(velocity immediately after impact)

i.e. $3840 = (1000 + 100)(v)$

from which, **velocity immediately after impact,** $v = \dfrac{3840}{1100}$ = **3.49 m/s**.

(c) Resistive force of ground = mass × acceleration

The acceleration is determined using $v^2 = u^2 + 2as$,

where v = final velocity = 0, u = initial velocity = 3.49 m/s and

s = distance driven in ground = 200 mm = 0.2 m

Hence $0^2 = (3.49)^2 + 2(a)(0.2)$

from which, acceleration $a = \dfrac{-(3.49)^2}{2(0.2)}$ = -30.45 m/s^2

Thus resistive force of ground = mass × acceleration = 1100 kg × 30.45 m/s²

$$= \textbf{33.5 kN.}$$

C. FURTHER PROBLEMS ON LINEAR MOMENTUM AND IMPULSE

(a) SHORT ANSWER PROBLEMS

1   Define momentum.
2   State the principle of the conservation of momentum.
3   Define impulse.
4   What is meant by an impulsive force?

(b) MULTI-CHOICE PROBLEMS (answers on page 157)

1   A mass of 100 g has a momentum of 100 kg m/s. The velocity of the mass is:
   (a) 10 m/s;   (b) 10^2 m/s;   (c) 10^{-3} m/s;   (d) 10^3 m/s.

2   A rifle bullet has a mass of 50 g. The momentum when the muzzle velocity is 108 km/h is:
   (a) 54 kg m/s;   (b) 1.5 kg m/s;   (c) 15000 kg m/s; (d) 21.6 kg m/s.

A body P of mass 10 kg has a velocity of 5 m/s and the same line of action as a body Q of mass 2 kg and having a velocity of 25 m/s. The bodies collide, and their velocities are the same after impact. In *Problems 3 to 6*, select the correct answer from the following:

(a) $\dfrac{25}{3}$ m/s;   (b) 360 kg m/s;   (c) 0;   (d) 30 m/s;   (e) 160 kg m/s;

(f) 100 kg m/s;   (g) 20 m/s.

3   Determine the total momentum of the system before impact when P and Q have the same sense.
4   Determine the total momentum of the system before impact when P and Q have the opposite sense.

124

5 Determine the velocity of P and Q after impact if their sense is the same before impact.

6 Determine the velocity of P and Q after impact if their sense is opposite before impact.

7 A force of 100 N acts on a body of mass 10 kg for 0.1 s. The change in velocity of the body is:
(a) 1 m/s; (b) 100 m/s; (c) 0.1 m/s; (d) 0.01 m/s.

A vertical pile of mass 200 kg is driven 100 mm into the ground by the blow of a 1 t hammer which falls through 1.25 m. In *Problems 8 to 12*, take g as 10 m/s^2 and select the correct answer from the following:

(a) 25 m/s; (b) $\frac{25}{6}$ m/s; (c) 5 kg m/s; (d) 0; (e) $\frac{625}{6}$ kN; (f) 5000 kg m/s;

(g) 5 m/s; (h) 12 kN.

8 Calculate the velocity of the hammer immediately before impact.

9 Calculate the momentum of the hammer just before impact.

10 Calculate the momentum of the hammer and pile immediately after impact assuming they have the same velocity.

11 Calculate the velocity of the hammer and pile immediately after impact assuming they have the same velocity.

12 Calculate the resistive force of the ground, assuming it to be uniform.

(c) CONVENTIONAL PROBLEMS

(Where necessary, take g as 9.81 m/s^2.)

1 Determine the momentum in a mass of 50 kg having a velocity of 5 m/s.
[250 kg m/s]

2 A milling machine and its component have a combined mass of 400 kg. Determine the momentum of the table and component when the feed rate is 360 mm/min.
[2.4 kg m/s]

3 The momentum of a body is 160 kg m/s when the velocity is 2.5 m/s. Determine the mass of the body.
[64 kg]

4 Calculate the momentum of a car of mass 750 kg moving at a constant velocity of 108 km/h.
[22 500 kg m/s]

5 A football of mass 200 g has a momentum of 5 kg m/s. What is the velocity of the ball in km/h.
[90 km/h]

6 A wagon of mass 8 t is moving at a speed of 5 m/s and collides into another wagon of mass 12 t, which is stationary. After impact, the wagons are coupled together. Determine the common velocity of the wagons after impact.
[2 m/s]

7 A ball of mass 40 g is moving with a velocity of 5 m/s when it strikes a stationary ball of mass 30 g. The velocity of the 40 g ball after impact is 4 m/s in the same direction as before impact. Determine the velocity of the 30 g ball after impact.
[$1\frac{1}{3}$ m/s]

8 A car of mass 800 kg was stationary when hit head on by a lorry of mass 2000 kg

travelling at 15 m/s. Assuming no brakes are applied and the car and lorry move as one, determine the speed of the wreckage immediately after collision.

[10.71 m/s]

9 A body has a mass of 25 g and is moving with a velocity of 30 m/s. It collides with a second body which has a mass of 15 g and which is moving with a velocity of 20 m/s. Assuming that the bodies both have the same speed after impact, determine their common velocity (a) when the speeds have the same line of action and the same sense, and (b) when the speeds have the same line of action but are opposite in sense.

$[(a) \ 26\frac{1}{4} \ m/s; \ (b) \ 11\frac{1}{4} \ m/s]$

10 Three masses, X, Y and Z lie in a straight line. X has a mass of 15 kg and is moving towards Y at 20 m/s. Y has a mass of 10 kg and a velocity of 5 m/s and is moving towards Z. Mass Z is stationary. X collides with Y and X and Y then collide with Z. Determine the mass of Z assuming all three masses have a common velocity of 4 m/s after the collision of X and Y with Z.

[62.5 kg]

11 The sliding member of a machine tool has a mass of 200 kg. Determine the change in momentum when the sliding speed is increased from 10 mm/s to 50 mm/s.

[8 kg m/s]

12 A force of 48 N acts on a body of mass 8 kg for 0.25 s. Determine the change in velocity.

[1.5 m/s]

13 In a press-tool operation, the tool is in contact with the workpiece for 40 ms. If the average force exerted on the workpiece is 90 kN, determine the change in momentum.

[3600 kg m/s]

14 The speed of a car of mass 800 kg is increased from 54 km/h to 63 km/h in 2 s. Determine the average force in the direction of motion necessary to produce the change in speed.

[1000 N]

15 A 10 kg mass is dropped vertically on to a fixed horizontal plane and has an impact velocity of 15 m/s. The mass rebounds with a velocity of 5 m/s. If the contact time of mass and plane is 0.025 s, calculate (a) the impulse, and (b) the average value of the impulsive force on the plane.

[(a) 200 kg m/s; (b) 8 kN]

16 The hammer of a pile driver of mass 1.2 t falls 1.4 m on to a pile. The blow takes place in 20 ms and the hammer does not rebound. Determine the average applied force exerted on the pile by the hammer.

[314.5 kN]

17 A tennis ball of mass 60 g is struck from rest with a racket. The contact time of ball on racket is 10 ms and the ball leaves the racket with a velocity of 25 m/s. Calculate (a) the impulse, and (b) the average force exerted by a racket on the ball.

[(a) 1.5 kg m/s; (b) 150 N]

18 A gun of mass 1.2 t fires a shell of mass 12 kg with a velocity of 400 m/s. Determine (a) the initial velocity of recoil, and (b) the uniform force necessary to stop the recoil of the gun in 150 mm.

[(a) 4 m/s; (b) 64 kN]

19 In making a steel stamping, a mass of 100 kg falls on to the steel through a distance of 1.5 m and is brought to rest after moving through a further distance of 15 mm. Determine the magnitude of the resisting force, assuming a uniform resistive force is exerted by the steel.

[98.1 kN]

20 A vertical pile of mass 150 kg is driven 120 mm into the ground by the blow of a 1.1 t hammer which falls through 800 mm. Assuming the hammer and pile remain in contact, determine (a) the velocity of the hammer just before impact, (b) the velocity immediately after impact, and (c) the resistive force of the ground, assuming it to be uniform.

[(a) 3.96 m/s; (b) 3.48 m/s; (c) 63.08 kN]

11 Work and energy

A. MAIN POINTS CONCERNED WITH WORK AND ENERGY

1 (i) If a body moves as a result of a force being applied to it, the force is said to do **work** on the body. The amount of work done is the product of the applied force and the distance, i.e.
Work done = force × distance moved in the direction of the force
(ii) The unit of work is the **joule, J** which is defined as the amount of work done when a force of 1 newton acts for a distance of 1 metre in the direction of the force. Thus 1 J = 1 N m.

2 If a graph is plotted of experimental values of force (on the vertical axis) against distance moved (on the horizontal axis) a force-distance graph or work diagram is produced. **The area under the graph represents the work done.**
For example, a constant force of 20 N used to raise a load a height of 8 m may be

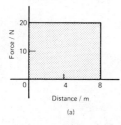

(a)

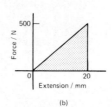

(b)

Fig 1

represented on a force-distance graph as shown in *Fig 1(a)*. The area under the graph shown shaded, represents the work done.
Hence work done = 20 N × 8 m = **160 J**
Similarly, a spring extended by 20 mm by a force of 500 N may be represented by the work diagram shown in *Fig 1(b)*.

Work done = shaded area = $\frac{1}{2}$ × base × height = $\frac{1}{2}$ × (20×10^{-3})m × 500 N = **5J**

The work done by a variable force may be found by determining the area enclosed by the force-distance graph using the trapezoidal rule, the mid-ordinate rule or Simpson's rule.

3 **Energy** is the capacity, or ability, to do work. The unit of energy is the joule, the same as for work. Energy is expended when work is done. There are several forms

128

of energy, and these include mechanical, heat, electrical, chemical, nuclear, light and sound energy.

4   **Efficiency** is defined as the ratio of the useful output energy to the input energy. The symbol for efficiency is η (Greek letter eta).

Hence, **efficiency**, $\eta = \dfrac{\textbf{useful output energy}}{\textbf{input energy}}$

Efficiency has no units and is often stated as a percentage. A perfect machine would have an efficiency of 100%. However, all machines have an efficiency lower than this due to friction and other losses. Thus, if the input energy to a motor is 1000 J and the output energy is 800 J then the efficiency is $\dfrac{800}{1000} \times 100$, i.e. 80%. (see *Problems 1 to 11*).

3   **Power** is a measure of the rate at which work is done or at which energy is converted from one form to another.

Power $P = \dfrac{\textbf{energy used}}{\textbf{time taken}}$ (or $P = \dfrac{\textbf{work done}}{\textbf{time taken}}$)

The unit of power is the **watt**, W, where 1 watt is equal to 1 joule per second. The watt is a small unit for many purposes and a larger unit called the kilowatt, kW, is used, where 1 kW = 1000 W. The power output of a motor which does 120 kJ of work in 30 s is thus given by $P = \dfrac{120\ kJ}{30\ s} = 4\ kW$.

6   Since work done = force $\times$ distance, then

Power $= \dfrac{\text{work done}}{\text{time taken}} = \dfrac{\text{force} \times \text{distance}}{\text{time taken}} = \text{force} \times \dfrac{\text{distance}}{\text{time taken}}$

However, $\dfrac{\text{distance}}{\text{time taken}} = \text{velocity}$.

Hence **power = force $\times$ velocity**. (see *Problems 12 to 20*).

7   (i) Mechanical engineering is concerned principally with two kinds of energy, potential energy and kinetic energy.

(ii) **Potential energy** is energy due to the position of a body. The force exerted on a mass of m kg is mg N (where $g = 9.81$ N/kg, the earth's gravitational field. When the mass is lifted vertically through a height h m above some datum level, the work done is given by: force $\times$ distance $= (mg)(h)$ J. This work done is stored as potential energy in the mass.

Hence **potential energy $= mgh$ joules** (the potential energy at the datum level being taken as zero).

(iii) **Kinetic energy** is the energy due to the motion of a body.

Suppose a resultant force F acts on an object of mass m originally at rest, and accelerates it to a velocity v in a distance s.

Work done = force $\times$ distance $= F s$

$\qquad\qquad\qquad\qquad\qquad = (ma)(s)$, where a is the acceleration.

acceleration.

However $v^2 = 2a\ s$, from which $a = \dfrac{v^2}{2s}$

Hence work done $= m \left(\dfrac{v^2}{2s}\right) s = \dfrac{1}{2}\ m\ v^2$

This energy is called the kinetic energy of the mass m.

i.e. **kinetic energy** $= \dfrac{1}{2} m\ v^2$ **joules**

8 (i) Energy may be converted from one form to another. **The principle of conservation of energy** states that the total amount of energy remains the same in such conversions, i.e. energy cannot be created or destroyed.

(ii) In mechanics, the potential energy possessed by a body is frequently converted into kinetic energy, and vice versa. When a mass is falling freely, its potential energy decreases as it loses height, and its kinetic energy increases as its velocity increases. Ignoring air frictional losses, at all times:

potential energy + kinetic energy = a constant

(iii) If friction is present, then work is done overcoming the resistance due to friction and this is dissipated as heat. Then,

Initial energy = final energy + work done overcoming frictional resistance
(see *Problems 21 to 26*).

B. WORKED PROBLEMS ON WORK AND ENERGY

Problem 1 Calculate the work done when a mass is lifted vertically by a crane to a height of 5 m, the weight of the mass being 75 N.

When work is done in lifting then:
Work done = (weight of the body) × (vertical distance moved)
Weight is the downward force due to the mass of an object.
Hence **work done** = 75 N × 5 m = **375 J**

Problem 2 A motor supplies a constant force of 1 kN which is used to move a load a distance of 5 m. The force is then changed to a constant 500 N and the load is moved a further 15 m. Draw the force-distance graph for the operation and from the graph determine the total work done by the motor.

The force-distance graph or work diagram is shown in *Fig 2*.
Between points A and B a constant force of 1000 N moves the load 5 m.
Between points C and D a constant force of 500 N moves the load from 5 m to 20 m.
Total work done
= area under the force-distance graph
= area ABFE + area CDGF
= (1000 N × 5 m) + (500 N × 15 m)
= 5000 J + 7500 J = 12 500 J = **12.5 kJ**

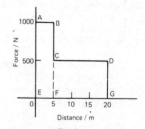

Fig 2

Problem 3 A spring initially in a relaxed state is extended by 100 mm. Determine the work done by using a work diagram if the spring requires a force of 0.6 N per mm of stretch.

Force required for a 100 mm extension = 100 mm × 0.6 N mm^{-1} = 60 N.
Fig 3 shows the force-extension graph or work diagram representing the

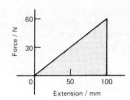

Fig 3

increase in extension in proportion to the force, as the force is increased from 0 to 60 N. The work done is the area under the graph (shown shaded).

Hence: **Work done** $= \frac{1}{2} \times$ base $\times$ height $= \frac{1}{2} \times 100$ mm $\times 60$ N

$$= \frac{1}{2} \times 100 \times 10^{-3} \text{ m} \times 60 \text{ N} = \textbf{3 J}$$

(Alternatively, average force during extension $= \dfrac{60 - 0}{2} = 30$ N and total

extension $= 100$ mm $= 0.1$ m.

Hence **work done** $=$ average force $\times$ extension $= 30$ N $\times 0.1$ m $= \textbf{3 J}$)

Problem 4 A spring requires a force of 10 N to cause an extension of 50 mm. Determine the work done in extending the spring (a) from zero to 30 mm, and (b) from 30 mm to 50 mm.

Fig 4 shows the force-extension graph for the spring.

(a) Work done in extending the spring from zero to 30 mm is given by area ABO of *Fig 4*, i.e.

Work done $= \dfrac{\text{base} \times \text{height}}{2}$

$= \dfrac{30 \times 10^{-3}}{2}$ m $\times 6$ N

$= 90 \times 10^{-3}$ J $= \textbf{0.09J}$

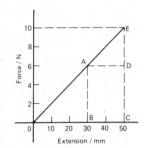

(b) Work done in extending the spring from 30 mm to 50 mm is given by area ABCE of *Fig 4*, i.e.

Work done

$=$ area ABCD $+$ area ADE

$= (20 \times 10^{-3} \text{ m} \times 6 \text{ N}) + \dfrac{1}{2} (20 \times 10^{-3} \text{ m})(4\text{N})$

$= 0.12$ J $+ 0.04$ J $= \textbf{0.16 J}$

Fig 4

Problem 5 Calculate the work done when a mass of 20 kg is lifted vertically through a distance of 5.0 m.

The force to be overcome when lifting a mass vertically upwards is *mg*.
i.e. $20 \times 9.81 = 196.2$ N
Work done $=$ force $\times$ distance $= 196.2 \times 5.0 = \textbf{981 J}$

Problem 6 Water is pumped vertically upwards through a distance of 50.0 m and the work done is 294.3 kJ. Determine the number of litres of water pumped. (1 litre of water has a mass of 1 kg.)

Work done = force × distance, i.e. 294 300 = force × 50.0, from which

force = $\dfrac{294\,300}{50.0}$ = 5886 N

The force to be overcome when lifting a mass m kg vertically upwards is mg, i.e., $(m \times 9.81)$ N

Thus 5886 = m × 9.81, from which mass m = $\dfrac{5886}{9.81}$ = 600 kg

Since 1 litre of water has a mass of 1 kg, **600 litres of water are pumped**

Problem 7 The force on the cutting tool of a shaping machine varies over the length of cut as follows:

distance (mm)	0	20	40	60	80	100
force (kN)	60	72	65	53	44	50

Determine the work done as the tool moves through a distance of 100 mm.

The force-distance graph for the given data is shown in *Fig 5*. The work done is

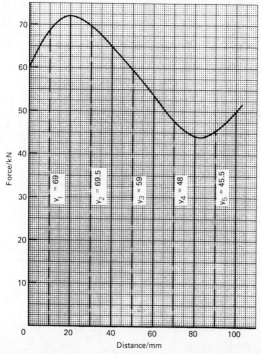

Fig 5

132

given by the area under the force-distance graph. This area may be determined by an approximate method.

Using the mid-ordinate rule, with each strip of width 20 mm, mid-ordinates are erected as shown, y_1, y_2, y_3, y_4 and y_5 and each is measured.

Area under curve = (width of each strip)(sum of mid-ordinate values)

= $(20)(69 + 69.5 + 59 + 48 + 45.5) = (20)(291)$

= 5820 kN mm = 5820 N m = 5820 J

Hence the work done as the tool moves through 100 mm is 5.82 kJ

Problem 8 A machine exerts a force of 200 N in lifting a mass through a height of 6 m. If 2 kJ of energy are supplied to it, what is the efficiency of the machine?

Work done in lifting mass = force X distance moved

= weight of body X distance moved

= 200 N X 6 m = 1200 J = useful energy output

Energy input = 2 kJ = 2000 J

Efficiency, $\eta = \dfrac{\text{useful output energy}}{\text{input energy}} = \dfrac{1200}{2000} = \textbf{0.6 or 60\%}$

Problem 9 Calculate the useful output energy of an electric motor which is 70% efficient if it uses 600 J of electrical energy.

Efficiency, $\eta = \dfrac{\text{useful output energy}}{\text{input energy}}$, thus $\dfrac{70}{100} = \dfrac{\text{output energy}}{600 \text{ J}}$

from which, **output energy** $= \dfrac{70}{100} \times 600 = \textbf{420 J}$

Problem 10 4 kJ of energy are supplied to a machine used for lifting a mass. The force required is 800 N. If the machine has an efficiency of 50%, to what height will it lift the mass?

Efficiency, $\eta = \dfrac{\text{output energy}}{\text{input energy}}$, i.e. $\dfrac{50}{100} = \dfrac{\text{output energy}}{4000 \text{ J}}$

from which, output energy $= \dfrac{50}{100} \times 4000 = 2000$ J

Work done = force X distance moved, hence 2000 J = 800 N X height

from which, **height** $= \dfrac{2000 \text{ J}}{800 \text{ N}} = \textbf{2.5 m}$

Problem 11 A hoist exerts a force of 500 N in raising a load through a height of 20 m. The efficiency of the hoist gears is 75% and the efficiency of the motor is 80%. Calculate the input energy to the hoist.

The hoist system is shown diagrammatically in *Fig 6*.

Output energy = work done = force X distance = 500 N X 20 m = 10 000 J

For the gearing, efficiency $= \dfrac{\text{output energy}}{\text{input energy}}$, i.e. $\dfrac{75}{100} = \dfrac{10\,000}{\text{input energy}}$

from which, the input energy to the gears = $10\,000 \times \dfrac{100}{75} = 13\,333$ J

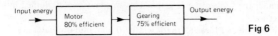

Input energy → Motor 80% efficient → Gearing 75% efficient → Output energy

Fig 6

The input energy to the gears is the same as the output energy of the motor.
Thus, for the motor, efficiency = $\dfrac{\text{output energy}}{\text{input energy}}$, i.e. $\dfrac{80}{100} = \dfrac{13\,333}{\text{input energy}}$

Hence the input energy to the system = $13\,333 \times \dfrac{100}{80}$ = 16 670 J = **16.67 kJ**

Problem 12 The output power of a motor is 8 kW. How much work does it do in 30 s?

Power = $\dfrac{\text{work done}}{\text{time taken}}$, from which
work done = power $\times$ time = 8000 W $\times$ 30 s = 240 000 J = **240 kJ**

Problem 13 Calculate the power required to lift a mass through a height of 10 m in 20 s if the force required is 3924 N.

Work done = force $\times$ distance moved = 3924 N $\times$ 10 m = 39 240 J
Power = $\dfrac{\text{work done}}{\text{time taken}} = \dfrac{39\,240 \text{ J}}{20 \text{ s}}$ = **1962 W or 1.962 kW**

Problem 14 10 kJ of work is done by a force in moving a body uniformly through 125 m in 50 s. Determine (a) the value of the force; (b) the power.

(a) Work done = force $\times$ distance, hence 10 000 J = force $\times$ 125 m,

from which **force** = $\dfrac{10\,000 \text{ J}}{125 \text{ m}}$ = **80 N**

(b) **Power** = $\dfrac{\text{work done}}{\text{time taken}} = \dfrac{10\,000 \text{ J}}{50 \text{ s}}$ = **200 W**

Problem 15 A car hauls a trailer at 90 km h^{-1} when exerting a steady pull of 600 N. Calculate (a) the work done in 30 minutes; (b) the power required.

(a) Work done = force $\times$ distance moved

Distance moved in 30 min, i.e. $\dfrac{1}{2}$ h, at 90 km h^{-1} = 45 km

Hence **work done** = 600 N $\times$ 45 000 m = **27 000 kJ or 27 MJ**

(b) **Power** required = $\dfrac{\text{work done}}{\text{time taken}} = \dfrac{27 \times 10^6 \text{ J}}{30 \times 60 \text{ s}}$ = **15 000 W or 15 kW**

Problem 16 To what height will a mass of weight 981 N be raised in 40 s by a machine using a power of 2 kW?

Work done = force $\times$ distance, hence work done = 981 N $\times$ height

134

$Power = \dfrac{work\ done}{time\ taken}$, or work done = power × time taken

$= 2000\ W \times 40\ s = 80\ 000\ J$

Hence 80 000 = 981 N × height, from which **height** $= \dfrac{80\ 000\ J}{981\ N}$ = **81.55 m**

Problem 17 A planing machine has a cutting stroke of 2 m and the stroke takes 4 seconds. If the constant resistance to the cutting tool is 900 N, calculate for each cutting stroke (a) the power consumed at the tool point; (b) the power input to the system if the efficiency of the system is 75%.

(a) Work done in each cutting stroke = force × distance = 900 N × 2 m = 1800 J

Power consumed at tool point $= \dfrac{work\ done}{time\ taken} = \dfrac{1800\ J}{4\ s}$ = **450 W**

(b) Efficiency = $\dfrac{output\ energy}{input\ energy} = \dfrac{output\ power}{input\ power}$

Hence $\dfrac{75}{100} = \dfrac{450}{input\ power}$, from which **input power** $= 450 \times \dfrac{100}{75}$ = **600 W**

Problem 18 An electric motor provides power to a winding machine. The input power to the motor is 2.5 kW and the overall efficiency is 60%. Calculate (a) the output power of the machine; (b) the rate at which it can raise a 300 kg load vertically upwards.

(a) Efficiency, $\eta = \dfrac{power\ output}{power\ input}$, i.e. $\dfrac{60}{100} = \dfrac{power\ output}{2500}$

from which **power output** $= \dfrac{60}{100} \times 2500$ = **1500 W**

(b) Power output = force × velocity, from which, velocity $= \dfrac{power\ output}{force}$

Force acting on the 300 kg load due to gravity = 300 kg × 9.81 m/s = 2943 N

Hence **velocity** $= \dfrac{1500}{2943}$ = **0.510 m/s or 510 mm/s**

Problem 19 A lorry is travelling at a constant speed of 72 km/h. The force resisting motion is 800 N. Calculate the tractive power necessary to keep the lorry moving at this speed.

Power = force × velocity

The force necessary to keep the lorry moving at constant speed is equal and opposite to the force resisting motion, i.e. 800 N

Velocity = 72 km/h $= \dfrac{72}{3.6}$ m/s = 20 m/s

Hence power = 800 N × 20 m/s = 16 000 N m/s = 16 000 J/s = 16 000 W or 16 kW
Thus the tractive power needed to keep the lorry moving at a constant speed of 72 km/h is 16 kW

Problem 20 The variation of tractive force with distance for a vehicle which is accelerating from rest is:

force (kN)	8.0	7.4	5.8	4.5	3.7	3.0
distance (m)	0	10	20	30	40	50

Determine the average power necessary if the time taken to travel the 50 m from rest is 25 s.

The force-distance diagram is shown in *Fig 7*.

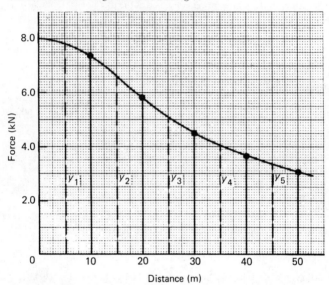

Fig 7

The work done is determined from the area under the curve. Using the mid-ordinate rule with 5 intervals gives:

area = (width of interval) (sum of mid-ordinate)
$$= (10)(y_1 + y_2 + y_3 + y_4 + y_5) = 10(7.8 + 6.6 + 5.1 + 4.0 + 3.3)$$
$$= 10(26.8) = 268 \text{ kN m, i.e. work done} = 268 \text{ kJ}$$

Average power = $\dfrac{\text{work done}}{\text{time taken}}$ = $\dfrac{268\,000\text{J}}{25 \text{ s}}$ = **10720 W or 10.72 kW**

Problem 21 A car of mass 800 kg is climbing an incline at 10° to the horizontal. Determine the increase in potential energy of the car as it moves a distance of 50 m up the incline.

With reference to *Fig 8*, $\sin 10° = \dfrac{h}{50}$,

from which, $h = 50 \sin 10° = 8.682$ m   **Fig 8**

Hence

increase in potential energy

= mgh = 800 kg × 9.81 m/s² × 8.682 m = **68 140 J or 68.14 kJ**

136

Problem 22 At the instant of striking, a hammer of mass 30 kg has a velocity of 15 m/s. Determine the kinetic energy in the hammer.

Kinetic energy = $\frac{1}{2}m\,v^2 = \frac{1}{2}(30 \text{ kg})(15 \text{ m/s})^2$

i.e. **kinetic energy in hammer = 3375 J**

Problem 23 A lorry having a mass of 1.5 t is travelling along a level road at 72 km/h. When the brakes are applied, the speed decreases to 18 km/h. Determine how much the kinetic energy of the lorry is reduced.

Initial velocity of lorry v_1 = 72 km/h = $72\frac{\text{km}}{\text{h}} \times 1000\frac{\text{m}}{\text{km}} \times \frac{1\text{ h}}{3600\text{ s}} = \frac{72}{3.6}$

$\qquad\qquad = 20$ m/s

Final velocity of lorry $v_2 = \frac{18}{3.6} = 5$ m/s

Mass of lorry, m = 1.5 t = 1500 kg

Initial kinetic energy of the lorry = $\frac{1}{2}mv_1^{\,2} = \frac{1}{2}(1500)(20)^2 = 300$ kJ

Final kinetic energy of the lorry = $\frac{1}{2}mv_2^{\,2} = \frac{1}{2}(1500)(5)^2 = 18.75$ kJ

Hence the change in kinetic energy = 300 − 18.75 = 281.25 kJ
(Part of this reduction in kinetic energy is converted into heat energy in the brakes of the lorry and is hence dissipated in overcoming frictional forces and air friction.)

Problem 24 A canister containing a meteorology balloon of mass 4 kg is fired vertically upwards from a gun with an initial velocity of 400 m/s. Neglecting the air resistance, calculate (a) its initial kinetic energy; (b) its velocity at a height of 1 km; (c) the maximum height reached.

(a) **Initial kinetic energy** = $\frac{1}{2}m\,v^2 = \frac{1}{2}(4)(400)^2 = $ **320 kJ**

(b) At a height of 1 km, potential energy = mgh = 4 × 9.81 × 1000 = 39.42 kJ
    By the principle of conservation of energy:
    Potential energy + kinetic energy at 1 km = initial kinetic energy

    Hence 39 240 + $\frac{1}{2}mv^2$ = 320 000

    from which, $\frac{1}{2}(4)\,v^2$ = 320 000 − 39 240 = 280 760

    Hence $v = \sqrt{\left(\frac{2 \times 280\,760}{4}\right)} = 374.7$ m/s

    i.e. the velocity of the cannister at a height of 1 km is 374.7 m/s

(c) At the maximum height, the velocity of the canister is zero and all the kinetic energy has been converted into potential energy.

    Hence potential energy = initial kinetic energy = 320 000 J, from part (a).

    Then 320 000 = mgh = (4)(9.81)h, or height $h = \frac{320\,000}{(4)(9.81)} = 8155$ m,

    i.e. the maximum height reached is 8155 m

Problem 25 A car of mass 600 kg reduces speed from 90 km/h to 54 km/h in 15 s. Determine the braking power required to give this change of speed.

Change in kinetic energy of car $= \frac{1}{2}mv_1{}^2 - \frac{1}{2}mv_2{}^2$,

where m = mass of car = 600 kg

v_1 = initial velocity = 90 km/h = $\frac{90}{3.6}$ m/s = 25 m/s

v_2 = final velocity = 54 km/h = $\frac{54}{3.6}$ m/s = 15 m/s.

Hence change in kinetic energy $= \frac{1}{2}m(v_1{}^2 - v_2{}^2)$

$$= \frac{1}{2}(600)(25^2 - 15^2) = 120\,000 \text{ J}$$

Braking power $= \dfrac{\text{change in energy}}{\text{time taken}} = \dfrac{120\,000 \text{ J}}{15 \text{ s}} = $ **8000 W or 8 kW**

Problem 26 A pile-driver of mass 500 kg falls freely through a height of 1.5 m on to a pile of mass 200 kg. Determine the velocity with which the driver hits the pile. If, at impact, 2.10 kJ of energy are lost due to heat and sound, the remaining energy being possessed by the pile and driver as they are driven together into the ground a distance of 200 mm, determine (a) the common velocity immediately after impact; (b) the average resistance of the ground.

The potential energy of the pile driver is converted into kinetic energy,

thus loss in potential energy = gain in kinetic energy, i.e. $mgh = \frac{1}{2}mv^2$

from which, velocity $v = \sqrt{(2gh)} = \sqrt{[(2)(9.81)(1.5)]} = 5.42$ m/s

Hence the pile driver hits the pile at a velocity of 5.42 m/s

(a) Before impact, kinetic energy of pile driver $= \frac{1}{2}mv^2 = \frac{1}{2}(500)(5.42)^2 = 7.34$ kJ

Kinetic energy after impact = 7.34 − 2.10 = 5.24 kJ

Thus the pile driver and pile together have a mass of 500 + 200 = 700 kg and possess kinetic enrgy of 5.24 kJ

Hence $5.24 \times 10^3 = \frac{1}{2}mv^2 = \frac{1}{2}(700)v^2$

from which, velocity $v = \sqrt{\left(\dfrac{2 \times 5.24 \times 10^3}{700}\right)} = 3.87$ m/s

Thus the common velocity after impact is 3.87 m/s

(b) The kinetic energy after impact is absorbed in overcoming the resistance of the ground, in a distance of 200 mm.

Kinetic energy = work done = resistance × distance

i.e. 5.24×10^3 = resistance × 0.200

from which, resistance $= \dfrac{5.24 \times 10^3}{0.200} = 26\,200$ N

Hence the average resistance of the ground is 26.2 kN

C. FURTHER PROBLEMS ON WORK AND ENERGY

(a) SHORT ANSWER PROBLEMS

1 Define work in terms of force applied and distance moved.
2 Define energy, and state its unit.
3 Define the joule.
4 The area under a force-distance graph represents . . . .
5 Name five forms of energy.
6 (a) Define efficiency in terms of energy input and energy output.
  (b) State the symbol used for efficiency.
7 Define power and state its unit.
8 Define potential energy.
9 The change in potential energy of a body of mass m kg when lifted vertically
  upwards to a height h m is given by . . . .
10 What is kinetic energy?
11 The kinetic energy of a body of mass m kg and moving at a velocity of v m/s is
  given by . . . .
12 State the principle of conservation of energy.

(b) MULTI-CHOICE PROBLEMS (answers on page 157)

1 An object is lifted 2000 mm by a crane. If the force required is 100 N, the work
  done is:

  (a) $\frac{1}{20}$ N; (b) 200 kN; (c) 200 N; (d) 20 N.

2 A motor having an efficiency of 0.8 uses 800 J of electrical energy. The output
  energy of the motor is:
  (a) 800 J; (b) 1000 J; (c) 640 J.

3 6 kJ of work is done by a force in moving an object uniformly though 120 m in
  1 minute. The force applied is:
  (a) 50 N; (b) 20 N; (c) 720 N; (d) 12 N.

4 For the object in *Problem 3*, the power developed is:

  (a) 6 kW; (b) 12 kW; (c) $\frac{5}{6}$ W; (d) 0.1 kW.

5 State which of the following is incorrect.

  (a) $1 \text{ W} = 1 \text{ J s}^{-1}$;

  (b) $1 \text{ J} = 1 \text{ N/m}$;

  (c) $\eta = \frac{\text{output energy}}{\text{input energy}}$;

  (d) energy = power × time

6 Which of the following statements is false?
  (a) The unit of energy and work is the same.
  (b) The area under a force-distance graph gives the work done.
  (c) Electrical energy is converted to mechanical energy by a generator.
  (d) Efficiency is the ratio of the useful output energy to the input energy.

7   A machine using a power of 1 kW requires a force of 100 N to raise a mass in 10 s.
    The height the mass is raised in this time is:
    (a) 100 m; (b) 1 km; (c) 10 m; (d) 1 m.

8   A force-extension graph for a spring
    is shown in *Fig 9*.
    Which of the following statements
    is false?
    The work done in extending the spring:
    (a) from 0 to 100 mm is 5 N;
    (b) from 0 to 50 mm is 1.25 N;
    (c) from 20 mm to 60 mm is 1.6 N;   **Fig 9**
    (d) from 60 mm to 100 mm is 3.75 N.

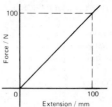

9   A vehicle of mass 1 tonne climbs an incline of 30° to the horizontal. Taking the
    acceleration due to gravity as 10 m/s², the increase in potential energy of the
    vehicle as it moves a distance of 200 m up the incline is:
    (a) 1 kJ; (b) 2 MJ; (c) 1 MJ; (d) 2 kJ.

10 A bullet of mass 100 g is fired from a gun with an initial velocity of 360 km/h.
    Neglecting air resistance, the initial kinetic energy possessed by the bullet is:
    (a) 6.48 kJ; (b) 500 J; (c) 500 kJ; (d) 6.48 MJ.

(c) CONVENTIONAL PROBLEMS

    (Where necessary, take g as 9.81 m/s²)

1   Determine the work done when a force of 50 N pushes an object 1.5 km in the
    same direction as the force.

                                                                        [75 kJ]

2   Calculate the work done when a mass of weight 200 N is lifted vertically by a crane
    to a height of 100 m.

                                                                        [20 kJ]

3   A motor supplies a constant force of 2 kN to move a load 10 m. The force is then
    changed to a constant 1.5 kN and the load is moved a further 20 m. Draw the
    force-distance graph for the complete operation, and, from the graph, determine
    the total work done by the motor.

                                                                        [50 kJ]

4   A spring, initially relaxed, is extended 80 mm. Draw a work diagram and hence
    determine the work done if the spring requires a force of 0.5 N/mm of stretch.

                                                                        [1.6 J]

5   A spring requires a force of 50 N to cause an extension of 100 mm. Determine the
    work done in extending the spring (a) from 0 to 100 mm; (b) from 40 mm to
    100 mm.

                                                            [(a) 2.5 J; (b) 2.1 J]

6   The resistance to a cutting tool varies during the cutting stroke of 800 mm as
    follows:
    (i) The resistance increases uniformly from an initial 5000 N to 10 000 N as the
        tool moves 500 mm.
    (ii) The resistance falls uniformly from 10 000 N to 6000 N as the tool moves
        300 mm.
    Draw the work diagram and calculate the work done in one cutting stroke.

                                                                        [6.15 kJ]

140

7   Determine the work done when a mass of 25 kg is lifted vertically through a height of 8.0 m.

[1.962 kJ]

8   Water is pumped vertically upwards through a distance of 30 m and the work done is 132.4 kJ. Determine the number of litres of water pumped (1 litre of water has a mass of 1 kg).

[450 litres]

9   A lorry is moving away from the rest and the force exerted by the engine varies with distance as follows:

Distance (m)	0	10	20	30	40	50
Force (N)	300	280	260	233	190	150

Determine the work done as the lorry moves from rest through a distance of 50 m.

[12 kJ]

10 A force is applied to a mass. The variation of force with distance moved is as follows:

Distance (mm)	0	1	2	3	4	5	6	7	8
Force (N)	0	14	27	45	47	43	37	19	0

Draw the force-distance diagram and hence determine the work done by the force when moving the mass through a distance of 8 mm.

[0.235 J]

11 A machine lifts a mass of weight 490.5 N through a height of 12 m when 7.85 kJ of energy is supplied to it. Determine the efficiency of the machine.

[75%]

12 Determine the output energy of an electric motor which is 60% efficient if it uses 2 kJ of electrical energy.

[1.2 kJ]

13 A machine which is used for lifting a particular mass is supplied with 5 kJ of energy. If the machine has an efficiency of 65% and exerts a force of 812.5 N, to what height will it lift the mass?

[4 m]

14 A load is hoisted 42 m and requires a force of 100 N. The efficiency of the hoist gear is 60% and that of the motor is 70%. Determine the input energy to the hoist.

[10 kJ]

15 The output power of a motor is 10 kW. How much work does it do in 1 minute?

[600 kJ]

16 Determine the power required to lift a load through a height of 20 m in 12.5 s if the force required is 2.5 kN.

[4 kW]

17 25 kJ of work is done by a force in moving an object uniformly though 50 m in 40 s. Calculate (a) the value of the force; (b) the power.

[(a) 500 N; (b) 625 W]

18 A car towing another at 54 km/h exerts a steady pull of 800 N. Determine (a) the work done in ¼ h; (b) the power required.

[(a) 10.8 MJ; (b) 12 kW]

19 To what height will a mass of weight 500 N be raised in 20 s by a motor using 4 kW of power?

[160 m]

20 The output power of a motor is 10 kW. Determine (a) the work done by the motor in 2 hours; (b) the energy used by the motor if it is 72% efficient.

[(a) 72 MJ; (b) 100 MJ]

21 A car is travelling at a constant speed of 81 km/h. The frictional resistance to motion is 0.60 kN. Determine the power required to keep the car moving at this speed.

[13.5 kN]

22 A constant force of 2.0 kN is required to move the table of a shaping machine when a cut is being made. Determine the power required if the stroke of 1.2 m is completed in 5.0 s.

[480 W]

23 A body of mass 15 kg has its speed reduced from 30 km/h to 18 km/h in 4.0 s. Calculate the power required to effect this change of speed.

[83.33 W]

24 The variation of force with distance for a vehicle which is decelerating is as follows:

Distance (m)	600	500	400	300	200	100	0
Force (kN)	24	20	16	12	8	4	0

If the vehicle covers the 600 m in 1.2 minutes, find the power needed to bring the vehicle to rest.

[100 kJ]

25 A cylindrical bar of steel is turned in a lathe. The tangential cutting force on the tool is 0.5 kN and the cutting speed is 180 mm/s. Determine the power absorbed in cutting the steel.

[90 W]

26 An object of mass 400 g is thrown vertically upwards and its maximum increase in potential energy is 32.6 J. Determine the maximum height reached, neglecting air resistance.

[8.31 m]

27 A ball bearing of mass 100 g rolls down from the top of a chute of length 400 m inclined at an angle of 30° to the horizontal. Determine the decrease in potential energy of the ball bearing as it reaches the bottom of the chute.

[196.2 J]

28 A 24 kW motor is used to drive a water pump. If the overall efficiency of the system is 75%, calculate the maximum mass of water that may be pumped per second from a depth of 20 m.

[91.74 kg]

29 A vehicle of mass 800 kg is travelling at 54 km/h when its brakes are applied. Find the kinetic energy lost when the car comes to rest.

[90 kJ]

30 Supplies of mass 300 kg are dropped from a helicopter hovering at an altitude of 60 m. Determine the potential energy of the supplies relative to the ground at the instant of release, and its kinetic energy as it strikes the ground.

[176.6 kJ; 176.6 kJ]

31 A shell of mass 10 kg is fired vertically upwards with an initial velocity of 200 m/s. Determine its initial kinetic energy and the maximum height reached, correct to the nearest metre, neglecting air resistance.

[200 kJ; 2039 m]

32 The potential energy of a mass is increased by 20.0 kJ when it is lifted vertically through a height of 25.0 m. It is now released and allowed to fall freely. Neglecting air resistance, find its kinetic energy and its velocity after it has fallen 10.0 m.

[8 kJ; 14.0 m/s]

33 A pile driver of mass 400 kg falls freely through a height of 1.2 m on to a pile of mass 150 kg. Determine the velocity with which the driver hits the pile. If, at impact 2.5 kJ of energy are lost due to heat and sound, the remaining energy being possessed by the pile and driver as they are driven together into the ground a distance of 150 mm, determine (a) the common velocity after impact; (b) the average resistance of the ground.

[4.85 m/s; (a) 2.53 m/s; (b) 22.87 kN]

12 Torque

A. MAIN POINTS CONCERNED WITH TORQUE

1 When two equal forces act on a body as shown in *Fig 1*, they cause the body to rotate, and the system of forces is called a **couple**.

2 The turning moment of a couple is called a **torque, *T***. In *Fig 1*,
torque = magnitude of either force × perpendicular distance between the forces,
i.e. ***T = Fd***.
The unit of torque is the **newton metre, N m**.

3 When a force *F* newtons is applied to a radius *r* metres from the axis of, say, a nut to be turned by a spanner, the torque *T* applied to the nut is given by

$$T = Fr \text{ N m.}$$

4 *Fig 2(a)* shows a pulley wheel of radius *r* metres attached to a shaft and a force *F* newtons applied to the rim at point P. *Fig 2(b)* shows the pulley wheel having

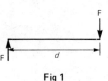

Fig 1

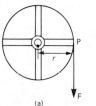

(a)

(b)

Fig 2

turned through an angle θ radians as a result of the force *F* being applied. The force moves through a distance *s*, where arc length $s = r\theta$.
Work done = force × distance moved by force = $F \times r\theta = Fr\,\theta$ N m = $Fr\,\theta J$.
However, *Fr* is the torque *T*, hence **work done = $T\theta$ joules**.

5 Power = $\dfrac{\text{work done}}{\text{time taken}} = \dfrac{T\theta}{\text{time taken}}$, for a constant torque, *T*.

However, $\dfrac{\text{angle } \theta}{\text{time taken}}$ = angular velocity, ω rad/s.

Hence **power, $P = T\omega$ watts**.
Angular velocity, $\omega = 2\pi n$ rad/s, where *n* is the speed in rev/s.
Hence **power, $P = 2\pi nT$ watts**. (see *Problems 1 to 9*).

144

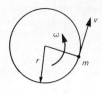

Fig 3

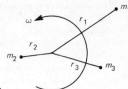

Fig 4

6 (i) The tangential velocity v of a particle of mass m moving at an angular velocity ω rad/s at a radius r metres (see *Fig 3*) is given by $v = \omega r$ m/s.

 (ii) The kinetic energy of a particle of mass m is given by:
 Kinetic energy $= \frac{1}{2} mv^2 = \frac{1}{2}m\,(\omega r)^2 = \frac{1}{2}\,m\omega^2 r^2$ **joules**

 (iii) The total kinetic energy of a system of masses rotating at different radii about a fixed axis but with the same angular velocity ω, as shown in *Fig 4*, is given by:
 Total kinetic energy $= \frac{1}{2}m_1\omega^2 r_1{}^2 + \frac{1}{2}m_2\omega^2 r_2{}^2 + \frac{1}{2}m_3\omega^2 r_3{}^2$
 $= (m_1 r_1{}^2 + m_2 r_2{}^2 + m_3 r_3{}^2)\,\dfrac{\omega^2}{2}$

 In general, this may be written as:

 Total kinetic energy $= (\Sigma mr^2)\,\dfrac{\omega^2}{2} = I\,\dfrac{\omega^2}{2}$, where $I\,(= \Sigma mr^2)$ is called the

 moment of inertia of the system about the axis of rotation.

 The moment of inertia of a system is a measure of the amount of work done to give the system an angular velocity of ω rad/s, or the amount of work which can be done by a system turning at ω rad/s.

7 From para. 4, work done $= T\theta$, and if this work is available to increase the kinetic energy of a rotating body of moment of inertia I, then:

 $T\theta = I\left(\dfrac{\omega_2{}^2 - \omega_1{}^2}{2}\right)$, where ω_1 and ω_2 are the initial and final angular velocities,

 i.e. $T\theta = I\left(\dfrac{\omega_2 + \omega_1}{2}\right)(\omega_2 - \omega_1)$

 However, $\left(\dfrac{\omega_2 + \omega_1}{2}\right)$ is the mean angular velocity, i.e. $\dfrac{\theta}{t}$, where t is the time, and

 $(\omega_2 - \omega_1)$ is the change in angular velocity, i.e. αt, where α is the angular acceleration.

 Hence $T\theta = I\left(\dfrac{\theta}{t}\right)(\alpha t)$

 from which, **torque** $T = I\alpha$, where I is the moment of inertia in kg m^2, α is the angular acceleration in rad/s^2, and T is the torque in N m. (see *Problems 10 to 16*).

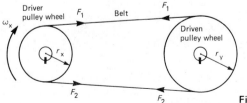

Fig 5

8 (i) A common and simple method of **transmitting power** from one shaft to another is by means of a **belt** passing over pulley wheels which are keyed to the shafts, as shown in *Fig 5*. Typical applications include an electric motor driving a line of shafting and an engine driving a rotating saw.

  (ii) For a belt to transmit power between two pulleys there must be a difference in tensions in the belt on either side of the driving and driven pulleys. For the direction of rotation shown in *Fig 5*, $F_2 > F_1$.

The torque T available at the driving wheel to do work is given by:
$T = (F_2 - F_1) r_x$ N m, and the available power P is given by:
$P = T\omega = (F_2 - F_1) r_x \, \omega_x$ watts.

  (iii) From para. 6(i), the linear velocity of a point on the driver wheel,
$v_x = r_x \, \omega_x$.

Similarly, the linear velocity of a point on the driven wheel,
$v_y = r_y \, \omega_y$.

Assuming no slipping, $v_x = v_y$, i.e. $r_x \, \omega_x = r_y \, \omega_y$
Hence $r_x (2\pi n_x) = r_y (2\pi n_y)$ from which $\dfrac{r_x}{r_y} = \dfrac{n_y}{n_x}$

  (iv) Percentage efficiency = $\dfrac{\text{useful work output}}{\text{energy input}}$ $\times$ 100, or

efficiency = $\dfrac{\text{power output}}{\text{power input}}$ $\times$ 100 per cent.

(see *Problems 17 to 21*).

B. WORKED PROBLEMS ON TORQUE

Problem 1 Determine the torque when a pulley wheel of diameter 300 mm has a force of 80 N applied at the rim.

Torque $T = Fr$, where force $F = 80$ N and radius $r = \dfrac{300}{2} = 150$ mm = 0.15 m.

Hence **torque T = (80)(0.15) = 12 N m**

Problem 2 Determine the force applied tangentially to a bar of a screwjack at a radius of 800 mm, if the torque required is 600 N m.

Torque T = force $\times$ radius, from which **force** = $\dfrac{\text{torque}}{\text{radius}}$

$= \dfrac{600 \text{ N m}}{800 \times 10^{-3} \text{ m}} = \textbf{750 N}$

Problem 3 The circular handwheel of a valve of diameter 500 mm has a couple applied to it composed of two forces, each of 250 N. Calculate the torque produced by the couple.

Torque produced by couple, $T = Fd$, where force $F = 250$ N and distance between the forces, $d = 500$ mm = 0.5 m.

Hence **torque T = (250)(0.5) = 125 N m**

146

Problem 4 A constant force of 150 N is applied tangentially to a wheel of diameter 140 mm. Determine the work done in 12 revolutions of the wheel. Give the answer in joules and in watt-hours.

Torque $T = Fr$, where $F = 150$ N and radius $r = \dfrac{140}{2} = 70$ mm $= 0.070$ m.

Hence torque $T = (150)(0.070) = 10.5$ N m
Work done $= T\theta$ joules, where torque $T = 10.5$ N m and
angular displacement $\theta = 12$ revolutions
$$= 12 \times 2\pi \text{ rad} = 24\pi \text{ rad.}$$
Hence **work done** $= (10.5)(24\pi) = $ **792 J**

1 J $= 1$ W s, thus 792 J $= 792$ W s $= \dfrac{792}{60 \times 60}$ W h $= $ **0.22 W h**

Problem 5 Calculate the torque developed by a motor whose spindle is rotating at 1000 rev/min and developing a power of 2.50 kW.

Power $P = 2\pi n\, T$ (from para. 5), from which torque $T = \dfrac{P}{2\pi n}$ N m,

where power $P = 2.50$ kW $= 2500$ W and speed $n = \dfrac{1000}{60}$ rev/s

Thus **torque** $T = \dfrac{2500}{2\pi(1000/60)} = \dfrac{2500 \times 60}{2\pi \times 1000} = $ **23.87 N m**

Problem 6 An electric motor develops a power of 3.75 kW and a torque of 12.5 N m. Determine the speed of rotation of the motor in rev/min.

Power $P = 2\pi n\, T$, from which speed $n = \dfrac{P}{2\pi T}$ rev/s,

where power $P = 3.75$ kW $= 3750$ W and torque $T = 12.5$ N m

Hence speed $n = \dfrac{3750}{2\pi\,(12.5)} = 47.75$ rev/s

The speed of rotation of the motor $= 47.75 \times 60 = $ **2865 rev/min**

Problem 7 In a turning-tool test, the tangential cutting force is 50 N. If the mean diameter of the workpiece is 40 mm, calculate (a) the work done per revolution of the spindle; (b) the power required when the spindle speed is 300 rev/min.

(a) Work done $= T\theta$, where $T = Fr$,
    force $F = 50$ N,
    radius $r = \dfrac{40}{2} = 20$ mm
    $= 0.02$ m
and angular displacement $\theta = 1$ rev $= 2\pi$ rad.

Hence **work done per revolution of spindle** $= Fr\theta = (50)(0.02)(2\pi) = $ **6.28 J**

(b) Power $P = 2\pi nT$, where torque $T = Fr = (50)(0.02) = 1$ N m

and speed $n = \dfrac{300}{60} = 5$ rev/s

Hence **power required**, $P = 2\pi(5)(1) = \mathbf{31.42}$ **W**

Problem 8 A pulley is 600 mm in diameter and the difference in tension on the two sides of the driving belt is 1.5 kN. If the speed of the pulley is 500 rev/min, determine (a) the torque developed; (b) the work done in 3 minutes.

(a) Torque $T = Fr$,

where force $F = 1.5$ kN $= 1500$ N

and radius $r = \dfrac{600}{2} = 300$ mm $= 0.3$ m

Hence **torque developed** $= (1500)(0.3) = \mathbf{450}$ **N m**

(b) Work done $= T\theta$, where torque $T = 450$ N m and angular displacement in 3 minutes, $\theta = (3 \times 500)$ revs $= (3 \times 500 \times 2\pi)$ rad.

Hence **work done** $= (450)(3 \times 500 \times 2\pi) = 4.24 \times 10^6$ J $= \mathbf{4.24}$ **MJ**

$\left(4.24 \text{ M J} = \dfrac{4.24 \times 10^6}{60 \times 60 \times 1000} \text{ kW h} = \mathbf{1.178 \text{ kW h}}\right)$

Problem 9 A motor connected to a shaft develops a torque of 5 kN m. Determine the number of revolutions made by the shaft if the work done is 2.5 kW h.

Work done $= T\theta$, from which angular displacement $\theta = \dfrac{\text{work done}}{\text{torque}}$

The work done $= 2.5$ kW h $= 2500$ W h $= 2500 \times 60 \times 60$ W s $= 9 \times 10^6$ J, and torque $= 5$ kN m $= 5000$ N m.

Hence angular displacement $\theta = \dfrac{9 \times 10^6}{5000} = 1800$ radians.

2π rad $= 1$ rev,

Hence, **the number of revolutions made by the shaft** $= 1800/2\pi = \mathbf{286.5}$ **revs**

Problem 10 A shaft system has a moment of inertia of 37.5 kg m². Determine the torque required to give it an angular acceleration of 5.0 rad/s²

Torque $T = I\alpha$,

where moment of inertia $I = 37.5$ kg m²

and angular acceleration $\alpha = 5.0$ rad/s²

Hence **torque** $T = (37.5)(5.0) = \mathbf{187.5}$ **N m**

Problem 11 A shaft has a moment of inertia of 31.4 kg m². What angular acceleration of the shaft would be produced by an accelerating torque of 495 N m?

Torque $T = I\alpha$, from which, angular acceleration $\alpha = \dfrac{T}{I}$, where torque $T = 495$ N m and moment of inertia $I = 31.4$ kg m².

Hence **angular acceleration**, $\alpha = \dfrac{495}{31.4} = \mathbf{15.76 \text{ rad/s}^2}$

Problem 12 A body of mass 100 g is fastened to a wheel and rotates in a circular path of 500 mm in diameter. Determine the increase in kinetic energy of the body when the speed of the wheel increases from 450 rev/min to 750 rev/min.

From para. 6, kinetic energy = $I \dfrac{\omega^2}{2}$

Thus, increase in kinetic energy = $I\left(\dfrac{\omega_2{}^2 - \omega_1{}^2}{2}\right)$

when moment of inertia $I = mr^2$, mass $m = 100$ g $= 0.1$ kg

and radius $r = \dfrac{500}{2} = 250$ mm $= 0.25$ m

Initial angular velocity, $\omega_1 = 450$ rev/min $= \dfrac{450 \times 2\pi}{60}$ rad/s $= 47.12$ rad/s,

and final angular velocity, $\omega_2 = 750$ rev/min $= \dfrac{750 \times 2\pi}{60}$ rad/s $= 78.54$ rad/s.

Thus increase in kinetic energy $= I\left(\dfrac{\omega_2{}^2 - \omega_1{}^2}{2}\right) = (m\,r^2\,)\left(\dfrac{\omega_2{}^2 - \omega_1{}^2}{2}\right)$

$$= (0.1)(0.25^2)\left(\dfrac{78.54^2 - 47.12^2}{2}\right) = \mathbf{12.34\ J}$$

Problem 13 A system consists of three small masses rotating at the same speed about the same fixed axis. The masses and their radii of rotation are: 15 g at 250 mm, 20 g at 180 mm and 30 g at 200 mm. Determine (a) the moment of inertia of the system about the given axis; (b) the kinetic energy in the system if the speed of rotation is 1200 rev/min.

(a) Moment of inertia of the system, $I = \Sigma\ mr^2$
  i.e. $I = \left[(15 \times 10^{-3}\text{ kg})(0.25\text{ m})^2\right] + \left[(20 \times 10^{-3}\text{kg})(0.18\text{ m})^2\right]$
  $+ \left[(30 \times 10^{-3}\text{ kg})(0.20\text{ m})^2\right]$

  $= (9.375 \times 10^{-4}) + (6.48 \times 10^{-4}) + (12 \times 10^{-4})$
  $= 27.855 \times 10^{-4}$ kg m^2 = $\mathbf{2.7855 \times 10^{-3}}$ **kg m^2**

(b) Kinetic energy $= I\ \dfrac{\omega^2}{2}$, where moment of inertia $I = 2.7855 \times 10^{-3}$ kg m^2

  and angular velocity $\omega = 2\pi n = 2\pi\ \dfrac{1200}{60}$ rad/s $= 40\pi$ rad/s.

  Hence kinetic energy in the system $= (2.7855 \times 10^{-3})\dfrac{(40\pi)^2}{2} = \mathbf{21.99\ J}$

Problem 14 A shaft with its rotating parts has a moment of inertia of 20 kg m^2. It is accelerated from rest by an accelerating torque of 45 N m. Determine the speed of the shaft in rev/min (a) after 15 s; (b) after the first 5 revolutions.

(a) Since torque $T = I\alpha$, then angular acceleration, $\alpha = \dfrac{T}{I} = \dfrac{45}{20} = 2.25$ rad/s^2

  The angular velocity of the shaft is initially zero, i.e. $\omega_1 = 0$

  The angular velocity after 15 s, $\omega_2 = \omega_1 + \alpha t = 0 + (2.25)(15) = 33.75$ rad/s i.e. **speed of shaft after 15 s** = $(33.75)\left(\dfrac{60}{2\pi}\right)$ rev/min = **322.3 rev/min**

(b) Work done = $T\theta$,

where torque T = 45 N m,

and angular displacement θ = 5 revolutions = 5 × 2π rad = 10π rad.

Hence work done = $(45)(10\pi)$ = 1414 J.

This work done results in an increase in kinetic energy, given by $I\dfrac{\omega^2}{2}$, where

moment of inertia I = 20 kg m^2 and ω = angular velocity.

Hence 1414 = $(20)\dfrac{\omega^2}{2}$, from which $\omega = \sqrt{\left(\dfrac{1414 \times 2}{20}\right)}$ = 11.89 rad/s.

Hence speed of shaft after the first 5 revolutions = $11.89 \times \dfrac{60}{2\pi}$ = **113.5 rev/min**

Problem 15 The accelerating torque on a turbine rotor is 250 N m.
(a) Determine the gain in kinetic energy of the rotor while it turns through 100 revolutions (neglecting any frictional and other resisting torques).
(b) If the moment of inertia of the rotor is 25 kg m^2 and the speed at the beginning of the 100 revolutions is 450 rev/min, determine its speed at the end.

(a) The kinetic energy gained is equal to the work done by the accelerating torque of 250 Nm over 100 revolutions,

i.e. **gain in kinetic energy** = work done = $T\theta$ = $(250)(100 \times 2\pi)$ = **157.08 kJ**

(b) Initial kinetic energy of rotation = $I\dfrac{\omega_1^2}{2}$ = $(25)\left(\dfrac{450 \times 2\pi}{60}\right)^2 \dfrac{}{2}$ = 27.76 kJ.

The final kinetic energy is the sum of the initial kinetic energy and the kinetic

energy gained, i.e. $\dfrac{I\omega_2^2}{2}$ = 27.76 kJ + 157.08 kJ = 184.84 kJ.

Hence $\dfrac{(25)\omega_2^2}{2}$ = 184 840, from which, $\omega_2 = \sqrt{\left(\dfrac{184\,840 \times 2}{25}\right)}$= 121.6 rad/s.

Thus speed at end of 100 revolutions = $\dfrac{121.6 \times 60}{2\pi}$ rev/min = **1161 rev/min**

Problem 16 A shaft with its associated rotating parts has a moment of inertia of 55.4 kg m^2. Determine the uniform torque required to accelerate the shaft from rest to a speed of 1650 rev/min while it turns through 12 revolutions.

From para. 7, $T\theta = I\dfrac{\omega_2^2 - \omega_1^2}{2}$, where

angular displacement, θ = 12 rev = 12 × 2 π rad = 24 π rad,

final speed, ω_2 = 1650 rev/min = $\dfrac{1650}{60}$ × 2π = 172.79 rad/s

initial speed, ω_1 = 0, and moment of inertia, I = 55.4 kg m^2.

Hence torque required,

$$T = \dfrac{I}{\theta}\left(\dfrac{\omega_2^2 - \omega_1^2}{2}\right) = \dfrac{55.4}{24\pi}\left(\dfrac{(172.79)^2 - (0)^2}{2}\right) = \textbf{10.97 kN m}$$

150

Problem 17 An electric motor has an efficiency of 75% when running at 1450 rev/min. Determine the output torque when the power input is 3.0 kW.

Efficiency = $\dfrac{\text{power output}}{\text{power input}}$ × 100, hence 75 = $\dfrac{\text{power output}}{3000}$ × 100

from which, power output = $\dfrac{75}{100}$ × 3000 = 2250 W

From para. 5(ii), power output, $P = 2\pi nT$,

from which torque $T = \dfrac{P}{2\pi n}$, where $n = \dfrac{1450}{60}$ rev/s

Hence **output torque** = $\dfrac{2250}{2\pi\left(\dfrac{1450}{60}\right)}$ = **14.82 N m**

Problem 18 A 15 kW motor is driving a shaft at 1150 rev/min by means of pulley wheels and a belt. The tensions in the belt on each side of the driver pulley wheel are 400 N and 50 N. The diameters of the driver and driven pulley wheels are 500 mm and 750 mm respectively. Determine (a) the efficiency of the motor; (b) the speed of the driven pulley wheel.

(a) From para. 8, power output from motor = $(F_2 - F_1) r_x \omega_x$
Force F_2 = 400 N and F_1 = 50 N, hence $(F_2 - F_1)$ = 350 N

Radius $r_x = \dfrac{500}{2}$ = 250 mm = 0.25 m

and angular velocity,

$\omega_x = \dfrac{1150 \times 2\pi}{60}$ rad/s

Hence power output from motor $(F_2 - F_1)r_x \omega_x = (350)(0.25)\left(\dfrac{1150 \times 2\pi}{60}\right)$

$= 10.54$ kW

Power input = 15 kW
Hence **efficiency of the motor** = $\dfrac{\text{power output}}{\text{power input}}$ = $\dfrac{10.54}{15}$ × 100 = **70.27%**

(b) From para. 8, $\dfrac{r_x}{r_y} = \dfrac{n_y}{n_x}$, from which,

speed of driven pulley wheel, $n_y = \dfrac{n_x r_x}{r_y} = \dfrac{(1150)(0.25)}{(0.75/2)}$ = **767 rev/min**

Problem 19 A crane lifts a load of mass 5 tonne to a height of 25 m. If the overall efficiency of the crane is 65% and the input power to the hauling motor is 100 kW, determine how long the lifting operation takes.

The increase in potential energy is the work done and is given by mgh, where mass m = 5 t = 5000 kg, g = 9.81 m/s^2 and height h = 25 m
Hence work done = mgh = (5000)(9.81)(25) = 1.226 MJ
Input power = 100 kW = 100 000 W

Efficiency = $\dfrac{\text{output power}}{\text{input power}}$ × 100, hence 65 = $\dfrac{\text{output power}}{100\,000}$ × 100 from which, output power = $\dfrac{65}{100}$ × 100 000 = 65 000 W = $\dfrac{\text{work done}}{\text{time taken}}$

Thus **time taken for lifting operation** = $\dfrac{\text{work done}}{\text{output power}}$ = $\dfrac{1.226 \times 10^6 \text{ J}}{65\,000 \text{ W}}$ = **18.86s**

Problem 20 The tool of a shaping machine has a mean cutting speed of 250 mm/s and the average cutting force on the tool in a certain shaping operation is 1.2 kN. If the power input to the motor driving the machine is 0.75 kW, determine the overall efficiency of the machine.

Velocity v = 250 mm/s = 0.25 m/s, force F = 1.2 kN = 1200 N
Power output required at the cutting tool (i.e. power output),
P = force × velocity
= 1200 N × 0.25 m/s = 300 W
Power input = 0.75 kW = 750 W

Hence efficiency of the machine = $\dfrac{\text{output power}}{\text{input power}}$ × 100 = $\dfrac{300}{750}$ × 100 = **40%**

Problem 21 Calculate the input power of the motor driving a train at a constant speed of 72 km/h on a level track, if the efficiency of the motor is 80% and the resistance due to friction is 20 kN.

Force resisting motion = 20 kN = 20 000 N; velocity = 72 km/h = $\dfrac{72}{3.6}$ = 20 m/s

Output power from motor = resistive force × velocity of train
= 20 000 × 20 = 400 kW

Efficiency = $\dfrac{\text{power output}}{\text{power input}}$ × 100, hence 80 = $\dfrac{400}{\text{power input}}$ × 100

from which, **power input** = 400 × $\dfrac{100}{80}$ = **500 kW**

C. FURTHER PROBLEMS ON TORQUE

(a) SHORT ANSWER PROBLEMS

1 What is meant by a couple?
2 Define torque.
3 State the unit of torque.
4 State the relationship between work, torque T and angular displacement θ.
5 State the relationship between power P, torque T and angular velocity ω.
6 Define moment of inertia and state the symbol used.
7 State the unit of moment of inertia.
8 State the relationship between torque, moment of inertia and angular acceleration.
9 State one method of power transmission commonly used.
10 Define efficiency.

(b) MULTI-CHOICE PROBLEMS (answers on page 157)

1 A force of 100 N is applied to the rim of a pulley wheel of diameter 200 mm. The torque is: (a) 2 N m; (b) 20 kN m; (c) 10 N m; (d) 20 N m.

2   The work done on a shaft to turn it through 5π radians is 25π N m.
     The torque applied to the shaft is: (a) 0.2 N m; (b) $125\ \pi^2$ N m; (c) 30π N m;
     (d) 5 N m.

3   A 5 kW electric motor is turning at 50 rad/s. The torque developed at this speed
     is: (a) 100 N m; (b) 250 N m; (c) 0.01 N m; (d) 0.1 N m.

4   The force applied tangentially to a bar of a screwjack at a radius of 500 mm if
     the torque required is 1 kNm, is: (a) 2N; (b) 2 kN; (c) 500 N; (d) 0.5 N.

5   A 10 kW motor developing a torque of $\dfrac{200}{\pi}$ N m is running at a speed of:

     (a) $\dfrac{\pi}{20}$ rev/s; (b) 50π rev/s; (c) 25 rev/s; (d) $\dfrac{20}{\pi}$ rev/s.

6   A shaft and its associated rotating parts has a moment of inertia of 50 kg m^2. The
     angular acceleration of the shaft to produce an accelerating torque of 5 kN m is:
     (a) 10 rad/s^2; (b) 250 rad/s^2; (c) 0.01 rad/s^2; (d) 100 rad/s^2.

7   A motor has an efficiency of 25% when running at 3000 rev/min. If the output
     torque is 10 N m, the power input is:
     (a) 4π kW; (b) $0.25\ \pi$ kW; (c) 15π kW; (d) $75\ \pi$ kW.

8   In a belt-pulley wheel system, the effective tension in the belt is 500 N and the
     diameter of the driver wheel is 200 mm. If the power output from the driving
     motor is 5 k W, the driver pulley wheel turns at :
     (a) 50 rad/s; (b) 2500 rad/s; (c) 100 rad/s; (d) 0.1 rad/s.

(c) CONVENTIONAL PROBLEMS

1   Determine the torque developed when a force of 200 N is applied tangentially
     to a spanner at a distance of 350 mm from the centre of the nut.

     [70 N m]

2   During a machining test on a lathe, the tangential force on the tool is 150 N.
     If the torque on the lathe spindle is 12 N m, determine the diameter of the work-
     piece.

     [160 mm]

3   A constant force of 4 kN is applied tangentially to the rim of a pulley wheel of
     diameter 1.8 m attached to a shaft. Determine the work done in 15 revolutions of
     the pulley wheel in (a) joules : (b) k W h.

     [(a) 339.3 kJ; (b) 0.09 425 kW h]

4   A motor connected to a shaft develops a torque of 3.5 kN m. Determine the
     number of revolutions made by the shaft if the work done is 3.2 kW h.

     [523.8 rev]

5   A wheel is turning with an angular velocity of 18 rad/s and develops a power of
     810 W at this speed. Determine the torque developed by the wheel.

     [45 N m]

6   Calculate the torque provided at the shaft of an electric motor which develops an
     output power of 2.4 kW at 1800 rev/min.

     [12.73 N m]

7   Determine the angular velocity of a shaft when the power available is 2.75 kW
     and the torque is 200 N m.

     [13.75 rad/s]

8   The drive shaft of a ship supplies a torque of 400 kN m to its propeller at
     400 rev/min. Determine the power delivered by the shaft.

     [16.76 MW]

153

9 A motor is running at 1460 rev/min and produces a torque of 180 N m. Determine the average power developed by the motor.

[27.52 kW]

10 A wheel is rotating at 1720 rev/min and develops a power of 600 W at this speed. Calculate (a) the torque; (b) the work done, in kWh, in ¼ hour.

[(a) 3.33 N m; (b) 0.150 kW h]

11 A force of 60 N is applied to a lever of a screwjack at a radius of 220 mm. If the lever makes 25 revolutions, determine (a) the work done on the jack; (b) the power, if the time taken to complete 25 revolutions is 40 s.

[(a) 2.073 kJ; (b) 51.84 W]

12 A shaft system has a moment of inertia of 51.4 kg m². Determine the torque required to give it an angular acceleration of 5.3 rad/s².

[272.4 N m]

13 A shaft has an angular acceleration of 20 rad/s² and produces an accelerating torque of 600 N m. Determine the moment of inertia of the shaft.

[30 kg m²]

14 A uniform torque of 3.2 kN m is applied to a shaft while it turns through 25 revolutions. Assuming no frictional or other resistances, calculate the increase in kinetic energy of the shaft (i.e. the work done). If the shaft is initially at rest and its moment of inertia is 24.5 kg m², determine its rotational speed, in rev/min, at the end of the 25 revolutions.

[502.65 kJ; 1934 rev/min]

15 An accelerating torque of 30 N m is applied to a rotor, while it turns through 10 revolutions. Determine the increase in kinetic energy. If the moment of inertia of the rotor is 15 kg m² and its speed at the beginning of the 10 revolutions is 1200 rev/min, determine its speed at the end.

[1.885 kJ; 1209.5 rev/min]

16 A shaft with its associated rotating parts has a moment of inertia of 48 kg m² Determine the uniform torque required to accelerate the shaft from rest to a speed of 1500 rev/min while it turns through 15 revolutions.

[6.283 kN m]

17 A small body, of mass 82 g, is fastened to a wheel and rotates in a circular path of 456 mm diameter. Calculate the increase in kinetic energy of the body when the speed of the wheel increases from 450 rev/min to 950 rev/min.

[16.36 J]

18 A system consists of three small masses rotating at the same speed about the same fixed axis. The masses and their radii of rotation are: 16 g at 256 mm, 23 g at 192 mm and 31 g at 176 mm. (a) Find the moment of inertia of the system about the given axis; (b) if the speed of rotation is 1250 rev/min, find the kinetic energy in the system.

[(a) 2.857 × 10⁻³ kg m²; (b) 24.48 J]

19 A shaft with its rotating parts has a moment of inertia of 16.42 kg m². It is accelerated from rest by an accelerating torque of 43.6 N m. Find the speed of the shaft (a) after 15 s; (b) after the first four revolutions.

[(a) 380.3 rev/min; (b) 110.3 rev/min]

20 The driving torque on a turbine rotor is 203 N m, neglecting frictional and other resisting torques. (a) what is the gain in kinetic energy of the rotor while it turns through 100 revolutions? (b) If the moment of inertia of the rotor is 23.2 kg m² and the speed at the beginning of the 100 revolutions is 600 rev/min, what will be its speed at the end?

[(a) 127.55 kJ; (b) 1167 rev/min]

21 A motor has an efficiency of 72% when running at 2600 rev/min. If the output torque is 16 N m at this speed, determine the power supplied to the motor.

[6.05 kW]

22 The difference in tensions between the two sides of a belt round a driver pulley of radius 240 mm is 200 N. If the driver pulley wheel is on the shaft of an electric motor running at 700 rev/min and the power input to the motor is 5 kW, determine the efficiency of the motor. Determine also the diameter of the driven pulley wheel if its speed is to be 1200 rev/min.

[70.37%; 280 mm]

23 A winch is driven by a 4 kW electric motor and is lifting a load of 400 kg to a height of 5.0 m. If the lifting operation takes 8.6 s, calculate the overall efficiency of the winch and motor.

[57.03%]

24 A belt and pulley system transmits a power of 5 kW from a driver to a driven shaft. The driver pulley wheel has a diameter of 200 mm and rotates at 600 rev/min. The diameter of the driven pulley wheel is 400 mm. Determine the tension in the slack side of the belt and the speed of the driven pulley when the tension in the tight side of the belt is 1.2 kN.

[404.2 N; 300 rev/min]

25 The average force on the cutting tool of a lathe is 750 N and the cutting speed is 400 mm/s. Determine the power input to the motor driving the lathe if the overall efficiency is 55%.

[545.5 W]

26 A ship's anchor has a mass of 5 tonne. Determine the work done in raising the anchor from a depth of 100 m. If the hauling gear is driven by a motor whose output is 80 kW and the efficiency of the haulage is 75%, determine how long the lifting operation takes.

[4.905 MJ; 1 min 22 s]

Answers to multi-choice problems

Chapter 1 (page 11)

1 (c); 2 (b); 3 (d); 4 (b); 5 (i); 6 (a); 7 (e);
8 (d); 9 (e) or (f); 10 (k); 11 (b); 12 (g).

Chapter 2 (page 22)

1 (c); 2 (c); 3 (d); 4 (a); 5 (c); 6 (j); 7 (i);
8 (d); 9 (g); 10 (f); 11 (a); 12 (h); 13 (e); 14 (k).

Chapter 3 (page 37)

1 (b); 2 (c); 3 (d); 4 (b); 5 (c); 6 (f); 7 (h);
8 (d); 9 (f); 10 (d); 11 (g); 12 (b).

Chapter 4 (page 47)

1 (d); 2 (b); 3 (a); 4 (b); 5 (b) and (c); 6 (a); 7 (c);
8 (b).

Chapter 5 (page 64)

1 (b); 2 (a); 3 (b); 4 (c); 5 (a); 6 (b); 7 (b);
8 (c); 9 (c); 10 (c); 11 (b); 12 (c); 13 (b); 14 (c).

Chapter 6 (page 78)

1 (c); 2 (d); 3 (b); 4 (g); 5 (b); 6 (c); 7 (j);
8 (k); 9 (a); 10 (c); 11 (a); 12 (d).

Chapter 7 (page 89)

1 (d); 2 (b); 3 (d); 4 (a); 5 (f); 6 (i); 7 (b);
8 (b); 9 (a); 10 (a).

Chapter 8 (page 104)

1 (a); 2 (d); 3 (b); 4 (b); 5 (c); 6 (d); 7 (b);
8 (c); 9 (c); 10 (b).

Chapter 9 (page 116)

1 (b); 2 (a); 3 (d); 4 (g); 5 (f); 6 (b); 7 (a);
8 (j); 9 (f); 10 (c).

Chapter 10 (page 124)
1 (d);   2 (b);   3 (f);   4 (c); 5 (a);   6 (c);   7 (a);
8 (g);   9 (f);   10 (f); 11 (b); 12 (e).

Chapter 11 (page 139)
1 (c);   2 (c);   3 (a);   4 (d); 5 (b);   6 (c);   7 (a);
8 (d);   9 (c);   10 (b).

Chapter 12 (page 152)
1 (c);   2 (d);   3 (a);   4 (b); 5 (c);   6 (d);   7 (a);
8 (c).

Index